TANA
MAGUIRE

TANA MAGUIRE

by
DIANA SAUNDERS

DONALD I. FINE, INC.
New York

PART ONE

CHAPTER
ONE

THERE HAD been an unauthorized parade earlier in the day, storming up busy, active Broadway, panicking the delivery horses, upsetting buggies, and sending the New York police into a frenzy of pursuit.

It was this wild melee that Antonia Maguire encountered when she came out the Fifth Avenue doors of the Waldorf-Astoria Hotel. The crowd, pouring along Thirty-fourth Street, away from the Broadway debacle, thrust her against the wall of the elegant hotel as if they could read her mind and knew she was their enemy.

Perhaps because she wanted to make a gesture to such men, she stooped before one swarthy, good-looking youth and lifted up the placard he had dropped in his collision with her.

The placard, read, as she knew it would:

"*Cuba Libre!* Down with Spain! Down with Butcher Weyler!"

She made no comment but handed it to him. He tucked the placard under his arm.

7

It was Antonia Maguire's smile more than her polite gesture that thawed his angry scowl. He muttered, "Thankee, ma'am," and started to run up Fifth Avenue. Finding that two police waving nightsticks were headed in that direction, he swung around, passed her with an astonished, "you're real pretty, ma'am," and hurried off along Thirty-fourth Street.

The compliment raised her spirits in spite of the irritating slogan on the placard. He had spoken to her in English. Evidently he hadn't recognized a fellow Cuban if, indeed, the boy was Cuban. His English sounded exceedingly American.

Reminded of her mission to New York, she told herself, they are being corrupted by the yellow press here in the United States. It isn't their fault. It's men like Mr. Joseph Pulitzer and that fellow—that William Hearst.

But the damage was done, and it grew more sizable every day.

It was up to loyal, Cuban-born Spaniards like herself to stop these newsmen and their informers, the smugglers that every American seemed to find so dashing. Even her Yankee Aunt Sybil did nothing but rave about this Captain Sanchez or that Captain Halloran, or more often the celebrated Captain Juan Diego.

Antonia had heard all about Juan Diego's suspected exploits in running both the United States and Spanish blockades while delivering weapons to the Cuban rebels. Though the Spanish customs inspectors in Havana and Santiago had never caught him with illegal cargoes, and he still sailed freely into and out of those ports, he was commonly considered a leader in the delivery of contraband weapons and goods to Cuban rebels.

He was said to be attractive to women. Cynically, she suspected that the blockade runner wouldn't have been half so popular in the American press if he hadn't possessed that particular quality of sexual appeal.

The resplendent doorman at the hotel's Fifth Avenue entrance saw her struggling to open her violet lace parasol against the spring breeze. He reached out to help her. Together, they fumbled with the catch but they had to give up.

"Seems to be broken," he admitted finally.

She agreed. "I must have struck it against the wall when the crowd came by."

"Pity. Excuse the liberty, ma'am, but it certainly is your color."

She appreciated his interest. She had chosen that particular shade for her parasol and the shot-silk walking dress with its inviting but not indecorous wide neckline, because the designer insisted the color matched her eyes. She felt that she needed all her assets to sway the notorious *Morning Telegraph* columnist, Quincy Kemp, to her family's cause.

It helped to know that Aunt Sybil's migraine kept her from accompanying Antonia on her "mission to the press" this afternoon. Antonia was fond of her aunt, but that elegant Irish-American lady, hostess to the best political dinners of the new McKinley administration, had spouted pro-rebel sympathies to everyone on their recent voyage up from Havana.

Since Sybil Maguire Revelstoke was returning to her home in the United States, Patrick Maguire had chosen his sister as Antonia's duenna in the old Spanish tradition. He had made the choice with some reluctance. He and the family knew all about Aunt Sybil's political views. They had agreed that while she visited her brother's family in Cuba, the less said among the family about "those scoundrelly rebels" the better. Sybil was sure to repeat the comments where they would do the most harm to the Spanish cause, in Washington. The "Spanish lobby" in Washington was proud of its quietly dignified conduct. It boasted that all the loud accusations and ungentlemanly conduct were the product of the regrettable minority of Cubans called "rebels."

The doorman, familiar with the careful upbringing of Spanish-Cuban aristocrats, inquired now, "Mrs. Revelstoke won't be accompanying you today, ma'am?"

Antonia knew she would hear this from other Yankees with their dangerous interest in Cuban affairs and Spanish customs. She said sweetly, "Oh, no. I'm sorry to say my aunt has a headache. Probably too much sea air on the voyage. But I went to school near Washington and I've become quite American in my ways. I often go out alone. By daylight, of course."

She had decided "Americanism" would be a better approach for these Yankees than to plead with them for fair play in writing about the Cuban revolt. In spite of their president's efforts, they had used very little fair play toward Cuba's Spanish queen and her government during the past two years.

Antonia gave up the problem of opening the parasol and started

across the sidewalk. There she hesitated, turned back to the doorman, realizing she wasn't sure just where she was going.

"I wonder if you could tell me which direction I take to reach
the *Morning Telegraph*."

He seemed surprised that she had not ordered a horse and
carriage like any respectable young lady of good family, but she
had no intention of being trapped in another traffic jam where
those violent "Free Cuba" protestors were blocking the streets. It
would be far easier to walk.

When she had explained this to him he gave her instructions to
go west on Thirty-fourth Street, then turn left on Broadway.

"Easy to find, Miss Maguire. About two, maybe three blocks.
It's one of those new skyscrapers. The first ten-story one across
the street. These buildings are quite safe, you know."

She didn't like the idea of skyscrapers, and especially those tiny
moving rooms they called elevators. Even those in the elegant
Waldorf-Astoria made her uneasy, but the memory of her father's
final instructions to her helped:

"It's these press vultures that give us the lie and call my friend,
General Weyler, a butcher. We Spaniards have got to make it clear
they aren't being told the truth. The Cuban people are loyal to
Her Majesty. No finer female than Queen María Cristina was ever
crowned. You've your mother's word on that. They went to the
convent school together."

Sometimes it amused Antonia, this attempt of her Irish father
to turn himself into a Spanish-Cuban. Patrick Maguire had made
his fortune running the Union blockade during America's Civil
War. Antonia suspected it was this fortune that had bought a wife
from among Cuba's most illustrious families; yet the two, Patrick
Maguire and Ysabel Guzman y Pontalvo seemed to have found a
lifetime of devotion in that arranged marriage.

No one in the somewhat shrunken empire, in Madrid itself, was
more loyal to the Spanish crown than Irish Patrick Maguire.

"Well, Father," Antonia reminded herself as she set out for
Broadway, "I told you I could serve your cause as well as Felipe
could, even if I am a female."

She knew her father's first thought was always for her younger
brother Felipe, but nineteen-year-old Felipe was at present going

through all the social amenities of a betrothal to Spanish General Weyler's favorite niece, and nothing could interfere with that.

Broadway was hazy in the golden afternoon. In spite of its cobblestones it smelled of stirred-up dust and horse odors. Like the traffic swarming up and down Broadway, they made her think of her island home. But this street lacked the beauty of Havana's flowers and greenery, and the ancient Spanish architecture that took the mind off the more mundane odors.

She and her Aunt Sybil had crossed Broadway in a horse and buggy yesterday after summoning a "cab" at the S.S. *Havana* docks. As always, New York seemed glamorous and intriguing to her. But yesterday she hadn't found herself down here among these people who hated everything her Spanish ancestors had built up during four hundred years of rule in Cuba.

Two passing gentlemen in homburgs and black business suits elbowed her aside without a word of apology. Very likely these were local manners. She wasn't too surprised. The jolt had knocked her perky lace hat askew. While she set it correctly on her blue-black cascade of hair, she resolved to show these bad-mannered creatures that they still had the Spanish Empire to reckon with.

She was relieved to see the ten-story skyscraper across the street, a gray monster festooned with overhanging cornices. She wanted to get this unpleasantness over. Then she and Aunt Sybil could go down to the lovely Revelstoke House in northern Virginia where they would once more enjoy the company of well-mannered, witty, charming people from Washington and the South. A far cry from the men she had met in the city this afternoon.

Crossing the street might have daunted any other provincial who visited this metropolis, but Antonia had crossed Havana's *malecón* and the Plaza de Armas many times. The vehicles might differ but the danger was the same.

The gloomy marble foyer of the building was crowded with men, all talking at once. They seemed to have one common subject of conversation: President McKinley's refusal to punish Spain's "atrocities" in her Cuban colony. The men were casually dressed. No homburgs or morning coats here.

One of them was saying, "Willie Hearst and his damned *Journal* are ahead of us already. Did you see his latest circulation figures?

They don't report the news. Hell! They make it. And we should do the same."

"Not the kind Wild Willie makes."

Another put in, "Hey, did you see the guy in the lobby? Had all the office girls on the floor hanging out every door watching him. Who the devil was he?"

"Some matinee idol probably. Looking for a little publicity. Costello? Warfield? I'll bet he's one of the cape-flingers."

Laughing, the five men poured out onto the sidewalk and into the saloon next door. Obviously these were some of Quincy Kemp's fellow reporters on the *Morning Telegraph*.

The elevator operator was a thin, academic-looking boy of sixteen or so who managed the alarming barred gate and each opening door of the floors they passed while he read a heavy book that lay open on his stool. It was a remarkable feat since the elevator had a dim light and he was forced to stop at three floors to let out passengers.

The several men and one woman who shared the elevator with Antonia took embarrassing note of her. Her common sense prevented conceit. She knew her main interest for them was her ill-chosen wardrobe, hardly that of a businesswoman. The other female sharing the elevator was neatly but severely dressed in a shirtwaist and black serge skirt; her iron-gray hair was piled high on her head above a stiff pompadour. Appearances were deceptive; she seemed to be on familiar terms with the three men around her and Antonia heard with wonder, even with envy, her raucous, free and easy laugh.

All the same, nudges and stares sprouted around Antonia. She gave the operator a nervous smile and was glad to step out onto the fifth floor hall away from all this curiosity.

The receptionist's booth, a stool at a high shelf, surrounded on three sides by glass, was empty. This appeared to be the haven of the forbidding person who surveyed all those wishing to enter Quincy Kemp's sacred portals. But not at this moment. Everyone at the *Morning Telegraph* had gone home or out to lunch. A dozen desks beyond were empty. A man in a far corner, wearing a green eyeshade and heavy-lensed glasses, busily hacked up other newspapers with a pair of gigantic shears. Probably collecting columns from rival newspapers.

Deeply aware of her unsuitability to this setting, where men, and a few women, molded the opinions of millions of Americans, she wished she had worn a batiste blouse and serge skirt. That would have shown them she "meant business," as Aunt Sybil was fond of saying. But she had been anxious to show Mr. Quincy Kemp, who pretended to know so much about Cubans, that they weren't all wild-eyed revolutionaries armed with bombs and blood-stained machetes.

She stood there looking around, wondering where to begin. The man cutting out clippings paid no attention to her, and she had a feeling that famed columnists must look just a little more important. Across the big room the scene seemed right. Two cubicles were cut off from the room by glass partitions and in one of them a man stood with his back to the open doorway, looking down at Broadway five stories below. He pushed up the window and leaned out. The sounds of the street, the hum of city life, an occasional shout, the rattle and thud of harness and hoof, the peculiar high toot of an auto horn reached Antonia as she crossed the room through the maze of desks and cuspidors.

There was an amateurishly carved wooden plaque on the man's desk reading "Q. Kemp." She studied the columnist's back as she approached. Tall and surprisingly trim. She had pictured him as short, pugnacious and middle-aged. But the man's hair was thick, dark, coarse and curly. All in all, he was a far more romantic figure than she and her family had been led to believe when Aunt Sybil first volunteered to introduce Antonia to him.

"Just a typical newsman," she had said. "Smart and ruthless, but reasonable if you handle him correctly. Bernard regularly lunches with him when he is down in Washington, and of course, we invite him occasionally to one of our soirees. He has the entrée at the White House and the Navy Department, you know."

The fact that he was Uncle Bernard Revelstoke's friend had pleased Antonia's parents, though Antonia was less impressed. Uncle Bernard's international investments gave him access to any number of unsavory characters, as Antonia had discovered on her occasional visits to Revelstoke House in northern Virginia. The spacious home, where many government affairs had been settled on the sly, was within an hour's drive of the fashionable Academy for Young Females Antonia had attended until she was eighteen.

With her excellent figure and modest height, she had thick, lustrous black hair, a magnolia complexion (due more to heredity than applications of soured milk) and her celebrated "violet eyes." These qualities gave her a reputation, not too wildly exaggerated, as the reigning beauty of a school famed for turning beauties out upon the Washington matrimonial market. But to the despair of her mother, she was still unmarried at twenty, having broken two engagements for the capricious reason that "she wasn't passionately in love."

It was all the fault of this Yankee influence in her formative years. As Señora Ysabel reminded in her gentle, loving voice, "Had you gone to convent school in Madrid, you might have been the mother of a fine brood by now and we should have no problems."

Whether Patrick Maguire agreed with this view was hard to guess. He had learned never to argue with a "Guzman y Pontalvo." The dispute would always lead back to Ysabel's ancestor, the one who rode with Cortes on the conquest of Mexico, or worse, the ones who supervised the secular punishment of heretics during the Inquisition.

Faced with the object of her angry search, Antonia lost courage. She was in Quincy Kemp's unfamiliar world now. She took a tight grip on her useless parasol, cleared her throat, and burst out:

"Mr. Kemp, there isn't a man in New York—even Mr. Willie Hearst—who knows less than you do about Cuba."

She was surprised at her own vehemence. Too late she decided that such a tone required a woman of greater height. She wasn't tall enough to carry off the haughty, imperious manner. She was revising her tactics when he turned, started to say something but stopped in mid-sentence at sight of her. He had appeared to be amused, but that smile faded with the unfinished sentence.

"I'm afraid you—"

She was sophisticated enough to suspect he may have been impressed by her looks. She was considerably younger than the women she had seen around this building, and they did little to show themselves at their best.

Quincy Kemp was a surprise. If he was Irish, as Aunt Sybil claimed, he must number among his forebears some of those dashing Spaniards of the Armada who were washed onto Ireland's shores.

She was sorry he had stopped smiling. It was a delightful teasing smile that suited the warmth and power of his deep brown eyes. His physical attraction surprised her because it wasn't like Aunt Sybil to overlook such a point in describing him. Sybil Revelstoke enjoyed flirtations with younger men almost as much as she enjoyed being present when major political decisions were made.

Antonia began again. "I beg your pardon, that wasn't very tactful of me. I shouldn't have blurted it out like that. I'm Mrs. Revelstoke's niece."

"Of course. You came to lay information? Or to make a complaint perhaps?"

He expressed himself so oddly and carefully, she wondered if he was making fun of her.

"In a way, sir. That is, I must take exception to your columns about Cuba."

He came around the huge beaten-up desk and waved her to the visitor's chair. Then, unlike some Americans of her acquaintance, he pulled the chair out for her but didn't sit down in his own big chair. Instead, he settled himself on the edge of the desk and looked down at her, making her keenly aware of his masculinity.

She had never felt so self-conscious. She shrugged or laughed off criticism from strangers. But now she bit her full lower lip, wondering if Quincy Kemp liked what he saw, wondering too what his lovemaking would be like. She could hardly avoid thinking about him that way; his physical appeal was overwhelming.

She wondered if he thought she had no business here, swooping into his office like Mrs. Astor, issuing an ultimatum without even an introduction. She cleared her throat, avoiding his eyes, pretending to study several framed citations on the wall, all of them proclaiming the wonders of one Quincy L. Kemp.

"I meant to say," she went on, "I understand that you Americans are sympathetic to rebels. Your own country was once a rebel." She looked up at him suddenly and had the satisfaction of startling him by her direct gaze. "But you surely respect the truth, sir. The truth is that the people of Cuba are not all suffering martyrs. And the gunrunners... those pirates who carry weapons to murderous rebel leaders—believe me, sir, if you knew those men you would despise them."

"You know these blockade runners personally?" he asked with interest, his black eyebrows raised.

"Not personally, of course. But my father is well aware of their crimes. And General Weyler is frank about calling them blood-thirsty pirates."

"Ah. So Weyler the Butcher calls them bloodthirsty." For some reason he seemed to find this conversation, and probably herself, amusing. He didn't smile but the amusement was in his eyes.

"Please don't call the captain general of Cuba a butcher. I know that is the name you Yankees have given a brave soldier, but Valeriano Weyler is a loyal subject of the queen regent and *she* would never permit the atrocities your columns and others charge him with."

Seeing that she had not impressed him, she added, annoyed by her own pompous tone, "My mother is a close friend and confidante of the queen."

"Queen Victoria? I would not have thought so, considering the old queen's age," he murmured, still the air of a man teasing a child.

"Queen María Cristina, of course!"

"Of course. Forgive me." Even his apology sounded as if he were mocking her, and yet his eyes managed that gentle amusement. He looked at her, obviously weighing his words, then leaned a few inches toward her. She stiffened and he retreated, but without amusement. His pleasant voice was suddenly tipped with ice, which made her far more uncomfortable. "I thought it might be worth-while to explain to you. Probably I was mistaken. I know a few of these blockade runners. Some of them are as you say. No better than pirates. But some, like Leidner and this . . . this Juan Diego, they risk their lives almost daily to feed starving women and chil-dren and bring an end of reconcentration."

His sudden intensity as much as his words puzzled her. Here was no casual male flirting and teasing, treating women like chil-dren as so many did. He spoke to her as if she were an equal, to be reasoned with. She found herself appreciating it.

"Then you do write about what you know, señor? . . . sir." she corrected herself.

"We try."

She sighed. "Then please tell me why you regard reconcentration as so shocking. I'm familiar with the word. Papa—my father explained that it was necessary to remove some rebel families from wretched squalor to decent cabins surrounding the army posts—"

"The *Spanish* army posts."

"Naturally..."

His building intensity was certainly surprising in a man with Quincy Kemp's reputation... Aunt Sybil had said that Kemp would go anywhere, take any side of a story, if he thought it would get a few more readers. Apparently he had decided Antonia was worth one of his better efforts.

"You must return to Cuba."

"I intend to."

"Ah, but next time, ask someone—not your precious papa—to take you to the camps of the *reconcentrados.*" He added, "I wish I could be the man to do that... I would dearly love to take you."

His dark eyes were no longer gentle or even warm. They burned. She was aware that her chin was raised. She did not mean to antagonize him but his absolute certainty provoked her. Any insult to her family would always make her react this way.

"And what purpose would that serve?"

He put out one hand. This time she remained rigidly in place. His forefinger outlined her lips with a light touch that she found disturbing. But hardly unpleasant. "You have a compassionate mouth. I don't think you'll be unmoved by what you see. In the past year the death rate in those so-called camps is over four hundred a week. Some camps report two hundred deaths a night."

She stared at him, honestly shocked. "But why, how—?"

"From starvation and exposure. Malaria and yellow fever spread like fire through those charnel pits where they're forced to live. The filthy conditions breed disease... and there's the brutality of some of your soldiers."

She persisted, if rather weakly. "They probably would have died in any case. Our climate is tropical. Even the *haciendados* sometimes..." Her voice trailed off. She was still put off by the conviction in his manner, but if it were all true... She knew little about the hundreds of thousands of country peons who had been rounded up with whips, cattle prods and rifle butts, forced to leave the cabins and belongings of a lifetime, and then resettle in "camps" clustered around the soldiers' barracks. She had always assumed that these wretched women, children and old people were being protected from starvation. Many of their active males were out in the jungle leading a treacherous revolt against their lawful ruler, the Queen Regent María Cristina. Patrick Maguire said the government had been benevolent in reconcentrating them. Besides, everyone knew what barbaric acts of cruelty were committed by the rebels against plantation owners, Spanish patrols and decent women left momentarily unprotected. A few reprisals...

Surely Quincy Kemp's figures were exaggerated. The camps themselves could not be as terrible as the columnist said. After all, he only knew these things from hearsay and prejudice. He admitted he was aware of Captain Juan Diego and Captain Leidner, two modern buccaneers suspected of repeatedly breaking through both the Spanish government blockade and the United States blockade in the Florida Straits. With a naïveté surprising in so knowledgeable a man, this Quincy Kemp claimed they carried food to the rebel families, but Antonia had her father's word that this was only a small part of their real activity. Gossip among Cubans had made them notorious for furnishing weapons to the rebels.

She pulled herself together, reached for her useless parasol, decided to behave with dignified understanding of his prejudices. "Well, Mr. Kemp, I am afraid it is you who are ill-informed. You should visit Cuba yourself and see the true situation. A man of your reputation really ought to leave Cuban matters to Cuban people. Meanwhile, señor, please *do* write about what you know."

He stood up and ushered her to the open door of the little glass office. She gave him her gloved hand. He took it in his palm—a callused palm unusual in a writer, she thought—and in the last seconds before she retrieved her hand he had kissed her bare wrist, just above the pearl button of her glove, creating an excitement in her far greater than anything her ex-fiancé and longtime admirer, Lloyd Hastings, had ever been able to produce.

She threaded her way between the cluttered rows of desks, spittoons and heavy typewriting machinery to the elevator, which opened abruptly. A stocky, fortyish man almost walked into her. He apologized. Then his bright blue eyes watched her until the elevator doors closed. Shrewd, clever eyes, she thought, and wondered if he was also here to argue something out with Quincy Kemp. And lose?

Because she was not at all sure that she herself hadn't been bested by the columnist she'd so confidently come to set straight.

CHAPTER
TWO

ANTONIA'S REFLECTIONS on her walk back to the Waldorf-Astoria were sobering enough to have delighted the pro-rebel columnist. She was annoyed by her response to Quincy Kemp's arguments, but they had been so vivid it seemed impossible to forget them.

So she welcomed the sight of Lloyd Hastings strolling with an elaborately casual air along the sidewalk outside the Fifth Avenue entrance to the hotel. He surely was not a spontaneous or passionate man, like her recent antagonist, Quincy Kemp, who had so dramatically described the supposed condition of the *reconcentrados*. Lloyd Hastings was far too careful. He had passed the bar in two states but his career centered in Washington, as one of the "conservative influences" in President McKinley's State Department. Which made him especially useful to Antonia's father at a time when Patrick Maguire's close friend, Captain General Weyler, the dictatorial ruler of Cuba, was being attacked in the Yankee press as "Weyler the Butcher."

Tall, slender, carefully groomed Lloyd Hastings was a perfect antidote to a man like Quincy Kemp. Antonia waved to him, remembering just in time not to wave her parasol. Lloyd did not approve of demonstrative women. Though she usually cared very little about pleasing him, today she felt the need of his support. Her self-esteem had been more than slightly dented by that newspaper columnist and she didn't want any tiresome disapproval even from Lloyd.

He responded to her wave with predictable enthusiasm, taking her hand in its lilac glove and asking her, "May I?" before his cool lips touched her cheek. She was sure Quincy Kemp would never have asked. Lloyd Hastings, of course, was a gentleman. She sighed. Her Aunt Sybil always claimed, "You can't have everything."

"My dear Antonia, you're looking especially well today," Lloyd told her as he escorted her into the perfectly named Peacock Row, a promenade area where the aristocrats of America and Europe, plus others with equal pretensions, exhibited themselves for the benefit and envy of their acquaintances.

She reminded him, "You may call me Tana, my friends do."

"But not your family, surely."

Good Lord. He was *so* solemn. "Well, if you want to treat me like a parent, it's no wonder we aren't married."

"Antonia, *really*." He looked uncomfortable but the chattering social magpies passing them were much too concerned with their own affairs to be shocked by this indiscreet young Cuban.

She nudged him. "Don't be so stuffy, Lloyd. Shall we stop and have tea? I adore those little cakes with the pink icing."

This casual suggestion was exactly what he had been edging around to. "Excellent idea. I have something to discuss with you."

They made their way among other strollers, especially females, several of whom had been sent to linger in the Peacock Row swathed in the latest fashions from their up-and-coming New York designers. Antonia eyed them all with interest, taking mental notes for her own benefit. During her visits to her home island she always noticed the French designer clothes worn by her brother Felipe's fiancée, Caris de Correña. Young Caris was not a female to be caught wearing last year's fashions. But the expensive garments that hampered movement seemed totally inappropriate to Antonia's busy life. She preferred to follow the lead of her soignée and extremely well-dressed Aunt Sybil.

After all, pretty, kittenish Caris needed only impress a select little group of Spanish-Cuban aristocrats. Aunt Sybil had entertained the presidents of the United States, Harrison, Cleveland and now William McKinley, along with all the important ambassadors, cabinet officers and the State and War departments. Sybil Maguire Revelstoke adapted her wardrobe and manners to her guests.

Antonia intended to follow in her footsteps, with almost everything but Aunt Sybil's husband. Antonia had never trusted Bernard Revelstoke, an unctious, overfriendly but oddly secretive lobbyist.

Over the elaborate tea service and her little pink cakes, Antonia prompted Lloyd about the matter he wanted to discuss with her. He reached for her fingers, burned the back of his hand on the elegant teapot and swore, but only under his breath. It was so like him.

She said impatiently, "You may say *damn*. I've heard it before. You ought to hear Felipe swear in Spanish. If you want to hold my hand, I've no objection. Just don't hold the one with this delicious cake."

Apparently her fingers were not all he wanted.

"Well, then, Antonia, have you given much thought to your age, and your family's plans for your future?"

She concealed her annoyance by plumping another of the petit fours into her mouth and chewing with gusto. She knew she had made him cross and was glad of it. At least, it was *some* emotion.

"My family's plans include you?"

"I wish—forgive me—but must you talk with your mouth full?"

She dabbed her lips and fingers carefully before saying, "That's me. You must take me as I am."

"Really, Antonia, you can be most provoking."

"And you are the stuffiest man I know. I suppose Father put you onto this idea. You will be happy to hear that he wants me to marry you too."

"Señor Maguire is very fond of me, I know."

To prick that bubble of conceit was her first concern. "He is fond of your influence with the State Department. You are against the

Cuban rebels. That's your great asset, dear Lloyd."

He glanced around again, hoping her voice hadn't carried. In this alcove of the busy hotel, however, her voice was easily drowned by the clink of silver on fragile china and the hum of many voices.

"I never made a secret of that. There are some who call me inflexible. I admit it. I have done everything I can, my dear Antonia, to prevent recognition of those Cuban animals." She raised her eyes, studying him with more curiosity than anything else, and he repeated impatiently, "Yes. Worse than animals. They've been burning crops and fields, even the haciendas of their betters. I can't begin to . . . I won't describe what happens to the respectable women of good family who may be alone on the outer plantations."

She should have been delighted at this fresh argument that demolished all Quincy Kemp's talk about the suffering Cubans. Perversely, his cold indifference to the fate of the Cuban people caught between the governing Spaniards and the Cuban rebels brought out all her obstinacy.

"Tell me, Lloyd, do the reconcentrated peasants fall into the animal category? Did you know that four hundred people a week are dying of starvation and disease?"

He opened his mouth, closed it abruptly. "Where did you hear that propaganda?"

"From Mr. Quincy Kemp of the *Telegraph*."

"Impossible. Quincy Kemp is connected with . . ."

Intrigued, she urged him on. "Why couldn't he have such facts? Heaven knows, he's written in favor of the rebels before."

He waved away the problem of the columnist. "Of course. It's his job. Good old Quin. Some government departments have been known to use old Quin to get ideas across. Sort of feeling the water temperature, so to speak."

It didn't sound like the Quincy Kemp she had just met. It was disappointing to think that the exciting, passionate man she had met today could be used by Washington politicians. She repeated her first thought aloud. "The Quincy Kemp I met didn't seem the type. Do you know much about him? His family? His background?" She added just a beat or two later, "His wife and children?"

It surprised her some that he knew so much. "Kemp's wife died some time ago. Galloping consumption, they called it. They were said to be devoted. He's never quite gotten over it, I understand."

Somehow, the columnist with the deep, warm brown eyes and the expressive hands had not behaved like a bereaved widower.

"Antonia, you haven't answered my question. Our engagement would delight your family. You almost said yes last year. I have your parents' approval. Both of them."

"What did you do? Write and ask them first?"

"I did what I thought a proper Spanish family of your mother's class would approve."

She waited until he insisted on accompanying her to her Aunt Sybil's suite before she blurted out, "Lloyd, haven't you ever in your life thought of marrying because of a great passion?"

"Well, certainly . . . it may be that I feel for you even more than your father felt for your mother."

She laughed. "Dear Lloyd, the truth is, Patrick Maguire's great passion was not for Ysabel Guzman y Pontalvo. It was for all those plantations, fields and town houses and haciendas she inherited."

"I hope you don't go around repeating this."

"Why not? They learned to respect each other. As a matter of fact, they are devoted to each other. Father doesn't even have a mistress." She considered this thoughtfully. "So far as I know."

"Antonia!"

By this time they were outside Aunt Sybil's suite, and Lloyd Hastings behaved toward the attractive Washington hostess with propriety plus a certain innocuous air of flirtation that might have won him a higher place in Antonia's affections if he had practiced it on her. It occurred to her that this ability might have been his greatest asset, being able to flatter females without arousing the slightest resentment in their husbands.

Antonia's Aunt Sybil had begun life as a red-haired colleen, developing at an early age into an admirably curved beauty. She had reached the age of forty-eight with her curves well corseted and her hair redder than ever. She still held the courtesy title of "a beauty," but her vast acquaintance had also begun to suspect there were brains in that charming head, despite her light, almost foolish laugh and her way of eliciting government secrets in the most innocent way.

Today she was reclining on a chaise longue in some kind of oriental brocaded green robe, and waving her ivory Chinese fan briskly as she accepted Lloyd Hastings' compliments.

Watching her, Antonia said mischievously, "Lloyd, I warn you, behind Aunt Sybil's fan lie a hundred secrets."

Lloyd's return was somewhat heavy-handed. "So long as that fan doesn't hide the handsomest eyes in Washington."

Sybil Revelstoke gave her niece an amused side-glance. Antonia stifled a giggle but was less pleased when Aunt Sybil suggested, "Dear Mr. Hastings, you see two ladies in distress. We are so in need of an escort down to Washington tomorrow. I know how involved you are in matters of national importance, but if you could put them aside, just this once, we would be so very much in your debt. And then, you must talk to us all about that delightful Mr. McKinley. Such a secretive little man. But I am persuaded you will unravel everything there is to know about him. You are so clever."

Lloyd hesitated, flattered but clearly conscience-stricken. Aunt Sybil saw his frowning look at Antonia and added, "Mr. Hastings, I shall be your cupid. Yes. You will accompany us and I shall never cease to remind our dear Tana of your splendid qualities."

She won, of course. Aunt Sybil always won. Antonia had no doubt the whole thing was staged so that Sybil Revelstoke could learn anything new about the cautious President McKinley. Antonia made a face at her but there was no getting out of it. Sybil was as devious as she was charming. As a girl, Antonia had often pictured herself playing a "spy" like Aunt Sybil. It seemed, even now, the most romantic job in the world.

Having resigned herself to a boring train ride down to Washington and then the Revelstoke carriage over bumpy roads to Revelstoke House, Antonia took very little trouble about her appearance for the occasion. She wore a last-year's deep blue taffeta gown and its tight jacket that hugged her bosom. She made no effort to be charming, and then, after all this nonpreparation, she walked into her fascinating opponent Quincy Kemp. Literally.

It was more than a little annoying. Also, remarkably coincidental.

She had rattled and stumbled from the diner of the train to Aunt Sybil's compartment to pick up her aunt's journal "for jotting down tiresome little details about the journey," as her aunt explained blandly to Lloyd Hastings. Antonia was just making her way back through three cars when the train lurched heavily around a curve in the green Maryland countryside and she fell against the corridor door, then was thrown the other way into the competent arms of the man who had occupied so much of her thoughts for the last twenty-four hours.

Before she saw anything but his shirtfront and felt his hands grip her forearms, she heard him say "Take care," in that curious way she remembered, which sounded faintly foreign, not the brisk Yankee "Careful, there." She apologized, but looked into his eyes, those unforgotten warm, dark eyes. There was a glow in them now that excited her and she almost forgot what she was saying. Well, why not let him know how much he attracted her? She had been a little spoiled by her easy conquest of most male admirers and saw no reason to deflect this man with imaginary airs.

"It's you, Mr. Kemp. How very nice."

That, at least, made him smile. "I'm delighted you think so, Miss Maguire. You have forgiven me then. I remember I made you quite indignant when I mentioned the *reconcentrados.*"

"Oh, that." She shrugged away the opinions of a lifetime, anxious to please him. "I like to hear both sides of every question."

"Admirably broad-minded. Beautiful young ladies are not always so wise." He spoiled this by adding, "Especially those with your background, Señorita Maguire."

"I didn't say I agreed with you." He was still holding her, and the Maryland scenery had relapsed into its familiar green fields and copses. She no longer needed his physical support. This was disappointing, but pride made her remind him, "I think you may safely let me go, Mr. Kemp."

He did so but to her satisfaction his hands proved reluctant. "Kemp. An ugly name, don't you think?"

She laughed. "I hardly know you well enough to call you Quincy."

Apparently he didn't like his first name any better. How odd! He wrinkled his nose at it. "Never. How they could give such a name to an innocent child... You are a Spaniard. Why not try some less formal name in Spanish... *mi amor?* But I leave the selection to you."

"You are being quite ridiculous. *Amor* means... never mind, I don't know you nearly well enough. And even if I did, I wouldn't." She saw that he was laughing at her silently and she laughed too.

She watched one of his hands, the lean dark fingers moving toward her face, but she pretended not to see them. After all, if she noticed, she would have to stop them.

He caught her chin between thumb and forefinger. She moistened her lips, managing a casual smile. None of her usual admirers went this far on such short acquaintance. This man was exciting.

"I enjoy pretty girls."

"I'm glad to hear you are normal—but I am not available for you—"

She tried to jerk her head away but his other hand moved up to the back of her head, reaching beneath the thick black hair and holding her in place. She found his lips as she had expected them to be, warmly sensual, their first touch gentle but titillating so that she was able to respond without thinking she'd signaled a greater involvement. That was the last time she underestimated him.

Having gotten her response in that kiss, a teasing one that she had often used with fumbling young men of the past, he now crushed her mouth, began to force her lips apart. She found herself too excited, all out of proportion to the kiss itself. She shivered under the impact of his hard, muscular body.

She was finally able to break away just as the train hooted its way into Baltimore's station. The pullman car rocked and shivered but she kept her balance and was able to laugh when she saw that the devastating Quincy Kemp was also a bit breathless. He laughed, too, realized she was studying him.

"*Bueno,*" he said surprisingly. "*Muy bueno.*"

She couldn't deny his effect upon her. Or hers on him. She knew he was playing a game. Well, let him be the loser for a change. Except she had to be careful she didn't play it too well...

She ignored his effort at Spanish dialogue. "Here we are at Baltimore. We'll soon be in Washington. I'd better be on my way. Lloyd will be wondering what—but who knows, Mr. Kemp, Washington is a small place. Perhaps we may meet again soon."

"Lloyd?"

"I was almost betrothed to a Lloyd last year."

"I see." He looked disapproving, as if he found her flippancy distasteful. She was annoyed by her own blunder.

"*Adiós,* Señor Kemp."

"Until we meet again, *mi amor.*"

She looked back and gave him one last smile as he reached over her head and pulled the door open for her.

She made her swaying, jolting journey back through the cars to the diner. Her first sight of the table where Lloyd sat talking earnestly to Aunt Sybil made Antonia once more ambivalent about conquering Quincy Kemp. He might be much too sure of himself but it was part of his challenge to her. Even if Lloyd Hastings actually felt a tepid love for her, he was obviously more interested in marrying the heiress to the Guzman y Pontalvo estate. Politically, too, he would profit by an alliance with the family of Captain General Weyler, the master of Cuba.

How clever her aunt was . . . Sybil Revelstoke seemed to be actually spellbound by Lloyd's conversation.

"Amazing! And to think Mr. McKinley confided it to you. He must trust you very much," she was saying to Lloyd.

"In confidence, ma'am. In strictest confidence."

Aunt Sybil placed one hand gently on his sleeve. "It won't go farther with me, dear Mr. Hastings. I'm not quite sure what it all means anyway. I'm afraid I've forgotten what it was about. So complicated. My poor head just spins when I think about international details. I really believe I don't know rebels from Spaniards." Antonia remained still until her aunt added, "Of course, at our house we are liable to see both sides. My interest, dear boy, is purely social."

"Naturally, ma'am."

Antonia made an appearance. Lloyd got up and would have seated her but she reminded him, "We had better return to our compartment. We'll be in Washington any minute."

"Too true." Aunt Sybil gave a little sigh, held out her hand to Lloyd. "Such a nice trip, thanks to our gallant friend here. You must come to visit us at Revelstoke. You will always be welcome." She gave Antonia one of her innocent asides, "Though I *swear*, I never understand all the fascinating things Mr. Hastings does. He's so knowledgeable, dear. Have you noticed?"

Antonia smiled. Aunt Sybil, she thought, if Lloyd Hastings has any secrets you still don't know about, they can't be worth knowing.

The two ladies with their escort left the train at Washington. While Lloyd was busy seeing them into the aged Revelstoke open carriage drawn by a matched pair of bays, Antonia saw Quincy

Kemp cross the road some thirty yards away. He looked back at her, grinned and went on with a very dark man. An Indian? Or Cuban? She nudged her aunt.

"Mr. Quincy Kemp just passed. You will invite him to Revelstoke, won't you? He can be very influential, we might even sway him to our side."

Aunt Sybil turned but too late. The two men had disappeared behind the columns of the busy station. Sybil agreed with her niece's thinking. "Very true, dear. Bernard and Quincy often have business to discuss."

Antonia was disappointed that the columnist should have any dealings with Uncle Bernard, whom she had mistrusted since her girlhood when he seemed much too interested in her and her low-necked ball gowns. Still, it was delightful to reflect that she would have a social excuse to be seen with Quincy Kemp.

CHAPTER
THREE

Antonia's long school years, added to the recent years of Cuban revolt when she had been left in her Aunt Sybil's care, had given her deep affection for Revelstoke House. It began to seem more like home than her birthplace, the three-hundred-year-old family *palacio* in Havana.

Antonia loved the mellow red brick house in its setting of Virginia pastures, distant blue hills and, across its long two-and-a-half-story front, a thick copse of trees. The Revelstoke Woods, as they were somewhat grandiloquently called, curtained off the house from those visitors who turned away from the busy Fredericksburg-Washington roads to enjoy the varied attractions offered by Sybil and Uncle Bernard. It was an estate purchased in Bernard Revelstoke's name but with money borrowed by Sybil from her brother Patrick. The money had never been paid back. Nor did Patrick expect repayment.

Aunt Sybil told her niece with unaccustomed honesty, "If you

31

could only regard Revelstoke as your home, my dear Tana, Patrick might never require payment, since Bernard and I will certainly have no heirs at this late hour."

Antonia laughed at the invitation. "You put it so delicately, I'm overwhelmed. But I adore it here. I always have." They were standing out on the front veranda, Sybil annoying the gardener with her hints about the cutting of the straggling honeysuckle hedge while Tana was exuberantly inhaling the sweet morning air. "It really is heaven."

"A matter of opinion. But it serves its purpose. By the way, the Quiet Little Man is coming tonight. That ought to set a special seal on the evening. Now, Tana, if you want to be a Washington hostess, you will be especially nice to him."

"President McKinley?"

"Of course. His wife won't be along. Not well, you know. They say she has—well—she swoons at awkward times."

Since they were being frank, Antonia challenged her. "Tell me, Aunty, do you have no compunctions about wheedling secrets out of the president of the United States? What will it gain you?"

"Compunctions? A big word for an amusing little game. No, darling, I don't mind. Besides, the Little Man is most secretive. I doubt if I'll learn—well, no more of that. I have a surprise guest tonight. I want the president to meet him. And the Spanish minister, that charming Dupuy de Lôme. Poor Dupuy. For all his beautiful manners and cleverness he is so dreadfully unpopular with the people. You Spaniards haven't made yourselves loved in this country."

"'We Spaniards,' as you call us, have no reason to love the United States government. They've grabbed up half of Spain's overseas empire in the southwest."

"Well, dear, that's politics. At all events, I can't wait for the explosion when Dupuy de Lôme meets my surprise guest."

"Quincy Kemp?"

"Quin? Good heavens, why would he be a surprise? Yes, he will be here. He may even write something about our surprise guest, who is a dashing fellow. Wait until you meet him. But I really don't see what you find so fascinating about Quincy Kemp. He's brilliant, I admit. Sometimes too clever for a simple newspaperman. But he can be useful."

Antonia ran a finger over her lips, remembering. "Among other things."

Aunt Sybil shook her head. "Tana, you certainly never learned such behavior from your mother or me. I can't imagine a daughter of the Guzman-Pontalvos behaving toward men with the freedom you use."

"Ah, but I am a woman of the twentieth century, Aunty. You belong to the nineteenth, and mother—well, mother belongs to the *sixteenth*."

"We haven't quite reached the twentieth century yet, I am happy to say. And I'll thank you not to rush matters. Heaven knows, I find myself old enough in 1897."

Antonia ignored the gardener's frown, broke off a tangled bit of sweet honeysuckle and tucked it into her aunt's russet-red pompadour. "You will never be old, Aunt Sybil."

Her aunt, no fool, readjusted the honeysuckle but didn't remove it. She accepted the compliment. "Of course. I will certainly use every weapon at my command to remain young. Come. I want to see what Calvin and the others have done with the preparations. Food is the greatest weapon of propaganda there is. Always remember that, my dear. I sometimes wonder what I would do if Calvin and the others were northerners. Calvin was born a slave, you know. Owned by that sad little war widow who sold us the place. Her family built Revelstoke in 1710. They called it Woodland Manor. Isn't that quaint?"

Antonia was used to the hundred servants of the several Maguire households at home in Cuba. Neither their condition nor their pittance of salary raised them much above slavery, but she was always shocked by the ease with which Sybil Revelstoke and her friends constantly referred to the previous servile condition of their black "retainers."

So many northerners who had moved south immediately after the Civil War and absorbed the vacancies left by the war's attrition seemed to feel that these black freedmen were part of war's spoils. However, Antonia decided it was not her affair.

Antonia did her best to absorb her aunt's teaching in the conduct of a great household. It was the one subject both her mother and her aunt agreed was vitally important to a young female in Antonia's position. But several hours spent inspecting the work of the ex-

cellent domestics and making picayune criticisms seemed excru-
ciatingly dull to Antonia. She escaped finally in the warm afternoon
when she had been ordered to "lie down, dear, and rest. We have
a long evening ahead and we want to look our prettiest."

With her aunt doing just that amid the faint laughter, chatter
and arguments of the busy servants throughout the house, Antonia
strolled out across the veranda and the pebbled road into the close—
overgrown woods that separated Revelstoke from the busy world
of Washington and the Virginia towns. Although spring was well
under way, the carpet of buttercups had not quite disappeared,
and she walked carefully, loving the delicate flowers, hating to step
on and crush even one of them.

Antonia pictured a harmless tête-à-tête with Quincy Kemp out
here on the edge of the woods, the scene faintly lighted by the
Japanese lanterns strung along the veranda, and the flaring, romantic torchlight that would illuminate the carriage road to the
house. The estate road needed something to spark it. It was mud
from December to May and full of dusty potholes the rest of the
year. How many tedious hours before Quincy Kemp rode over
those potholes? She realized he was not a man she could play fast
and loose with, which made the challenge even more irresistible.

She made her way very carefully among the buttercups and other
tiny field flowers until she could hear traffic on the Washington
road, the jingle of harness, the rattle of wagon wheels and the clip-
clop of dray horses. Any other kind of mount would come later in
the cool of the early evening. She passed the keeper of the warped
wooden gate across the Revelstoke estate road and began to hear
heavy, distant sounds. Although an occasional automobile chugged
its way along the road every other noise suddenly appeared to have
been swallowed up by a distant thunderstorm.

She scowled up at the piercing blue sky whose only disturbance
was a fleecy white cloud over the hills to the west. No storm there.
But the rumbling sounds came on. It seemed clear now that the
noise was on the road, probably this side of Woodland Rectory.
She walked along the edge of the road, avoiding the line of dogwood
trees that hovered low over the meandering, leaf-choked stream.
The confused noises grew clearer, like a parade. An unpleasant
parade. Screams. Yells. Catcalls.

The road took a detour around a huge old water oak. Beyond

the turn she made out a fretting, nervous horse and closed buggy surrounded by a yelling parade of people. Most of them had squeezed onto a hay wagon. Others rode bicycles, and a few ran along the sides of the black buggy. Some appeared to be Latin, but many of the youthful crowd looked like the labor union members she had seen in the New York parade. They probably represented a dozen nationalities. Whatever their identity, their object was obvious: the person in the black buggy.

Three pretty girls in the wagon held up a homemade, rather amateurishly printed sign on a strip of butcher paper that fluttered in the breeze. It read: "Labor for Our Amigos! Cuba Libre!"

Antonia stared at the black buggy. She recognized the handsome, dark-bearded face of Spanish Minister Enrique Dupuy de Lôme, whom she had met several times. While he seemed to be conservative like most of her father's Spanish friends, he was also a trusted envoy of the more liberal Queen Regent, María Cristina. Obviously, the buggy was headed for the Revelstoke turnoff. She hurried back to help this early guest. There was the old wooden gate a hundred feet up the estate road. The aged gatekeeper was on duty; she had seen him leaning against a gate post and smoking his pipe, and the horse and buggy might trot through, leaving this noisy crowd behind. But if there should be a delay, Señor Dupuy would be in trouble. Not to mention the United States for having failed to protect their ambassadorial guest only an hour or two out of Washington.

Antonia picked up her cumbersome lawn skirts and ran up the estate road but the crowd kept pace beside the buggy. The old man at the gate shuffled to attention but misunderstood the situation and started to chain the gate shut. Antonia called to him to open for the buggy. *"Only* the buggy."

There was a pile-up at the gate. Antonia elbowed her way to the front of the crowd, avoiding the nervous horses. She waved her arms, shouting in Spanish, "Down with Spain! Cuba for the Cubans!"

Most of the crowd stopped yelling. A young Cuban looked down at her from the wagon. "You are with us, señorita?"

Antonia thought, If Aunt Sybil could see me now... I'm more of a hypocrite than she is. Aloud, she said in Spanish, "Certainly. Why do you think we invited the gentleman here? We hope to persuade His Excellency to see the problem of the *reconcentra-dos*."

"Let him report this demonstration to his precious queen," a girl called out in English. "It'll do her good."

Antonia made a great show of laughing. "We'll tell him that. And more, *amigos*. A great deal more. Her Majesty should know the truth about those poor people in the camps. This cruelty must be stopped." For good measure she added, "*Viva Cuba Libre!*"

The temper of the crowd had been soothed, and after some muttering the wagoneer began to back his team, preparing to turn around. Several men on bicycles hesitated, exchanged glances and, to Antonia's intense relief, likewise began to turn back.

She waved to them, tried to give the situation her coup de grace. "Leave him to us, *amigos*. I will personally straighten this gentle-man's thinking."

The young Cuban grinned. "I do not doubt it, señorita. You might straighten any of us, as you say. Good luck. The rest of you, *andale!*"

"*Adiós, amigo*," she called after him as he led the retreat, and she added to herself, "*Madre de Dios*, forgive me for my lies today," and then she laughed, much pleased with herself.

With the gate closed and the chain dropped around the fence post, the ambassador's buggy was safely inside the Revelstoke grounds. Señor Dupuy's companion, a white-faced, scared male of middle years, possibly a secretary or valet, opened the buggy door on a word from his autocratic master and bowed to Antonia, who was hurrying along beside the buggy.

In Spanish he murmured shakily, "His Excellency asks if the señorita will join him."

Antonia was happy to do so. She had always admired the Spanish minister's polished manners. She knew he could be brutally frank to his confidants like her father and General Weyler. It was said that he had little respect for President McKinley himself, but it was easy to forget these small matters when he treated her with so much respect. And it was warming to hear the sonorous Spanish language again as it should be spoken.

She was quick to take advantage of his invitation. With a tilt of his head Señor Dupuy indicated the noisy, retreating crowd behind him. He remarked in Spanish, "I believe it was an English general at Waterloo who said, 'That was a near-run thing.'"

"Not from them, Excellency. They were young and enthusiastic. They just wanted to let our government know how they feel about the forcible concentrating of thousands of people who haven't committed any crime." That sounded, as nearly as she could remember, like the charge made by Quincy Kemp.

He looked at her sharply. There was no anger but something more disconcerting in his eyes. He seemed to be analyzing everything she said, probably storing it away to tell her parents. "Then I am to believe you meant those obscenities you uttered to that mob?"

"No, no, that was a charade—"

His smile was chilling. "I assure you, I do not regard my assassination as a charade."

She retreated. If he made trouble for her with her parents, she might have to return home even before her brother's wedding in the broiling heat of early summer. "They had nothing like that in mind, señor. They just wanted to annoy you—"

"They succeeded."

"If they had intended violence they would never have left us at the gate." She remembered his close ties with her father and added quickly, "But I am certainly glad they turned around. Her Majesty needs you, señor."

Again the sardonic smile. "I confess I share your feeling. I sometimes wonder if anyone else in Washington realizes how dangerous the rebels have become. If Washington continues to encourage them, their fine wooden-headed *presidente* may find a new rebel army grown up around him. It is little more than thirty years since the last rebel army—the so-called Confederates—threatened Washington."

"True, very true..." But all this didn't explain why the queen's army felt it necessary to lock up and starve hundreds of thousands of civilians. It was all very perplexing, and though her mind and a lifetime of family loyalties told her the Spanish minister was right, her imagination had been touched, had been opened by Quincy Kemp's remarks. Besides, there was a certain ring of truth about those passionate young people today...

In a few minutes she surrendered Señor Dupuy de Lôme to her Aunt Sybil, awakened by her tall, efficient majordomo, Calvin Jepson, whose dignity was fully equal to the occasion. Nor had Antonia ever admired her aunt so much as at this time when, awakened suddenly and in her casual afternoon garments, she was able to be gracious and charming to her early guest.

Dupuy explained that he had arrived early in the hope of throwing "troublemakers" off the scent but they had followed him anyway, almost to her door. While Aunt Sybil digested this with proper shock, he went on, "I was saved by your lovely niece. In a somewhat unorthodox fashion. But we will say nothing more of that."

Antonia ran up the light maple staircase to dress. She had no intention of being caught disheveled and dust-stained by Quincy Kemp.

She needn't have worried. He did not arrive that evening until after the quiet, secretive arrival of President McKinley himself. Antonia met the president in the big kitchen, almost behind the newly purchased gas stove with its trash burner on the side. He had come in behind three advisers, or perhaps they were guards. They entered through the rear cool-room and pantry just as Antonia, wearing her best watered-silk grosgrain ball gown, was bending over to pick up her swansdown fan. Her bodice was much too low-cut for this kind of display and the president got an abundant view of her shapely breasts before she quickly got up, covering her decolletage with the feathers of the opened fan. She curtseyed, murmured some feeble excuse for being in the kitchen where the busy, bustling cook, Sapphira Bacon, clearly did not need her. She couldn't very well explain to the president that she had come to get a glass of water because champagne made her thirsty. Who wanted to appear so hopelessly gauche before the most important man in the United States?

When it came to that, she hadn't realized before that the president might be in any danger himself during these lively times. But why else would he arrive in his hostess' house by way of the kitchen and pantry?

He accepted her presence, however, without question. He had an unimpressive, rather blank expression on his clean-shaven face. Then she remembered a comment of Aunt Sybil's, unflattering but very possibly true:

"He is not a stupid man, and I doubt if his advisers can use him, though I'm sure they think so. There are wheels within wheels behind that wooden facade."

He looked taller than he was. Perhaps he was also smarter in his quiet way.

Antonia would like to have asked about those unfortunate civilian prisoners in Cuba while she had him here in the kitchen but she wasn't at all sure which side she defended currently. She told herself that she needed more information about the matter before she made up her mind. Information from Quincy Kemp...?

Mr. McKinley murmured a compliment and moved on. It was clear to Antonia that he hadn't the least idea who she was. As the president and his lackeys moved out of the kitchen (the lackeys giving her the contemptuous glances they saved for nonentities), she heard the comment from a man and woman near the hall doors.

"Quincy Kemp. He's that columnist with the New York *Telegraph*."

"Know-it-all."

He was that. Antonia pulled herself together, brushed off her skirts and strolled casually into the hall, then across to the long double drawing room. She threaded her way between chattering, noisy groups, the women dazzling in their jewels and stiffly corseted figures. Eventually, as Quincy Kemp was ushered into the room, Antonia managed to be standing under the main chandelier with its newly polished glass lusters that reflected her own more modest pearl-and-diamond set.

She watched her Uncle Bernard approach President McKinley accompanied by a stocky, graying man with a rugged face and Irish blue eyes. She frowned, stood on tiptoe, wondering where Quincy Kemp had disappeared to.

She tried not to have any more to do with her uncle than necessary, but this was one of those necessary times. Uncle Bernard's stocky friend seemed extraordinarily popular. He was already surrounded by several eager guests, leaving Uncle Bernard alone. Uncle Bernard's chubby face creased into his thick-lipped professional smile, but his small eyes were busy as always, observing, noticing everyone, every face.

Antonia watched him a minute before she went to him. He seemed to make mental notes of more than faces. He watched

men's hands, noted when they slipped into pockets or touched a
woman. He also took an interest in the groupings of his guests,
noting who spoke to whom. Maybe he even guessed what they
said.

She waved her fingers at him. He reached her before a hopeful
young State Department man could do so. Bernard Revelstoke's
roving eyes took in her splendor in an obvious fashion that put her
off but she tried to ignore the feeling.

"Uncle, they said Quincy Kemp was here. I wanted to thank
him for a kindness the other day in New York. Did you by chance
lose him along the way?"

He was surprised and she knew he didn't like to be taken by
surprise. Recovering, he was especially polite and avuncular. He
tapped the shoulder of a man in the group behind him.

"Quincy, you have a grateful admirer. I didn't know you and my
niece were acquainted."

The stocky man with the grizzled hair and Irish face turned
around. He grinned, his face lighting up. She recognized that face.
She had seen it at the elevator in the New York *Telegraph* offices
only a minute after she left the man she knew as Quincy Kemp.
He reached for her hand, took up the limp fingers. She was still
nonplussed.

"Well, well, so you like my work, Miss Maguire. Mighty pleased
to hear it. I figured, considering your family's close connection
with Weyler the Butcher that you'd be after my scalp."

Aware that a dozen people were watching them, she managed
a forced smile. She let the real Quincy Kemp shake her hand while
she murmured something inane. She had a suspicion he knew all
about her mistake.

Before she had fully recovered, her Aunt Sybil's voice called
everyone to attention. She rapped on a champagne glass with a
spoon and then, more loudly, rapped on the sideboard beside a
punch bowl.

"Mr. President, Your Excellency (to the Spanish minister), dear
friends all, when my husband and I invited you here for an unusual
evening, we promised you a fascinating guest. And here he is, the
bravest seaman on the Florida Straits. Some call him one of those
naughty rebel filibusters, but we know his only concern is humanity
... All those valiant trips to Cuba with food have saved hundreds,

perhaps thousands of lives. I give you Captain Juan Diego, the humanitarian, of the good ship *Baracoa*."

The tall man, all in close-fitting black, stepped out from behind the staircase. He seemed to give each of the upturned faces a penetrating look before he bowed and smiled.

Why not? Antonia asked herself, understanding at last. He had done everything superbly, and nothing more successfully than the way he made a fool of her. How could she ever have believed this dark Spanish-Cuban whom she had met in the *Morning Telegraph* office was an Irishman named Quincy Kemp?

CHAPTER
FOUR

HE CERTAINLY looked appropriately dashing in his close-fitted black outfit. Not a suit. It was very like the simple clothing worn by the mate of a deep-water sailing vessel, but even the buttons on the short Spanish jacket were black. Oddly enough, the lack of color was not oppressive, his own personality dominated it.

Aunt Sybil went on: "Whether we believe in Captain Diego's cause or not, we have all been touched by the sufferings of the civilian families in Cuba who have been reconcentrated into camps under guard of the Spanish army."

Several in the crowd gave Señor Dupuy curious side-glances, but though his features tightened he gave no other sign of offense.

Aunt Sybil held up a graceful hand. "You must have guessed that we are going to ask for donations. But surely you will not want to be found behind the rest of us in your generous charity. Captain Diego will answer any questions personally."

Uncle Bernard, well-primed, raised a hand with one finger up. "Let me open the drive with a thousand."

"Dear Bernard," Aunt Sybil murmured. "And you, Ethel? You, senator? You, my old friend—Commander Beckland?"

The rustle of billfolds being opened, however reluctantly, filled the night air.

Antonia watched Juan Diego, who stood by, impressed by his hostess' manipulation of her guests. The crowd now pressed around him, cutting him off from Antonia's view. She was grateful for the opportunity to recover her composure. She looked around, found there were others who hadn't rushed forward to greet and question "the hero."

Two State Department men had President McKinley cornered and were arguing with him in low if vehement tones. He remained calm, unmoved, and when they finished he signaled to Aunt Sybil and nodded. He would speak to the man whose little ship had committed several crimes against American laws by operating out of Florida waters, delivering goods, undoubtedly including guns, to the Cuban rebels.

A cool voice spoke to Antonia in Spanish.

"Your father is acquainted with his sister's treason against our queen, señorita?"

Antonia had been thinking something of the same but she resented the Spanish minister's reminder. She turned to him. "Now then, Señor Dupuy, Aunt Sybil is an American citizen. But aside from that, you know her better than some people do. Anyone who claims to be a public figure is her victim." She doubted if he believed her.

His fingers stroked the small, neat, V-shaped beard that added to his distinction but also gave him a slightly satanic look. "And you, señorita? Are you one of Señora Revelstoke's victims?"

"I?"

"Forgive me. I have an old affection for your parents. I dare to speak frankly. The fact is, you seem distracted tonight. Is it possible that what I heard today was a facade? That you are acting on behalf of your parents and Her Majesty the queen regent?"

Actually it had been one of her girlhood dreams to be a merciless, beautiful spy for some cause or other. She gave him her sweetest smile. "You heard my aunt say Captain Diego doesn't run contraband. He is a humanitarian. And if I remember correctly, no patrol boat, Yankee or Spanish, has ever proved otherwise."

"Perfectly true. He sailed into Santiago harbor last month in broad daylight with perfect freedom. It is said he carried wheat for the Spanish garrison. It is the voyages he does not make by daylight to government-controlled harbors that I question." He kissed her hand, adding, "Who knows, I may persuade this pirate to change his ways. He looks like a creature who would kill for a Yankee dollar. No matter who pays it."

"Who knows, indeed," she said, as he left. She was laughing when Captain Juan Diego, who had just been introduced to President McKinley, must have heard her. And he was caught by the sight of her. He knew she would be here, and she couldn't mistake the flash of approval in his eyes. She was far more pleased than she meant to be.

After all, he had fooled her shamefully.

He resumed whatever he was saying to the president, but the interruption proved unfortunate. One of the State Department men whispered something to McKinley, who nodded slightly to Captain Diego and turned away.

Not much hope for the Cuban rebels there. Still, the captain failed to approach Antonia. Quincy Kemp backed away from his group, caught the captain by the sleeve and drew him into a chattering tangle of admirers. Everyone moved to question the romantic newcomer. He did not look at Antonia again.

Señor Dupuy was still behind Antonia, and now said, "If, as I believe, you are loyal to your parents and their traditions, you might discover the plans of this pirate. Pardon . . . this humanitarian. You could, for example, find out the date of his next voyage. His cargo. Where he intends to deliver the weapons . . ."

She was revolted. "I hardly know him. Besides, there are a hundred possible shorelines in Cuba where he might land rebel supplies."

"Weapons and ammunition."

She shrugged and moved away from him, trying to make the withdrawal unobtrusive, and began to flirt with one of Lloyd Hastings' State Department friends. It was something to do.

Half an hour later Antonia saw the Spanish minister make his way over to an alcove where President McKinley stood alone, looking a little overwhelmed by one of Aunt Sybil's gigantic Chinese vases on a table behind him. Two of his advisers stood off like guards, just out of hearing. The alcove was very near the two hall doors which were ajar, but neither the president nor Dupuy de Lôme seemed aware of the slight movement Antonia thought she saw between those partly closed doors.

She pretended to listen to a young man who had once led the Lancers with her when she attended the Young Ladies Academy, but her thoughts were not there. Because so many intrigues took root in this house, she was especially intrigued by the possibilities of those hall doors that stood ajar. She was positive something had moved behind them... someone who would be listening to the conversation between the president and the Spanish minister.

Who would be most concerned by this close exchange between the president of the United States and the one man closest to the government of the queen of Spain?

Juan Diego came quickly to mind.

There were others, of course, but none with as much to lose by any understanding reached between McKinley and Dupuy de Lôme.

She looked around the long double drawing room, figuring to make out Captain Diego's distinctive black-clad figure. He had disappeared. What she saw was her Aunt Sybil talking to a heavyset woman whose brown foulard gown and unfashionable braided hair made her look very much out of her element here in this fashion-conscious gathering.

But Adelaide Heffernan, who had been Antonia's history and government teacher, was never troubled by the vagaries of fashion. Miss Heffernan was a passionate follower of the rebel *guerrilleros* in Cuba, not so much for their politics but because their families suffered such hardship. She had been the first person at the academy to teach the girls about the activities of Miss Clara Barton and the Swiss-born organization called the Red Cross. According to Adelaide, who had last year made a plea for pin money from the rich young students, Miss Barton and her handful of nurses were now trying to help the suffering thousands among the civilians concentrated in Cuban camps.

Though no longer in the academy, Antonia had given money liberally because Adelaide Heffernan asked for it. Her parents would have done the same. Their intense loyalty to the Spanish government didn't mean they weren't humane. Antonia hadn't understood the cause but she understood Miss Heffernan. Funny, stout Adelaide had often been referred to by the girls of the academy as "the Fat Saint," yet curiously enough, the girls were only half-joking. The truth was, they loved and admired her.

Antonia had no doubt Miss Heffernan was here now to meet her hero, Captain Diego. And was her hero at this very minute sneaking behind doors to eavesdrop on the president and the Spanish minister?

Antonia excused herself to the surprise of her love-struck admirer who had thought her violet eyes were misty over his compliments. She crossed the room to her aunt and Adelaide Heffernan. She teased, "Don't tell me Aunty hasn't introduced you to the dashing filibuster?"

Miss Heffernan lit up. "Tana, my dear child." And they embraced.

Over her shoulder Antonia scolded her amused aunt.

"You mean you haven't introduced her to our hero yet? Shame on you, Aunty. I only hope he appreciates her."

"Now, now," Miss Heffernan disclaimed modestly. "All the same, if Captain Diego agrees to take me, I can join Miss Barton's ladies in Havana. If you could come with me, Tana... you must return home soon for your brother's wedding. Why not at the hands of our hero?"

Antonia was captivated by the idea but very likely her parents would see it differently.

"The government is being most difficult," Miss Heffernan said. "They'll let me go on a steamship as a tourist, but not for any practical reason. It doesn't make a mite of sense."

Antonia said, "Why waste time with underlings? You can always ask President McKinley. He's over in that alcove."

Since Miss Heffernan showed every sign of following this suggestion, both Antonia and her aunt were forced to stop her, gently but with a certain firmness.

"Not quite yet," Aunt Sybil urged, holding her back with an arm across her ample bosom. "Another day, I think. The president is about to leave. I thought he and Captain Diego might accomplish

something but he has very little time. I believe he and Señor Dupuy
also had a brief discussion so at least it was all worthwhile."

Still suspicious about the listener behind those double doors,
Antonia asked, "Is Captain Diego in the room now? I don't see
him."

Aunt Sybil shrugged. "Who knows? Everyone wants a private
word with him. He might be anywhere in the house. Or on the
grounds."

Hoping against hope that Juan Diego hadn't been the person
behind those double doors, Antonia moved slowly on around the
room. There was a hall doorway in the north living room. A diplomat from the Austro-Hungarian Empire was flirting with a State
Department wife in the doorway. They shifted their positions,
making room for Antonia without letting their attention wander
from each other. The hall appeared to be empty. Whoever had
been listening to the president and the Spanish minister was gone
now.

Antonia walked the length of the hall, wondering just where
Captain Juan Diego was at this moment. One would think, with
all his popularity tonight, that he might be at the center of the
crush in the big drawing room. Maybe, though, he had heard what
he needed to hear and then simply left.

Perhaps she wasn't being fair thinking he was so devious, except
that he *had* deceived her, making her think he was the columnist
Quincy Kemp... She turned and started back. Uncle Bernard's
library door was open and across the room she saw the French
doors with their moonlight view of the pastures and an old stile
that she had sat on many times during her school years. The doors
opened on the south veranda. And then she saw a tall, lean man
on the grass below the veranda, staring out at the same view. She
recognized Juan Diego instantly. Her first reaction was pleasure.
Next, she realized that it had been only a few steps from the double
doors of the drawing room to that place below the veranda. It was
almost a straight move. Her suspicions hardened.

Suspicion, however, did not seem to subdue her weakness for
the captain, a weakness she excused on the grounds that he could
help Miss Heffernan. She walked silently across the room. At the
same time the captain shifted his position out on the grass and
proceeded in long, slow strides toward the pasture. He was heading

for the stile that had once been Antonia's special world when she sat on the top step and dreamed girlhood dreams of gallant heroes riding by to seize hold of her and set her up before them in the saddle.

The captain stopped with one hand on the wooden fence beside the stile. She reached up, tapped his shoulder with her closed fan.

"Good evening, Quincy Kemp. Written any more columns glorifying those murderous filibusters?"

He turned and looked down at her, soberly, as if he intended to read every nuance on her face. She would not be put off and tried again.

"I could tell you such a story about a pirate called Juan Diego ... But why bother... you've already told me what a fine fellow he is."

He finally allowed a smile and took her hand in his. "I am certain I didn't say it in quite those words."

She released her fingers from his strong clasp, after a suitable pause. "Our pirate friend Diego owes me an apology. Of sorts."

"For fooling you or for kissing you? I am happy to apologize for the time at the newspaper office. As for the kiss..."

She studied her fan, pulling at one of the feathers. She was more casual than coy when she said, "Well, that was a deception of sorts, at the newspaper office."

"And the other? Or are you kissed so many times by strangers in railway cars that it leaves no impression?"

"Ah, but you see, that was not a stranger. I had met the gentleman in New York."

"I surrender, Miss Maguire. I am no match for you. What is my forfeit?"

Which was her chance to speak up for Miss Heffernan. "I have a friend who wants to join Miss Barton and her Red Cross workers. I believe they intend to help your *reconcentrados*. Those civilians you were so eloquent about. She merely asks to be landed at a safe rebel harbor on the coast."

The warm Virginia night suddenly took on an electric atmosphere. He looked at her as if he had not seen her before. The moonlight made his dark eyes sparkle and she wondered if she had hurried ahead too fast.

"You surprise me, Miss Maguire. I had no idea you were interested in dull, suffering humanity."

"I *merely* wondered if you could take a friend of mine, a teacher, who wants to work with Miss Barton."

"So I'm not to have the company of the unpredictable Miss Maguire after all. I had thought she surely might actually care. Never mind."

"If you mean to say I'm afraid—"

He cut her short, he really seemed to have been disappointed by her refusal. "Afraid? Do your feelings run that deep, señorita? You are perhaps afraid of your own feelings, but I suspect you are more afraid of losing a few good meals. You might also wear out your second-best pair of shoes, or be scolded by your noble papa."

She avoided his eyes, turning her head in a way that seemed abysmally coquettish, even to her.

"I can't imagine anything less likely. But I do respect my parents' wishes and it happens they don't expect me home for almost three weeks."

He put out one arm, resting it against the stile behind her. "I sail in seventeen days. As you Yankees say, I'm calling your bluff."

"I am not a Yankee. I happen to be a loyal subject of the Spanish throne—"

"You are avoiding the issue. Tana Maguire, I have thought many things about you but not that you might be a coward."

"Only my friends call me Tana."

He put out his other arm, locking her within his loose embrace. "I've never wanted to be your friend. Come, now, I dare you to sail with me."

She raised her chin, enjoying the glow in his eyes that was at least part anger. The other part she could feel. He might disapprove of her but he wanted her. She broke the spell of the moment with a laugh. "This is the first dare I have ever refused. But I think, under the circumstances, I must."

"Coward." He leaned nearer. "Politics have nothing to do with it, have they? It's you. Who knows, I might agree to deliver your precious teacher to Miss Barton's group in Havana."

And suddenly, it occurred to her . . . "If they found any contraband in your ship, you would be taken and hanged."

"Shot."

"Well, much as I admire Adelaide Heffernan, I wouldn't ask you to risk your life"—she went on lightly—"or mine, if it came to that. Suppose your ship were attacked by the United States Navy. Or the Spanish navy. I don't especially want to get blown up. So..."

In spite of her words her eyes invited him. He accepted the invitation but prolonged his approach so that she very nearly gave up before he lowered his hands to her shoulders and, to her astonishment, shook her.

"Don't play this childish game with me." Which amused and excited her. In the past her hopeful lovers hadn't the nerve to make demands—

The force of his mouth on hers stopped childish comparisons and made her think on the possibilities that would present themselves if she took his dare and sailed home to Cuba with him. Besides, there could be no more highly respected duenna than Adelaide Heffernan, nor a woman more easily fooled...

While his mouth held hers, his fingers moved over the back of her gown, edging the satin and heavy silk off her smooth shoulders. *Por Dios*...was he going to undress her in full view of any one who happened onto the veranda?

His touch was fire and she didn't want him to stop. She dug her fingers into his shoulder muscles, holding him, guarding this instant, knowing all the time that it had to end, and quickly. But surely *this* must be what passion was meant to be... He released her mouth and she gulped the night air, regaining her breath only to be trapped again when he bent his head and his lips touched her bared shoulder, which she felt all the way down her body.

The pressure of him made her body arch back against the stile, and she wondered for the first time in her life if she had invited more than she could handle. His hands still bit into her upper arms, but he drew back a few inches, reading something of her possible resistance in her narrowed eyes. He smiled, not a pleasant smile. His voice sounded harsh.

"I'll finish this, you know"—her eyebrows went up—"when I wish. But I never land my catch when it is immature. I throw it back." And abruptly he let her go.

She realized he probably expected her to go into a tantrum and thereby further betray her immaturity. She refused. Her answer was a light, silvery laugh and: "Only a fisherman. Not a pirate after all." She swept the train of her gown away from his legs where it had become entangled. "Good night, *captain*."

Still he managed to get in the last word as he called after her, "I pay my forfeits. Tell your Miss Heffernan I will carry her to Cuba."

She knew she should have ignored this but couldn't resist. She turned as she reached the veranda, "Thank you, and I really hope they won't hang you."

"Shoot me," he called back.

Without looking back again, she called out, "That, too."

Seconds later she almost walked into Señor Dupuy de Lôme, who stood in a shadowed corner, smoking a cigarette.

As a loyal Spaniard she decided she would have to warn the Spanish minister that his conversation earlier with president McKinley had apparently been overheard. Also, this might take his mind off the sight of his friend's daughter kissing a rebel pirate. She would not, though, tell him that she suspected the man she had kissed with such enthusiasm.

Dupuy spoke first. "Clever of you, señorita. You have been learning the details of Captain Diego's next voyage, no doubt."

She heard the sarcasm, but it didn't trouble her as much as the fear that he himself had heard the captain's mention of a voyage in seventeen days.

She laughed and quickly agreed. "My father wants me home within three weeks, for my brother's wedding. Captain Diego kindly offered to take me. He wants to prove to the Spanish authorities that he is a loyal Cuban and that all the gossip about him is a lie spread by the real fillibusters."

"Ah . . . ?"

She didn't much like the sound of that and hurried on. "He suggested a duenna, Miss Adelaide Heffernan, and he expects to pass the Havana customs." She added this, hoping to offset his suspicions; after all, the captain would hardly let himself be caught running contraband while carrying a young aristocrat related to the captain general of Cuba and a respectable Yankee like Miss Heffernan.

Dupuy studied the glowing tip of his cigarette. "So Juan Diego is not a filibuster. Her Majesty—not to mention the captain general—will be relieved to hear that. You may assure Diego, however,

that General Weyler himself will be at the Havana docks to supervise the customs inspection—and to greet you."

In spite of her family's insistence on the noble character of Captain General Weyler, whose niece would soon enter the Maguire
y Guzman family, Antonia could not forget his nickname of "the
Butcher." Either Juan Diego must abandon this trip, or it was
crucial that Tana Maguire and Miss Heffernan should be aboard
the *Baracoa* when it reached Havana.

CHAPTER
FIVE

THOUGH THERE was nothing Antonia would rather do than become Captain Diego's passenger on the *Baracoa* to Havana, she had enough common sense to know she couldn't make even this short voyage of half a day alone with such a man and his crew, which made the idea of using naive Adelaide Heffernan as her duenna and chaperon so appealing. Miss Heffernan might not be nearly as lively a companion as Aunt Sybil, but under the circumstances that could be an advantage.

Meanwhile, the Revelstokes became a problem. To Aunt Sybil any secret in which she had no part became a challenge, and she seldom veered away from the subject of Miss Heffernan as a passenger on the *Baracoa*. Antonia was quite sure she would disapprove of Antonia's involvement, but she simply had to know any secrets.

"Tana, dear, a birdie hinted to me that our dashing captain might carry Adelaide to those Red Cross females in Havana. I daresay she is quite a bit too old to tempt Juan Diego, but one wonders."

"Aunty, don't be silly. Miss Heffernan is a spinster going on fifty. Captain Diego would never—" She hadn't managed that with such finesse, she realized too late.

"I too am going on fifty and I do not consider myself in the grave, thank you very much."

Antonia stared at the trim figure, the carefully arranged auburn hair and barely lined face of Sybil Maguire Revelstoke and backtracked in a hurry. "But, Aunty, you are quite a different matter ... everyone knows you could attract any man in America, if you chose, that is."

Aunt Sybil was mollified, but in the days to come she was far from silent. Uncle Bernard, fortunately, asked few questions, even when he delivered a letter to Antonia and saw her cheeks color as she red the two words: TEN DAYS.

It was Sybil who said, "That sheet looks empty. Tana, have you become a spy or something?"

Uncle Bernard, who had caught the women at their breakfast, barely glanced at the sheet. All the same, Antonia began to sense that he knew exactly what those two words were.

This worried her almost as much as the nagging feeling that the Spanish minister to Washington might also know about Juan Diego's next voyage and be planning to intercept the *Baracoa* at sea.

When Uncle Bernard had lunch with Dupuy de Lôme the very next day, Antonia took a chance on Aunt Sybil's often expressed admiration for the Cuban filibusters. While she waited for Lloyd Hastings to take her to an Alexandria patriots affair, she asked her aunt, "Do you really like those men the newspapers call filibusters?"

Aunt Sybil was surprised. "But you know my sympathies, dear. Captain Leidner is an attractive young man—"

"And the others? That what's-his-name ... the one who met President McKinley here the other night?"

"What's-his-name? You knew his name well enough yesterday when we discussed him. To answer your question, yes, I like Captain Diego. And speaking of the captain, I hear on the best evidence that Adelaide expects him to carry her across the straits."

Adelaide Heffernan would be a rigid duenna ... still, Antonia told herself, if she sailed in the *Baracoa* even with Miss Heffernan, the gossip about her might injure her family. Captain Diego's political reputation preceded him. What if he persisted in carrying contraband? The Maguires and Guzman-Pontalvos might look like rebels too. The reputations of some of the most highly placed families in the Spanish Empire had been destroyed on less evidence. And worst of all, it really was a possibility that the captain might be shot. The Pulitzer and Hearst press had made clear the picture of the rebels with their arms tightly bound from shoulders to wrists, standing above their own graves, waiting for the volley that would spin them around and drop them as bleeding rags. Nor had the jingoist press spared the public some hair-raising sketches of women, supposed American citizens, stripped to nakedness, ogled and pawed over as they were searched by Spanish officials. True, the more subdued press had indicated these were untruths perpetuated by fake sketches and the so-called reports of Richard Harding Davis, among others. But even so, the horrible images were seared into the minds of all who saw the sketches in the Hearst *Journal*.

Aunt Sybil looked hard at Antonia, ignoring the butler Calvin's throat-clearing before he gave Antonia her morning mail and announced the arrival of Lloyd Hastings. "Tana, I hope you don't plan to do anything foolish."

"No ... I know what I owe the family. Calvin, did you want to speak to me?"

"Mr. Hastings, Miss Tana. He says there isn't much time. You'll miss the flag raising."

Aunt Sybil said, "Go along, dear, enjoy yourself, but remember ..."

Antonia ignored that. She felt that her aunt had urged her into an ephemeral relationship with the filibusterer and now was retreating. It was especially annoying since it found an echo in her own dealings with the captain.

"Ask Mr. Hastings to wait, please."

With her forefinger she tore open and read the most important of her letters, the one from her father:

Tana, my girl,

Your mother orders me to warn you that our temperamental little bride doesn't expect her trousseau from Paris for another

three weeks, so we will remain at the hacienda during those
weeks, arriving in Havana in time for the wedding.

In these unsettled days I want to keep an eye on the field
hands. There have been only a few defections to the rebel
bandits but you never know.

So delay your coming for three weeks and we will meet you
and your duenna at the Havana docks. Let us know by telegraph before you embark.

Love, from Papa.

P.S. Madre and Felipe join me.

Antonia folded and put the letter away, feeling let down, and
obliged to admit to herself that she had seriously considered sailing
with Captain Diego, using Adelaide as her chaperon. But that
would be pointless after this letter. She would have to wait until
the last minute or must spend the extra days in Havana at the old
deserted *palacio* until the family came.

"I hope that wasn't bad news," her aunt said.

"No, nothing important..."

Knowing Sybil's prying ways, she stuck the envelope into her
handbag, gave her aunt a brisk parting embrace and hurried off to
meet Lloyd Hastings.

She was surprised and a little shaken when Lloyd handed her
into the buggy and immediately began to question her about "those
pirates you complained about in New York."

Antonia swore she remembered no such thing. "And I resent
your implying that I'm interested in people you call 'those pirates.'
You'd think I'd been attacked or something."

"I only meant to say, the president has heard that Captain Diego
wants to take you home for your brother's wedding. I hope you
realize what that would mean to your family. *And* your country."

Yes, she knew, and she resented others reminding her. Lloyd
was worse than the rest. She flashed all her teeth, smiling sweetly.
"I do know what it means, darling Lloyd. But it was so good of
you to remind me. It makes me understand how well you would
run my life if we were married."

He squeezed her hand. "I'm so glad you see it at last." And then,
looked at her. "Are you making fun of me?"

"Lloyd, what makes you think so?"

He sat up ramrod-stiff, his eyes on the dusty road where the stream and the dogwood border were gradually succeeded by open fields and fresh green pastures.

The pleasant town of Alexandria with its pre-Revolutionary aura and quiet, almost secretive houses and gardens had suddenly been inundated by picnicking groups from Washington and other capital areas. The gathering now spread across the hill above the town. To Antonia's surprise many in the crowd carried placards favoring home rule for Cuba. Evidently the whole outdoor gathering had been sponsored by the New York and Washington juntas for Cuban autonomy.

"I didn't know they had this kind of money," Antonia said as Lloyd turned his horse and buggy over to the blacksmith's boy. They walked up to the picnic grounds. "Even if contributions come in, it costs a good deal to organize and advertise."

Lloyd pointed to the long plank table laid over numerous saw-horses, all under a canopy that kept out the sun but not the sweet breezes of late spring. In the center of the table huge pitchers of lemonade and fruit punch sweated off their ice on sheets of the New York *Journal*. The napkins beside the mounds of sandwiches read: COURTESY OF WILLIAM RANDOLPH HEARST AND THE NEW YORK JOURNAL.

"Yellow journalism at its worst," Lloyd said.

She supposed she agreed in theory, but so many people had spread *Journals* on the grass to sit on, or were reading Mr. Hearst's latest diatribe against Spain, it was clear that his part in today's political picnic had surely paid off.

Still, most of the crowd seemed to have come to the gathering for the fun, the food and even the drinks. Antonia had little doubt that there were kegs of beer and hard liquor around for most of the males, who didn't strike her as lemonade drinkers.

Just as Antonia and Lloyd joined the others, mostly women and children, at the long table, a fight broke out between two Cubans and a burly red-haired man who flailed away on all sides with the handle of a Free Cuba sign. Peacemakers rushed to break up the fight.

"I don't understand what he hopes to gain by all this turmoil," Antonia said.

"Who?" Lloyd asked while he poured lemonade.

"Mr. Hearst. What does he really care about Cuba?"

A well-remembered voice behind her provided the answer. It was Captain Diego, of course. "He hopes to outsell Señor Pulitzer's New York *World*."

She shook her head, at the moment feeling angry at both sides. "Captain Diego, we all know your views, but frankly, you all remind me of dogs fighting over a wounded animal."

Her voice, especially the Spanish she was talking, had attracted some of the young rebels and their sympathizers. They closed in around Diego and Lloyd Hastings but couldn't get to her to argue their cause.

It was the captain who said quietly, "Animal? No, *cara mia*, we are talking about a people who are not to be owned or fought over. Cuba asks only for home rule. Spain is no longer able to provide justice or safety or even food. Cuba needs, deserves, her own local government, not the Spanish *cortes*. It is too far away. The queen doesn't know what conditions really are in Cuba."

She looked around at the faces crowding behind Diego. These were friendly decent people, most of them very like those workers at home that she had for so long thought of as "good peons," who needed guidance. But maybe Diego was indeed right. They should have their home rule. But under the benevolent hand of her mother's friend, Queen María Cristina . . . ?

"You may be right, but it isn't easy to solve."

She certainly hadn't meant to amuse them, but as the Cubans translated to the Yankees, the laughter rolled through the crowd. To save face she joined them, then nudged Lloyd, who was looking glum. He drank the lemonade himself, muttering in answer to her nudge, "This is no place for you."

"Then why did you want to bring me?"

But she already knew. He had to be here for reasons connected with his job in the State Department. She was along to make his visit look reasonable. As an escort. She turned her shoulder to him, proceeded to become terribly interested in those eager, chattering Cubans and their American sympathizers trying to convert her and anybody else on hand to their cause.

Diego stood by with his arms crossed, watching her. She was almost relieved when someone called him away, although it amused her to see how Lloyd sauntered after him. As a spy, Lloyd would certainly be a flop.

She managed to absorb a good deal of the argument of the rebels around her, and managed not to be prejudiced against them. At least she absorbed their sincerity. They were not stupid or naive, by any means. But her thoughts began to wander, and she was surprised by the appearance of Miss Heffernan and another much younger woman, with a coltish grace and the cheerfulness of a girl without a care in the world whom she introduced as "our dear Mary-Belle Burford, a very young widow lady."

Stocky Mrs. Burford wore a blue cotton scarf draped over her forehead and hair. Across the forehead of the scarf was a hand-sewn red cross on a white field. She was doing all she could to become one of Miss Clara Barton's Red Cross ladies. The two women were as earnest as the rebels around Antonia. Mary-Belle Burford now effectively managed to wedge herself between an impassioned young rebel and Antonia.

"Miss Maguire, in the name of humanity!"

Antonia assumed this was the girl's way of asking for a donation. "Yes?"

"Get us on to the *Baracoa*."

"*Into* the *Baracoa*," Miss Heffernan corrected her. "Dear Captain Diego always says—"

Antonia felt that she'd had enough pressure and suggested coolly, "Why not ask the captain? He's around here somewhere."

The ladies exchanged knowing smiles, and the young Red Cross woman explained, "He might refuse us, he might think it too great a responsibility. But we must get to Havana and then the western provinces, wherever we're needed. The steamers refuse us transportation. The *City of New York* says there is no room. No room, indeed! On a vessel that size, loaded with tourists?"

"I'm sorry, but I have no influence with shipowners. Or ship captains. Maybe the tourist steamers really are booked up—"

"Miss Maguire, no one goes to Cuba in the broiling summer."

Antonia resented being used, even by Adelaide Heffernan, who must have been turned down by Captain Diego, and she resented even more this effort by Miss Heffernan's friend. She remembered Don Diego's knowing smiles, his male superiority when he thought he sensed that she wanted to make the voyage with him. Doubtless, he thought if he had her alone she would be easily seduced. All that tantalizing "ten days" business. If only she hadn't received instructions from her father, she might play an interesting trick on Juan Diego and have her voyage as well. Suppose she hadn't received the letter. No one else knew about it. And it occurred that she would decide later what to do in Havana when she arrived more than a week before her family.

"Ladies, we may all arrive in Cuba together. Leave it to me."

They were delighted to do so. It was Miss Heffernan who first saw the captain when he returned to the table. She warned Antonia, who put on her most gracious manner. "Captain, how very good of you. But you were always a charitable man."

Captain Diego looked wary. He sensed the trap and said as much. "I don't trust that wide-eyed innocence of yours, señorita.".

Someone laughed. A dozen people must have been listening.

Antonia went on, "I feel I shall be perfectly safe in your care. On the voyage, I mean."

"I am delighted. What brought about this sudden faith in me?"

She waved a hand toward the eager ladies. "I never dreamed you could make such a beautiful gesture to Miss Barton's Red Cross."

He knew he was trapped. His voice acquired its now familiar cynical edge.

"Oh, that. A trifle—"

"Hardly a trifle to transport three of us ladies all the way to Cuba."

"A trifle, as I said. A day out of Tampa if the wind is right. If it is not, then ... but you ladies have strong stomachs, I'm sure."

He was smiling, and Antonia felt sure he would choose the roughest course across the straits.

Well, it was done. She could only be thankful that her father was a poor correspondent ... A new letter telling her to stay in her aunt's household another two or three weeks was most unlikely, she hoped.

Antonia had never been entirely certain of what she wanted from Juan Diego. A flirtation, yes. Controlled familiarity, yes. More? Yes. She wanted Diego to make love to her. She also wanted to reform him sufficiently to the government's side ... so that ... she could marry him? Marriage?

She thought about it the next few days while she secretly packed her things for the voyage home. She did not see Captain Diego again, but she had decided what she wanted. And she had nearly always gotten her way.

On the other hand, Captain Diego must *not* know what she wanted. Not yet. No doubt he didn't think she was ready for marriage. He'd called her immature, and she had behaved like a tease. It was up to her to show him how mature she was, yet not lose her self, her own personality the way so many of her academy friends had done when they plunged into marriage immediately after their debuts. She knew they'd pitied her, wondering what Antonia Maguire lacked, or how it was she had failed to win a husband by the ripe old age of almost twenty-one.

Antonia was sure now ... she wanted Juan Diego in a way she'd never wanted any other man. He followed a dangerous profession and she wanted him alive. She also wanted him to be accepted by her family, which would certainly not be easy. Well, she'd never lacked self-confidence. Or had such respect for short odds.

Curiously enough, she'd received support in her plan from Lloyd Hastings. He'd unnerved her the day he arrived at Revelstoke and told her calmly that Mary-Belle Burford had confided in him her ambition to join the Red Cross ladies already in Cuba. ... "Timothy Burford was an old friend of mine. They were newlyweds when Tim passed on in that yellow fever epidemic a year or two ago. She could be a chaperon when Diego is around. A fellow like that, he might try to ... to harm you."

"Yes, I suppose you're right."

"Well, don't look so complacent." Lloyd had actually taken out a leather notebook and read off another of his hectoring orders. "Be certain to telegraph me when you are safe with your family. You are certain they will be in Havana when you arrive?"

"Felipe's April letter said so," she told him with perfect truth.

When Lloyd left her, still without having betrayed her plan to Aunt Sybil, she thought so well of him she accepted his kiss more enthusiastically than usual and even kissed him soundly in return. Until the night before Antonia left Revelstoke with her two duennas

on the railway cars to Florida, Aunt Sybil was under the impression
that her niece would sail on the steamer *City of New York,* with
Miss Heffernan and Mrs. Burford. When she learned the truth,
she finally resorted to a threat:

"I shall telegraph your father. I can't believe Patrick would permit you to sail with a man he suspects of breaking the laws of two
countries..."

"But, Aunty, you welcomed him into this house, you made col-
lections for his cause—"

"That was an entirely different matter. It was necessary to make
a gesture toward the rebels so we could—" Aunt Sybil broke off,
but what she had left unsaid could be even more unpleasant. Apparently Sybil and her husband were not sincere in their sympathies. Antonia suspected that the two of them were in the pay of
lobbyists who wanted nothing but trouble for Cuba, the "Pearl of
the Antilles." She knew many Yankees had sugar interests on the
island. If enough trouble could be caused between Spain and her
prize colony, these investors might buy the island itself. Unofficial
offers had already been made from the United States and refused
by the imperial Spanish government. So much for this Yankee
sincerity about "Spanish brutality" and "Cuban freedom." Sugar,
not freedom, seemed to be the answer.

After the threat to telegraph Patrick Maguire in Havana Sybil
coldly accepted her niece's good-bye kiss on the cheek, and Antonia,
feeling depressed over the rupture in their friendship, left the
Washington station with the two would-be Red Cross ladies.

During the long overnight ride and transfer to Florida's Tampa
Bay, the ladies were annoyingly optimistic, though Antonia never
let them suspect her irritation. They meant well, and she recognized that their motives were far more admirable than her own,
but she saw as little of them as possible on the trip.

Antonia had often come into Tampa Bay from Cuba, staying with
Aunt Sybil or her father at the elaborate Tampa Bay Hotel, which
somehow always made her laugh... it was like the setting of a
musical comedy in some Moorish never-never land. Minarets,
mosques, porches galore had been added to every conceivable inch
of space.

This time, since Antonia and her duennas barely arrived at the
harbor in time to sail, there was no chance to spend the night in

the musical comedy hotel. Antonia was relieved but Adelaide Heffernan sighed in disappointment.

"If I were getting married, I'd want to have the ceremony right here, I swear. And you know how I love fishing. We could fish right from one of those porches, or the seaside windows."

Antonia laughed, then hustled the women into an open carriage, and the driver drove them around the harbor to the dilapidated longboat whose rough-looking oarsmen turned out to be their future crewmen.

"Not too appetizing," Mrs. Burford muttered, "but beggars can't be choosers."

The women had envisioned a splendid Spanish galleon waiting for them in the sparkling blue waters of Tampa Bay, or if not a galleon, at the very least a modern steamer like the S.S. *Havana* or the *City of New York*. What they found in the harbor was an old, frail-looking, three-masted schooner without even the impressive square-rigging of a windjammer.

The ladies were rowed out under the long bowsprit, where they saw the name *Baracoa* crudely painted in white on the black hull. Staring up from the waterline, Antonia thought it looked rather imposing but knew her friends were disappointed. Well, they'd make the best of it. Mrs. Mary-Belle Burford, in her blue head scarf and slim unadorned skirts, climbed up the boarding ladder with an ease that surprised Antonia, who was being helped up the ropes behind her. The lady was something of an athlete.

Captain Diego met the women in the waist of the ship. He looked hard and all business, with none of the charm the ladies remembered from the picnic near Alexandria. Still wearing black, including a short pea jacket though the day was warm, he looked over Mrs. Burford with an interest that Antonia found annoying.

"You did very well, ma'am," he congratulated Mary-Belle Burford, who seemed embarrassed by everyone's surprise.

"It comes from riding the bicycle. Most useful."

The captain told her, "Not in the Cuban jungles," while he caught Antonia just under her breasts and lifted her down to the deck. Antonia enjoyed it, regretted that his hands moved away from her body too soon as he reached for the flustered Miss Heffernan.

The *Baracoa* got under way almost at once while a handsome blond young man the captain called Felix took the three women below to the small after-cabin that he referred to as Juanito's Sanctum.

The crewman Felix aroused the curiosity of Mary-Belle Burford, who told Antonia and Adelaide when he was gone that "that lad uses mighty big words for a deckhand."

In fact, Felix was hardly a common name in these latitudes, and Antonia realized what Mrs. Burford was getting at.

"There's a Captain Felix Leidner that Captain Diego spoke of as a friend. He's another filibusterer." She retracted quickly, "I mean . . . some people call him that."

Miss Heffernan was nervous. "Do you think they're carrying contraband?"

"Let's hope not."

Mrs. Burford looked around. "Where do you suppose they hide it?"

"If it's here, and I hope it isn't, I'd rather not know," Antonia said sharply. She knew how dangerous it would be if these two chattering women started talking to others about the cargo. Ashore it would be dangerous for Captain Diego if he ever landed again in Havana, and if they mentioned it on board the *Baracoa*, one of the crewmen might just take it into his head to toss them overboard.

Mrs. Burford considered the tiny cabin with its single bunk, its Cuban rocking chair and the inlaid table with a framed shaving mirror. "Wouldn't it be funny if we were standing right on top of a whole shipment of rifles?"

"Not so funny, ladies, and most unlikely. I hope you are not disappointed."

At the moment Antonia once again thought Captain Juan Diego looked very much like the pirate the Spanish minister had called him.

CHAPTER
SIX

THIS WAS no time to play games with Juan Diego. They owed him their thanks and their loyalty. Mrs. Burford's stupid behavior angered Antonia.

"I'm awfully sorry, Captain. This young lady seems to be amusing herself at our expense and I agree she isn't very funny."

Flustered, Miss Heffernan added to the apology. "Please, sir, it's not our concern, no *indeed*. You may carry any cargo and we won't make the slightest objection, I assure you."

"Thank you, ma'am. You are very kind."

"I was only teasing, Captain. Never for a minute would I dream of—well—good heavens, I'd be the last to betray you."

Diego shrugged. "Please, no more protests. You are quite free to search to your heart's content, if it entertains you."

Without looking again at Antonia he stepped back into the passage. The schooner heeled over sharply, caught by the cross-currents at the mouth of the harbor. The door slammed shut,

67

making the women jump. Antonia wished, not for the first time, that she hadn't saddled herself with her two companions.

Shortly afterward the young crewman Felix arrived and announced that the door had jammed and he was there to fix it. He made a fine drama out of forcing the door open but Antonia caught his knowing expression and had little doubt he was there to see that the women made no unfortunate discoveries of contraband.

Mary-Belle Burford settled down grumpily in the rocking chair while Miss Heffernan began to knit. Antonia walked up and down as best she could while the schooner plowed its way through the choppy seas. After congratulating herself that she had begun to develop sea legs she was suddenly thrown against the hard wooden bunk, painfully cracking her elbow.

Felix stopped tinkering with the door and went to her.

"Let me rub it, ma'am. Only thing to do. A good, stiff rubbing." He waited while she rolled up the sprigged lawn sleeve and then set to work with vigor. "Captain Diego would have my hide if anything happened to you while you were in my care."

Her spirits rose at this. "You two are old friends, Captain Leidner?"

Still working vigorously, he answered without thinking. "Since a long time. With Juanito it's patriotism. With me it's strictly—" His hands dropped as he noticed Mrs. Burford's fixed attention. She stopped rocking and his friendly blue eyes looked harder, like the blue waters of the Gulf that appeared so deceptively calm at a distance.

"You know me, ma'am?" he asked Antonia.

"I know you are said to be quite a hero in the United States, Captain Leidner."

Felix Leidner looked grateful and would have continued to rub her elbow but she freed herself. "Thank you. That feels much better."

Before he could go back to his work at the door she was past him and out in the passage. She heard him call to her from the doorway, but she merely waved one hand behind her and started up the steep, narrow companionway. Buffeted from side to side, she made her way to the deck. The wind had come up while the women were belowdecks, and Antonia found her skirts billowing and her carefully arranged hair beating around her face. She knew she looked like a hoyden but it was necessary that Juan Diego be warned of the danger. It might be greater than he suspected.

The captain was standing in the bow with a spyglass in one hand. He didn't seem to be in a good mood and occasionally beat the glass against his left hand, but his attention was focused on the horizon where a large paddle-wheel steamer crossed the path of the *Baracoa*. The man at the *Baracoa*'s wheel, an elderly Cuban with a weathered dark skin and liquid eyes that looked as though they had seen the sorrows of a long life, followed her with his gaze. She felt uneasily aware that these men must resent or even despise her, and she couldn't really blame them. Had she ever done anything in her life that was not selfishly concerned with herself?

While she hesitated, Captain Diego turned away from the sight of the rapidly disappearing paddle wheeler and saw his disheveled passenger. The sight of her surprised him. He just stood there for several moments and she wondered if she'd angered him again. She started toward him, ignoring the warm salt wind that whipped across her face and whirled around her body.

"Captain, forgive me," she called out. "I know I've no right here but I wanted to warn you—"

"Oh?" He closed the spyglass but made no effort to join her.

She managed to cross the slanting deck but when she finally got to him she was staggering. Almost in spite of himself he held out his free hand but she had already clutched the salt-stained rail.

He looked her over. "You do well for a landlubber."

She ignored it and got to the point. "I recognized Captain Leidner. I hope you don't plan anything, well, anything risky..."

"Now why should I do that, Miss Maguire? I am simply taking my friend Felix to Havana. He has business there." He took a long easy step that brought him unexpectedly close to her.

"I'm afraid I've aroused Mrs. Burford's suspicions again. I called Captain Leidner by his name and she noticed. She's too curious. I just wondered if she might cause you any trouble..."

"You met this somewhat southern belle at the picnic?"

"Yes. Lloyd... Mr. Hastings spoke for her."

"That should certainly provide an entrée to the best society, if not the best ships."

She took hold of the gritty rail, started to edge away. This time he stopped her.

"Felix will keep an eye on the lady." Close now, with one hand on hers, he asked, "Did you see much of Mrs. Burford on the trip down?"

It was an odd question. Naturally, the three women had eaten several meals together and there had been some conversation. Most of the friendship, however, was between Adelaide and Mary-Belle Burford, as Antonia now told him.

"She met her last week after Adelaide talked to some Red Cross ladies in Washington." What was this all about?

"Did you ladies have separate sleeping arrangements?"

"Adelaide and I shared a compartment. Mrs. Burford preferred to sleep in her chair. She felt strongly about saving money for the Cause, as she put it."

"I don't doubt it."

She thought his attitude was strange. If he mistrusted Mary-Belle Burford, why not simply say so and act upon it. She tried again. "You aren't carrying contraband, I hope."

This time he seemed to take her seriously, and his voice held more warmth, as he thanked her.

He let her go, reluctantly. She started below and he opened the glass again to watch another ship on the horizon, much smaller and faster than the paddle-wheel steamer. His attention was so fixed that Antonia stopped at the companion-ladder and watched the small sleek gunboat.

Unlike the steamer it seemed heading on a collision course with the *Baracoa*. After a minute or two, Antonia heard the watch bellow to Captain Diego, followed by running feet that slapped the deck as the crew came to their stations.

Antonia shaded her eyes. Was it the United States Navy or the Imperial Spanish Patrol? If Diego was found guilty of carrying contraband by the Cuban courts, which were under Spanish law, he would be shot. There had even been reports recently of torture in Havana's Morro Castle, that ancient symbol of Spanish defiance against the pirates of the Caribbean.

But instead of her own familiar crimson and gold, the flag of Castile and Spain, she made out the stars and stripes of the U.S. Navy. And instantly she found herself in the way as hurrying men shoved her aside and the patrol boat came on.

Was the *Baracoa* going to fight? It could hardly argue with the guns of the patrol boat.

Captain Leidner ran up the companion-ladder past Antonia, ignoring her. His blond hair seemed to stand on end and there was a light in his eyes. Like his friend Juan Diego he obviously enjoyed the smell of danger.

From the passage below Miss Heffernan stared up at Antonia. "Dear, what is it? Are we being arrested?"

"Probably." Antonia tried to pull herself together.

"Oh, my God..." Adelaide circled in a panic. "I'm only grateful my parents aren't alive to know, they would be horrified... What will Miss Barton say?"

Antonia looked past her into the dim recesses of the passage with its weathered wood that smelled of salt and age. "Yes... where is your friend, the noble young widow? She doesn't seem very frightened."

Miss Heffernan shook her head. "I don't understand Mary-Belle. The minute that young man Felix left she started pounding on the walls. She even tried to dig up some of the planks in the deck. Lord, she could sink us all if she tore the bottom of the ship out."

Antonia smiled. "I imagine she would have to go some to do that. Anyway, she is a spy of some sort and I mean to give her a spy's wages." She thought this over for a minute. "She must be a Yankee spy, because Lloyd knows her..."

She started down the ladder, hurrying, catching a heel in her skirt hem, tearing the voile folds. Ignoring the tear, she rushed along the passage to the captain's cabin. Belowdecks there seemed to be little room for anything but the captain's cabin and what she assumed were the men's quarters in the fo'c'sle.

It was a curious choice for its purpose—a sailing vessel without even an auxiliary engine like so many other Caribbean vessels used to transport contraband. How had Juan Diego ever thought he could outrun two navies in this crude vessel?

From a distance over the water an indistinguishable voice was magnified by a voice horn. She thought the language was English but she couldn't really make it out. She moved quietly to the captain's cabin, aware that the ship had somehow righted itself. The decks were almost level except for a fore and aft movement.

The *Baracoa*'s anchor chain ran out with a terrific rattle and roar. They must, she decided, be fairly close to shore.

She found Mary-Belle Burford busy as Miss Heffernan had predicted, actually trying to pry up some of the deck under Captain Diego's bunk. She could sign on as crew somewhere.

Antonia went at her, caught her by that handy blue head scarf and yanked her head back. Miss Heffernan came in behind Antonia and squatted firmly on Mrs. Burford's flailing skirts. A minute later, as Antonia pulled tighter, stretching the woman's neck, Miss Heffernan managed to get out... "My God, she's a *man*..."

"Of course." Antonia herself had only realized the spy's gender a few minutes before, thanks to Juan Diego's leading questions. She was still furious with herself for not having paid more attention to the annoying chatter and babble of the young "widow." It hadn't taken Juan Diego long to figure it out. She couldn't forget how he had looked "Mary-Belle" up and down with such interest, an interest she only understood now.

"Who are you, really?"

Grabbing handfuls of his hair, she got the blue scarf off his head, but he had apparently counted on a possible exposure and wore his shock of red hair very long.

"T-Tim Burford... they sent me... hope to find guns before patrol challenge..."

It made some sense. This man must be the very person Lloyd Hastings had claimed as a friend. Hastings... she had a score to settle with that so-called gentleman.

"You have found nothing?"

"N-nothing, ma'am."

Miss Heffernan began to experience her usual maternal qualms. "He's a boy, Tana, I think we might let him up. He can't hurt anyone, the captain is innocent—"

"Of course, he's innocent." But she was deeply aware of all the confusion, the tramping of boots, the slap of bare feet and the shouting that came from the deck overhead.

She helped the young man to stand up in his skirts and padded basque blouse. Antonia wanted to push him toward the door, but he did have a certain bumptious charm that she had to admire under the circumstances. His eyes took on a lively sparkle as Antonia heard the heavy ring of boot heels on the deck in the passage. She and Miss Heffernan had barely smoothed their skirts when a lanky young man in a navy blue uniform appeared in the doorway. He was a startling presence in this part of the world where almost all participants in the Cuban revolt, including the Spanish army, wore either white or an off-white homespun.

The U.S. naval officer in blue cultivated a deep voice, probably to make himself more impressive in the company of seamen like Captain Diego who needed no such theatrical props. The Cuban captain strolled in behind him. To Antonia's eyes he seemed almost abnormally calm.

The officer saluted the ladies, then said to the boy, "I am told you may have a report, Mr.—uh—Burford." He studied the boy.

"Well, sir, I was a-tearing up planks under the bunk here where the guns was hid last month in the *Cora K.*, but there's nothing I could see. Or get ahold of, anyway."

"That is our responsibility. If the ladies will wait on deck—"

Antonia watched Juan Diego, who seemed undisturbed and now leaned against the door as if this search meant nothing to him. Overhead the search proceeded on deck as well. Apparently, the deck was being attacked by axes. The screech of rotting timbers made her grit her teeth, but Miss Heffernan was leaving after an uneasy look around the room. Before Antonia followed Adelaide into the passage Diego murmured, "I'd have given a thousand dollars to know what was going on in here before we arrived."

She said, "I haven't the faintest idea what you are talking about."

When she was halfway down the passage, he called to her: "We should be entering the Havana Channel soon. You will be with your father before moonrise."

Antonia knew quite well Patrick Maguire couldn't possibly be on the Havana docks tonight. He and the entire family were still at the hacienda in the country outside Santiago. The only person she could be sure of meeting was Captain General Weyler, the man Juan Diego and half the United States called "the Butcher."

The naval officer cut in, "If no laws have been broken, Captain, you may make your promises. I'm afraid your reputation precedes you."

"My reputation or the gossip of my enemies?"

Antonia climbed up the companion-ladder, figuring that for once Juan Diego must be innocent, but when she got to the deck, the

U.S. Navy and the *Baracoa*'s crew were lugging up huge packing
cases out into the afternoon light from the cargo hold.

Miss Heffernan said to Antonia in a piercing stage whisper, "Don't
tell me that man really is smuggling... where does that leave us?"

One of the sailors from the patrol boat stopped running, said
straight-faced to Adelaide, "You'll be next, ma'am. You know how
them Spanish stripped and searched the American ladies on the
Olivette?"

Antonia told him angrily, "They proved that was a lie."

"Hush, dear. Don't antagonize them."

Under the supervision of a grizzled naval lieutenant the sailors
and the *Baracoa*'s hands pried open the first box and then a barrel
behind it. Curious objects made of tin, most of them cylindrical,
poured out across the deck. Antonia recognized them as tin cans
of food. She'd never bought any herself, but her friends at the
academy had sworn by them the last days of her senior year at
school. While sailors ran to stop the rolling cans and rescue the
rectangular tins that proved to be filled with meats, Captain Diego
and the young naval officer stepped out upon the deck. Antonia,
watching the scene, noted the exchange of looks between Diego
and the mate, William Pullitt. She could read nothing in that
exchange.

The lieutenant reached for one of the cans, took it up, and read
the pasted white label aloud: "Tomatoes... *por el—*"

"Spanish, sir," a sailor told him, glancing at the label. "For
the Army of Spain, care of Captain General Valeriano Weyler y
Nicolau, from the friends of Her Most Catholic Majesty, the Queen
Regent. For delivery to the Customs House, La Habana... That's
Havana, sir."

"So I gathered."

Antonia looked at Captain Diego. He was staring innocently at
the myriad colors of sunset over the Gulf of Mexico. She would
have liked to have kicked him for having put her and Adelaide
Heffernan through this horror. The U.S. Navy shared her sentiments. The lieutenant threw down the can of tomatoes, picked up
another and another, tossed them down. A sailor reached for a can,
read aloud, "Pork and beans. Kind of carrying coals to Newcastle.
And this's hamburg-beef, whatever that is."

It didn't take too long afterward for the navy to collect its boarding crew and surrender control of the *Baracoa*, leaving broken crates and barrels scattered across the deck. The Cuban crew had to rescue these cans, slats and broken staves. While they worked, Diego walked with the naval officer to the boarding ladder near the unwanted passengers. Antonia heard the lieutenant say, "They'll tear this old tub apart when you reach Havana. If we've missed something, don't bet on the Spanish customs doing the same. You will have the Butcher to deal with there."

Diego saluted and thanked him politely. Turning away from the rail, he almost stepped on Antonia.

"He isn't really a butcher, you know. Very shortly he'll be a member of my family—"

"By marriage. Well, to each his own." He made a sweeping wave toward the rolling cans that were still scattered over the deck and running into the scuppers. "But look at all our gifts to him. How can he resist our generosity? They say the Spanish soldiers get little to eat when they are out in the field."

She tried not to smile. "You're a conniving—"

"And you are a well-known heartbreaker. But I've no intention of being your latest victim. I am counting the hours until I turn you over to your father in Havana."

This time she did laugh.

He would have a long wait.

CHAPTER
SEVEN

THE *BARACOA*'s voyage up the channel into Havana's spacious harbor was serene, if not unguarded. The little schooner had been escorted by two Spanish gunboats that lay in wait at the entrance to the channel, but otherwise Antonia could give herself up to enjoyment of the beautiful night scene.

She leaned against the rail studying and identifying each separate light for the benefit of Adelaide Heffernan and Tim Burford, now wearing a pair of the cabin boy's breeches with the late "Mary-Belle's" ruffled blouse. He seemed awed by the ring of lights around the busy harbor, the ships at anchor, an astonishing number of steamers but there was also no shortage of windjammers, a five-masted barkentine and any number of schooners as large as the *Baracoa*. Tim and Miss Heffernan were surprised by the blazing lights of the city itself on its gentle hills in the distance. The old section of Havana, which Antonia preferred, was darker, but she pointed out the roadway following the harbor line which she called "the *Malecón*." Her Yankee friends were impressed.

"But the big castle that we passed across the bay," Miss Heffernan said, "it's that Morro Castle I've heard so much about, isn't it? I saw it from miles out to sea."

Antonia shook her head. "If you're thinking of torture, we Spaniards have a dozen other nice gory old castles. The fortress we passed on the city side and—oh, don't be so silly." Antonia tried to make out the various Spanish colonial buildings of the ancient Plaza de las Armas near the Palacio Guzman y Pontalvo, her birthplace. But here and there in the city whose buildings were so brightly colored by day there were pools of darkness. Deep in the center of the old quarter, which rose on the tapering hills, would be the poinciana, the bougainvillea and hibiscus planted by her mother when the laurels didn't grow as she wanted around the heavy outside walls of the palace. She imagined she smelled the yellow roses that were her mother's favorites. All growing things, including both plants and children, were the Señora Maguire's delight, and Antonia felt homesick just thinking of those yellow-and-salmon roses.

Tim was sniffing too. "Sure can tell you're in a hot climate. Smell that garbage in the bay?"

"It's not garbage, it's the foliage, the greenery. In the tropics it rots quicker."

"I'm afraid our young spy has you there," Captain Diego said. He had come up behind her and placed both hands on her shoulders. "Our beautiful bay does carry the odor of death."

"If you're being political, save yourself the effort. You could say the same about any harbor."

"But any harbor doesn't have the Butcher in control." To avoid further argument he informed her companions that the crew was straightening his cabin. "I'm afraid they are moving your luggage around rather carelessly."

Tim Burford left promptly, with Miss Heffernan hurrying across the deck after him. Diego remarked, "The fellow is an actor, did you know that? He was hired by your friend Hastings and a few of his political friends in the State Department. I imagine at least half of the department is trying to get President McKinley to side with the Spanish government."

"And the other half wants him to recognize the insurgents." It was a reminder that her politics were still not his.

"Probably. But the boy failed to help them out when the U.S. patrol arrived. I'd say his spying days seem to be over."

"Lucky for you he did fail. You would be in irons now if he'd succeeded."

Diego squeezed Antonia's shoulders. Her head was close to his cheek. "What happens after you return to that old dungeon of your mother's?"

"It isn't a dungeon. It's actually a very old house. Some of it was originally adobe. The conquerors of Mexico lived there. So did the Spaniards who took the gold back to Seville. Legend says our home is one of the six original palaces in the New World."

"Impressive. My house was smaller. But pleasant in many ways. My mother grew flowers and pigs and goats and sheep. My father only went into action when there was a revolt to be fought in."

"He sounds like quite a troublemaker."

"Oh, all of that. He followed José Martí. My father was one of the first to call for home rule for Cuba. Autonomy under Spain was all we asked. Now, who knows?" His dark eyes were abruptly serious as they looked out over the waters streaked with light from the mastheads of so many ships.

"What happened to him?"

"He died in an ambush, with Maceo, the great black Cuban. You don't hear so much about Maceo these days. It's all Cuba for the Cubans, but there were others. Like Antonio Maceo... Do you really care?"

"Of course I care. If the queen only knew about the injustices we could live in peace... and your mother?"

"When Weyler came to rule the island he removed most of the families from the farms in Oriente and Camaguey provinces, put them in camps beside the troops. I was sailing at the time. *Not* contraband. Unless you call food a contraband."

She took a breath. "What happened to her?"

"To her and to my little sister, Manuelita. How long do you think a girl of fifteen, a pretty girl, and virginal, would be safe in the camp of enemy soldiers?"

She wished she hadn't asked. She didn't want to know, except she had a need to share his feelings.

He went on, "When I crossed the *trocha* they were digging in the province, one of those no-man's-lands of Captain General Weyler. I found my mother and Manuelita had been dead for over two weeks and buried in the common pit beyond the urinals of your precious queen's soldiers. My mother died of yellow fever two days before my little Manuelita was taken by the scum. Well, it is over now."

It wasn't over. She saw it in his hands as they gripped her shoulders painfully, and in the bitter hardness of his features. She understood his bitterness against her people, but at the same time she wanted to tell him that he shouldn't blame the whole Spanish Empire because a few soldiers had behaved like barbarians. As for General Weyler digging *trochas* and reconcentrating homeless people, she didn't understand all of that and wasn't ready yet to decide what she thought. The word *trocha* was as foreign to her as the real meaning of *reconcentration*.

He must, though, have felt her empathy. He raised his hand, ruffled her thick windblown black hair and kissed her forehead.

"My own papa couldn't have done that better."

"For a lady, lady, you're shameless. But you know that."

"Tell me, Captain, where do you stay in Havana?"

He hesitated, looked at her. "Since I have not been welcome in some time, I have no permanent address."

"But how am I to see you?"

"I will call upon you. Like one of your respectable young admirers."

"Tomorrow. Early. I will be ... tolerably interested to find out whether you're free or being shot for piracy."

"Then, *buenos noches* until tomorrow. Unless, of course, I have been shot."

She watched him turn away and give orders for signal replies to a harbormaster in one of the Spanish gunboats. Obviously the unobtrusive little *Baracoa* was of considerable importance to the customs officers and others waiting on the docks. The Customs House itself was well lighted and there seemed to be a greater crowd than usual milling around the area devoted to customs inspection.

One of Juan Diego's men, darkly bearded but scarcely older than Antonia, stopped to warn her in Spanish, "Best get your passport papers out, señorita. We are here at La Habana."

It was good to hear a part of Havana's true name, San Cristóbal
de la Habana, which reminded her of her mother's teachings when
she was very small. Antonia called her thanks to him and went
below to get her handbag.

Minutes later, while she stood on the foredeck with Miss Heffernan and an uncomfortably conspicuous Tim Burford, Captain
Diego stopped enumerating the canned cargo with a newly arrived
customs officer to tell Antonia, "The captain general has been told
about you being on board, señorita. And your friends. He will send
a launch if you wish, or you can go over the side and ashore in one
of our boats."

Antonia said, "We'll go immediately, in the first boat. I need to
prepare him for you."

"You think he needs preparation? I assure you he is expecting
me."

"I only wanted to tell him that you helped the ladies who wanted
to join the Red Cross—" Out of the corner of her eye she became
aware of the absurdly clothed Tim Burford and amended, "Well,
one Red Cross lady. And to remind him of all the tins of food you're
bringing to the Spanish army—"

"Thank you."

He went over the side and reached up to help her down the
ladder, enfolding her blowing skirts as he lifted her into the boat
below. She wondered if, in fact, he was afraid of the confrontation
that would soon take place with his enemy, the captain general of
Cuba. She only hoped he wouldn't ruin all their combined efforts
to make him acceptable in her family's circle, including General
Weyler.

Miss Heffernan had been peering into the black waters that
lapped at the boat as the oarsmen approached the docks. "It looks
beautiful, but is it safe? I thought I saw something down there."

"Sharks, señora. They make good eating," one of the oarsmen
called out, and the others smiled, not adding that the reverse was
true too.

"True," Antonia said, "but you needn't swim in the bay. And
let's hope we never need to find out at first hand."

Among the crowd waiting on the dock at this late hour of the
night were a number of newspapermen from the United States,

who now rushed at her and Miss Heffernan with a dozen questions.

"Is it true, Miss Maguire, that the filibuster Diego saved your life?"... "Señorita, what's your real opinion of Governor Weyler?" ... "Ma'am, are you in love with this rebel?"... "Señorita, do you believe in reconcentration of the Cuban peasants? Did you know hundreds of thousands are dying?"...

She swung around in confusion. A half-dozen Spanish soldiers made a sudden foray into the crowd, and she had to be grateful to see Juan Diego's great enemy, Captain General Valeriano Weyler y Nicolau, who now moved along the aisle made by the soldiers' rifles. The noisy Havana night was suddenly so quiet Antonia could hear the waters of the bay washing against the long shoreline.

She had seen General Weyler only on several informal occasions when he settled back in her father's favorite rocking chair, refused all tobacco and even wine and reasonably... or so it seemed... discussed the need of firmness in dealing with the Cuban rebels. He was considerably more formidable-looking now. Though still the same short, dark, black-bearded man, hard-eyed and with a thin, set mouth, he clearly inspired fear in those around him, including some of his own men. The authority of his Germanic ancestors underlay the Latin good manners he greeted Antonia with, bowing and taking her hand while she felt his eyes boring into her. She became voluble, feeling foolish, knowing he expected her to behave like his niece, Caris, who was engaged to her brother.

"Surely, you were not in danger, Señorita Maguire. This Diego ... did he dare to—"

Miss Heffernan was the one who came in with her mediocre Spanish, "No, no, he saved us."

"That patrol boat... the United States Navy stopped us," Antonia added in a hurry. "They might have sunk us all. They actually questioned Captain Diego's right to bring food to our Spanish garrisons." Tim Burford stood by, impressed or surprised by this rush to defend.

General Weyler seemed to accept all this, though his eyes closely studied each of the *Baracoa*'s three passengers. Now he signaled to the customs officer, who stood at attention, then bowed to the ladies at the general's nod. The general said, "It appears we owe the young man our thanks."

"And Captain Diego, too."

She detected a pause before Weyler said, "A valuable acquisition, if the fellow is sincere in his reformation..."

General Weyler made her uneasy. She wondered what it was going to be like to have this man's niece in the family for a lifetime. Not to mention the man himself.

A soldier in homespun field outfit topped by a palmetto hat with a wide brim turned up all around, elbowed his way through the crowd, sandals slapping the ground in his hurry. He whispered something in the general's ear. General Weyler replied impatiently in Spanish.

"Yes, let him wait. And his crew. For personal interrogation." He took Antonia's hand once more. "I have business in the Customs House but I shall pay a call upon your honored family at the first opportunity."

"My—family?" What on earth possessed them to be in Havana when her father had told her they would not make the journey for three weeks?

"My niece has not had a message from them yet, but I assume they arrived at the *palacio* today or you would not be returning at this time." He was about to follow the messenger but said with a slight edge to the words, "That is the fact, I assume."

"I assume so," she agreed nervously.

"My niece will pay you and your family an informal visit tomorrow, perhaps with me, if time permits."

"Yes, we'll be most... honored to receive your call."

Although this man was the ruler of Cuba, he still possessed the bourgeois Spaniard's awe of Antonia's family and her distinguished heritage. He seemed willing to accept the social superiority of the Guzman y Pontalvos as embodied in Antonia's mother. He looked around now. "I don't see the family carriage."

She said vaguely, "Perhaps they mixed up the time. One never knows how long it will take for the anchoring and docking and inspection, and it's so late. They may have given me up for tonight." He started to make an offer when she hurried on, "But Miss Heffernan's carriage will be here. I think I see it over beyond the crowd. It may be on the Malecón waiting for us."

When she first manipulated this whole affair, Antonia had only thought of excuses for Juan Diego so that he would be forced to sail on toward Santiago, where he might get her home in a day or

so if the little train to the sugar mill was running, but it hadn't
occurred to her that General Weyler would carry on about the
absence of her family. Or worse, that her future sister-in-law, Caris
de Correña, would visit the *palacio* as early as tomorrow. She and
Caris had never exactly been close. There were jealousies on both
sides.

Meanwhile there was nothing for it but to hire a carriage and
go to wait at the empty old *palacio* for Juan Diego's visit. The idea
that he could be detained for some reason still held her. She very
much wanted to follow the captain general and perhaps be a discreet presence to help Juan Diego while he was questioned, but
Weyler had forestalled her, either by chance or design. Just as the
New York Times and the *New York Journal* surrounded her again
with awkward questions, the customs inspector who had brought
the word about Captain Diego's arrival pushed his way between
her questioners and offered to escort her.

"His Excellency wishes to relieve you of annoyances, señorita
. . . señora." As an afterthought he included Miss Heffernan. "Your
parents will be happy to see you safely home."

"I must stay. I may be able to speak for Captain Diego, he was
kind to us . . ." Antonia was still looking back and arguing when
two of General Weyler's men formed a protective guard against
the local citizens and the press. The sight of swords stuck through
their belts impressed Tim Burford, but Antonia was embarrassed
for her people who still lived in the past splendor of the empire
. . . their courage was fine but would it be enough in a world of
Gatling guns and cannons? From what Antonia could make out,
there were rebel sympathizers among the crowd and they were
outraged over the notion that their hero, Juan Diego, should be
bringing supplies for the Loyalist army that supported the Spanish
throne.

Antonia resisted leaving all the way to the *Malecón*, the busy
harbor road that followed the line of Havana's seawalls. Here the
soldiers flagged down a wide, low-seated *volante* drawn by a mare
and used mostly for Yankee tourists. Antonia and her two companions watched the gradual change from the lighted harbor area
to the quiet dark streets lined by palm trees interspersed with
endless cool shrubbery and flowers.

Antonia sat forward, hardly noticing the once-familiar scene of stone and stucco, the many churches and palaces looking like fortresses, the narrow *calles* opening into the world-famed plazas but showing only glimpses of what Antonia knew were enchanting walled gardens perfumed by jasmine and roses. If there were other less romantic smells, as she heard tourists complain so frequently, she ignored them. This was her birthplace and she loved it, though she thought she would now be much more at home in that Virginia countryside of Aunt Sybil.

And her thoughts were on whether Juan Diego would be free by sunrise, or had Captain General Weyler's attitude been a performance to cover his intent on revenge?

Tim Burford surprisingly seemed to sense her suspicions, and he said, "Excuse me, miss, but that Weyler isn't going to hurt the captain. I mean, I think the general wants to believe Captain Diego ... he has to if his daughter is marrying into your family—"

"His niece."

"Whatever she is, I think he'll convince himself the captain has changed coats on your account... I mean, well, he could tell you were friendly with the captain ... and how could this Weyler have a rebel pirate in his own family... ?"

Miss Heffernan nodded. "I do believe the boy's right. Or could be, Tana. Now don't protest too much. It makes one almost forget the trick he played on me, pretending to be joining the Red Cross, and all."

"My father was on the stage," Tim said proudly. "And I played females from the time I was twelve, not having much beard. But I can do males. I read for Ben-Hur for Klaw and Erlanger but they wanted somebody taller."

"Tim," Antonia said, really considering him for the first time, and not being reassured by him or Miss Heffernan, "what are we going to do with you? What had Mr. Hastings and your naval connections planned for you after you'd exposed Captain Diego as a rebel leader?"

"They said I'd be met by ladies in the Red Cross and I was to say I was seasick and take the next steamer back to Key West. But they never met me."

Antonia wondered if anyone had ever intended to meet Tim

Burford. He'd simply been used and discarded. "If I pay your passage back to New York on a steamer sailing tomorrow, would you promise to leave Havana at once?"

"I've got a few dollars, but I could always use more. Captain Leidner's promised me a part on some job later. Truth is, I'd leave here the very first minute I can get off this jungle that calls itself an island. I thank you for your offer."

So that was solved. Miss Heffernan coughed. "I hope you won't think me rude and ungrateful, dear, if I too leave you after a short rest. I really must report to the Red Cross."

Antonia was sorry to lose her, but it had been inevitable and, in any case, Adelaide would never go overland to the Guzman hacienda.

The carriage had passed the great cathedral where Antonia's brother Felipe would marry pretty, golden-haired Caris de Correña within the month. She noted briefly the magnificent old municipal palace that was the headquarters of the captain general, the queen's civil and military representative in the Americas, and soon they were wandering into one of those dark *calles* that were hidden and unknown to the casual passerby.

The *volante*'s mare pulled up in front of the darkened old stone and stucco building in the little square not far from the Plaza de las Armas, which had once been the heart of the Spanish Americas. Antonia was helped out of the carriage, relieved to be home, or at least relieved to have reached her first destination, but the tension and sleeplessness of the last twenty-four hours had worn on her nerves. And no one knew better than she that there would be no warm reception by her family when she touched the bell at the barred gate between the high, forbidding stone walls; the Palacio Guzman y Pontalvo had few windows in the outer walls and those that existed were high, small and barred.

Pablo, the old caretaker, shuffled to the gate over the tiled stepping stones imported from Portugal. He peered at Antonia, then at Miss Heffernan and Tim Burford, seeing with difficulty through his blurred vision. "Eh, who is it?" he demanded in Spanish. "The mistress is away in the country." He'd never learned to include Patrick Maguire as master of the house. To Pablo, whose ancestors came to Cuba with the early Pontalvos and Guzmans, there was only the single owner, Antonia's mother.

"It's the señorita, Pablo. I'm Tana, come home with friends from the States."

"We have no friends from the States," he grumbled, but the single, dim electric light over the gate illuminated enough of Antonia's face to make her recognizable. He bowed his already bent back. "Señorita Tana, welcome," and added, "you were not expected."

She led the way through the fragrant garden which was surrounded on three sides by the house itself. All its barred windows overlooked the garden below, and Antonia remembered that on the hottest days there was always a breath of air from the perennially moist and sheltered garden.

"Lucky for you, Señorita Tana, the cook is here. She came back early from her people in Regla across the bay. They argued about the rebels. She'll have the rooms made up. I'll tell her you are here. Much too soon."

Antonia knew it was always wise to go along with the pride, and annoyance, of the help. "I'm sorry, Pablo. I don't want to cause anyone any trouble. My friends and I will be leaving shortly—"

"Tomorrow, if you'll forgive me, Tana," Miss Heffernan murmured, and Tim Burford added, "Me too. Soon as I can get some clothes. Anything you want to give me for my performance, well, you can send to Timothy Burford, care of the Players Haven, Washington, D.C."

Antonia smiled. Clearly he still regarded the whole masquerade as strictly an acting performance. . . . By the time they reached the dusty bedchambers on the upper floor, Miss Heffernan was still remarking on the scent of jasmine that pervaded the rooms with windows overlooking the garden. She settled onto a bed, asking only that she not be disturbed until midmorning. "I won't trouble you when I leave," she said, "but as soon as I am settled in, I'll write you all the particulars."

Tim Burford was put in a room with a Moorish arch that had always pleased Felipe's friends, and then Antonia went back to her own bedchamber and curled up in the worn, high-backed chair by the window. Now that she had a chance to relax, she found it more difficult than ever. She huddled there, reliving every word of Captain General Weyler's conversation, trying to read into his words an optimistic future for Juan Diego. Or at least, a future. Eventually, she closed her eyes and dozed off, only to dream of jasmine and mimosa-covered walls and a man standing with his back to one wall, his arms bound with cords from above the elbows to his wrists. She screamed silently, her throat ached from the effort, shots rang out—

The sound awakened her. She raised her head, realized that what she had heard must have been the heavy front door banging shut after Pablo.

Minutes later, his irritable voice called to her from the hall: "Señorita, you wish not to be disturbed?"

"Yes, I wish *not*."

Pablo said incomprehensibly, "There! It is the truth."

But the door opened. Antonia turned around. And Juan Diego stood there only a few yards from her.

"Not twenty-four hours after our farewells. Well, how soon we forgot..."

She quickly unwound herself from the chair and tried to regain some dignity.

"Not soon, Captain. Several hours late, as a matter of fact. I plan to start for my father's hacienda as soon as Miss Heffernan is safely within the arms of the Red Cross."

She might have known he would be ahead of her... "Then we leave at once, señorita. I have just escorted our good Adelaide to her friends. Miss Barton was up-country, but the others welcomed her, and me, with open arms."

"I believe it," she said drily.

It seemed too good to be true that he had managed to fool Valeriano Weyler. But at least he was here, very much in the flesh. And as soon as Pablo stepped back from the doorway, she greeted Juan Diego with open arms, hoping, wondering, if he understood that this meant a commitment, by her—and by him.

CHAPTER
EIGHT

"**I**T'S A perfect disguise." Antonia was fascinated by the peasant stranger she saw looking back at her in the long pier glass.

"Your friend Timothy Burford's performance gave me an idea," Diego said, studying Antonia's reflection. "I'm afraid—no, glad—that your natural assets make it impossible for you to play a young male, but this will do well."

She had been a little surprised that he agreed so easily to escort her home to the hacienda. He had a few objections when she assured him that General Weyler would not allow her to leave Havana "for personal reasons." "What personal reasons?" And she had looked evasive. "I'm afraid the general has some thoughts about me. He wants to . . . you know."

"I don't believe I do."

"To ally himself more closely with my family. He made it fairly plain when I met him outside the Customs House gates last night. I found him repulsive, but he intends to pursue matters during

89

these next three weeks. He'll be here for a visit this afternoon. He admitted as much. I have to get away before he finds out I've gone."

She had never been able to fool Juan Diego so easily. She decided it was because he hated "Butcher" Weyler so much that he found her farfetched scenario easy to believe. Actually, the puritanical Weyler would shudder at the notion of seducing and marrying a young woman her age. He was less squeamish about other matters, of course.

Juan Diego had immediately begun to lay out a plan. "You can hardly cross the country in your Maguire finery. The provinces are full of *mambises* who would like nothing better than to get their hands on a likely future member of the Butcher's family, even if the connection is only by marriage."

"But if I'm just a peasant girl, and with you ... don't the rebels consider you their leader?"

"Not if they find—hear that I delivered a cargo of food to Weyler's armies. And Weyler expects me to stay in Havana until I am issued a permit to travel."

"Then it seems we must both go disguised."

He took everything in stride, looked pleased, as if this suited his own plans. Within two hours it was all arranged, thanks to Diego's charm and the cook, Zerlina's, susceptibility.

Antonia tried the somber, beaten-down look she had seen on the scullery maid, whose dress was furnished by the cook. The dingy black blouse and skirt were brightened by the scarlet head scarf she had knotted at the nape of her neck to hide her hair. When Diego set a cane worker's dirty white hat over the scarf, she fingered the woven straw brim and felt that her own father wouldn't know her, much less General Weyler's men.

Zerlina, thin, hard-boned, with gypsy blood, looked her over critically. "It is not so pretty as you, señorita, but you will be more safe. At least you won't attract those rebels." Zerlina had known Antonia since her infancy and was used to her odd fits and starts. If the señorita chose to sneak off and visit her family in the country, then there must be a good reason, and though Zerlina was loyal to the Spanish authorities, her own *infanta*, the princess of the Maguire-Guzman house, came first.

Antonia would have been perfectly willing to shock General

Weyler by traveling cross-country, but not when she knew his men would be watching Juan Diego's activities ... and Diego had some reason for this trip besides just escorting her, she was sure of at least that much. What it was and what she would do about it ... she preferred not to think about that just now ...

Juan Diego wore the caretaker Pablo's loose seersucker shirt over a pair of baggy-legged breeches, and sandals that looked as if they had seen better days some ten years ago. His own big palmetto hat completed his getup. The sight of him made her laugh, but his nearness, in spite of the sweat-stained old outfit, was as exciting as ever to her.

Sizing them up as they stood together, the cook shook her head. "The señora will never receive you. You must not tell her it was old Zerlina who dressed you so. But this Señor Hastings, he is a smooth fellow."

Diego did not look too happy at being named for a man he despised, but it was the first name that had occurred to Antonia when she introduced him to Zerlina, and there was no question of letting her know his real identity. Zerlina was too much of a loyalist.

Antonia thanked her again and took Diego's arm. "I'm looking forward to our ... adventure."

He was less exuberant. "I hope you can still call it that by the time we reach your parents. Incidentally, let's hope that Señor Maguire accepts ... he may not believe in my reformation. After all, I'm not bringing him a cargo of food for his troops—"

"Well, I hope I'm worth more to my father than a cargo of tomatoes."

Diego became the bent and aging Pablo as they left the old house by the servants' gate. No one was in the shady *calle* at this siesta hour except a cart, a strong horse and a driver looking dejected in a huge sombrero. Beneath the sombrero Captain Felix Leidner's lively eyes looked out at them. He affected a cracked voice as he asked, "You hire me, friend? You have your papers?"

"We are loyal subjects, we always carry our papers. Here, my good wife, in you go." Diego picked Antonia up, lifted her over the high wooden side of the cart with a whirl of skirts, then swung in beside her. "Onward, friend."

From the time they rattled across the city and until they faced the Loyalist inspection of their papers, Antonia was still exhilarated by their "adventure." But it faded when they were stopped by one of the soldiers, with a new and effective Krag-Jorgensen carbine quite different from the soldiers she had seen with their aging rifles and the swords stuck through their belts.

When all had apparently passed inspection the horse clip-clopped on through the outskirts of the city toward the westerly coves that were impossible to patrol twenty-four hours a day...

Antonia's plans to have Diego escort her home had so far gone well. She was grateful for the cook's explanation to him that the family hadn't been expected for three weeks, which seemed easier then to blame the delay in mails between Cuba and the U.S. mainland for her mistaken arrival. She was nonplussed, though, when he said calmly, "I guessed that when the Butcher—pardon, General Weyler—said he had been surprised by the news you were aboard the *Baracoa*. It seems your family had also neglected to inform him they were arriving in Havana three weeks early."

"But you can see, they weren't arriving early at all."

"Then why did you hurry to Havana?"

"Oh, well, as I said, early this year Felipe wrote that they would be in Havana this week and I simply failed to receive father's letter about the delay."

"How do you know he wrote you a letter if you did not receive it?"

"Don't be silly, he must have."

"I see. And now you are determined to travel across half the island, through jungles and fields, past Cuban rebels with good reason to hate your family, all so that in three weeks you can return to Havana with them?"

"I thought I might hire some of Pablo's friends or some unemployed Havana men. There are so many, what with the revolt and all."

"Local men wouldn't last an hour in those areas. Whole platoons of Loyalist soldiers have been wiped out in Oriente and Camaguey provinces. In Santiago last week—"

"I thought General Weyler's *trochas*, that's what they call those long bare strips of land, isn't it? I thought they kept them back." She was delighted when he read her mind and mentioned the jungle areas between the coast and the Guzman y Pontalvo plantations . . . it meant he would know that only he could get her safely home to her family.

He gave in. "I will take you myself, since you seem determined to do this idiotic thing. Felix is sailing to a cove near Santiago. He can save us a part of the trip overland. We will move inland for the last two days. But you cannot make that trip in Tana Maguire's finery."

Antonia had agreed. "I'll dress any way you please. If Timothy Burford could play a female, I could play a boy."

"You can rule out that idea. Can you trust any of the household?"

And so Zerlina had been brought into the conspiracy to help Antonia and her "faithful betrothed, Señor Hastings."

Antonia knew she would have to be careful around Felix Leidner's crew . . . since they had no idea of her real identity, and being for the most part U.S. citizens, they might assume this "native girl" was brought aboard for their pleasure. Felix had warned her about this as they waited for the shore boat.

"You'll have to excuse my lads if they don't show you too much respect. They're in this gunrunning for the money, like me, and most of them think all Cubans are savages."

"I understand, I'll be careful." But it was one more obstacle to what she now realized had been a self-indulgent notion of romance that was supposed to end in Juan Diego's proposal. What lay ahead could be highly dangerous, with little if any of her romantic fantasies.

She increasingly felt this when they reached the coast and were hustled by silent fishermen into a tunnel carved out of the cliffside. The tide was in, roaring through the tunnel and showering Antonia as it raced for the inner walls. One of Felix's shore boats bounced up and down on the waters, and before Antonia could catch her breath she was huddled in the center of half a dozen filibusterers, including the two captains, Leidner and Diego. The Leidner ship was anchored surprisingly close inshore, and it took only a few minutes for the crew to haul in the boat and set the engines chugging and clanging.

As Captain Leidner had warned, Antonia, on board the *Frederika*, his fast little steamer that was once a Confederate gunboat, got a firsthand taste of what women less fortunate had to endure.

In spite of Diego's protection he couldn't be with her every minute of the short coastal voyage. He did, although, keep her with him as much as possible, and several times her presence seemed to handicap the two captains. They talked in a kind of code. For example:

"The Betancourt group are fighting with the old Gomez armies." She recognized those as the present and former presidents of the so-called Cuban Republic. "If you deliver to one of them on the beach the others may put in a word to the nearest garrison." Felix shrugged. "Can't keep the stuff on board, even if we count on the Santiago patrols running last week's schedules." "Why not try Paloma? The patrols usually ignore it. Too small. And I know the fishermen. The patriots there are Gomez men."

On the bunk across the cabin Antonia pretended to be asleep, but though the men had begun to speak in low tones, even the noisy engines did not entirely blur the meaning of the conversation between them. She did not want to hear about their filibustering activities. In spite of her feelings for Juan Diego she became aware now that what she heard was, in fact, a kind of treason against her family and what she'd believed in. What her father believed in. Cubans aren't educated, he'd said. Can't govern . . . Once when she was younger, she'd ventured, "But isn't that true of the people in Spain too?"

Patrick Maguire had not been amused. "Antonia, if you learned this sort of nonsense in the United States we must bring you home to stay, in spite of this rebel madness."

Antonia had said no more, tried to go along with her father and the other Loyalists, but her ambivalent feelings were sharpened in the *Frederika* now when she heard these plans laid by what she'd long heard were violent, murderous rebels.

Eventually Captain Leidner went up on deck to argue the matter with his mate, who according to Felix wanted to sell the entire cargo to the first bidder. "You know Bagley," he said as he left the cabin, "he'd sell his mother for a silver dollar if he thought we were losing his little scuffle with your precious Mother Spain."

"Not my precious mother," Diego said.

Antonia made excuses to herself for the man she loved. After all, he'd lost his family in a horrible way. It was natural his feelings should be this way. She would have felt the same way if . . .

The long tropic evening that had softly framed a sea of gold, salmon-pink and fire when Antonia was young, now looked dangerous, threatening. The clear Caribbean night made the *Frederika* a perfect target for Spanish patrol ships. Antonia spent most of that night looking out the stern porthole and hoping that none of the ships whose running lights she made out faintly through the gathering darkness was connected with the Imperial Spanish Navy.

Juan Diego was frequently called on deck to give advice or bare a hand during a fight between two particular crewmen, a German and a Cuban. It grew stifling in the night. The Caribbean breeze died down. The world beyond the clamor of the engines seemed far away, a part of the past. Even that quiet world brought danger ... it made the *Frederika* audible to any ship creeping by in the blue dark.

Morning brought a troubled sea, clouds rolling in, and a wild spring storm that swept along the rugged and beautiful Cuban coast, blotting everything from sight except the wild seas. The *Frederika* pitched and tossed for hours, lashed by the wind-driven waves that left Antonia and several of the crew thoroughly seasick. In the end she almost wished for a return of those calm, clear seas that would prove so disastrous if a Spanish patrol caught sight of them.

At last, late in the day, she felt that she would live. She unwrapped the dirty, sea-stained red kerchief and began to comb her hair with Felix Leidner's comb.

Diego and Leidner were still working out plans for the delivery of a deck-load of long wooden boxes when Leidner's mate Bagley, a burly fellow, stopped by the cabin to tell Antonia, "Best hustle yourself up on deck, girl. We'll be moving fast when we let go the boats." About to go on along the passage, he stopped, his heavy face wrinkling in a squint. "For a country girl you ain't hard to look at. How come you to cover up your hair like a cane worker? It's right pretty when it's all spread out around your face."

She tried to ignore this and began to tie the red kerchief around her hair. Bagley looked up and down the passage, then stepped inside the cabin.

"Yeah. Real pretty. Where'd that *cholo* find a nice little country mouse like you?"

Trying not to make it obvious, she looked for a weapon. Nothing within reach occurred to her except her own fingernails and the unladylike knee that her school friends had taught her. Still, her lungs were probably her best defense . . . in spite of the *Frederika*'s engines she was sure she could bring Diego to her with a few shrieks. It was a very small ship.

She poured out in Spanish her opinion of anyone who called her man a *cholo*.

Bagley looked a bit surprised but came on slowly, playing her like a fish on a line, she thought.

"You got a real temper, you Cuban tramp. But old Bagley, he's heard it all. Come on, now. Gimme a little'a that sweetness you got hidin' in them big eyes." He reached for her. She ducked away but one of his ham fists went across her body. He liked what he felt under that damp and clinging bodice, her breast heaving in her nervousness. She braced herself as he reached into the gathered neck of her bodice, his hand groping for her right breast.

"Nice. Real nice and full like all them greasers."

She shrieked, at the same time brought her knee up hard against his groin, then kicked his shinbone. He doubled up, grabbing his crotch and calling her a "dirty little *culch*," whatever that was. She ran for the doorway, but she underestimated his long legs. He caught her skirt, pulled her back while she screamed again. The next minute she found herself on the deck of the cabin with Bagley wriggling around on top of her, fumbling to separate her bodice from her skirt. His sweating hands were already on her flesh, pinching her stomach, grabbing at her thighs. "Curly black hair, like this warm little body . . . the way I like 'em."

She called out again and he quickly took one hand from her body and slipped it over her mouth, too close to her nose. She couldn't breathe. In panic now, she wriggled under his body—

Abruptly the mate had tumbled off her body in a V-shape, huddled up with his knees jammed against his chest. Clutching his shoulders, he squatted in the middle of the cabin, breathing hard and looking up at Juan Diego.

"Do you want to go over the side, you goddamn scum?" The threat was made in English, and Bagley's small eyes, squeezed into his fleshy face, continued to stare up at Diego. He also began to recover his senses.

"No, sir. It was just a . . . well, a sudden temptation . . . I mean, you know them Cuban tramps, they'll go after you, no matter what—" Diego kicked him in the face.

Antonia flinched in spite of herself. The mate crawled away but by the time he got to the doorway he was halfway to his feet, still bent over, and he made a dash for the companionway.

Revolted by the business, Antonia had a momentary wish that she could be alone for a while, untouched by any man, even Diego. But she also wanted to soften that look on Diego's face, the rage. She said quickly in Spanish, "He didn't hurt me, he was only here a minute."

When he pulled her to him she made an effort, subdued the little shiver as she relived those awful minutes in a man's hands that had made her feel like a dirty object. He was the first man who had gotten that far in possessing her, and it was hardly what she had hoped sexual possession would be.

Trying to blot it out, she ran her arms around Diego's neck and clung to him until she stopped shaking.

"I should have killed him," he muttered, his mouth against her hair.

She silenced that idea by touching his throat with the tip of her tongue. "You taste salty. I like the taste of you, sir."

My God, this was some strange proper lady . . . He'd been un-inhibited enough with the *Frederika*'s mate but during the minutes afterward he seemed more reserved with her. Was it out of respect for her inner feelings that he thought she must be trying to cover up? Or maybe he had never intended more, she thought. It was even possible she had been used on this whole trip, beginning in Washington, to disguise his real purpose in delivering her to her parents. It wouldn't hurt him to have the entry and freedom of Havana once more. As soon as he brought her home, he could see that her parents made his peace again with General Weyler and he would be a hero of sorts for having safely escorted the young lady who would soon be a member of Weyler's family. The story was to be that he had prevented her kidnapping and rescued her from filibustering pirates, and meanwhile he would have spied over half of Cuba, perhaps delivered messages, committed other crimes for the rebels . . . ?

She reminded herself he'd feel justified to avenge the death of his mother and sister. She also told herself she needed to make him understand that what had happened between the mate and herself couldn't sour her feelings for him... She needed to convince herself of that too. And stay convinced that in the long run Juan Diego would believe she was the only woman for him.

She became aware of the muscles of his body and thighs tightening against her. She knew it was necessary to love him now or there would always be the shadowy memory of the first mate's brutality to her.

She freed herself from him. He let her go, watching her. She bolted the cabin door and pressed back against it as if to hold him here. She was shaking inside but she gave him her most impudent smile.

"I couldn't let that animal take what was yours... show me... make me love you. Now..."

A pulse pounded in his throat as he watched her, then he finally said, "I warned you not to play this game."

She was sure she would never have the courage to behave like this again. It must be now. "It is not a game. Are you afraid of me?"

"More afraid for you... come here."

She did. He picked her up and swung her high in his arms.

"I believe I promised you once I would make you come to me."

Well, if it made him feel better to think it... When it all happened it was much quicker, less planned with mood and seduction than she had thought possible in a man she could love. He unceremoniously put her onto Felix Leidner's bunk, and while she tried to get her breath, he dropped onto her body. She had few seconds to regret or rethink her impudent seduction of a man who had been careful to treat her with a reasonable amount of respect in spite of their situation, first on the *Baracoa*, then the Palacio Guzman and now the *Frederika*. She was aware of a tightening nervousness, a fear that the memory of the first mate's near-rape would make her freeze. For a moment she even tried to struggle, but Diego was already on her. He had freed himself from the loose trousers and while her heartbeat threatened to suffocate her, she felt the welcome hardness against her warm, moist flesh.

Wondering at her own reaction, she opened to him, cried out only once when he entered her. As she writhed with his own twisting force, an unknown elation invaded her senses and she heard herself gasp out, "Stay, stay, part of me..."

She bathed in a delicious shower of heat, heard him say, "Love me, no one else. Not ever. Swear it..."

Of course she swore it. And meant it.

When they finally parted, they lay there for several minutes, staring at each other. He ran his finger over one long black strand of her hair, caressing it. She tucked her fingers gently around his genitals, bedding them in her palms.

He had propped himself on one arm, watching her, but she thought there was still some doubt in the black depths of his eyes.

"You are mercurial, my love. In the same circumstances, would you have enticed that fellow Hastings to your bed?"

Her hands clenched and he yelled, "ouch!"

"Never provoke a lady with your future in her hands." And then, with complete sincerity, "I could never feel this way about anyone but you. I swear it by the Holy Virgin. Does that satisfy you?"

"It must," he said, "especially under the circumstances," but she had a feeling that he still wasn't sure of her. He added, as he got up and dressed, "Actually, I suspect you love your family more, and maybe your idea of Cuba, and even that ignorant Hapsburg, the Spanish queen."

She wanted to shout, "I don't," but she restrained herself and said quietly, "All my life I will look back and say this was my best moment. I mean that, Juan Diego, and I mean it when I say I will never love another man."

He studied her, then leaned over her, kissed her, and said, "Well, back to being the scullery maid again. We will soon be dropping anchor and there isn't much time."

Still holding one of her hands, he reached for her big hat, set it on top of the red kerchief that he rescued from the back of her head. He tied the kerchief under her chin and smiled at her. "That's better. We don't want any more of the men seeing you as yourself." Over his shoulder he slung the bundle of what a casual inspector would assume were their life's belongings.

On deck they were assigned the second boat that headed for the shore of an inlet with heavy jungle growth to the water's edge. The first mate, Bagley, still nursing a swollen mouth and jaw, had been put in charge of the first boat and was busy loading long boxes onto the backs of Cuban fishermen when the second boat reached shore. Everything was completed in silence.

There was no beach, just a frothy shoreline where the tide was receding, and Antonia felt her sandals sink into the wet sand over her instep as she tried to keep up with Diego's stride. Though he ignored the first mate, she was aware of his little eyes in that pudding face, following her movements. She was still afraid of him, not so much for what he could do to her, but the danger he represented for the two captains. They might tend to forget him...

Diego did not look back. In five minutes they were out of sight of the shore and high on the bluff, making their way inland, Diego ahead of her, occasionally hacking away at the undergrowth with his machete. Straight palm trees and pines had proved to be guardians of the coast, but once the coast was left behind the jungle closed in around them. There seemed to be no path across the endless slippery palm fronds, the ferns and wild vegetation that still dripped from the day's heavy storm. She knew the thick-textured black earth of her native land well enough not to be surprised when her feet began to sink in the viscous, clinging mud. In other circumstances she would have called out, but with Diego plunging ahead of her, the need for stealth, she kept quiet. She was learning.

The farther they went, the less they saw of the sky. Palm trees and mango and great red flowering plants were invaded by unknown webs of jungle growth, tangled lianas that made the going slower. She became aware of new sounds, the hoarse chatter of parrots and the ubiquitous doves cooing.

She felt he must be pleased by her attempt to live up to his own cool strength. She was determined not to disappoint him, would have slogged on, but he stayed where he had stopped, studying the plant life and fungus around them. He dropped his bundle on what appeared to be a pile of clean-picked bones.

"Sit on top of this. It has been a rough hour for you."

"Only one hour? I don't believe it." But though the light overhead was dim and filtered through the lattice of green, she realized that it was not yet sunset and would probably rain again soon. She started to drop onto the pile of bones, but he stopped her.

"Have you never traveled in the jungle before? Tuck your skirts around you, unless you want scorpions crawling all over you."

She quickly drew her skirts up, not concerned with the considerable length of bare limb, as he scattered some of the bones and knelt there beside her.

"What are we sitting on," she asked, trying to finger the broken bits of shell that had fallen away from the little mound.

"Crab shells. Among others, probably some rebel *mambises* moving through here stopped for a meal."

She shifted her feet. Even when she was a child and spending weeks on the plantation she had never wandered into the jungle areas, leaving these adventures for her father and her young brother. She'd worried that one day she would come face to face with those armies of giant crabs that infested the areas south and east of the plantation. It was bad enough seeing them at a distance, in the brush that lined the old unpaved roads as the family carts and mules with all the family comforts moved either to Santiago or to Havana.

Minutes later, while she was trying to face down such old fears and pretending to find this trek an everyday experience, she felt her heart sink when he got up, stretched, and turned to offer her a hand up, saying, "Take care you don't step on that fellow. He's quite harmless."

A furry dark mass moved across the toe of her sandal. A *tarantula*.

Felipe was always telling her how harmless most of the tarantulas were, but she never stayed in their vicinity long enough to find out.

Juan grinned. "You certainly can move in a hurry when you choose. We should be on the Guzman land by nightfall at this rate."

He plunged on through the heavy undergrowth and she plodded after him, her teeth clenched, her eyes fiercely concentrating on his back.

Suddenly he stopped. "*Sangre de Cristo.*" His low voice frightened her more than his sudden stop. She had seen and heard nothing but the chattering, twittering jungle sounds.

"What is it?"

"Loyalist soldiers. Must be clearing a *trocha* across the area. I didn't know they'd gotten this far."

She tried to concentrate her tired brain on what this meant. The queen's soldiers were leveling ground, digging ditches, creating a no-man's-land ahead that they would guard, making it impossible to cross. Even in the middle of the night silhouettes could be made out by the starlight. Her knees felt watery.

He studied her. "Here, now. Where's your faith in me? I've been in worse spots. Take a breath, that's it."

Terrified, she gave him the best glint of a smile she could manage, and hoped he appreciated the effort.

CHAPTER
NINE

H E TOOK her hand. "There is no Spaniard who will outfox us."

This it is, she thought... I'm now officially included among his rebels.

She didn't make the mistake of arguing. She waited like a good soldier. He moved stealthily forward and to the right. The birds made so much noise neither Diego's steps nor Antonia's could be heard against the chatter. She hoped. It seemed they'd changed their course to a ninety-degree angle. He must be hoping to out-flank the workers on the lengthening strip of ground that was intended as a barrier. They were close enough now to hear the soldiers complaining and cursing as they chopped away trees, fo-liage, underbrush, flowers, wildlife, everything that grew in the way of their road.

Overhead the green world darkened. Night wouldn't help them ... the previous night, before the morning storm, had been starry with a three-quarter moon. But this was Juan's world, surely he would know how to escape the trap...

Going was much slower now. He couldn't use his machete with its noisy betrayal of their presence, and was forced to push aside the vines and branches that barred their path. The barriers were slippery, yielding, often unbreakable by hand, and Diego made little progress. Meanwhile Antonia could still hear the Spanish soldiers chopping away at roots and vines, dragging palm branches to thatch what she could faintly make out were sentry boxes at regular intervals along the ground and at the edge of the ditches.

She continued to move cautiously after him. Once, she made out the bright crimson-and-gold banner that belonged to her country and half of her ancestors. It fluttered from a new blockhouse. It was difficult to think of them as the enemy. Those were her people, her flag...

A drop of water on her hand and then another. She pulled her big hat lower. Within moments the downpour began. Diego raised his head and smiled. "A good sign. We should have dark skies for several hours."

She realized then how it gave them an advantage. The Spanish soldiers would seek shelter at night. They seldom if ever slept out in the field like the homeless insurgents who were used to this outdoor life, and the scattered guards might fail to see their silhouettes as they crossed the line.

As she thought, the soldiers ran off, some leaving their tools and some not even stopping for the tethered horses.

Twilight had fallen over the jungle world, but the bright glow of firelight and lamps was concentrated in one area half a mile beyond Diego and Antonia. It appeared to be a partially constructed stone blockhouse. Diego stopped in the shelter of a mango grove and shifted his machete to the hand that held the bundle. He pulled Antonia close to him. She could hear the pelting of rain on the leaves overhead and on her hat, but after her first shiver at contact with his wet shirt, she felt the warmth of his body and clung to him. Suddenly she felt him stiffen.

"Quiet."

His warning came just in time. She heard a volley of shots, followed by distant shouting of the sentries.

"They are bringing in *reconcentrados*."

She stood on her toes, trying to see into the darkness around the lanterns at the opening in the blockhouse that would eventually be a doorway. Soldiers in the pale uniform of the Spanish colonial troops appeared in the flaring light, herding a rain-soaked group of twenty or more people huddled against each other at the blockhouse, mostly children and women. Some of the women wore blouses; some, like many country peasants, were naked above the waist. There were two shuffling men, very old, judging by the effort it took them to move.

At least they'll get shelter, she thought, as several children ducked into the blockhouse, but soldiers inside routed them out and pointed to the fresh-turned ground beside the three-story stone wall of the building.

While Antonia and Diego watched, the peasant women and children, with the two old men, were forced into a tight group against the blockhouse wall. One by one they began to squat in the mud, some pulling down the children to sit in their laps. They'd been driven out of their houses or cabins or jungle lean-tos and shifted from place to place with rarely enough food and never enough shelter.

While she watched, hot with anger, two soldiers came out and passed around chunks of something, probably bread. The reconcentrated group grabbed at every piece and began to gnaw at it like starving creatures. The soldiers talked together, apparently not hardened to such sights... One of them brought out a jug and poured a cup full of some kind of liquor that was passed around until it was empty. It was a tiny consolation to Antonia that her people had at least shown *some* signs of humanity.

Diego felt her fingers move as she rubbed her eyes. "Don't cry. There are good and bad in every army." She had seen very little of the good today.

He hoisted his pack, let her go, and raised his machete again. She hurried along after him as he veered toward the east in the direction of the *trocha* line. Clearing of this strip of ground had only begun and it was deserted now, but there had been some tramping around through the jungle's edge. At least the going was easier here, even in the half-dark.

They arrived at the *trocha* before she was ready for it. She could never have made out the area if she hadn't been going in the dark for the last hour. The rain had let up, ending in a drizzle accentuated by the dripping of trees, wild hibiscus and foliage unknown

to her. Skeletal branches caught at her hat and blouse. She realized
that this was now an area bordering on the lengthy dead zone.
Many trees had been hacked away or burned to clear the barren
strip of no-man's-land that Captain-General Weyler called his *trochas*.

"Your hat," Diego whispered. He had slipped his own hat back
on his neck and pointed toward the lamps and fires of the distant
blockhouse they had left behind them. There was always a chance
their pale hats would catch a ray of light from those fires. She
pushed her own hat back and got a taste of misty rain on her face.
The barren, unfinished *trocha*, like a dead path carved out of field
and jungle, lay before them. Two sentries walked its borders opposite each other, their new Krag rifles slung over their shoulders.
They apparently expected nothing in this wet darkness, and from
the uneasy way they looked across at each other they wanted to
find nothing. One of them, slight and young judging by his sil-
houette against the blockhouse, seemed especially nervous. The
other, a stocky man with the decisive voice of a veteran, called to
him.

"Forget these rebel lice. Think of Seville and that sweetheart of
yours."

"It's those things," the other said. "Those crabs. We killed
hundreds on the march. Never saw anything so big. And the clack-
clack of them in the dark . . ."

Antonia grimaced in some sympathy. She and Diego huddled in
the ditch west of the line. He was waiting for a moment when the
attention of both men would be directed toward the blockhouse.
It came quickly when the veteran said, "Water, *amigo?* You will
piss blood before this campaign is over. Here. Shade me for a light.
You need a cigarette."

Diego nudged her. The two men were close together, their
palmetto hat brims joining as they tried to light one cigarette between them. Antonia scrambled after Diego, running over the
ground in a crouch.

The young Sevilliano swung around, his comrade listened. "Crabs,
nothing but your crabs," he called out, angry that the other's sudden movement had left their cigarette unprotected and sodden.
He stuck it into his cartridge belt and under the protection of their
hats the soldiers tried to light another.

Diego drew Antonia quickly into the foliage beyond the easterly side of the bared ground. He seemed to know exactly where they were and where a trail ran east and north. She followed him with a confidence in him that was exhilarating, as though she'd drunk a good deal of wine. Crossing the *trocha* had also made her stronger, more confident. Now at least she knew something more of what she was capable. She could count on herself to follow the directions of Juan or even—perhaps—to help herself if it became necessary. She trudged on behind Diego through the heavy jungle that was interspersed with wild growth where someone had tried to lay out wheat or rye and then let the ground return to its original greedy master—the jungle.

It must have been just before dawn. There was a lightness in the sky when he stopped in a small clearing where others had camped. Squinting through the blue light of false dawn, she could make out the cold remains of fires. Flapping soggily from a young coco palm was a piece of canvas.

Diego pointed to it. "Headquarters for General Gomez when he came through here last year."

"Headquarters? A piece of canvas?"

"Let me tell you, this clearing, small as it is, held two hundred men at one time. The true *mambises*, the trained insurgents."

She thought of the captain-general's palace in Havana with its great heavy walls and ancient banners, a citadel for the leader of an army. But he couldn't conquer this ragtag army for all his high walls and expert tools like the new rifles the Spanish had been equipped with, far newer and more efficient than the Springfields of the Yankee army, as Lloyd Hastings had grumbled one day.

She was thinking on all this when Diego removed the bundle, laid down his machete and piled a place for her with a cushion of palm fronds and the bundle.

"Well, my recruit, you have learned the first lesson in warfare. This is Cuban ground. We have an advantage. Your Yankee friends found out about that a hundred years ago when they fought their own crown ruler. They fought on their own ground, for their own land. It gave them the edge, the knowledge of the field . . . well, rest now. We're safe, I think, from your friend. Let's hope we don't meet any of mine."

She tucked her sodden skirts around her legs and settled on the little throne he'd arranged for her. She dropped her head forward over her arms and to her surprise almost went to sleep. She was aware of him standing over her. He knelt down. She felt his hands massaging the back of her neck.

"You've been brave, sweetheart." His voice was as much a tonic as his hands. "Go to sleep."

Her eyes were already closed. She dreamed of warm velvet darkness, and had just settled into it when someone began to juggle wooden blocks. It must be Felipe. Her little brother loved to get up early, knowing she was what he called a creature of the night, and the more noise he made the better *he* liked it. Click-clack . . . click-clack . . . She opened her eyes. At the same instant she knew that what she heard was not her little brother and the wooden alphabet blocks Aunt Sybil had brought him. In spite of the humid air her flesh felt as if it were tipped with ice. She knew what the click-clack meant.

She whispered, "Where are they?"

The mist had stopped. The flicker of light illuminated the little clearing. Juan Diego had dug up some canvas-covered brush and lighted it in the dead embers after losing several matches. He had more trouble lighting the heavy branches that were still damp. Antonia understood what they were for. She looked about. Within the depths of the jungle that laced itself around them she saw in every direction the glimmer of movement.

Diego took a smoking ember and tossed it into a clump of ferns whose heads curled like young cobras. Immediately, creatures began to scuttle around. The glimmer of firelight made the gigantic crabs more visible. She saw the claws first, feeling their way out toward her, twisting and winding, like razor-sharp mouths. She got up, stood as high as she could get on the mound of palm fronds and clothing.

Diego threw out another stick in a different direction. This one burned well and the underbrush came alive with scuttling, clicking noises. The whole glade was surrounded by the awful things. They did not care to cross the clearing where the fires burned but they seemed to grow bolder in the areas where the grassy soil remained damp. They scuttled along like bloated spiders in their rainbow colors, moving forward, then, when she bent over and threw muddy grass at them, they scrambled sideways. And all the time their claws reached out, searching, snapping at her. Gleaming little eyes peered out at her malevolently from under hard, sunset-colored shells.

It seemed impossible but Diego managed to find enough smoking, burning brands to surround a small circle in the clearing. She tried not to think of what would happen if this smoke attracted soldiers—rebel or loyalist.

"Hungry?" Diego asked as he dried off his clothing by the flickering fire.

She shook her head.

Diego reached behind her, took a can and a sheathed hunting knife from the bundle on the palm fronds and punctured the can in several places, then peeled them back. The crabs went on clack-clacking as they scuttled around the ring of smoking branches. Diego held up the can.

"Peaches?"

In spite of the crabs and whatever other jungle denizens were watching them from the dark recesses of the forest, Antonia found that she actually was hungry.

They scooped out the fruit between them, eating it with their hands. It was discolored, but once the moist, sweet slices were in her mouth they tasted just fine. She marveled at the can that had proved so useful.

"It may prove still more useful." He cleaned it out reasonably well with the drying leaves nearby and tucked it back into his bundle.

It was within minutes of dawn but nothing discouraged the nervous, hungry crabs. They circled the still-smoking debris until they could break through. No matter where Antonia turned to avoid seeing them, they were incessantly moving, shifting, clack-clacking as they tested ways to reach Antonia and Diego inside the circle.

"I always knew you would introduce me to a new life, with exotic surroundings."

He had been stirring up the fire, had taken out another smoking branch, but he stopped with it in his hands and looked at her. Even in the blue dawn she couldn't mistake the depth of feeling in his eyes.

"I confess, I meant to test you, sweetheart. But I never intended this—" He threw the next burning stick at the army growing around them. "Never mind. We'll start on. There's a path north beyond a little stream I know."

How were they going to get through their circle of tormentors, she wondered. A pair of clicking claws reached for her. The first crab scout had broken through. She jumped closer to the dying fire and heard a revolting crunch as Juan beat off the bold scout with his machete and finished the job with his heavy sandal.

The crabs panicked too, with an almost rhythmic clatter as their claws twisted and groped toward Antonia. Diego had thrown the bundle on his back and still had the machete in his other hand. *"Jump!"*

She leaped over the most venturesome crab, feeling the razor-cut as one of his claws grazed her calf. She followed Diego out of the glade and along a path scarcely wide enough to move single file through the underbrush, and marveled that the crabs didn't attack her as she hurried after Juan Diego, a pale yellow dawn showing the way overhead.

The creatures had not given up.

With every step she heard the scuffling noises among the roots, tangled lianas and fronds that covered the jungle floor. She tried to follow in Juan's footsteps but his long stride was not attuned to her shorter steps, even when he had to hack a way for them through the tangle of vines and overgrown brush. She spent valuable time leaping to bared spots only just vacated by the ubiquitous crabs in Juan's wake. She was forced to stop and brush off the things that crawled over her or fell from the foliage overhead. They seemed to have a special affection for her.

Diego often stopped for her but she waved him on. She couldn't wait to get out of this noisy green world. Thighs and feet aching, back bent and hurting, she moved along, thinking of nothing but one step ahead. Abruptly, a web of vines swung across her path. A strong spider web? She clawed at it as she tripped and fell across the tangle of vines, found herself flat on the ground, fingers groping through decayed plant life and mud.

Her fall had drawn the crabs out of the filtered green light of the jungle all around her. She called to Diego, but he was chopping away at some barrier and overhead a parrot chattered in protest. Her left temple and cheek in the mud, she opened her right eye. One of the monstrous, clacking creatures was within inches of her face. Tiny eyes glowed at her from under that hard, sunset-colored shell. When she lay flat on the ground the crab loomed over her, its claws moving in rhythm to join each other and her.

She shrieked, getting a mouthful of mud. The creature scuttled backward, mandibles clicking, but others came on. She could see herself being ripped up by these monsters, torn and sliced and shredded and . . . then Diego was there. Finally. A huge crab moving across her leg went flying through the air and into the tangled foliage. Diego moved more carefully with the creature that now threatened to embrace her. She hardly breathed until he had scooped the crab off her body with his machete.

He reached for her hands. She barely had strength to raise them but he managed that, pulling her up to her feet and putting her over his shoulder and going off along the trail he had cut through. Now mosquito bites were driving her mad. She wriggled to scratch, still being carried slung over his shoulder like a Springfield rifle.

Finally when she stopped hearing the clatter of the crabs, Diego set her down.

"Think you can walk?"

"Thank you. Yes."

"Good. On our way."

And they were off again. However threatening the Loyalist soldiers at the *trocha* may have been, she felt that Juan had really saved her when he rescued her from the crabs, so monstrous they had actually towered over her when she lay flat on the ground. . .

Gradually now the tight jungle growth gave Antonia and Diego more breathing space, and they came to the rush-covered stream he had mentioned. He stepped carefully around a busy hill of multi-legged, translucent green insects and went down to the bed of the stream, where he dipped the peach can into the bubbling water that looked surprisingly clean, considering its surroundings.

Dazed with fatigue, Antonia leaned against the bare, lean trunk of a palm tree and watched him. When he brought the peach can up the muddy bank and offered it to her she took it in both hands, which shook, and drank it all, gulping until the can was empty. She couldn't believe it when she looked into the can and handed it back to him.

"I'm sorry. Greedy, I guess."

He too looked tired, the faint lines in his face creased with dirt, but when he took the can back he suddenly kissed her fingers, then went down the embankment again. She had been enormously touched by his gesture.

Returning, he told her they'd rest soon, that there was an abandoned house not too far down the road. She followed him, often stamping her feet to shake off numbness. He was right about the abandoned house. Its red tile roofs loomed up beyond a fallow field that had once grown experimental tobacco, but nothing remained of the crop now except the muddy runnels and wild stalks swarming with tobacco worms. The trail widened into a road, overgrown but still wide enough to carry a wagon and mules. It was bordered by trees and red-flowering bushes. She made out the occasional rasping cackle and chatter of parrots in the trees overhead, began to recognize certain landmarks, and warm relief crept through her aching body. She was coming onto familiar ground. There would be fields of maize ahead, then a cane field beyond the sluggish stream. Off to the east below the mountain range was an old sugar mill.

Patrick Maguire and a neighbor, Raul Guttierez, had an interest in the mill, a matter of contention with Antonia's mother, who considered the mill workers harshly dealt with. To Señora Maguire all workers were her children, her kindly treated property. They were paid the going wage, but she claimed the mill itself was a great smoky horror, a place that should remain invisible to a daughter of the *hidalgos*. Antonia had once sneaked over with Felipe during a visit to the Guttierez hacienda, and remembered now coughing and gasping over the sulphur fumes that had almost obliterated sight of the mill itself.

The abandoned old house belonged to the Guttierez family. Where had they gone? María-Rosa Guttierez, who was Felipe's age and two years younger than Antonia, had adored Antonia's handsome brother. For several years during their childhood it was generally assumed by the two families that a marriage would be arranged, but during Antonia's school years the idea had died out and this spring when she returned home for a visit everyone talked about the advantageous connection with Captain-General Weyler, the ruler of Havana. Patrick Maguire had waved aside the Guttierez connection as "impractical."

Could this desolate hacienda be the reason? Even at a distance it appeared to be burned out, a shell of the lovely place she had known in her girlhood. Diego waved her back into the protection of an abandoned orchard whose overgrown foliage, newly watered by the rain, had completely eclipsed Señora Guttierez' prized apple trees. No one had thought she could harvest apples in this arid little patch of soil and it seemed that the pessimists had been right in spite of the recent torrential downpour.

Diego had disappeared inside the hacienda's stucco garden walls. He would be crossing the garden at this moment, and she remembered the glorious bougainvillea and hibiscus, the jasmine from Señora Guttierez' native Córdoba, and the rope swing hung from a bent coco palm. She could see the curving trunk and part of the foliage above the hacienda wall.

Those had been good times in her childhood, but they were a dream, curiously unreal. More and more, she felt that she was merely visiting this lush, beautiful, terrible island, and was relieved when Diego came out again and waved his hat to her.

She took a deep breath and began to run slowly along the muddy wagon ruts, but something in the way he held out one arm to her, then glanced behind him and frowned, spoke to her. He was trying to warn her.

CHAPTER
TEN

ANTONIA WENT around him to enter the garden but Juan
Diego kept his hold on her arm.

"Tana, wait."

"Enough. I'm a woman who has lived half her life span. I'm
almost twenty-two years old. Let me see whatever it is. Come on."

He shrugged. "I am sorry... the hacienda was raided. About
two days ago, I would say."

How could he be so precise if he judged by nothing but the
debris of a partial fire? She looked around the wall and through
the blackened wooden gate into the garden that was surrounded
by the tile-roofed portico, the rooms were lighted only by the
louvred doors and windows opening on the portico, most of them
burned and smoked. It was like her own family's plantation house,
excellent in the tropic climate, seldom too hot even on the most
humid day. She expected to see the flowers killed by the heat or
trampled by those men who must have fought the fire that had

blackened the gate and the doors and the windows as well as the smoke-stained beams under the red tiles.

The garden was deserted, the grass beaten down, and the swing hung by one rope, but most of the flowers against the walls still bloomed though the heavy hibiscus heads sagged after the night's storm. Puzzled, Antonia looked to Diego. They would share this disaster and whatever was inside the house.

Inside the gate the garden air smelled of sickly sweet decay. She hurried to the open double doors in the center of the portico, saying, as she went, "This was the Guttierez' salon, the big formal center of the house. You could walk straight in from the garden..." The louvred doors had been forced inward. One of them hung by a single hinge. The other had been pushed against a barrier. A body lay inside the standing door. Evidently it held the door in place.

She heard herself make a retching sound in her throat as she knelt and started to turn the body over. She suspected from his small chunky size and the extreme youth of his hands that he was the boy being trained as a butler by Señora Guttierez two years ago.

"I think he's Luis Sanchio. He used to work in the garden. He was ... very good ..."

"And loyal, it seems."

"He adored the señora." She moved away. The corpse had nearly been decapitated by a sharp instrument, probably a machete. The head was severed under the jaw. Ants and other jungle scavengers had done their work.

She swallowed, cleared her throat. Diego had a mud-stained handkerchief ready and she pressed it so hard against her nose and mouth that the muscles in her fingers ached. Her voice was muffled. "How many others?"

"A tall man. Lean. Well dressed. An old scar across the knuckles of the left—"

"Señor Guttierez. Were there any women?"

He hesitated, then pointed to the far right, where the kitchen and storage area had been added back of the dining room. "A girl."

Oh, God, not her childhood friend María-Rosa. "Tall? Chestnut hair?"

He maneuvered her around the boy's body. "No. Small and black-haired. Don't go out there."

Long, panicky strides took her across the room from Luis Sanchio. In the hall, striped with shadows from the broken louvres of a window, she found the little Guttierez family dog, a bronze-colored spaniel. One blow with a machete had disemboweled it. Beyond the dog, half in and half out of the master's study, lay Raul Guttierez. She could not see his face but the floor beneath appeared to seethe with movement. The bloodstains had long since become faded blotches.

Diego's arm was around her waist, propelling her out the nearest door onto the portico.

"But we must bury them . . . a priest . . ."

He ignored that until they had crossed the garden and moved her along.

"We just can't leave them there. *Stop!*"

The water-stained bundle of clothing, cans and other items lay where he had dropped it beside the wall. He picked it up, glanced around the desolate scene. Buzzards circled lazily overhead, waiting for their departure to do what they did naturally.

"Where is the well?" Diego asked.

She was confused by his odd movements but stammered, "One is behind the kitchen. They had a . . . new one but the kitchen well is closer."

He hoisted the bundle and machete. "Can you run?"

The danger finally penetrated. "You think they may still be around?"

"Possible." He hurried her along the wall around to the back of the house, removed the wooden cover of the well that Raul Guttierez' father had put in as an imitation of those in the American West. It was overgrown with the lush plant life of the jungle. The wooden cover fell apart in Diego's hands, eaten away by insects. He dropped the bundle down into the black, echoing depths and took her hand. "Nothing in sight. Ready?"

She seemed to have acquired a sudden nervous strength. She no longer seemed to feel around her ankles the sharp scratch and cut of the underbrush in their path as she headed toward the wagon road that would lead by nightfall to the lands of her own family.

But Diego swung her toward the jungle encroaching on the pastures where no sheep or pigs or cattle remained. Everything useful had been carried off.

"We must stay away from the road," he told her.

"Not the jungle again!" But she knew he was right. She braced herself, took his hand again and he plunged into the brush.

Before they made their way off Guttierez land Diego was already hacking their way through thickets to the swampy river and an area now returned to nature that had almost been tamed years ago by Patrick Maguire and Raul Guttierez. When the sun was high overhead he stopped abruptly. Antonia leaned against a wild tangle of cane and palm fronds. She had a cutting pain over her ribs and was breathing hard. Diego was listening, watching something through the jungle beyond the curtain of vines. She was sensible enough not to speak.

He pointed westward through the jungle growth dappled with sunlight so hot the green fronds and wild blooms drooped in the humid air. The road between her family's estates and the Guttierez lands must have been nearer than she thought. She listened, heard heavy sounds in the distance followed by the closer flutter and scuttling of animals, birds and insect life, which told her even before she heard the rattle of wooden wheels that a heavy force was moving along the road. And now she made out the shouts of running men:

"Half the Butcher's assassins were waiting." . . . "The Spanish devils were everywhere." . . . "Couldn't move beyond the *trocha* . . . Guzman land can't be reached with any force." . . . "The Irishman was ready . . ."

Antonia caught her breath. Diego waved her to silence. At least she had learned that her family was safe.

When Diego was satisfied none of the small insurgent army had been dawdling behind the main force, he allowed Antonia to rest and joined her, knowing she would want explanations. She sat on a boulder in the stream. She could hear the stirrings of the gigantic crabs again in the underbrush, even over the gurgle of the stream.

"You should be safe at home in a few hours."

"Safe." She looked down at him. He sat on a lower, flat rock with one foot in the water, his sandal dangling in one hand. "Did you have any idea all this would happen?"

He avoided her eyes, seemed to be mesmerized by his dangling sandal. Finally he said, "Everything went wrong. Neither Felix nor I expected to land in such a dangerous place, but I couldn't take a risk staying on the *Frederika*. I had counted too much on the loyalty of his crew. I judged them by my own. I thought if it came to the worst and the Spanish patrol caught us, you would be safe because of your father. And the Butcher, but"—he shrugged— "Bagley couldn't be trusted. I had to get you off. There would have been other Bagleys."

"And then, you were surprised by the new *trocha* line being built."

"A bad time. The line might have been finished. Almost four hundred yards across. We could hardly have run four hundred yards without being spotted."

"Are we all right now?"

"We must not let ourselves be seen until we meet your family."

"I understand... You do think they are safe?"

"According to these rebels the Maguires are being protected by your admirer's army."

She colored a little, remembering her lie, the lie that persuaded him to escort her on this hellish trip. She guessed she deserved everything she'd gone through.

"Was it your people, those rebels, who killed Señor Guttierez and the others?"

He barely nodded. He was not looking at her.

Antonia felt it was only fair to add, "My own people, those Loyalist soldiers, were at the blockhouse last night, herding the poor wretches to some reconcentration camp."

He reached up and squeezed her hand. "You need to eat. Try chewing this jerky."

She took the hard, dry, stringy thing that looked like a wide shoelace, began to chew on it and found it surprisingly satisfying. He took another ribbon out of his stained bandolero and joined her.

They were silent for a while, too tired to talk. Soon, though, they should be home with those she loved, and she could introduce Captain Juan Diego as the man who saved her from kidnappers. All the same, it took every ounce of strength for her to get to her feet. She accepted his hand in trying to leap from rock to rock upstream, their movements starting a clatter among the crabs.

Once they were in a desert bush and beyond the sound of the crabs, she saw familiar landmarks in the open country. "I could almost show you the way from here. There's a *fonda* beyond that grove of mangoes and the tall palms. The owner was my father's friend in the old days. Maybe we could borrow his mule and cart." She shaded her eyes against the crimson light from the western horizon. "I think I see a little trail of smoke above the trees."

He shook his head. "That platoon on the road at noon came through here. They wouldn't leave him if he was friendly to the Loyalists."

She stared anxiously at the trail of smoke. "You don't think they've burned him out . . . ?"

"No. It's a typical smoke fire from a *fonda*, but I think you will find he has gone over to the Republic, if he is the same man."

"The Republic?"

"We think of it as the Republic of Cuba. You people think of us as insurgents, rebels."

So it was still *you* and *us*. But she at least understood his feelings after the blockhouse episode, just as he must hers after the monstrous thing they found at the Guttierez estates.

Under cover of the forgotten orchard they had made good time until they passed nearly opposite the *fonda*, which was now visible through the trees. It would take only a few minutes to pass out of sight of the *fonda* in the long shadows of afternoon, but Antonia was shocked when she heard the challenge:

"Where do you go there? You in the grove?"

Diego glanced at her. "Is it your father's friend?"

She shook her head, frowning as she tried to study the man who had hailed them from the road. It was difficult at first to make out more than the bloody red aura around a muscular man with his homespun shirt flapping over his trousers. Two crossed bandoleros held bullets and he carried an old Springfield rifle in his hand, not the new smokeless Spanish army issue. The new Krags did not betray every firing by black smoke like the Springfields.

The bloody aura was caused by the sunset behind the man, but she did not need Diego's warning. "A rebel. For God's sake, don't give your right name."

She nodded.

He pushed aside the giant palm fronds of the thicket, waving his machete.

"Making our way home, my woman and me. Can you help us?"

Antonia knew he was feeling out the political waters, but his disheveled condition and hers, doubtless the smell of them as well, after over twenty-four hours in the swamp and jungle, had provided them with a ready-made passport to satisfy a fellow insurgent.

"Come on closer. Both of you." His dark eyes looked them over. It would be hard to find two more wretched specimens. "You must have been running from the Butcher's men."

"Then we're among friends, señor." Diego knuckled back his big hat, bowing in the old, gracious Spanish way still common to the people of Cuba in spite of the troubles. "We crossed a *trocha* they were clearing. Over Santiago-way."

Which was all they needed as an open-sesame.

"Welcome, friend. That is always something to boast about, beating Butcher Weyler's *trochas*."

He introduced himself as Pablo Morales and waved his rifle, urging them toward the broken-down adobe-and-brick shelter farther along the road. Its palm frond roof was in the last stages of decay, but it was the *fonda* Antonia remembered from her childhood. More dilapidated, certainly less respectable, but the rebellion that had torn the island intermittently after 1893, with fresh violence since 1896, had left nothing as it was.

Antonia always found it difficult to play the subservient and maltreated female so easily dismissed by the *fonda*'s owner, but she trudged along after Diego and Pablo Morales, her head down, her shoulders bent. She knew Diego must be as anxious to get on as she was, but it wouldn't look well if he hurried off toward what the innkeeper thought was certain danger so near the Maguire-Guzman estates, where General Weyler's men waited.

Only one patron remained in the little roadside cafe, a cane worker asleep on a three-legged stool and snoring loudly, his big-brimmed hat pulled down over his face. Morales' dog, a short-haired bitch, wagged her long rope tail and hung around the newcomers hopefully.

Antonia knew there was a good two-hour walk ahead, and when Morales asked if he could get them something to eat, she looked so hopeful that Diego got out several small coins, considered them one by one for the owner's benefit, and agreed. Morales brought them coffee and beans, his menu for the day, probably the year.

Nothing had ever tasted so good. She didn't like to imagine what shreds of meat went into the bowl with the beans and tomatoes, but it was what she needed to give her strength, that and the thick black coffee whose power might almost have propelled her the rest of the way home. She said nothing while Diego and Morales exchanged gossip and opinions about the progress of the "revolution" and the next move of Captain General Weyler.

"They say the Spanish prime minister has ordered him home to Spain," Morales said, though Antonia had heard nothing of this. "The queen is trying for clemency. Much good it may do her while Canovas is prime minister. Home rule be damned. We're going to demand complete independence now."

Diego grunted. "They say the junta has organized Peanut clubs in New York to get money for the cause."

An item Juan had not confided to her.

Morales was frank. "There are uses for the money. Some of the men, not our leaders but some, have talked about using force against the greatest of the tyrants."

Antonia thought, Surely what they did on the Guttierez estates was force. But Diego raised his head. Antonia could see his eyes narrowing as he asked in a flat voice that did not fool her, "Assassination? And the victim?"

"There was talk of the queen regent herself. Or the young king."

Antonia barely held back a gasp.

"A bad idea," Diego said. "Do we want the world to hate us as an army of murderers? And against women and children?"

Morales agreed, though Antonia thought he seemed reluctant to give up the idea. "So they say, but there are other candidates. Then too, the assassin wouldn't be Cuban. It couldn't even be traced to this hemisphere. There are those available with no political loyalties. Anarchists."

"I know General Gomez would never have approved. To count on anarchist assassins... that's no way to freedom. I tell you, we would be outcasts in the eyes of the world."

Antonia was grateful to hear that. It would have been unforgivable if Juan had agreed to such an idea.

"So they say, but Angiolillo is such a likely little monster. I heard talk here and there that he might be interested. Neither Spanish nor Cuban. Nor French, when it comes to that. They say he's somewhere in southern France right now. Probably just waiting to be called."

"Not by *our* leaders, señor."

Morales shrugged, changing the subject as Juan Diego finished his coffee. "Aren't you walking into the butcher shop if you keep on this road? Weyler's men are waiting at the line they've drawn up along the borders of the Guzman estates."

"We've a shelter... near the Maguire-Guzman properties. Used in the old days by Maguire cattlemen. We keep goats when times are better."

The drunken customer on the stool in the corner raised his head, staring at Diego and Antonia with bleary eyes.

"You said Maguire? The Spanish. Knew them well, those Guzman-Pontalvos. Black Spaniards, everyone of them."

Antonia lowered her head, trying not to attract his attention. She didn't remember him, but it was probable he'd been one of the many workers on the estates. In which case he would know Antonia by sight. She felt the gooseflesh rise on her arms.

Diego got up, pulled his hat down over his eyes. "I best be on my way. Wouldn't like to run on the Butcher's men by accident, after sunset. Come along, woman."

Antonia trudged after him, hunched over, much of her face concealed by her hat. The drunk sat up.

"You there. That's a fine set of ankles. Young, too..."

Juan ordered her in a loud voice: "Hurry. Always a slow one. Half-witted." He took her arm and hustled her away.

The drunk kept leaning forward, staring after them.

"You with the ankles, don't I know you?"

She shot a quick look at Diego, who pushed her in front of him and out the door. Over his shoulder he called to the drunk. "The Guttierez kitchen, but I made her quit. Them with their Spanish friends. Loyalists, they call them. Loyal to what? Not to Cuba."

The drunk and Morales agreed, and by this time Juan and Antonia had left the *fonda*.

They scuffed along in the hardening ruts of mud that marked the road until they were out of sight of the *fonda,* then cut into the tangled brush on the edge of the jungle.

Out of breath but still running, Antonia reminded him, "We should get to the line inside of an hour. I ought to make myself presentable, so they'll recognize me. I don't want to be shot."

He grinned. "Anyone less like the daughter of the Guzman-Pontalvos . . . of course"—he looked her over—"you might still be one of the bog-trotting Maguires."

She raised a dirt-stained fist and shook it at him, but though she had been almost too tired to respond, she was grateful for his mood.

"What do we do, then?"

"We will manage. If you recognize any of the guards, and if any are from the estate, that will help."

"If not?"

"Then we will think of something else. You must know the area well enough to find a break in the line somewhere."

She did recall a little cave in the hills where she and Felipe used to hide from each other. It opened onto the side of the hill, ran as a tunnel into some tangled mesquite. Maybe it would serve. She told him about it.

He studied her. "It may do. Let's hope we don't need it. You look exhausted."

Night came down suddenly in the valley that they soon after entered. The tension reached a climax when they saw lights ahead, flaring torches that cast the shadows of scores of men across a wide strip of cleared ground. At first Antonia thought this human barricade was crazy. Couldn't dozens be mowed down by gunfire from the jungle dark? But she discovered that the shadows were deceptive. No man remained where he seemed to be, and the shifting figures were behind brick-and-stucco barricades. Even a devilish "infernal machine" planted below the walls would have difficulty reaching its target.

For an instant a youthful figure with a delicate profile, the face pale against coal-black hair, was illuminated by one of the flares. Antonia grabbed at Juan Diego's arm.

"It's my brother Felipe," she whispered. "There, near the brick barricade on the left."

"We'll have no chance if he doesn't believe you. Might be better to go around the line, to that tunnel you mentioned."

"It's a cave, and we can't. He's right there, so close I know he would recognize me."

"I still think—"

Suddenly she was waving the dirty white handkerchief he had given her at the Guttierez hacienda.

"Felipe ... it's Tana, *Tana* ..."

Excitement back of the no-man's land that separated them from the soldiers and Felipe Maguire. Someone shot but there was no volley. The men were arguing. Evidently Felipe had heard her call. She tried again.

"Felipe, I didn't mean to knock you down that day in the cave, but you made me angry..." That should identify her.

Diego and Antonia could hear arguments. One of the soldiers wanted to get his senior officer. Felipe became visible again.

"Tana, take care. Come out into the torchlight. Keep your hands high until we can see you."

She made her way out of the brush, almost too exhausted to care.

"I have someone with me, Felipe. He saved my life." She raised her voice. *"He saved my life. Don't shoot."*

Her brother was calling to her. Someone held him back and they were arguing... "I know my own sister when I hear her"... "We have not examined her papers yet, señor."

She started across the bare churned ground. Felipe waved to her. She called behind her to Juan Diego.

"Come on, they've seen us."

She heard his footstep on the ground at the same time she heard the sharp splat close to her ear.

Felipe called out, "What the hell are you doing? That's my sister," and at the same time Diego muttered, *"Jesu,"* and lurched against her.

She went down with him, holding on to him. He sank to one knee, Antonia beside him. Her shoulder was moist and red with his blood. He looked at it, surprised.

"Not too friendly, your family. I seem to have been shot."

CHAPTER
ELEVEN

THE SEÑORA Ysabel Maguire Guzman y Pontalvo kissed her daughter's sunburned forehead and said in her calm fashion, "The young señor is quite himself, Tanita. He has the good manners one approves. It is not usual to find a person of his class with the manners of an *hidalgo*. Your influence has been excellent."

Antonia had to laugh. "His manners are better than mine by far." She hugged the plump, regal little woman. "You ought to thank him for making a lady out of me." Or rather, a woman, which was considerably better.

Her brother Felipe slapped his sister's bedpost. "Tana would be a handful for any man. Poor fellow, he deserves our thanks for not having thrashed her."

"Not amusing, such jokes," their mother told them. "You will give the *capitán* a false hope. He may think he can aspire to—"

Antonia's eyes were bright. "Yes, he might. All right, *mamacita*,

I will sleep. My bath was heaven, all that clean warm water. I hope you saw to it that Captain Diego got a bath after they took the bullet out of his shoulder."

Señora Maguire assured her daughter and Felipe that "this Yankee humor is not to my liking. Felipe, you are as bad as your sister. You encourage her."

Actually, Felipe could do no wrong, so far as his mother was concerned, and when he coaxed her to let him stay with his sister a few minutes, the señora gave in. He was her baby. His childhood had been marred by too many diseases, stomach upsets and colds, so that she had long been used to giving him his way.

Antonia watched her leave, blew her a kiss and promised to send Felipe after her very soon.

"Dearest Mama, she's a great one for protocol but her heart isn't in it when she scolds you, Felipe."

Felipe, a slender youth whose entire life had been filled with love, had more innocent self-confidence than conceit. He knew he was not the most intellectual of men and that his redoubtable sister was his superior in a good many qualities. Part of his charm was that he had always accepted the idea of his headstrong sister's dominance and never grudged it. He pushed aside the veil of mosquito netting around his sister's bed and settled lightly on the edge of the counterpane.

"Mama always thinks her friend the queen is watching her every move. As if Mama didn't have more aristocratic blood in her little finger than all of María Cristina's thin Austrian blood."

"I wouldn't care how thin her blood was if I could be sure she cares about the welfare of Cuba. I saw things on this journey, Felipe, that make me wonder."

"And where did you get such rebel talk, from your dashing pirate?"

"He is not a pirate." She hugged her shoulders, remembering the moments in his arms. "I'm as bad as you are, Felipe."

Felipe smiled and asked, "Did you see Caris when you were in Havana? Prettiest thing you ever saw. She makes other women look like clumsy oxen. How did you happen to be kidnapped right out of mama's house onto that filibuster ship? Why didn't Pablo sound the alarm? Surely, there was time. When they made you change into those awful clothes... All the same, I envy you your adventure."

"You wouldn't have liked it, I assure you. Those awful crabs, and scorpions. And Bagley." She thought of the moments in the Guttierez hacienda but couldn't bring herself to mention them again. She had heard Juan Diego's brief description while one of the soldiers made a sling for his arm as they entered the protection of the Maguire grounds. At the time she had tried to concentrate on Felipe's apology for the idiocy of the soldier, a recruit who had shot so wildly, or perhaps deliberately, to impress the absent General Weyler, and struck Antonia's "savior."

"It definitely wasn't the sentry, I promise you," Felipe said. "We don't run that bad an operation here."

When Antonia was asked to verify Diego's story of the Guttierez massacre she did so, but they understood the pain it caused and did not pursue it with her.

So long as she didn't relive it in her mind, or speak of it, she could pretend it hadn't happened. It was all part of a nightmare.

"I wish Father had been here. I wanted him to tell General Weyler how brave Captain Diego was. Papa shouldn't be out shooting people, haven't we had enough of that?"

"He isn't out shooting. He rode to meet a platoon of the general's soldiers. They're coming to escort us all into Havana for the wedding." Felipe punched the bed in his excitement. "Won't Caris make a gorgeous bride? She's so delicate, like a little flower."

Antonia rolled her eyes, said nothing. He knew perfectly well that Caris de Correña's so-called delicacy always annoyed his sister, who believed it was a performance to make others wait on her. Felipe watched Antonia, his mischievous expression fading. "Am I keeping you awake, Tana? I'm sorry, but you aren't ever home any more. Sometimes I think you've forgotten us. The Yankees have corrupted you, they say."

She stifled a yawn. "It's not true. Nobody cares more about Cuba—"

"Well, just so we haven't lost you..." He got up. "Caris is anxious to see you."

She raised up on her elbows, suddenly remembering the Guttierez hacienda. "Felipe, do you ever see María-Rosa any more?"

He was puzzled for a minute. "You mean our María-Rosa Guttierez? She has always been a friend. Mama is very fond of her."

"And you?"

He fumbled with the mosquito netting. "I feel terrible for her and Señora Guttierez, if what you and the *capitán* say is true. I mean, the massacre. But we hadn't really seen each other for years except in passing. They've been living with relatives across from Havana at Regla. Why?"

"Nothing, just memories."

Felipe began to fidget. "You know I'm sorry for the señora and María-Rosa. But ever since their fields were burned two years ago and then the old man—I mean Señor Guttierez—was refused by the Spanish banks, they've drifted away from all our old friends."

"*They* have drifted away?"

"That's how it is . . . I'll leave you to sleep, Tana." He kissed her cheek and left.

The Caribbean night was hushed. She knew they had put Juan Diego in a guest room on the far side of the main building, she had made it a point to find out. It was her suggestion that he be placed there since it was farther from her family's quarters and most unlikely that her mother would visit him. Which suited Antonia's own plans.

She awoke halfway through a stifling hot day when Gavi, the gypsy Zerlina's daughter, brought her sweet chocolate and rolls with marmalade from Sevilliano oranges, and asked what the señorita would like for her lunch.

Each one of Antonia's muscles seemed to ache separately, and her legs stung from the slap of brush, palm fronds, bare twigs and the razor-sharp touch of the crab claws. However, she was soon up, washed, dressed, combed and curried, as she put it, so she could show Juan Diego what kind of stamina and recuperative powers she had. She intended to be his *permanent* companion.

While the servant girl went off to report Antonia's menu to the hacienda cook, Antonia made her way, avoiding family and servants, to the captain's room on the stucco side of the compound. She knocked gently, picturing the wounded man as he lay on his rawhide bed of pain, pale but brave, of course, dreaming of her.

He was awake, his voice brisk as he told her to enter.

"Set it there," he went on, obviously assuming she was a servant with his morning coffee. He did not look like a "chocolate man."

She slipped in, closing the door carefully behind her. He was up and dressed in a pair of her father's casual trousers and a white shirt that looked odd on him... She was so accustomed to seeing him in black. It must have been painful to get on that shirt with his sore shoulder. He was really impossible, he might have started bleeding again.

She crossed the room as he eased on a short, close-fitting jacket that her father had long since outgrown. He grunted but managed to get it on over his bandaged shoulder.

"You *are* a fool." And as she realized the significance of all this, said, "You're leaving, sneaking away like a thief in the dead of night without a word to anyone?"

"But, my darling, you seem to have enough words for both of us. And as for the dead of night..." He nodded toward the sun pouring across the patio and garden beyond.

"You know what I mean."

He grimaced as he adjusted the collar of the jacket and leaned toward her, kissing the top of her head. "You know I am not welcome here. They aren't sure what your precious Butcher Weyler will say."

"Be *quiet*. Haven't you *any* sense. That's all they need to hear, this sort of talk about Butcher Weyler." She pronounced it in English for emphasis.

"Say that again."

She repeated the name "Weyler" and his lips caught hers, silencing her and sending a delicious excitement through her. He held her there as she separated them, or tried to. What would he do next? She wouldn't put anything beyond him. Actually, she was quite willing to be "ravished and plundered," as they said, right here in her father's own house. But unfortunately he showed no signs of carrying this to its natural conclusion.

She had to challenge him. "You see, you can't leave me."

"Sweetheart, we have a long, long road to run, jungles to hack our way through before we can hope for anything in our own future."

"No matter. Whatever your plans, I can help you... with my name and the family's reputation. If you insist on sailing your broken-down old ship, which any Spanish gunboat can outrun, I won't prevent you."

He sighed. His hands seemed to enjoy kneading her upper arms. She loved his touch.

"Antonia..."

"Sir, you may call me Tana."

He ignored her flippancy, but his lips brushed the bridge of her nose. "Antonia, that pathetic wreck is stronger than she looks. And we have hidden compartments no one has ever uncovered. I've been searched before, in port, and no one found contraband."

"You mean I worried about you for nothing?"

"They found what I wanted them to find. I deliberately keep the *Baracoa* looking like an old mud scow. This time, along with all those lovely things to please General Weyler, I transported three ... well, two and a half... respectable females to their equally respectable and important friends in Havana. It was a plan to impress the captain-general of Cuba and I am happy to say it worked."

"I wondered why you agreed to take us. It was so dangerous. For you and for us."

"There was to be no danger. I knew the cargo. It was deliberately chosen." He was being all too honest. She would rather keep a few illusions. "Then you never did trust me," she said. "After all we've been through—"

"On the contrary. You are in a position to do me in now."

"Which, of course, I would *never* do." Not if her life depended on it. It wasn't as if he had hurt her or her family. She knew nothing about "General Garcia" except that he was a rebel and operated in an area east of Havana's province. Until recently that province had been secure to the government forces.

"You did risk both our lives on that mad journey."

"I never intended that, as you know." He pulled her against him, pulling the muscles in his bandaged shoulder at the same time. Antonia saw him grit his teeth.

"Oh, God, are you hurt?"

"I guess I deserve it. I thought it would be simple. There was a safe trail beyond Paloma. But the new *trocha* line, and the gang of murderers around the Guttierez hacienda, I hadn't counted on them."

"But you did count on the crabs."

"Ah, well, that." Before she could react, he reminded her that he was a wounded hero. "I'm happy also to say your queen's soldiers seem to be amateurs. I lost a little flesh but nothing of consequence."

"You bled all over me."

"I bleed easily." Then he became serious. "Listen to me. Your mother has asked me not to see you again until I make my peace with the . . . with General Weyler. I told her I would ride with the soldiers to meet your father and the general. Your brother is going to present my case. I went with you to save you from your fiendish kidnappers, there should be no problems—"

"But us . . . you and me. We're engaged, aren't we?"

"I so considered myself, but with that unpredictable behavior of yours I have more to worry about than you do. If we are never man and wife, it will be your doing, not mine."

"Never—"

He cupped her face between his hard lean hands. "I know that you mean that, but never is a very long time. And I have met your brother and the señora. I honor them both, but I also know they are utterly sincere in what they believe. I think you are too . . . and I can't change my beliefs. My sister's blood cries to me for justice."

"Vengeance."

"You don't know, sweetheart. It has never happened to you. I pray God it never will. Do you understand what I am telling you?"

"Of course I do. I am not deaf. You are saying we must wait until the rebellion is over."

"Kiss me, then."

A part of her, the part that remained childish, self-centered and spoiled, wanted to deny him, but an adult core wanted otherwise. That and the determination to give him a farewell that would haunt and tantalize him afterward when he remembered that he might lose her. She twined her arms around his neck to avoid the bandaged wound just above his armpit. She opened her lips to his. They clung together, her body tight in the embrace of his thighs.

And her darling brother Felipe opened the door and walked in. He had the grace to look embarrassed, but whether at what he saw or at his awkwardness in interrupting them, Antonia couldn't guess.

In either case his presence and the precious moments he had cut short infuriated her.

"Are you quite satisfied, little brother? You always were a wretched spy. Run away to mother and tell her what you saw your big sister doing. Go on, *run...*"

"Tana, I didn't... it was an accident. I came to get Capitán Diego. Didn't he tell you?"

Diego nodded to him. "And I am ready." He kissed her once more, this time quickly. "Señor Maguire is right. I arranged to leave with him. He is obliging enough to speak to the captain-general about me."

Antonia watched as the two of them passed her, Diego's hand brushing hers, his fingers curling over hers for just an instant. Felipe looked at her, smiled his winning little-boy smile, and she put her arms around him.

"I will guard your *capitán* with my life," he promised.

Looking from her slight, delicate brother to Juan Diego's lean, battle-hardened figure, she had to smile and tried to keep that mood while she watched them cross the patio toward the stables. Minutes later she ran after them to watch a little troop of unsuspecting Loyalist soldiers ride out with one of their most resolute enemies in their midst.

It was then that the undercurrents of terror surfaced around her. Could he be safe with his enemies? Would she ever see him again? What would happen when his rebellion failed and all his *recon-centrados* gained nothing? They had already suffered so much. Would they ever be together?

She knew Juan Diego was not a man to abandon his people. Perhaps, she thought better for her if she could love him less for that. But of course she only loved him all the more for it.

CHAPTER
TWELVE

ANTONIA WAS not a woman to be depressed for long. Not that she loved Juan Diego less during his absence, but with all the wedding talk around her she was able to convince herself once more that she and Juan Diego would be married once the troubles were settled. She felt extremely sorry for the poor people she had seen herded around the Spanish blockhouse that night she and Diego crossed the *trocha* line, but she was sorriest of all for the Guttierez family, the widow and daughter left virtually without resources after the appalling death and destruction at the hacienda. During the nights that followed she often woke up in an icy sweat, seeing Señor Guttierez and his little dog cut to pieces by Juan's people.

When Patrick Maguire reached home with General Weyler, the captain-general said he would escort the entire family into Havana for the wedding. He and other *haciendados* were setting up a fund to support Señora Guttierez and María-Rosa. There would, though, be very little left to make a dowry for María-Rosa and the thought of marriage at a time when she was mourning her father had shocked the girl and her mother.

From this remark, repeated by General Weyler, Antonia suspected that María-Rosa also mourned the loss of Felipe Maguire, whom she genuinely loved. For Antonia the fate of the Guttierez family cast a shadow over Felipe's wedding. She just couldn't believe Caris de Correña was a good substitute for the warmly sincere María-Rosa. It was clear, however, that all the Maguire family did not share Antonia's dislike of the kittenish bride-to-be. Antonia's father made that plain when he called her into his study to discuss her role as Caris's chief bridesmaid.

Patrick Maguire was a compact, impressive man of middle height, whose good looks had proved of less importance than his native shrewdness and ambition. He had begun his climb to affluence by a brief filibustering career, running Confederate cotton to England and the Continent during the Civil War. He was not a seaman and still could scarcely tell bow from stern or foremast from orlop deck, but he knew how to get products cheap and where to sell them dear. His pleasant blue eyes were seductive. He used them now. "Mavourneen, you've behaved badly. You would never find little Caris acting so disgracefully. All this running about through jungles with a filibusterer, a pirate who may or may not eventually prove loyal to General Weyler. We can only hope none of your suitors hear about it. We've done our best to defuse gossip, but I'm afraid such stories have a way of coming to the surface at awkward times—"

"Like Felipe's wedding."

"Yes." He reached out and touched her shoulder. He was not a demonstrative man with his children. He loved his children but inside him some barrier kept him from saying so. He was deeply attached to his volatile sister Sybil and his marriage to Ysabel Guzman had been remarkably happy, but he *showed* little feeling to them either. Antonia had often been spanked by her various, long-suffering governesses, but Patrick Maguire had never raised a hand to her, and her mother, though loving, was of too indolent a temper to use such punishment.

"Tell me what you want, *padre mia*. I'll be good." But her grin made him suspicious.

"You couldn't be good no matter how hard you tried. You are a mischievous monkey. And that brings me to my point. During the wedding festivities little Caris de Correña will be her usual sweet self. The captain-general has been recalled to Spain by Prime Minister Cánovas. He will leave immediately after the wedding. If all goes well there may be some interest there on behalf of our family. I am trying to bid in the Guttierez properties to join ours. General Weyler may be received at court. He will put in a word."

She didn't like it. Any profits from Guttierez land would be blood money. But this was business and her father knew what he wanted. "I hope you aren't going to put Felipe in charge of the Guttierez plantations."

"As a matter of fact, that was in my mind."

"Oh, Father, it's so insensitive. At one time María-Rosa was in love with Felipe."

"This is business, my girl. Marriage settlements have nothing to do with love. Do you think your mother loved me when we were married? She had only seen me twice."

"And adored you, Father. She told me so."

"Well, we'll say no more. General Weyler was impressed by Diego's education, it seems he worked his way at sea to pay for it. His command of English is as good as my own, better than your brother's. The general thinks he may be useful to us before we've finished, but men like that are unsuitable to young ladies with your background."

She was prepared to argue that but he got up, rang his small pewter bell for a servant and waved Antonia out. She knew her few minutes with him had ended. His blue eyes were always a little intimidating and she thought it wise to wait until he was less preoccupied with business.

The family left for Havana the next day. Along with oxcarts and carriages a troop of General Weyler's horsemen and the general himself, the groom's half of the wedding party arrived in the great Caribbean city with none of the problems Antonia had encountered on their journey. The wild fauna of the jungle scattered at the approach of this army, and even the weather held off until they were at home in the Palacio Guzman.

Felipe was excited over the possibility of becoming his own master. Much to his sister's annoyance, he couldn't talk of anything else, especially when he saw how it impressed his bride-to-be. On the other hand, there were moments when Antonia was prepared to push her brother anywhere, even onto the bloodstained Guttierez land if it would get Caris de Correña out of the Palacio Guzman.

Hardly two minutes after Caris was escorted into the cool, leafy *palacio* garden by her uncle she managed to antagonize Antonia. She arrived clinging to the general's arm, her little fingers fastened into his uniform sleeve, her green eyes gazing up at him soulfully.

"Dearest uncle," she said to the Maguires as much as to him, "how can I give him up, even to go to my handsome Felipe?"

All smiled graciously. Felipe rose to the occasion. "You make me jealous of the great señor capitán-general. I will have much to live up to."

"Not at all, my boy. You have good blood." The Señora Maguire set her strong jaw along with her smile, and the general added, sensing undercurrents, "the very best blood."

Señora Maguire then gave him her plump, small hand and he bowed over it with a Latin grace superimposed over his stiff German manner. Shortly afterward Patrick Maguire drew the general into his study to discuss the acquiring of the Guttierez properties for the bride and groom.

Caris de Correña suggested with her tight little smile, "Now, if the dear Señora will be so good as to show me around my future domain."

This shook Antonia. She had always assumed that her brother, as the only male heir to the Maguire-Guzman name, would inherit all the properties except Antonia's own dowry, but this merely indicated that Felipe would have the final word in their operations. Of course, all the family would live here as always. The Palacio Guzman would remain Antonia's home in Cuba, wherever else she might live. Clearly, Caris de Correña saw it as her exclusive domain. She was petite, golden-haired, with a body so slight that she built up her tiny breasts with bits of cotton sewn in cloth and her hips with old-fashioned semicircular pads like those used to support bustles of an earlier day. She seemed especially fragile to most Latin males, who found her irresistible.

She went about the garden now, and then along the portico

escorted by an enraptured Felipe and, in their wake, Señora Maguire, leaning on her daughter's arm.

"Felipe, *mi amor*, I do not like this too sweet jasmine. It will
be torn down, I think. And a larger marble fountain. Yes. With a
long marble bench. They are very popular on the Continent now.
And, Felipe, the old furniture must go. I can never be happy with
articles that saw the conquistadores, those tiresome noisy creatures..."

Felipe gave his mother a nervous, sidelong glance. "Later, *car-
isita*, but now, it is as *madre* wishes. She likes the careless look of
the garden and the old furnishings. They are home to her."

Caris was quick to pick it up. "That's understood, dear señora,
do not think we wish to hurry. I only speak of a time far off."

"Very far off," Antonia put it.

"Come, Tanita," the señora ordered. "It has been a long day. If
our dear little Caris will forgive me, I think I must retire. Perhaps
a little broth and warm wine later."

Before they were out of hearing Caris had cuddled up to Felipe,
her silvery voice ringing out. "My sweet Felipe, there is so much
we can do. We Spaniards must be prepared to show the Cubans
how life is lived in the great world. They're so out of fashion here.
Even in your beloved Havana. But between us, we will set the
fashion."

Felipe mumbled something, which Caris answered with what
Antonia thought of as a titter. "Oh... Tana... well, we must not
be too concerned with that. Do you know, at poor Tana's age we
should consider a convent. What else is possible?"

Antonia wanted to kill her. Her mother's heavy jaw became a
little heavier. She whispered, "Come along, Tanita, we will not
pay attention to her. She is of the New Spain. Even her uncle"—
her voice roughened—"do you know what the German is called in
some quarters? The Butcher. One of the servants, I forget who,
told me he has driven two hundred thousand Cubans to their death.
Shameful... but perhaps it's not true. Your father would not let
my Felipe marry into such a family if it were..."

Much as Antonia loved her father, she suspected he certainly
would marry into Weyler's family if it served his business purposes.
Of course she didn't say so now.

Antonia waited while her mother was bathed by half a dozen girls, all fluttering around to make her comfortable. It was an old familiar routine, one that marked Ysabel Guzman's entire life, but it still seemed foreign to her daughter, who felt that such buzzing like so many bees would drive her crazy. Eventually, her warm broth and wine were brought, and she slept, with visions of Juan Diego dancing in her head.

Next day the wedding plans were put into action. Caris insisted that she must have a fashionable wedding like those in New York and Paris; so there were six bridesmaids outfitted in styles to complement the bride. Unfortunately the bride's pale skin looked best in oyster-white and she decided all her attendants must also wear oyster-white. It was a color, or lack of it, that clashed with Antonia's own olive flesh tones. The high-waisted Empire style chosen by Caris likewise disguised the most flattering points of Antonia's figure, her high, well-curved breasts, small waist and rounded hips.

"I look all of a size, and it's all dreadful," she told her mother.

"My little one, does it not occur to you that this child wishes to have all eyes on herself for once? I have heard it said all your life that you were the most beautiful infant in Havana. This thin little creature comes from Spain and hears nothing but the beauty of Don Felipe's sister. She wishes to make you less and herself more."

Antonia decided she had one special consolation: Whatever her faults of face, figure or disposition, Juan Diego loved her. He wouldn't lie about that. He'd better not.

But all the self-assurance went out the window on the morning of the wedding when she saw herself in the long mirrors, looking sallow and dressed like a whitewashed bundle, her hair piled high in a rigid pompadour made still higher by her white lace mantilla. She felt ridiculous and more and more self-conscious as they neared the cathedral, a huge forbidding palace of religion that looked what it was, a relic of a medieval day. Its walls were as thick as those of Havana's Morro Castle, that fortress known to every mariner on the Spanish Main. It was not a church Antonia would have favored for a wedding. Certainly there was nothing romantic about it. But it did exude power, the eternal power of the Spanish Catholic tradition.

The wedding party was escorted through a crowd that had gathered about the cathedral steps. The Maguires were met at the great doors by another early arrival, the United States consul, Fitzhugh Lee, a stout jovial man, nephew of the late Confederate Commander Robert E. Lee. Actually the Spanish governing powers believed he was responsible for a great deal of his country's pro-rebel newspaper attacks on the rulers of Cuba. But Antonia noted that her father and most Loyalists welcomed him politely; too many sugar interests were involved in the relationship between the two countries for either party to shun the other.

General Fitzhugh Lee greeted Patrick Maguire with his usual bluff effusiveness, and congratulating the young bridegroom on his luck in winning "that pretty child." The American diplomat had just bowed over Señora Maguire's hand, his bristly white beard tickling her knuckles, when the Spanish ruler of Cuba, Captain-General Weyler, arrived on horseback, guiding his mount through the crowd that had suddenly grown hostile. He dismounted, gave over the reins of his mount and greeted the Maguires.

Antonia's nerves tingled uneasily. She couldn't fail to hear the muttering, the hissing and booing that spread among those varied faces, some black Africans, some as light as Caris de Correña, but most of them square, attractive faces, predominantly men, whose black eyes smoldered with hatred of "the Butcher," Valeriano Weyler y Nicolau.

The captain-general ignored them, shook hands with the American consul while behind him the tides of hatred collected. He saved his special greeting for Felipe.

"I bring Her Gracious Majesty's own congratulations to you, young man. They were telegraphed to me this very morning. She rejoices in the joining of both our loyal houses."

Antonia could see that Felipe was nervous. Watching him as a proud sister, she felt that he had never looked better, a graceful caballero. Weyler's niece would be the envy of every Cuban female.

While the ladies waited in the broiling Cuban sun Weyler, the American consul and Patrick Maguire exchanged opinions on the progress of the latest diplomatic notes between the queen regent and President McKinley about United States intervention in the Spanish province of Cuba. The American consul reminded Weyler,

"Unfortunately, there is always the chance that troublemakers on both sides will force the break. I happen to know there is a campaign on to demand complete independence from the mother country. It looks like that's next on their agenda."

Weyler dismissed such arguments. "An old story. The mistake is to yield to anything in the first instance. Her Majesty will discover that shortly from me when I return."

Patrick Maguire nodded but Antonia wondered if he altogether agreed. She wanted to interrupt, to tell these men what she and Juan Diego had seen at the *trocha* line, those huddled, starving, suffering women, children and old men. But even her education in the United States had not shaken her from her Spanish upbringing.

Consul Lee, however, spoke for her. "Excuse me, Excellency, but you might be doing Her Majesty, and your government, a real disservice. This bloody business has gone beyond the question of punishment. You'll be fortunate to come out of it by Cuban self-government under the Empire."

Weyler's features stiffened. Then: "What are we thinking of? The bridegroom must be impatient. We'll exchange sour war talk for the sweet vows of love." A real phrase-maker, the Butcher, thought Antonia.

The little group moved toward the massive doors that opened for the captain general. Antonia glanced down before entering the cathedral—and saw Juan Diego making his way through the crowd to the steps. His injured arm still appeared to be slightly stiff. He did not use it as freely when he strode along. Of course he refused to wear a sling.

He was with a newspaperman she had thought she knew so well—Quincy Kemp. Quincy's short stocky figure had some difficulty keeping up with him. They were either wedding guests or about to cover the ceremony for Quincy's New York newspaper column. Antonia stopped, blocking everyone's way, and waved to them. Juan Diego looked up, saluted her with his free arm. Quincy waved as well.

At the same minute there was a stir in the crowd that now packed the plaza. Someone shouted. A whirring noise followed. Then screams a shade before the explosion.

"An infernal machine," Weyler shouted, pushing his little group inside the cathedral's great walls.

The bomb went off halfway up the steps, but the smoke engulfed the wedding party and floated into the cathedral around them. Felipe doubled over with racking coughs while the church full of wedding guests eventually gave in to the same spurt of coughing.

Antonia kept looking toward the massive cathedral doors. Where was Juan Diego? Had he been hurt? He and Quincy Kemp were awfully close when that bomb went off. She tried to reassure herself. Diego had nine lives, he had already lost one when Felipe's trigger-fingered sergeant shot him, and it had hardly slowed him down.

The family was all concerned with Felipe, but the great walls of the cathedral echoed to running, panicky footsteps. Other wedding guests either crowded toward the distant altar or tried to leave by the main doors. Antonia, anxious to find out about Juan Diego, pushed toward the doors.

She was relieved to catch sight of him elbowing his way toward her. When they met and he took her in his arms, they were both nearly knocked over by running, panic-stricken or just curious wedding guests, but neither of them cared about such jostling.

"*Madre de Dios*, I was afraid for you," he said as he looked her over.

"*You* might have been hit. Oh, my darling..." There were moist spots—blood?—on his homespun jacket and sleeves, but he seemed unhurt. She clung to him and when he kissed her, she responded with all her heart.

A heavy hand closed around Antonia's shoulder. She raised her eyes over Diego's shoulder and saw her father.

"Antonia, you are making a display of yourself. Your family is leaving now. *Come.*"

Diego managed to sound both calm and authoritative, nor did he release her. "Señor Maguire, at some date soon I will ask your permission to pay court to the señorita. I wish to marry her, with your permission, of course."

Maguire ignored this. "Come, Antonia, your mother and the captain-general are waiting."

Outside in the plaza the shouts and screams had dissolved into a general pandemonium. Quincy Kemp now squeezed his way in through the big doors and shouted to Diego that "they've caught the bomb throwers. Two *reconcentrados*. Escaped from a camp over near Oriente. Five casualties. Two dead. Three wounded. A lot of blood out there on the steps."

"Well, thank God they were captured," Maguire said, and turned to General Weyler, who had brought his niece out of hiding along with five shaken bridesmaids. Caris de Correña still presented a pretty if frightened picture.

As for Antonia, now that it was all over the full realization of their danger came to her. She knew it wasn't Juan Diego or Quincy Kemp but her own family and General Weyler who had been the special targets of that bomb.

Weyler was now saying to her father, "My men are well trained. These people will see how quickly Spain acts toward anarchists They'll receive their reward by sunset." He glanced around, feeling that the subject was unsuitable to the surroundings, and cleared his throat. "We must get the ladies out. The Señor Maguire suggests the wedding be moved to the Palacio Guzman, where the ladies may have more seclusion to recover in."

Antonia began to object, but Juan Diego nodded to her and she was hustled away by her family through the nave and past the still shaken wedding guests. No one hinted that there might be other bombs waiting for General Weyler and his guests in any of the narrow, crowded streets between the cathedral and the Palacio Guzman.

Antonia looked back again, unable to make out Juan Diego among the hundreds who had crowded into the cathedral to escape the carnage in the plaza. But the whispers were beginning among the wedding guests . . . nervous tales of bad luck, of frightening blood omens for this marriage.

CHAPTER
THIRTEEN

"**B**UT UNCLE is sailing for Spain in two days," Caris was complaining. "I won't be married without my own family. I won't."

Felipe added his indignant plea. "We've already postponed it for twenty-four hours. We shouldn't let these assassins make cowards of us. We're Spaniards, not Cuban peons. We must show them..."

While the men argued Antonia wondered uncomfortably about their reasoning. Felipe had never seen the mother country, yet he called himself a Spaniard. Worse, he denied four centuries of Cuban blood. It had been little more than a day since the anarchist bomb. There had been injuries to half a dozen innocent people who were very probably sympathetic to the side of the assassins who had thrown the bomb.

Antonia was not surprised to hear that the two criminals had been hanged at Morro Castle four hours after their capture, but she was concerned when Zerlina, the cook, confided some servants' gossip to her.

"Señorita, they whisper it in the markets. Even the orange seller this morning in the street told me... those two who were hanged yesterday afternoon, they have friends and they have sworn vendetta against the Butcher and his family... señorita, you are part of his family."

When Antonia tried to get this across to Felipe they got into an argument.

"I am not a coward. No man with the blood of the Guzman-Pontalvos was ever a coward. You think I'm going to humiliate Caris now by refusing to marry her?"

"Stop blustering. How do we know those two assassins don't have other friends? There was no trial."

"You couldn't understand, you're a woman. My honor is involved—"

Honor. The final word to a Spaniard, as Antonia knew only too well. Oh yes, Felipe was now a man. "Honor isn't going to do you much good, brother, if you are dead."

Before he could answer, their father arrived in the patio and told Antonia quietly, "We are all in danger, Mavourneen. But we have lived through these times before, during all those years you were safe in Virginia... You must agree that we know the situation better than you."

"Yes, I realize that. But maybe, Father, just because I have been away, I can see it more clearly. Can't you leave Havana at least until the rebellion is settled? Mother always wanted to return to Spain to visit her school friends. Including the queen regent," she added as an inducement that might move him.

"Later, I hope, but the wedding will have to take place today. Here at home. Your mother is supervising the arrangements for an altar, the prie-dieu in the garden, she says, over in that corner."

"Caris won't like it. She hates jasmine." A funny argument, she knew.

Her father pinched her cheek. "If I know your mother, there will be so many roses she won't know the jasmine exists."

Felipe's eyes brightened. His father smiled. "Hurry and make yourself presentable. And you, Tana. The bridesmaid gown." Antonia made a face but was touched as always by her brother's enthusiasm.

He went off at a run to make himself irresistible to his bride and Antonia was starting for her room when her father joined her, putting an arm around her.

"I think, my dear, it is time you returned to your Aunt Sybil. At least until this rebellion is settled. As long as you remain in Havana you may be a target for, well, insults. You are much too pretty, and the fact that you are an heiress is well known."

She would be glad to return to the States, so long as Juan Diego knew about it . . . he had been less inhibited in his attentions there.

"No one in Havana has exactly been assaulting me for my inheritance."

"What about Diego?"

"Oh, Father, even General Weyler believes he's pretty much come over to our side."

"General Weyler, if I may remind you, hasn't seen his daughter in the fellow's arms. Nor his niece, when it comes to that."

She decided now was not the time to lay down her ultimatum. Her father might even put in a bad word about Juan Diego to the general, so she smiled at her father and hurried to her bedroom to call her maid Muriella and dress for the wedding. As soon as she could excuse herself after the ceremony, she would find Diego and tell him about going back to the States. Since he was with Quincy Kemp he was bound to be staying at the popular old Inglaterra Hotel in a *paseo* within walking distance of the docks, where all the newspaper correspondents had their headquarters. The hotel was not far from the censor's office. No stories could be telegraphed to the United States without undergoing the rigid examination of the Spanish censors.

Meanwhile, though, there was no escaping the detestable oyster-white gown. When Muriella, slumbrous and slow-moving, began to pile her hair up, Antonia told her just to knot it on her neck.

"And the other young señoritas? They do not come to the wedding?"

"It all happened so fast we had no time to notify them."

Antonia did not think it wise to admit that the parents of the five other bridesmaids were too terrified to join the party again.

She wished she could share her own fears with Juan Diego. There was no one in the household she could talk to about her real feelings. True, Aunt Sybil was rather shallow but Tana could hold long chatty conversations with her. She looked forward to that.

Against his preference, but for security's sake, the bride's uncle arrived by small, alleylike *calles* on an ordinary mount that had none of the parade ground splendor popularly associated with a general's horse. His niece and her duenna, the stout, nervous wife of a Weyler aide, had already been escorted from the governor's palace during the busy morning hours before the siesta with no effort made to display any trappings of a wedding.

Between Antonia's mother and the duenna the bride was once more made ready. Her twenty-yard lace mantilla-and-train had been mended, her heavy white satin gown, doubly heavy in the Havana heat, had been cleaned and pressed. Even Antonia admitted to herself that Caris de Correña had never looked better.

The much shrunken bridal party arrived in the garden to the melancholy strum of a guitar played by the nephew of Pablo, the caretaker. Antonia found it more romantic than the solemn cathedral music, but it was uncomfortable to think about why all these changes had been made. She kept looking over her shoulder, wondering if any of the rebel terrorists would dare climb over the high garden walls to get at them, or to throw one of those "infernal machines." Nor was she reassured by the knowledge that almost everyone present in the garden wedding party shared her apprehensions. Standing a little behind the bride, with her own parents and the general close by, Antonia noticed how often General Weyler's narrowed gaze slipped away from the nervous priest and focused on the garden walls.

She knew her father was also uneasy when everyone else was kissing the bride or congratulating the groom and Patrick Maguire asked Pablo in a low voice, "The soldiers—are they still in place outside?"

"No one notices them, señor. They look like peddlers. One is a pomegranate seller, another a beggar. And, señor, the family is well loved in Havana, it is only the captain-general who—"

"Quiet. No more. He is our guest."

General Weyler glanced their way, and Antonia suspected he

had overheard, but he only leaned over, kissed his niece on the forehead and bowed over Señora Maguire's hand.

The wedding party returned to the less perfumed atmosphere of the long parlor, a salon whose heavy overhead beams darkened the atmosphere, though the wooden shutters permitted a certain amount of cooling air to pass through. The few articles of furniture, equally heavy, always made Antonia think she had been transported back to the sixteenth century. The big canopied chair which the general accepted as his due, the long chest which held an entire household's goods, the monstrous sideboard that must have been a king's desk, the Portuguese-tiled floor, all represented a life that seemed alien and exotic to Antonia.

In spite of the danger around them, how happy her family all were now . . . her mother, with plump cheeks pinker than usual, a drop too much sherry, perhaps; her father looking so proud and happy; Felipe beside himself with his bride.

I'm lucky, Antonia thought. No wonder Juan Diego is so bitter. He lost all of this. Well, I will bring him my family. He just must be patient, that's all. They will come to love him as I do. They have to . . .

Meanwhile, Caris de Correña Maguire and Felipe were discussing their very modern honeymoon, which they intended to enjoy at the Guzman hacienda.

"Completely surrounded by a platoon of General Weyler's picked troops," Patrick Maguire put in.

The general agreed. "In fact, the wedding party will be met at the crossroads south of the city. They are safe as long as they are in sight of Havana and its environs. But once the road moves into mesquite and jungle, we take no chances. Not even with the cane fields."

Antonia was somewhat reassured by that, though she privately felt that no place on the island was safe from isolated acts of terror. She had become increasingly nervous as time passed while the wedding party gorged on sweet Spanish and North African bonbons, sticky little cakes, nuts, and the excellent homeland wines. Several times Antonia opened the small gold watch she wore on a chain around her neck.

Would Juan be at the Hotel Inglaterra, or had he maybe gone

off on some secret mission connected with the rebel cause? If
Quincy Kemp was there he could take a message for Diego. Antonia
was sure he knew about her affair with Diego. The important thing
was to find an excuse for her unexpected departure from the Palacio
Guzman. She decided to plead an unoriginal headache from too
much wine, the mixture of champagne toasts and the sipping sherry,
which would amuse everyone and they would understand when
she demanded to be left alone and locked her door. But she must
be quick. As usual, she turned for help to her gypsy friend, Zerlina.

The cook was willing to help her. "But you take care, señorita.
No foolishness. You go very fast and come back quick. And not in
those bride clothes."

No one was more conscious of the danger than Antonia. She
made her excuses to the wedding party and was annoyed by Felipe's
joking remark: "You should not drink, Tana. You don't have the
head for it."

Much you know, she thought. She also caught the patronizing
smiles exchanged by her father and General Weyler, but none of
this caused as much difficulty as her mother's insistence on trying
to help her.

"A cold cloth on the brow, that should make you feel better,
Tanita *mia*. I'll prepare one for you."

Antonia hugged and kissed her, assured her she must not leave
her guests, and finally persuaded the good señora that she would
be quite comfortable "with an hour of quiet."

Once free of her mother, she called the waiting Zerlina and
together they eased her out of the hooks, eyes and buttons of her
boned bridesmaid gown and into an old blue dress she wore when
bargaining with the street peddlers and bazaar vendors.

"I'm becoming quite an expert at these quick changes," she said
to Zerlina.

"Like my brother, Francisco. He was quick as a wink. He could
fool the police in half of Andalusia. Go, quickly. I called my friend
Pedrito. He will take you in his cart."

Pedrito looked like a cutthroat but he proved to be friendly and
best of all he asked no questions. He helped her into the cart whose
floor was covered with straw and set off with his obliging mule.

It was just after the siesta hours when Antonia made her bumpy
ride across Havana. The city was coming to life again, a noisy

combination of perfumed beauty and the ugliness of decay and poverty. They approached the long waterfront and the ever-exciting Havana Bay and Channel. They hadn't quite reached the elaborate Pension-Hotel Inglaterra when Antonia saw Quincy Kemp seated at a sidewalk cafe near the busy turn into the *malecón,* which followed the line of the waterfront. He was enjoying what appeared to be a gigantic stein of beer.

Surprisingly, in spite of cavalry horses, riders, walkers, sailors of every nationality, peddlers and dozens of international correspondents, Quincy Kemp recognized Antonia. Thank God he had enough sense not to call her by name, but he set down his stein and came out on the street to the side of the cart.

"Señor Diego?" she asked.

Kemp made a big display of unrequited love, clutching his bosom just north of his considerable stomach. "You wound me, ma'am. You have no words for me, only for another?"

She leaned over the warped side of the cart. "I have a message for our friend, and stop the clowning."

The columnist sighed. "Then my case is hopeless?"

"I am being sent back to my Aunt Sybil."

"Ah. That clever Sybil." When she frowned, he reached up and touched her hand. "Be careful of that dear Aunt Sybil."

"But I've seen you at her evening parties—"

"Quite true. The kaiser's boys are meddling around the Caribbean at this very minute and I'll dine with them too if I think they can tell me anything I want to know, but that doesn't mean the kaiser and I are boon companions."

She studied his seemingly innocent, pudgy face, and decided to be as frank as he was insinuating. "Mr. Kemp, my aunt thinks you're with the United States naval intelligence. Is that true?"

His vivid blue eyes opened wider. "Charming woman, your Aunt Sybil. And what an imagination! Be sure to give her my best regards."

Had she touched a nerve? He seemed to confirm her aunt's suspicions by his evasion. So far, in the bloodletting between Spain and her Cuban colony, the biggest contribution of the United States seemed to have been an effort to keep the kettle boiling. Obviously, powerful sugar interests in the States would like to see Cuba free of Spain. Was the sharpest intelligence in the States, the U.S.

Navy, involved on the side of the rebels? Or merely using them
to stir up further trouble? Or both? Did Juan know what his friend
was up to...? Still, she couldn't help liking Quincy Kemp. She
didn't trust him, but then she didn't entirely trust Aunt Sybil; yet
she liked both of them. Maybe she was drawn to devious people.
At least, Juan had been honest—well, almost—with her about his
own politics.

"Señor Kemp, please tell your friend I must return to Virginia.
Promise me that."

He seemed irritated by her apparent doubts about him. "My
dear lady, whatever you and your precious aunt may think of me,
I have been known to tell the truth on occasion."

"I'm sure of it...and thank you." She was ready to give Pedrito
the word to turn and head back toward the Palacio Guzman when
she saw Juan walking up from the waterfront, apparently to meet
Quincy Kemp at the sidewalk cafe. Even while Kemp and Antonia
talked, the cafe had been filling with men, mostly Cuban businessmen or foreign reporters, ready for their afternoon drink and
good conversation. For a minute Diego didn't recognize the girl
in the cart, then grinned, spoke to Quincy Kemp, careful not to
stare at Antonia.

"Buying from natives, Quincy?"

Fitting into her role, Antonia called out, "Best oranges, señor.
Expensive, but the best. Bananas all gone. More soon."

He came close to the cart, pretended to look inside. His voice
was low as he told her. "You are in some danger here, sweetheart.
These people are bitter about the hangings."

"They were assassins."

"In a democracy even assassins have trials. I want you to go back
home now and stay there. I'd better ride with you."

Quincy Kemp said, "He's right, believe him."

Antonia was, of course, delighted to have Diego's company and
gave in quickly, though her pride demanded some show. "They
may hate the Butcher, but we Maguires haven't hurt anyone. We
have been very charitable, as a matter of fact."

Diego ignored that for the moment, climbed in beside her and
sank down on the straw, pulling her onto his lap.

Quincy Kemp waved him on, saying in English, "Take the byways and alleys."

The mule began a turn, neatly avoiding the wild traffic around him, and started back up toward the old colonial plazas.

Antonia was about to explain why she had risked this visit in broad daylight when Juan stopped her with his mouth. A delightful interruption, but after a few minutes she again tried to explain: "I'm being sent back to my Aunt Sybil."

"I'm glad. Every minute you stay in Cuba I'm worried about you."

"Me, but what about my family?"

"They know the danger..."

She thought of the honeymoon. Of Felipe and his bride at the hacienda. She told him so, adding, "Thank God there will be soldiers guarding them."

His fingers traced her face, he seemed to be memorizing the look of her. "And on the journey? They will be protected then?"

"The minute they leave Havana and enter the countryside. We don't dare to have a procession through the city, it will call attention to the family."

"True. But you will remain at the *palacio* until your steamer sails for Key West. Promise me that."

"Only if you promise I will see you in Virginia."

"Within a month. I am walking a thin line until the new governor arrives to take Weyler's place. He should be more moderate. If he is, I'm willing to carry any message to the New York junta. Otherwise it means a trip to Spain."

So far away... anything could happen before she saw him again.

She tried to be light about it. "Juanito, no. All those Spanish beauties..."

He liked that, and she promptly leaned over and kissed him. But he was looking very somber. "Sweetheart, what about the temptations for you in the States?"

She only smiled. She was smart enough to keep her mouth shut when she was ahead.

CHAPTER
FOURTEEN

ANTONIA SPENT most of the night reliving those final moments with Juan Diego. She knew that any minute her mother would try to enter her bedroom only to find her missing. But somehow this made her good-byes with Diego more precious.

They held each other as if it were the last good-bye. She told him, "And we'll have all the days in the future. In Virginia and Washington and—"

"But that may be weeks away. Well, you won't be leaving for a few days. I'll see if we can't still meet, officially, some way. Maybe at Weyler's sailing. *That* should be a happy moment for all concerned."

"Please, no politics."

Zerlina appeared then at the gate of the kitchen garden. "Señorita, we must hurry."

Juan Diego lifted her out of the cart and kept her in his arms, not wanting to let her go. "Be careful."

"I will." She loved his anxiety.

"Don't leave this place."

"Then how can I meet you by accident at the general's sailing?"

"I'll visit you here. With a message for—your Aunt Sybil."

They kissed again and she hurried in through the gate. When she looked back Juan was still standing there by the cart, watching her. She kissed her fingertips and waved them to him.

She had barely undressed when Señora Maguire came to see whether she would join what remained of the wedding party. "The gentlemen must find it very dull without you, Tanita. The bride and groom have gone across the patio to Felipe's apartment. You understand."

"Perfectly, mama. I'm coming. I wanted to take off that awful white satin thing."

After her time with Juan Diego she knew the evening would be an anticlimax but she felt her parents' loss when she returned to the long parlor. She herself had been in the States so long they probably would not miss her as they already missed Felipe, who had been with them during these recent tumultuous years. After the honeymoon, Felipe and Caris would share the same large household with the Maguires, but Antonia knew nothing would ever be quite the same again, with two mistresses of the house. Remembering this, and sensitive to the well-concealed feelings of her parents, Antonia tried to show them all her love and devotion at this time when she could help to soften their loss.

It was a beautiful evening, with a rare perfumed breeze, and it ended with a fine display. The caretaker's guitarist-nephew was called to the garden and the Maguires with General Weyler and Caris' duenna, Señora Lopez-Cordera, all joined in Andalusian melodies. General Weyler seemed in excellent spirits, though he was the only member of the group who did not touch the wines the others enjoyed. In such a setting it was difficult to see him as "the Butcher." But settings, Antonia knew, could also be camouflage.

Only one presence was missing to make it a beautiful night, but she told herself that Juan Diego would be a member of her family by this time next year, perhaps sooner if the rebellion could be settled in a short time. She went to bed a trifle tipsy but warm with thoughts of the future.

In the morning Antonia discovered that her father and General Weyler had arranged for the honeymoon party to leave at the moment the general was taking ship for Spain. "To confuse any troublemakers," Patrick explained to his wife and daughter. "It means we may safely accompany Felipe and Caris to the crossroads, where the troops will take up their posts for the rest of the journey."

Patrick Maguire himself looked over the area outside the Palacio Guzman with Pablo the caretaker. Everything seemed normal. The forbidding windows with their iron bars were as formidable as they had been three hundred years ago. The alleys and muddy byways were heavily shaded by lime trees on both sides of the building, and around the minuscule plaza below the heavy formal entrance no one used, a cheerful hedge of red hibiscus bushes bloomed, interrupted once near the street by palm trees too high to cast any useful shade.

The only people abroad that hot morning seemed to be the street peddlers in loose blouses and palm leaf hats. But they were always around. Antonia, who returned from early mass with her mother and Caris, thought there were more peddlers than usual but she was assured by the señora's calm voice.

"It is always this way at this hour. They sell more fruit in the morning heat."

Caris was looking very much the new and prosperous matron in her black mantilla, which set off her golden hair so well. She bowed to everyone they passed in the hired carriage that had been chosen because the Guzman y Pontalvo crest was not emblazoned on its doors.

"Your trouble, Tana, is that you are not a true daughter of Spain. You have been corrupted by the conspiracy of the United States with—"

"Must you be so stupid?" Antonia snapped, too nervous for good manners. "You've never even been in the States."

The señora tried to make peace. "Children, these are dangerous times. We must not quarrel when the whole world is against us. I hope both of you did as I asked and offered a candle to peace for our unhappy Cuba."

Caris assured her mother-in-law virtuously. "Oh, yes, dear *mamacita*. Peace *and* victory for Her Majesty. Felipe says we may go to Spain this fall. It is months since I saw Madrid and he says we will be presented to Her Majesty. Uncle always promises but with him it is forever business. He wants to prove to the Cortes and all the others in government that his methods of dealing with Cuba are correct. And of course they are."

Antonia, who remembered Juan Diego's remarks on the subject, was further drawn to his side by her dislike of her new sister-in-law. As they passed the brightly painted houses of the district she saw two soldiers striding along in their light uniforms of seersucker, their dark eyes shadowed by their cockaded hats, and she wondered if they really were superior to the rebels who were not Spaniards but Cubans. Yes, the new Krag-Jorgensen carbines slung over their shoulders were superior to the old U.S. Springfields furnished the rebels by Juan Diego, Felix Leidner and the other filibusterers, they made these soldiers seem more skilled...

In the wake of the soldiers came a banana seller carrying over one shoulder the huge, long, brown fruits on their stem. The two soldiers had gone but two others, taller and younger, sauntered out of a *calle* and walked behind the carriage and horses of the Maguire women. It was reassuring to know they were nearby in case of trouble.

When the women reached home they found two water peddlers looking too young, too straight-backed to be what they seemed, and Antonia had little doubt they carried pistols in the water containers they wore on yokes. Still, she felt better inside the garden.

Felipe rushed to meet his bride, and the señora stood by the vases of wedding roses a few minutes, breathing deeply, echoing Antonia's relief. Both women knew how rare a large interior garden like this was in Havana, where most of the ancient buildings were erected with an eye to defense, not comfort. But now, with danger everywhere outside the *palacio*, the garden walls became doubly welcome. Two oxcarts had gone ahead on the way to the hacienda, almost entirely filled with the bride's belongings, including a trousseau wardrobe that would certainly astonish the few peasant field workers who were the hacienda's neighbors. She had also chosen all the new household furnishings, with which Caris intended to surround herself at the hacienda.

The family was ready before noon, the two married women in their black lace mantillas and shawls, Antonia more comfortable in grass-green lawn, her hair worn free like a peasant, barely covered by an old green shawl. They rode in the worn, hired carriage with Patrick and Felipe seated opposite them. Two horsemen accompanied them looking like caballeros fresh from a Seville *feria* in the mother country. Felipe confided to her that they were excellent shots, but she wished they didn't look quite so obvious. Luckily there were other carriages abroad, most of them headed toward the open country or the many coves on the long Caribbean shoreline.

As the family moved away from the *palacio*, Antonia, with her thoughts on Juan Diego, envied Felipe his ability to show his love for his bride. He kept leaning forward to take her hand, and Caris reminded him as she released her fingers. "Please, it's so warm, lover. Wait until the shade, no?"

Everyone laughed to relieve the awkwardness of the something less than romantic reaction, but Antonia sensed that her father's thoughts were elsewhere, concentrated on every face he saw as the carriage rumbled through unpaved byways of the city.

Presently, the pastel-painted houses began to scatter, and the bright, tropic foliage was smothered by the beginnings of an abortive effort at growing tobacco plants by local entrepreneurs. These were half-grown but straggly, the soil bad and many leaves rotting.

"Those crossroads we've chosen for the meeting," Patrick Maguire pointed out suddenly about a mile ahead of them. Antonia saw that the road wound past the tobacco plants and onward beside a cane field. Another road crossed it, headed toward the westerly coast and the coves between the piercing blue waters of the Caribbean.

At the beginning of the coastal road on the near horizon Antonia made out a pleasant grove of trees, brush and high banana leaves waving in a vagrant breeze. That must be the setting for the *merienda* they'd planned earlier, a perfect picnic spot.

They rode on while Antonia shook her head over the wasted tobacco field. "I've heard Uncle Bernard say tobacco makes the soil poor after a time. You can't keep growing tobacco in the same soil as they appear to have done there."

Her father shrugged. His thoughts were still elsewhere. "Very likely, though, there seem to be field hands out there now, probably pinching off tobacco worms. Well, we ought to see the troops coming along soon. Beyond the cane fields and that weatherbreak of palms and bananas."

By the time they reached the grove and meeting place it was past noon. The workers in the dying tobacco field had stopped and were gathering up bundles of lunch and leather bottles of liquor. The two caballeros dismounted, and while the ladies were being helped down from the carriage they laid out an old white linen cloth on ground that they first covered with palm fronds and banana leaves.

They all knew as they looked over the feast that this was the last time the family would dine together as one unit. When Felipe and Caris left them under guard of the troops they would go to form another unit, and when they returned to the Palacio Guzman they would be their own masters, no longer an intimate a part of the Patrick Maguire household.

It soon became, though, a jolly family time. It also was infectious. Even the cane workers in the field beyond the crossroads had stopped slashing their big shiny machetes through the long cane fields and began slowly wending their way across the road past the several tobacco field hands. Antonia assumed they were on their way to pick up their own lunches somewhere along the crossroad.

Her father interrupted the happy scene briefly when he asked one of the caballeros strolling back and forth outside their little family circle if he'd seen the troops yet.

The two young men looked out from under their flat-brimmed, flat-crowned black hats and one of them reported, "I don't see them so far, señor. But soon . . . with so many cane workers in the road at siesta time they may have been a bit delayed."

Caris called their attention to the ring Felipe had given her over their breakfast chocolate that morning. It was truly impressive. Antonia had seen the enormous emerald framed in diamonds as long as she could remember her mother's warm and comforting hand. It made her slightly ill to see it now on Caris' scrawny little finger, obviously much too big and sliding around absurdly, but she looked up at her mother's eyes, read the love in them and knew it did not matter. Caris could keep the ring . . . maybe it made up for the loss of her parents at an early age. Antonia had her mother's affection, and knew she was the more fortunate . . .

Two of the tobacco hands, dark, sweating and scowling under their big hats, approached the picnic grove while heading toward the coast road. There was probably a cafe or *fonda* farther along toward the sea. One worker's muscular brown hand swung a dull-bladed cane knife. The other worker pressed a machete close against his thigh. Antonia tried not to look at the men or otherwise provoke them. She saw that the rest of her family did the same, all but Caris who stared at them over her hand while admiring her ring, which caught the piercing noon sunlight. The two caballeros were also fascinated by the ring, or perhaps by Caris' flirtatious manner. They crowded around her.

The señora leaned forward over the remains of the feast and confided to Antonia, "You must not mind, Tanita *mia*. It means more to her than to you or me."

"I know, Mama. Besides," she repeated her thoughts aloud, "she has the ring but I have you." She took up her mother's stout little hand. The sight of it brought back memories of so much tenderness and kindness that she squeezed it and raised her eyes to her mother's face—

She was stunned by her mother's sudden change. Her face had drained of color. Her flesh looked pallid. Her smile was frozen into a near grimace while her eyes were nearly all whites as she stared at something behind and above her daughter.

Antonia turned away, pushing her mother down in the middle of the white picnic cloth. Her quick glance over her shoulder encompassed a field hand towering above her as he brought down his machete with a slicing motion and the *whish* of a scythe through grass. He sliced into her sleeve and her skirt and missed her neck, which had evidently been his target.

A trap... the tobacco workers only pretending to work at a dead field. She had one momentary comfort... the workers in the cane field beyond would see what was happening and come to the rescue...

Neither Antonia nor her mother was capable of making a sound. The man above her pulled the machete's curved blade out of cloth, palm fronds and earth in one gesture and raised it again. In the same moment one of the caballeros fired his pistol twice. The field hand staggered but his momentum brought the machete down again, whirring through air and cloth, missing Antonia's body by a literal hair, the sound this time muffled by the melee around the rest of the picnic party.

The other two field hands were swinging their weapons. The second caballero was there one instant, admiring Caris' ring, and the next instant there was nothing but blood, a headless thing fallen across Caris' body, and more flashes as the blades cut everywhere through the hot noonday light.

Antonia had fallen across her mother's right shoulder, now heard a thud from the other side, then a sigh, and her mother writhed briefly before lying still underneath her.

A shriek was in her throat, unable to get out. Felipe... Where was he? Antonia tried to scramble up but stumbled over her mother's body and fell again.

... Not Felipe too. Holy-Mary-Mother-of-God help us...

She thought she made out the place where her brother had sat, just in front of some low dry bushes. Now the place swarmed with a dozen people wielding knives and machetes. The men from the tobacco field must have been joined by friends from the cane field, their loose, pale blouses already soaked and stained. The minutes were passing. The blood of their victims turned black on them.

One voice registered through her dazed brain. A cane worker shouting as he raised his knife over Felipe: "He said 'the more they hang, the better.' This one said it. About my son. Give it to him, again..."

She tried to get to her knees. Her father's voice, weakly: "Don't move, Tana. Don't—"

Again that scything noise, the *whish* and whirr as blades cut through the air. A sandaled foot kicked the side of Antonia's head, she fell into a blessed unconsciousness...

The sound of running feet, some of them bare, crunching dry palm fronds aroused her. They were hurrying off, they must have been warned that the escort troop was coming. She couldn't seem to get up. She didn't feel any wounds, only an incredible weakness. She raised her head a few inches. Her forehead was bleeding but it did not hurt. The muscles in her neck ached. It didn't matter, only one thing mattered. Had any of her family survived?

Felipe? She remembered that sickening moment when half a dozen of those men surrounded him. And that one tearing, wrenching shriek from inside her. She closed her thoughts to the memory.

She fumbled at the quiet body beside hers, the clothing already scorched by the sun, so hot her fingers burned when she tried to drag her mother into the shade.

"Mama?"

She had seen the bodies at the Guttierez hacienda, but this was different. Her mother could not die. No wounds. Nothing. Gently, she turned her mother over and saw the bloody cane knife buried to the haft in the hard knot of flesh and bone at the nape of her neck. Somewhere, from another and saner world, came the noise of horses sauntering along the road. The escort coming from the country hacienda to pick up Felipe and Caris.

Antonia got to her feet, fell down. Got up again, grabbing at a dry bush. There were no injuries except a bleeding cut on her left thigh, the one on her forehead, a near miss from the machete, and a long thin bloody line across her left shoulder where her sleeve had been cut away but also a near miss.

Over the buzz of insects she heard scrabbling noises, like a creature digging in the earth and leaves. Then moaning. Felipe? Father? Caris? Or one of their two escorts, the soldiers disguised as caballeros?

She raised her head with an effort. Nothing moved in the little picnic glade except flying insects. Bloody bundles of torn clothing everywhere.

Everyone I love is gone, I'm alone . . .

Felipe, father . . . which of these bloody bundles covered them?

Again moaning. Beneath the bloody trunk of the beheaded caballero. Caris. She started across the glade, fell down, began to crawl. She turned her head away when she scrambled around the place where Felipe had gone down under the knives of half a dozen of them.

Caris had pressed her face into green leaves and earth. Except where the caballero's body had fallen across her skirt she did not seem to be stained with blood.

"They've gone, Caris. Open your eyes. The escort troop is coming. Someone has to meet them," Antonia managed to get out.

Caris raised up on her elbows. her face was covered with dirt. She murmured in a kind of awe, "I'm alive, oh, Tana . . ."

"Listen to me, Caris. I need help. I want to see if anyone else is alive. Maybe we can save them."

Caris leaned away from her. "I can't look at them. I'll stop the soldiers. You . . . you look."

She slipped from Antonia's hands, apparently unhurt, skirted the mounds of bodies in the glade and hurried out to the crossroads, where she began to wave both arms. The hem of the girl's skirt was weighted with the caballero's blood.

Antonia found herself still kneeling where Caris had left her. Her knees had given out. She looked around her, reached out and tried to shift the trunk of the luckless caballero guard.

A body lay beyond, the upper torso and the head covered by the corner of the blood-drenched tablecloth that had blown across the body. She wanted to lift the cloth. To be sure. But her fingers were stiff. She couldn't make them obey her. The cloth did not cover the right arm and hand. A young hand. Male.

Lord . . . how well she knew those slim fingers, the scar across the first joint of the thumb and the base of the forefinger where the child Felipe had dropped his grandfather Guzman's sword when he was practicing a mock duel. How angry and frightened father had been at this danger to his only son and heir . . .

She saw Felipe now, in her mind's eye, his sassy grin, the way he wheedled himself out of punishment and then had the heroic experience of going around with his hand heavily bandaged. María-Rosa Guttierez had cried over his danger, which made him strut all the more . . .

She lowered her head, touched the scarred hand gently with her lips. She raised her head again. There was still one other.

Her father.

When the troopers dismounted and poured over the blood-drenched glade they found her stumbling blindly over the bodies, turning up leaves and brush that the gentle breeze had blown over them.

"My father," she explained without emotion, with astonishing calm, as they afterward reported to the new Governor Blanco. "I have to find Papa. He's around here somewhere. You will find my brother there. *Madre* is over near the palm. That hand you stepped on this side of the palm, it's one of them . . ."

They'd destroyed all she loved today. *They* had to be destroyed. They and their so-called cause . . . "We were betrayed by someone in our own household, I heard them repeat something no one could have heard but the servants at the *palacio*."

"Yes, yes, señorita, but later..." The soldier, like his companions, had been appalled by what they found. Half a dozen rode off after the assassins, down the road to the sea, several with carbines in hand. Others were trying to wrap the bodies of the dead in saddle blankets, serapes, even a blouse one of the soldiers had peeled off.

One of the soldiers hurried to help her as she tried to stand up. She shook him off. The world all around her was hot and spinning like a fireball. But she was ice cold.

Not one of them, including Caris, who sobbed in a captain's arms, understood Antonia's cold implacable hate. She walked several yards toward her mother and her legs gave out again. Darkness shrouded her before she reached the ground.

CHAPTER
FIFTEEN

THE SECRETIVE, challenging message from the queen regent arrived for Antonia after the most rapid Atlantic crossing in the steamer's history. It came to her in the Palacio Guzman when she badly needed to find some way of occupying her thoughts and accomplishing her sworn vengeance.

With her deep body cuts healing and her neck and shoulder recovering from the pressures of the assassin's body as he fell, only her mind was left to be healed. Claiming to be in excellent health, she went to the high mass held for her family at Havana's great cathedral and then home. But one idea she kept sacred through it all. Her first priority—the capture and execution of the traitor in the Palacio Guzman, and she had to return home to find out who he was.

The afternoon of the murders the rescue troop had taken Antonia and Caris to a small hospital run by Sisters of the Poor Clares, to whose order the Señora Maguire had contributed regularly. The hospital was on a hill west of the old colonial plazas, overlooking the distant masts, sails and steamer smokestacks in the sparkling Havana harbor. Antonia had never deviated from her passion for revenge. She awoke the evening of her arrival in the hospital to find Juan Diego bending over her, eyes anxious, holding her unbandaged right hand. She managed a smile for him.

The hospital room had formerly been a nun's sleeping cell but its austerity was relieved by flowers everywhere. When she thanked Diego he pointed out that only the roses on the altar across the room were his. The others had come from her Aunt Sybil and her uncle, as well as many friends of the Maguires, and from Miss Barton's new Red Cross member, Adelaide Heffernan.

Antonia now knew without the slightest doubt that she and Juan Diego must be on the same side. This monstrous crime would certainly have shaken his faith in those horrors who called themselves "rebels" and talked about "the Cuban Republic." It was impossible that any decent human being could condone that bloody scene at the crossroads.

She did not discuss it with him or with anyone else she cared for. Aunt Sybil was on her way to Cuba but the voyage would take her three days. Meanwhile, Antonia only gave the details to Señor Hernán de Noriega, who represented the new governor, Captain-General Ramón Blanco. She had heard the General Blanco's views were more moderate than his dreaded predecessor's, and she wanted to be sure there was no moderation used when the assassins were captured.

She did, however, spread the word, even before she left the hilltop hospital, that she would offer one thousand American dollars for the name of every "cane worker" and "tobacco hand" who had been in the crossroads fields that day, at that hour. She told the governor's aide, Noriega, that she could recognize four of the faces of the assassins and would offer another thousand dollars to each person who betrayed any of the four.

She added with a chilling smile, "Don't worry, Señor de Noriega. Once one is captured, he will betray the others, and it will soon all be unraveled. A thousand, maybe two thousand Yankee dollars ... What have the police found so far?"

He had no satisfactory news. "Your regular household servants remain. It seems unlikely they would stay to be questioned if they had had any part in betraying your brother's words—"

"One of them did."

"Perhaps a temporary servant. You would not permit us to question your cook, the gypsy woman, or your caretaker, as emphatically as we would have liked."

"Because I would trust my life to Zerlina and Pablo."

"Well then, we have learned nothing. Of course, there are others, peddlers, musicians, doctors who were in and out of your house recently."

She shook her head. "It has to be someone who heard my"— she cleared her throat—"my brother's words the night before the picnic."

Noriega made the vigorous if vague promise, "The police will exhaust every possibility, you may be sure. The army is on the road, investigating every phase of the crime. Sooner or later one of the cane workers will betray his comrades, it is inevitable."

When Juan came in to take her to the cathedral for the commemorative high mass she motioned Noriega to silence. Diego would now agree that the rebel cause had been reduced to terrorist assassins, but she still didn't want him to see how strong—tough— she could be. He might not find her so attractive, and he was her whole life now, the only one left that she really loved.

Her feelings for her only living relative, Aunt Sybil, remained in their place, secure and companionable. For Caris de Correña Maguire she felt as she might feel for an co-conspirator. The two women belonged to a tight little "Masonic lodge" of secrecy. They were joined by their desire for what Señor Noriega called with unctuous understanding "revenge," but which Antonia also now liked to think of as "justice."

Whatever, it was not a picture of her that she wanted Juan to carry around with him.

She had insisted on returning to the Palacio Guzman because she knew that if she did not go home at once, she could never return to this place with its agonizing memories.

The high mass, with its memories of other services here with her mother, Felipe and her father was almost unbearable. She spent the long hour with her mother's ancient wood-beaded rosary so tight in her fingers that she found her hand numb when the tribute ended. Juan never asked questions, never discussed her loss, yet she knew he understood. Perhaps, in her suffering, he relived his own loss.

Diego took Antonia and Sybil home after the cathedral services. He had offered to include Caris but the young widow refused. When he was called away by Quincy Kemp, who jotted down notes in the boiling hot plaza before the cathedral, Caris told Antonia and her Aunt Sybil, "I can't forget what that man has been. I could never forget. But I will have a surprise for you. A charming surprise that should make you forget that wretched man. It . . . arrived at the end of the service. Evidently you didn't see it."

Sybil was curious and later remarked acidly to Antonia, "She cried a good deal, but one can't help wondering how deep her feeling for poor Felipe was."

Antonia had seen Caris in hysterics at the hospital hours after the murders and didn't doubt the girl had been shaken, but she suspected the horror of what she had seen was deeper than her sense of loss. Caris' "surprise" must be some sort of commemorative flowers. She despised the triviality of Caris' mind and wondered if her own had been this superficial before . . .

She arrived with Juan at the garden gate during the long summer twilight, steeling herself against memories when she heard Felipe's green parrot squawking away on his perch near the stone bench where the señora had often sat making the little circles of silk thread with her tatting shuttles. Juan held her, supporting her with his strength and his understanding, but there was also help from Adelaide Heffernan, who waited with arms outstretched and a wordless sympathy.

They tried to take Antonia's mind off her memories by discussing the new governor of Cuba, General Blanco, and arguing whether the jingoists, the warmongers in the United States, would drag President McKinley into a war neither he nor Queen María Cristina wanted.

Aunt Sybil had been badly shaken by her brother's death, and her presence also made it easier for Diego to be accepted as a visitor in the household, partly because Sybil was determined to flout any of Caris' opinions and especially Caris' assumption that the *palacio* was now hers, as the widow of Patrick Maguire's only heir.

For the first and, Antonia devoutly hoped, the last time in her life she found herself holding private conversations with Caris. It was Aunt Sybil who kept Miss Heffernan and Juan occupied with girlhood memories of her adventures with her brother Patrick, how they first came to New York from the Old Country and then moved on to Virginia during the hectic winter of 1860. Antonia, who heard a little of this, found it hard to picture her self-possessed and glamorous aunt as a scrawny poor-white child of twelve. Thanks to Patrick's shrewdness and her own intelligence, plus a talent for intrigue, Sybil had come far since 1860. But even today it was clear that she still credited her big brother Paddy with her present splendor. Antonia was touched by that devotion, and from Juan Diego's sympathetic attention she guessed he was too. After all, he had known Sybil Revelstoke far longer than he had known her.

She was briefly lost in her own memories of the family when Caris signaled to her from the darkness of the patio and she left Juan with Aunt Sybil and Miss Heffernan to join her.

"The surprise I told you about, Tana. Come quickly. I have already talked to him today. He arrived at the cathedral while you were with the archbishop. I told him we would talk to him privately. We never know who our enemies may be."

"Certainly not in this house," Antonia agreed.

She was aware of Juan watching her, ready to help her, but in this matter he was the last person she could turn to. However much he must despise them now, he could hardly become involved in the punishment of men who had once been his allies.

She had spent hours in the hospital going over everything she knew about the servants at the *palacio*. One by one they had appeared before her mind's eye and she dismissed them as suspects. She tried to recall every detail of that last evening, with special emphasis on the time when Felipe had made that unthinking remark, "The more they hang, the better." Then, as he looked around at the patio beyond the louvred doors of the parlor, he had added, "if they are guilty, of course."

Were any servants near the doors at that minute, or in the long patio around the garden?

She remembered Felipe's green parrot chattering, and another noise that ended abruptly, the quick, strumming sound of a hand across the strings of a guitar. Pablo's nephew, Carlos Melina, the guitarist. He had been very close to the doors with their slatted panels. Carlos had certainly heard Felipe's remark.

Carlos also stood behind the carriage and waved his guitar after the family as they escorted the wedding pair to the crossroads. Could that have been his signal to one of those street peddlers that the Maguires passed? Was it his way of saying good hunting to the assassins?

"Where is your precious surprise?" she asked Caris as they walked along the patio through shadows and lantern light and the haunting scent of jasmine.

"You'll see. He wants to help us, so don't be discouraged. You look very grim, Tana."

"I feel grim. I think I know who—" She broke off. No need to tell Caris yet. She was not exactly her idea of a discreet colleague.

Caris knocked three times—not a very original signal, Antonia thought—on the last door along the west patio. The room was beside the servants' staircase to the ancient upper floors. In her mother's day it had been used only when the *palacio* was filled with guests. Antonia didn't know what to expect of the "surprise" and cared less. Her thoughts were still on the possible guilt of the guitarist.

The door opened and Caris looked into the austere little room. The rest of the old-fashioned house was still lighted with oil lamps and the double-globed lamp with its pink glow revealed a surprising sight to Antonia.

Lloyd Hastings stepped forward to take Antonia's hands. His usually neat suit coat was unbuttoned, his white shirt collar pulled up around the back of his neck and open in front, the tie crooked. His light hair had blown into a tangle in the evening breeze.

"Quite the hero," she murmured. "You're also the one who sent Tim Burford to spy on Captain Diego."

He dropped her hands. "I thought . . . I really believed it was for the good of the cause, but the president himself has taken me to task." She looked skeptical and he added quickly, changing the subject, "I know I'm a disgrace, Antonia, but I was caught in that mob outside the cathedral this afternoon. Then I couldn't get to you, they had you surrounded. At any rate I've been trying to pull myself together. This country, and the climate . . . why anyone wants to fight over it I can't imagine."

Caris agreed. "That may be true, but I'm sure my sister-in-law isn't interested in your view of Cuba, señor. Can you help us? That is the important thing." She took care to speak in English. Obviously, she didn't want him to misunderstand.

Lloyd Hastings kissed Antonia's cool cheek. "I want you to know, Antonia, that you have considerable support behind you. What happened to your family . . . that whole terrible shocking business . . . well, maybe their martyrdom was needed to wake up the United States."

Caris put in, "Let Señor Hastings tell you how you can get direct action and clear away this whole monstrous conspiracy."

Like a room in a religious Spanish parador, the room held only a single bed placed next to a candlelit prie-dieu. The altar was a solemn reminder of Spain's religious teachings. The narrow, slatted window and door looked out on the lovely green vista of the garden. Otherwise there was nothing to recommend it to a young man like Lloyd Hastings, accustomed to the crowded, overdecorated rooms of Washington and its environs. He looked around for a chair to offer Antonia but found only a three-legged stool.

"Never mind." She sat down on the edge of the stiff hard bed. "Tell me what you have in mind."

Caris settled herself at the end of the bed, making a face at its unyielding hardness. Hastings pulled up the three-legged stool.

"I'm relieved to see how well you've taken your awful loss, Antonia. You're so . . . self-possessed."

She said nothing.

"Well, in any case, unfortunately my ship docked late today but I was lucky enough to speak with Mrs. Maguire, your sister-in-law, and I understand you two ladies will be sailing for Spain shortly to . . . to lay your family with their illustrious ancestors."

"Lloyd, you haven't changed in the least."

"Antonia, I still wish——"

"You are just as pompous as you always were."

It was cruel and she heard Caris gasp, but she was beyond caring. While Lloyd's good-looking face reddened, Caris defended him.

"*Really*, Tana. Your tongue runs away with you sometimes. Señor

Hastings has been exceedingly gracious. No one could be more kind in our hour of grief."

They were a pompous *pair*, Antonia amended her first opinion. She could not imagine describing how she felt and her loss as her "hour of grief." There were *no* words for the loss. All the same, Caris was right. Lloyd might be of help. She reached for his hand and said quietly, "I'm sorry, it was a stupid thing to say."

"I understand. But to get back to important—I mean more immediate problems. Do you think it's possible you may have an interview with the Spanish prime minister, Cánovas del Castillo? You could point out that a few of us are working very hard on President McKinley. He must see that the conservative cause is our cause. They say General Weyler was too harsh. I think we need someone to point out he was too lenient."

This went against everything Juan Diego believed in. Antonia also had felt that General Weyler's ruthless policies were a mistake. But that was before the massacre of her family. Juan had been wrong supporting the rebellion... Couldn't he have been wrong calling Weyler a "butcher"?

"General Weyler will soon be speaking for himself, but I might add what I know, what I've seen..."

"There is one very crucial matter, Antonia. You are moving in ...well, dangerous company these days. You must be very careful that he doesn't learn about your plans. There's no doubt he is in this with them."

Her anger at this advice was greater because she had to wonder if there could be any truth in it. About Juan ... she hadn't yet heard his opinion of the men who committed the atrocity on her family. But that was unfair, of course he was as shocked ... she had to believe that.

"Lloyd, if you say one more word along that line you can forget any help I'd have given you in Spain."

"Tana, I don't understand. How deeply are you involved with this Quincy Kemp? You know he's one of the worst jingoist-warmongers in the newspaper game."

Antonia covered her mouth to hide her relief and managed to retreat nicely.

"You may be right. I hadn't considered it in that light. Quincy Kemp does act like a spy and a provocateur at times. As a matter of fact, that's how I met him. I went to his office to protest a column he'd written."

But the tall, lean man she met, the man with his warm dark eyes and intensely vital personality, turned out to be someone else entirely. How would her life have gone if Quincy Kemp *had* been in his office that day?

"And that pirate filibuster is Señor Kemp's friend," Caris put in so quickly she forgot Lloyd Hastings had spoken in Spanish.

Lloyd understood enough of the language to add, "Very true, they're friends. I'm sure Kemp gets much of his propaganda from that pirate." He saw Antonia's cheeks flushing and added, "However, that's not the real danger. Quincy Kemp has great influence in Washington. Surprising influence, for a newspaperman."

Antonia remembered Quincy Kemp's odd reaction, or rather his lack of reaction, when she accused him of being with U.S. naval intelligence. Surely if it had been false he would have laughed or made some witty comment but that little stunned silence had told her more ... yes, the columnist might have been all right to trust before his rebel friends murdered her family, but now it would be a blow if he guessed her thoughts ...

"I agree," she said, "he must not know any of our plans from this moment on."

They all heard the approaching footsteps along the Portuguese tiles that lined the patio. Caris got up and went to the door, all smiles. "Capitán Diego. Have we been too long? We have an unexpected guest. Señor Hastings came in on the *City of Washington*. Unfortunately it docked too late for the señor to reach the cathedral in time."

Antonia passed Caris in the doorway and went to Diego, who looked tense, and she wondered if he'd heard any of their conversation.

He kissed her and greeted the uneasy Hastings. She was not surprised that his manner was correct but chilly. He'd probably known in Washington that Lloyd Hastings was his enemy.

"I'm sure you will agree, señor, that Miss Maguire has had enough today. She could use a little peace and—"

Lloyd Hastings was all indignation. "Are you implying that I could upset Miss Maguire? I've never had anything but her best interests at heart—"

Antonia broke in, "I know, Lloyd, and I appreciate it. I'll see you again before you return to the States. But now I really am tired, so if you don't mind we'll talk about our Washington memories some other time."

She and Diego walked away then, along the patio, arm in arm, and Diego suggested for the first time, "If you want to talk about it..." He looked at her, then drew her close against him. "Or if you like, we can just sit out here in the garden and listen to the night sounds."

But there were too many memories here where the wedding party had sat joking and laughing, with the guitarist Carlos strumming a romantic song. The guitarist. She shivered.

"Memories?" he asked her.

"That last night."

They reached her father's study, a masculine room whose walls were crowded with camera pictures of Patrick Maguire being awarded or bestowing honors. The camera pictures, including one with newly inaugurated President McKinley, overshadowed the paintings, commemorating Patrick's friendships with various captains-general of Cuba as well as two showing him receiving handshakes from presidents Cleveland, Harrison and Arthur. Obviously the fashionable camera meant more to him than the paintings "done by hand."

Antonia said, "I'd like to sit here a few minutes and talk. Do you mind?" She motioned to Patrick's long mahogany desk, which had once belonged to an American secretary of state. "Father keeps... kept an excellent sherry."

Diego found small sherry glasses in the paneled cabinet behind the desk, settled on the arm of the leather couch where she sat. His searching eyes troubled her. She hated even the notion that she had to weigh very word with this man that she loved. She drank down her sherry.

"Juanito, I know you're no longer... I mean to say, this horror has shown you what they're capable of..."

He reached for her empty glass, looked at it as though he expected to find his answer there. "I think you know, sweetheart, I was never against your family. Only what they stood for. I am sure the señora and your brother had no idea that over a hundred thousand Cubans have died as a result of Spain's policies here and in Puerto Rico and the Philippines. Some claim that figure is double."

"But they're criminals, Juan, enemies of Spain—"

"A quarter of a million women, children and grandparents? Think, Tana. We aren't talking about a few crazed, isolated assassins."

"You're still defending the rebels? Even after what they did to my family?"

The sherry glass was upside down in his hand and a dark golden drop splashed on his finger. He tasted it, remarked apropos of nothing, "I never liked sherry. Too sweet."

"Well? Are you going to continue delivering weapons to these assassins?"

He didn't remind her that the weapons used against her family had not been his guns, but the assassins' own cane knives and machetes. "I believe in autonomy for Cuba," he said quietly. "I may even believe in an independent Cuba. I don't know. But you would despise me if I turned from everything I believed in—"

"There have been *five* terrible crimes, I include the two soldiers."

He took a deep breath. "Five, yes. And there are others. I haven't forgotten the Guttierez hacienda. But against that there are thousands committed in the name of the government... Tana, if we are not true to what we believe in, what are we?"

The room was so silent Antonia thought she could hear the low murmur of voices in the big Spanish parlor. The slats in the doors and windows were all open, as they had been the night Felipe's words were overheard.

... I must tell Señor de Noriega about the guitarist, she thought ... I've waited too long, listened to too much ... and now Juan ... oh God, he's the man I thought he was before I let him charm me out of the truth. But I can't count on Caris or Lloyd either. They cling to me just to get their revenge. As for Juan ... it's over, it has to be, nothing's left but the pain ... it's over ... I must believe that. I *must* ...

"Tana? Is there any future for us?"

She looked up at him. "You made the terms. You said when this rebellion is over."

"Yes, but that was before—I don't want to leave you here alone. Sweetheart, I may have to make a voyage to Cádiz. I want you to come along so I can look after you. We could be married in Spain, very quietly. We needn't announce it until your mourning time is over."

Don't be charmed again, she told herself. And don't let him know her intentions about going to Spain. "It sounds tempting, Juan, but no, I want to spend some time alone. A retreat, I think. There are several . . . one across the harbor here, one in the States. Maryland or Delaware. I've forgotten. Maybe then I'll get my . . . my perspective back and see that you"—she wet her lips nervously over the lie—"see that you were right."

He drew her close and kissed her. There was a tentativeness in it, but then her old feelings took over and she gripped his back and shoulders, her fingers digging into his flesh. She was at war with herself, with him. Love and hatred went into that farewell kiss.

And she knew if they met in Spain she would need to lie again and keep lying. She might not be able to stop loving this man. Accept that for now. But at least she could learn not to trust him . . .

PART
TWO

CHAPTER
SIXTEEN

LONG AGO the Señora Maguire had advised Antonia that keeping occupied was the best way to forget sorrow.

"Tanita *mia*, I have lost three babies before their birth, and each
time I have dreamed their poor little souls were lost in perdition.
Only one thing helped me. Not sympathy, not friends, not even
the church. But our Holy Mary, Mother of God, she lost her son.
And she seemed to say to me, 'work is the answer.' Keep the
thoughts occupied. I say this now to you, if sorrow ever comes,
keep the thoughts busy on new things. New sights..."

Antonia slept little the night she discovered that the man she
loved still supported those who had destroyed her family, even if
in the name of his grand cause. The next morning the letter came
to her from a Condesa de Montemayor, lady-in-waiting to Her
Majesty, María Cristina, the queen regent. It appeared that besides
being lady-in-waiting, the condesa was also Her Majesty's secretary
and confidante.

The letter:

In greatest confidence, this communication.

Her Majesty commands me to offer her deepest sympathy in the bereavement you have suffered. The news was received through the telegraph only hours ago. Her Majesty is mindful of old and dear friendships which she treasured, especially the friendship with your mother.

Since your loss was suffered in the Cause of Spain, Her Majesty believes you might wish to act in a capacity known only to Her Majesty's few confidants and perhaps, His Excellency, the President of the United States. Of this, no more can be said until your audience with Her Majesty. The audience itself should be kept in strictest secrecy.

Her Majesty commands me to ask that you burn this communication upon reading it. Captain Villedo, who delivers this to you, is the brother of the person who has the honor of signing this missive and can be trusted.

> Albinia de Serra,
> Condesa de Montemayor

Since Antonia and Caris would be returning to Spain where the Cuban branch of the Guzmans was buried in the family tomb near Córdoba, the queen's order was a blessing. Surely, it would occupy all her thoughts, just as Mama had advised long ago.

She couldn't confide to Caris the information in the royal letter, but Caris accurately assumed that Antonia, at least, would receive a royal audience, and so she and Lloyd Hastings were at great pains to advise Antonia about her replies to the queen's inevitable questions when she saw her.

"You must be firm," Lloyd told her. "Describe exactly what you saw, what was done by the murderers. Don't mince words."

"And," Caris added, "don't let her liberal advisers talk her out of the advice Uncle Weyler must have given her already. Perhaps she will receive me too. I must write to Uncle Weyler... Tana, you must tell her my uncle is right. No compromise. Remind her of the disasters when terrorists get in control. Tell her to remember what happened to other Austrian queens in Latin countries. Like Marie Antoinette."

Antonia said dryly, "I doubt if that would win me the royal friendship but I'll do my best to make the point. If, of course, I get the chance." She thought of Juan's argument and was curious to see Caris' reaction. "Did you know that some say your uncle's policies have killed several hundred thousand people?"

"Terrorists, murderers—"

"Women, children, old people...?"

Caris looked annoyed. "Did *you* know, Tana, that in every good fight a few innocent people are bound to suffer?"

Lord, how cold she sounded... Antonia suspected that in other circumstances Caris would have dismissed the Maguire family's death with equal ease... well, she had done all she could, given the description of Carlos the guitarist, and could only hope he would be captured before her return to Cuba.

That same day Juan came to say good-bye to her. He was sailing for Cádiz. Pretending... actually it was more than pretense... that all was well between them, she became interested in his mission to Spain.

He silenced her with one finger on her lips. "I can't tell you now, but someday I believe you will approve."

She doubted that, but she smiled and agreed, and felt sick and lost when he left her. She badly wanted to follow him and make things right between them, but everything stood in their way and now there was Her Majesty's own hint that Antonia could be of service to the Spanish Cause, against Juan's people.

Although Antonia did not know Juan's business in Spain, and he certainly wouldn't be seeing the queen regent, she knew she and Caris must reach the mother country first. They must also avoid southern Spain until she had had her royal audience and the entombment of the three heavy, silver-edged coffins that would be stored in the hold of the ship for the voyage.

Captain Villedo's fast steamer, the *Santa Cruz*, landed them in France on the Bay of Biscay, giving Caris time to buy French perfume before they crossed the Spanish border at Irun.

Having sent the coffins through Spain to Córdoba on a cart owned by her mother's Cousin Rafael Guzman, Antonia and Caris crossed from the modern French train over a mist-bound river in the evening. The two young women in black mourning gowns attracted attention among other travelers. The hour was late. The men were nervous over rigid Spanish customs inspection, and among the eleven waiting for their baggage to be examined only this pretty blonde and the equally attractive brunette spoke Spanish. Caris' Spanish was excellent Castilian, Antonia's more provincial, though a foreigner would not guess that.

While a trim, elegant gentleman with a wispy red mustache tried to make his English clear by raising his voice to the inspectors, the other travelers behind him exchanged uneasy grins and feeble jokes. The Englishman's difficulty was made evident when one of the customs officers, with the profile and steely courtesy of a grandee, brought a large-bore hunting rifle out of its case and raising it to his eye, sighted along the barrel, making several of the crowd duck hastily.

Caris exclaimed, "*Madre de Dios*, that thing would bring down an elephant."

Several travelers agreed, exchanging opinions as to where the Englishman expected to bring down his big game. One slightly built young man just ahead of Antonia and Caris inquired hesitantly, in heavily accented Spanish, "Is it permitted to bring firearms? I was not aware."

"It is strictly forbidden, señor," Caris said. Then she apparently discovered that the dark, Italianate young man was handsome and asked with her tight little smile, "You are visiting our beautiful Spain for the first time?"

"The first, señorita. But I am sure it will be most instructive. And who knows, perhaps even profitable." He gave some study to her black taffeta gown, jacket and hat with its tantalizing nose veil. He added, "I beg pardon. It is señora?"

"Widowed," she murmured softly.

Antonia wanted to throw up. And almost did when the man added, "So young, what a tragedy."

Antonia noted that that Italianate man wasn't the only one who spoke Spanish with an accent, her own broad Cuban dialect leaving much to be desired. Meanwhile, the Englishman had left the counter, complaining that his hunting rifle had to remain behind.

A pair of French businessmen moved up to the counter as Caris chattered away to the good-looking dark young man. Antonia had little interest in him except for his surprising attention to the Englishman's rifle, which was out of reach on a scratched, unvarnished table behind the inspectors.

When Caris' dark young man stepped up to the customs inspectors and opened his valise Antonia saw that he carried one change of underwear and books on the history of Spain. It made Antonia a little uneasy when one of the inspectors took up a book, riffled through its pages and calmly ripped out at least an entire chapter, probably the history of the First Republic, which had ended with the return to the throne of the present boy king's young father. Antonia knew such things went on in Cuba, but Cuba was at war. She wondered if the queen knew about this sort of censorship.

The Italian didn't seem to object. He took back the book, paying far less attention than Antonia would have done to the mutilated pages that the inspector now put on the table with the rifle. "Señor Angiolotti," the inspector read from the young man's passport. "How much money do you bring into Spain?"

Nervously, "Five hundred francs."

"They must be changed to pesetas."

"Yes, señor . . . I mean, *sí* señor."

The young man turned away from the counter, Antonia took his place. Her black mourning with white ruching impressed the inspector so that he was especially kind.

"*Señorita*, welcome to Spain."

She turned away just as Angiolotti was picking up his valise, her elbow struck his and he dropped two books. Apologizing, she tried to help him pick them up but Caris had already rescued them by their marbled board covers and handed them to him. He fastened them inside his valise, sealed it with its buckled closing and hurried away.

"How odd," Caris murmured, frowning, as Antonia pointed out their great pile of luggage and the brawny porter hung each valise, case or portmanteau on his back and shoulders. Impatient over her interest in the little dark Signor Angiolotti, Antonia ignored Caris' puzzled comment.

"We haven't much time, our carriage isn't going to wait forever." They would be lucky if the coachman waited at all. The border inspection had taken much longer than they'd expected.

The town of Irun at this hour was shrouded in foggy blue darkness, with no signs of life except a lean dog loping homeward across the unpaved street. Two of the travelers who had cleared customs now stalked down the deserted main street of the town, casting shadows taller than most of the shuttered white buildings they passed. Where was the nightlife and the flirtatious "paseo" that Antonia had heard so much about? Not at this border town, evidently.

"Carriages. Imagine, after the amenities of a train in France," Caris said, but hurried along after Antonia and the porter.

A ponderous closed coach thirty years behind the times was stationed alongside a little drinking establishment. Its four vigorous black coach horses looked to Antonia like Arabians who had been just barely tamed. Felipe would have loved them . . .

The horses rattled their harness as the two young women passed, and a stout little coachman in red-and-gold livery calmed them as he opened the coach door. A tall, imperious woman, made taller by her black lace mantilla draped over an impressive comb, looked out at Antonia and Caris, signaled to them with one gloved finger. Antonia stopped but Caris nudged her.

A watchman in black with a stiff stovepipe hat strolled by swinging a lantern and calling the hour. He acted as if he hadn't seen them.

"You don't see that any more in the States," Antonia said.

"We aren't in your precious States," Caris told her in her usual charming fashion.

Meanwhile the coachman had waddled toward them at an order from the frozen-faced female, and Antonia noted the crest on the coach door by the carriage lights. She hesitated. "Caris, it seems we're being given a royal summons."

Caris was startled, disappointed too. "That can't be Her Majesty. I saw her one summer at San Sebastián. She was quite a good-looking woman. Elegant and gracious, uncle said."

Their porter stopped and set down their seven cases.

"She is the Condesa de Montemayor, señora. Close to the royal family, they do say. A lady of the chamber, or some such. She wishes you to come to her."

Caris nudged again. "We may have been a trifle hasty."

Antonia remembered very well the name of the woman who had written to her in Queen María Cristina's name but she had never discussed the destroyed letter or the *condesa*. She decided to pretend she had never heard of the woman.

"I suppose we must speak to her."

They walked back to the old-fashioned carriage, avoiding the mettlesome team. Before the *condesa* could address them in her arrogant, lisping Castilian way, as she showed every sign of doing, Antonia said abruptly, "We have arranged for our own horse and buggy to take us to a parador, señora. I am Antonia Maguire. This is the Señora Felipe Maguire. We are in Spain on family business."

The *condesa*'s wrinkled eyelids descended over her pale eyes, then went up again. For a minute Antonia's abrupt manner had come as something of a surprise to her. Then she understood that Antonia was only keeping the bargain of silence.

"You are the Señorita Guzman-Maguire. Never forget it. And you, young woman, you are the widow of a Guzman-Maguire. You are also Her Majesty's guests. She has learned of your tragedy in her service. Please to take your seats." She pointed one bony finger at the stout little coachman who let down the carriage steps and then bustled off to claim their luggage from the Spanish porter.

Under her breath Antonia said to Caris, "I wonder if we're being kidnapped," but Caris refused to see the humor of it.

"Don't be ridiculous. It is Her Majesty who invites us. I told you your American notions of traveling without duennas would shock any aristocratic Spanish woman."

"Señora Guzman-Maguire is quite right," the *condesa* said. "Her Majesty would never approve."

Antonia laughed. "Don't concern yourself, *condesa*. On every possible occasion my sister-in-law explained to the world that our duenna was seasick. When we landed our duenna had a severe attack of gout. We were forced to leave her at Bayonne. Or Biarritz, or some such place. We now leave her at the border."

Aided by the flaring glow of the carriage lights, she thought she detected a humorous glint in the *condesa*'s frigid eyes, but Caris was too busy noticing such important matters as the heavily padded interior of the coach that looked faded but unquestionably regal with its red-and-gold fittings, the colors of Spain's glorious past.

The ancient elegance of the coach was not quite impressive enough to overcome the discomfort of covering half of Spain, rattling and tumbling and jolting around in the tight airless interior when, as

Caris reminded everyone at every occasion, "We might have taken a train, if only this were France."

The *condesa* had an answer. Once, on the arid Castilian high plains, "if pigs had wings they would fly."

Which made Antonia and even Caris laugh. The only thing that cheered up Caris for very long, however, was the occasional attractive male among the hosts who entertained the royal guests on various nights. These nightly visits were made to structures that would have been castles in the medieval world and remained castles of privilege on the brink of the twentieth century. It shook Antonia that there was so much of the Dark Ages in those gloomy habitations and in the lives of those who lived there.

Several times when the mood seemed genial and friendly and the nobles who were her hosts would talk to her as to a human being and not a "sheltered female," Antonia found herself pursuing the subject of Cuban autonomy.

"But a loyal part of the Spanish Empire, of course, locally ruled by Cuban landowners like my father, and the loyalist merchants in Havana and Santiago."

While the Marquesa de Palma fanned herself rapidly, the marqués skimmed over Antonia with a tolerant smile and dwelt with genuine warmth on the sight of a kittenish golden Caris.

"And you, señora, do you share these radical views?"

"*Madre mia*, you are making a joke, I think. Antonia knows no more than I do about politics. She is teasing you, Excellency."

Antonia had a quick answer. "Since my parents and my brother were butchered by the radicals I can hardly be said to sympathize with them. On the other hand, if Spain can't protect Cuba, I'm suggesting the United States will."

The marquesa closed her fan with a snap of ivory sticks. "Of what concern is that to Spain? The United States is a collection of peddlers and riffraff, the dregs of every nation, no purity of bloodline there. The scum swept up on the shores of an aboriginal land." She leaned forward, all her many teeth gleaming. "You cannot suggest that we, Imperial Spain, First Daughter of the Church, should be bullied by such a rabble."

Antonia knew it was less than diplomatic but she couldn't help saying, "I'm afraid it's already happening."

The marques coughed over his Cuban cigar and suggested they

all adjourn to the music salon to be entertained by his twelve-year-old daughter's piano rendition of music from a new Madrid *zar-zuela*. "Entertain" proved to be a questionable description.

"They are operettas in the tradition of Lehar and Kalman," he expounded for the benefit of the "provincial" Antonia. Apparently he had no idea that every *zarzuela* was heard in cosmopolitan Havana's many cafes long before it ever reached his noble Castilian ears. Spain itself had few cities the size and magnificence of Havana, and none she could see that was as beautiful or busy and exciting. She already longed for the moment when she could return to the Washington environs or even Havana, in spite of its memories.

Caris spent most of her time comparing the males she saw one day with those she had seen the day before. "In some ways the marques was better looking than that young man at the border, though not as handsome as the captain of the *Santa Cruz*. Strange, the captain doesn't look in the least like that old gargoyle, the *condesa*."

"Personally, I sort of like the *condesa*." Antonia was surprised to find that she meant it. The *condesa* was sharp and salty but there was a sly humor about her as well. Small wonder, the queen regent trusted her. She was intelligent and not likely to betray secrets.

Caris, as usual, paid little attention to Antonia's response. "I wonder what his first name was."

"Whose?"

"Angiolillo's. The man at the border."

Antonia was packing for the next day's journey and only looked up to say, "He said his name was Angiolotti, didn't he?"

"That's not what it said on the frontispiece of his book. Angiolillo . . . You forgot to pack your new mantilla, the package is on your left."

Antonia grabbed up the package and threw it into the valise, wishing for the hundredth time that she could stay at a public hotel on their next stop so that there would be decent, modern rooms and amenities, not these thick walls and cell-like rooms.

She had her way when they reached one of their goals, the city of Córdoba where she insisted on taking rooms of their own at a modest white stucco hotel near the Great Mosque. Caris never stopped complaining at the narrow streets, the high walls with their forbidding little balconies and barred windows. She even attacked the presence of the old mosque itself, with its glorious moorish patterns, its endless columns that trailed off into infinity and made one forget the patchwork Christianity placed in its midst.

"It's obscene. I don't approve of idolatrous non-Christian ornaments, or those black creatures who worship Allah. I can't wait to get back to the *palacio*. Now I can make changes I've always wanted. And another thing, here in this patio we have more of that sickening jasmine. I detest it."

They were seated beside a fountain that saved the scene from the broiling heat of midsummer. Antonia took her hands out of the cool water and stared at Caris for a long moment. They would hear the Guzman-Maguire wills read tomorrow after the entombment in the family mausoleum, and doubtless Caris was entitled to the Havana house, but every time she mentioned all the changes she would make, Antonia flinched with anger. Her early changes were a slap at Antonia's mother and all those who had died.

"If you object to what you call 'black creatures,' you aren't going to want to live in Havana. A considerable part of our population is black, as you may have noticed. Are you sure you don't want to stay in Spain?"

Caris gave the patio and the ancient Moorish world of Córdoba a wave of the hand. "No. I don't feel at home here any more. I'm sure it will be the same in Seville. It has changed dreadfully since I was born but it isn't...you know, modern. Besides, Lloyd says—"

"Lloyd?"

"Señor Hastings says one is really alive only in Washington. A heady place."

"I thought you didn't like the States."

"I don't. That is, I've never been there. But I make friends easily, and there is always your Aunt Sybil."

Aunt Sybil and Caris had not shown any affection for each other during their brief time together in Havana. On the other hand, Lloyd Hastings seemed to have become an important character in Caris's conversation. With Felipe not dead a month she obviously was already considering a successor.

In a burst of fury Antonia hated this little golden feline who could demean the memory of both her mother and her brother in so short a time. Did these people—this Caris, the de Palmas, Lloyd Hastings—stand for anything Antonia was about to fight for? But the answer came quickly to bury these doubts. She saw again in memory that noonday when she had crawled over the stained luncheon cloth and identified each body...

She saw Caris looking at her. Even Caris had noticed that the tears were running down her cheeks. Well, what difference did it make? A least she could weep for her loved ones.

Her mother's second cousin was a sympathetic little man named Rafael Guzman, who looked astonishingly like Antonia's mother. Now he took the two young women out to the Guzman mausoleum in the austere yellow landscape beyond the old Roman ruins where the three elaborate silver-handled coffins were laid beside ancestors from the days of El Cid.

"I believe half the population of the province must be here," Caris said proudly as she looked around the hillside that baked in the high, dry sunlight.

Cousin Rafael Guzman said, "We seem to be a popular family." Antonia was aroused from painful thoughts by her cousin's boast as he went on. "The Guzmans live everywhere. They have married into many great families, but our branch returns here for their eternal rest. My cousin Ysabel would be proud."

Antonia made an effort to smile. "I'm sure she would be." She turned away to avoid seeing the heavy, iron-studded door close, and saw hundreds of eyes staring at her, most of them simply curious. A man stood a short distance away with a camera on a tripod. He draped a black cloth over his head—someone trying to photograph both the mausoleum and the mourners in one shot. Antonia remembered her father's interest in this method of preserving events for posterity but she resented it too much at this moment to appreciate any art involved.

She said abruptly, "Can we return to the hotel?"

"As you say, Cousin Antonia. I regret that your friend could not arrive in time for the entombment. He wrote to us most kindly. But transportation from Cádiz is very uncertain. However, he may be here on Friday with the captain of his vessel."

Her heartbeat quickened at the mention of the captain and Cádiz, but she felt something ominous as well. "Which friend is this?"

"Why, Señor Quincy Kemp, of course. I am told he is a very

important gentleman of the press. He will want to know all your plans."

She and Caris looked at each other, sharing a fear of this man who was probably an enemy, certainly a spy. Worse, the man she loved would be there with him . . . to help him destroy her cause?

She put the thought, but not the excitement, out of her mind.

CHAPTER
SEVENTEEN

"**D**ID SEÑOR Kemp mention an attempt to get an audience with Her Majesty?" Antonia appeared more calm than she felt.

Her cousin Rafael was puzzled. "I do not see how that is possible. Protocol is very strict at court and even though Señor Kemp is our family's friend, he is unlikely to be granted an audience." Then his brown eyes lighted with pleasure. "Unless he seeks an audience through the new emissary from the president of the United States. A Señor Woodford has just arrived in Spain. Señor Kemp's letter says he is to meet with Señor Woodford today. That should be the key to an interview."

The two women discussed it as soon as they could politely free themselves from Cousin Rafael. Caris urged, "You must ask the Condesa de Montemayor for an immediate audience with the queen."

Antonia pretended to hesitate. "Yes, I suppose you're right. I'll ask the *condesa* if it's possible. But it will take days to reach the summer court at San Sebastián."

The *condesa* was ready for Antonia. "Do not concern yourself. You will have your audience. And at once. Her Majesty is fully aware of this Woodford's arrival. She has granted him an audience." Antonia groaned. The *condesa*, who evidently enjoyed leaving her victims on the edge of suspense, added with her dry smile, "It is arranged for next week. Her Majesty intends to make her wishes known to you first."

Antonia was relieved but puzzled too. She couldn't imagine what secret commission the queen might have for her. "Is there anything I should do? Anywhere I should go to meet Her Majesty? San Sebastián is a long way from Córdoba."

The *condesa* merely shook her head. It was all very mysterious, and Antonia returned to Caris, who was wild to know when they'd leave for San Sebastian and did the *condesa* appreciate the need to hurry?

Antonia tried to calm her. "She must know how prejudiced Quincy Kemp's column has been."

"Well, they say this Señor Woodford comes from the Yankee president," Caris complained. "I don't like that."

"The queen is not a stupid woman. She has been a balance wheel in the government ever since the little king was born. I doubt if very many men could have kept the conservatives, the liberals, the Carlists and Republicans from each other's throats as well as she has. She'll know what to do."

But Antonia had her own private worries which Caris could only suspect. She did not want to face Juan Diego until her audience with the queen was over. She had almost fallen under the influence of his arguments once before and she recognized his power over her. How much she wanted him, and wanted in spite of herself to believe in him.

Late that afternoon when the siestas had finally ended in the hot dry city, Antonia was summoned again to the *condesa's* suite, by far the most lavish in the simple, almost monastic hotel.

"We shall stroll in the old quarter, past the Mesquita. The Old Mosque," she explained, imperious as ever, "you will be impressed."

Antonia walked out with her, hoping the woman would not lose them both in this labyrinth of tiny streets that reminded Antonia of native casbahs in North Africa she had read about. She missed the thick, jungle greenery of her native land, not to mention the green hills of Virginia, but this city with its ancient glory as the capital of Moorish Spain intrigued her by its difference from everything she had known. The air was silent through the night and often during the daytime as well, a far cry from Havana, which remained passionately alive twenty-four hours a day.

The few women who passed were accompanied by males and each of them had her face partially concealed by her veil or her mantilla. Antonia had seen women in Santiago and even Havana who were veiled, but in the Cuban cities there were the North American tourists and so many young local women who imitated them that the old Spanish customs seemed merely exotic. Here she felt herself in the heart of medieval Spain, as if time had carried her back to another era, both terrifying and glowing with that rebirth the Moors had brought to Spain over a thousand years ago. Could this Spain, fascinating as it was, ever compete with the young colossus across the Atlantic, that hungry United States with its forward-looking politics and its *very* forward-looking navy?

She caught the *condesa* looking back over her shoulder. It wasn't the first time, but Antonia saw no one except a peasant carrying home a bundle of overripe fruit in his faded jerkin.

"He doesn't look very dangerous."

"You think not, my innocent friend? And yet if one of us were accosted at this moment, you would see a dagger in an extremely useful hand, and very likely a pistol as well."

Antonia studied the peasant with new interest . . . this secret audience business had interesting sides that she had never suspected. It gave her an excitement she found both attractive and disconcerting. If only she could talk to Juan about it. Or Felipe. When she was a girl she would have confided the whole story to her little brother and he would have shared her excitement. They were always sharing secrets from the rest of the world. Felipe . . . she missed him more every day.

"It's strange," she said aloud but more to herself, "I didn't miss my brother all those years in Virginia. Now, it seems almost unbearable."

The *condesa* was gruff as usual. "All the more reason for you to join Her Majesty's service."

If I ever see her, which begins to look doubtful, Antonia thought.

Minutes later, with the last light of day dissolving into the lantern-lit darkness, the *condesa* said abruptly, "This way, through the alley."

Like many of the white lines of adobe houses with single walls between, this wall had a narrow, grilled door. Through the grill-work Antonia glimpsed a fountain, a partially tiled garden and either mimosa or jasmine climbing the adobe walls. "Am I being kidnapped," she said, not altogether joking.

"Don't be flippant. Ah, Pedro, is it you?"

The gate squeaked open. A nervous young man stepped aside with a bow. Behind him stood an elegantly gowned female, her head swathed in the elaborate mantilla and comb that reminded Antonia of the *condesa*'s old-fashioned formal look. The youthful Pedro especially surprised Antonia. He wore the red-and-gold livery of Spain, and she couldn't imagine what the livery was doing in provincial Córdoba, in the middle of an extremely unregal casbah. She was less surprised by the obeisance the regal Spanish lady made to the *condesa*, who seemed to have that effect on everyone.

"Wait here," the *condesa* ordered Antonia, who obediently seated herself on a stone bench against a wall of mimosa. She wasn't used to obeying such an autocratic creature. Neither her father nor her mother had ever been so dictatorial, but she had finally begun to suspect the truth . . . However farfetched it might seem, the queen regent of Spain must be somewhere nearby, and Antonia was being taken to visit her in secret. The garden was dark except for the bright stars overhead and one lantern hanging in the moorish archway leading to the interior of the ancient house. The youth Pedro stayed at the gate across the patio, and seemed to find her intriguing. At least he kept staring at her and every time she caught him at it he looked away in embarrassment.

Suddenly, though she hadn't heard anything, he straightened like a little tin soldier and faced toward the lantern-lit interior of the house. He bent over, as if in pain, at the instant the *condesa* and the woman who had received Antonia stepped out from under the red tile roof of the cloister around the patio and sank to the ground.

The sight of all these cases of sudden collapse warned Antonia that—unbelievable or not—the queen regent of Spain must indeed be very near. She got to her feet and swung around. A young woman had stepped silently into the patio and stood by the fountain, running the fingers of one hand through the water spray. In rich black from her mantilla and comb to her shoe tips, she might have been any aristocratic, youthful widow, but her poise and her strong profile announced the Hapsburg blood and the ancient pride of Spanish royalty.

Antonia was annoyed at the awe she felt. Surely she had spent too much time in the democratic United States to be overpowered by the sight of one tired, hardworking woman who happened to be the mother of a boy king. Nevertheless, Antonia was aware of a weakening in the knees as she sank in a curtsy every bit as deep as that of the Condesa de Montemayor. Her skirts rippled out around her, the hems skimming the wet ground around the fountain, and she could think of nothing more inspiring to say than, "Your Majesty?"

María Cristina had a light and charming laugh, almost a chuckle, Antonia thought. It reminded her of Aunt Sybil's contagious laughter. The queen moved across the patio, offering her hand.

"And you, of course, are the brave daughter of my dearest friend, Ysabel Guzman y Pontalvo." Antonia touched the queen's fingers with her own as she rose from her curtsy. Her Majesty added in her faint Germanic accent, "Come, my dear. Sit with me. I am afraid it must be a very brief meeting. At this minute I am supposed to be back in San Sebastian recovering from a" —she looked over to the *condesa* for help—"what is my problem, Albinia?"

The *condesa's* pale eyebrows raised. She glanced at the young lady-in-waiting, who murmured, "I believe it was a bad chill, Your Majesty. Compounded by a severe migraine. Too severe for Her Majesty to conduct audiences. For the moment."

The queen nodded. "If I had received you there all Spain would know of it in a matter of hours. This absurd cloak-and-dagger business was necessary, you may be sure, although I imagine your dear mother would have been shocked. There was nothing secretive about my friend Ysabel . . . we met at a convent school one summer. Not near Vienna, I am afraid, but sufficiently far for us to enjoy the privacy of youthful friendship." She sighed. "There are many times when I wish we might have returned to those days. We corresponded for years, until the responsibilities I inherited when the late king died."

"A tragedy, Your Majesty. Alfonzo the Twelfth was a great man, I'm told, in spite of his youth."

The queen nodded. "He would have been a great man. He died so terribly young. An appalling thing for Spain. And for those who loved him." She took a deep breath, then clapped her hands as if she thereby gained new strength. "And now, we all must do our best to carry out his hopes for Spain." She raised her voice in spite of the quick signal by the *condesa*. "Above all, that means peace, not war. War would be disastrous for the empire. And, I think, for the United States as well. Their President McKinley understands this. We have had some little private correspondence on the subject. Our problem is that so few Americans know or understand our problems. We need Cuba and her industry, we need the Philippines and Puerto Rico. These are a *part* of Spain. In return we understand the problem of these colonies. But does the United States know or understand any of these problems?"

Antonia probed at the queen's intentions. "I'm afraid I have a rather biased view of the rebels in Cuba. I can't forget what they did."

Her Majesty's penetrating gaze had none of the sweet warmth that Antonia remembered seeing in her mother's brown eyes. How the two women had become friends was a mystery. This woman knew what she wanted and just as she had so carefully balanced the four parties that wanted to tear Spain apart, she was able to convey her point to Antonia.

"Your feelings are surely understandable, my dear. But we must think of our country's needs." Antonia wondered where this was leading. She couldn't imagine anything that Antonia Maguire could do to save Spain. On the other hand the queen regent's letter, through the *condesa* as intermediary, had suggested that Antonia "act in a capacity known only to Her Majesty and her few confidants."

What capacity?

She asked aloud, "How can I serve you, ma'am?"

María Cristina examined her fan briefly, running her finger over each shiny black stick that was joined to the others by stiffened lace. "In confidence," she began.

Antonia looked around the little patio and fountain that were sheltered by high, thick white walls. Everyone had disappeared, even the all-knowing *condesa*. "I understand, ma'am," she said, and noted a silver crucifix in a niche of the wall near the alley gate, that glimmered in the starlight.

"What I want you to do is very simple. And of the utmost importance. I can trust no one for this purpose except, perhaps, our Spanish minister to Washington, who will be your partner, in a manner of speaking."

"Señor Enrique Dupuy de Lôme. I know him. While I was staying with my aunt in Virginia recently he and I were confronted by some noisy members of the Cuban junta."

"So he told me. You may have saved his life, I believe, by your quick wits."

Antonia laughed at the exaggeration. "Hardly that. They meant no physical harm, they simply wanted to present their case."

The queen waved aside this explanation. "Well, that is as may be. You are also acquainted with President McKinley."

"Slightly."

"In brief, I am in secret correspondence with the president. He has been intelligent enough to send me coded messages on occasion, to avoid those warmongers around him. He wanted to preserve the peace as I do, but the Cortes of the United States—their Congress—is filled with jingos."

"Jingoists. Yes, those who want to make trouble. The newspapers sell more papers. The sugar lobby wants control of Cuban sugar. The tobacco people want to handle the Cuban cigar industry." It was Antonia's chance to remind Her Majesty about Quincy Kemp. "The columnist, Mr. Kemp, is a likable man, but most of his columns glorify the rebels."

She need not have worried. María Cristina was well aware of her adversaries. "Quincy Kemp, yes. I am familiar with his work. Another American emissary has arrived in Madrid. He wishes to bring Señor Kemp when I receive him. This Señor Woodford brings stern warnings from the United States, making many demands on Spain. I shall hear him out, I will hear out Señor Kemp as well. But on occasion I wish to send messages in code and directed to

Señor McKinley's eyes only. A brief appraisal of my true thoughts—
not the lies diplomats exchange."

"In code?" Antonia had never even seen a coded letter. This
whole conversation reminded her of the hints she had gotten from
her father about Aunt Sybil's methods of earning money during
the Civil War in the United States. Being a teenage girl, and
apparently a clever actress, Sybil Maguire had carried messages
several times between the lines in northern Virginia. But I could
never do things like that, she thought . . . I'm just not the sort to
keep secrets . . .

The queen seemed to guess her doubts. "My dear, I haven't
asked you here to make death-defying journeys across two hemi-
spheres with secret messages."

Antonia pulled herself together. "I'm here to help you, ma'am.
In anything that will stop the rebels and put an end to all this talk
of war."

"Exactly so." María Cristina clapped her hands, fan and all. "I
knew I could count on Ysabel's daughter. You will return to that
home of your family's, near Washington, where our Minister de
Lôme may borrow your services when there is a message to be
decoded. You will have half the code. Señor Dupuy de Lôme will
retain the other half. That way there is no likelihood that these
jingoists—*thank* you for your correction—in Washington and New
York will read my personal correspondence with the president and
twist my words to their own purpose, as they have repeatedly
done."

"I see," Antonia said, though she didn't really. "I'm to hold half
the code. But what if it's stolen? I can't be certain of everyone in
Aunt Sybil's house." As a matter of fact, she would have to be
careful around Aunt Sybil herself.

"Because the key, in your case, will be one of several Spanish
books of travel and history." María Cristina looked anxious for the
first time. "These messages may not be frequent. I cannot say as
to that. But you do enjoy reading?"

"Of course. And they will simply fit in with the other books I
carry to Revelstoke. I see now . . ."

The queen was pleased. "They contain no markings. The code
will be in numerals and the correct book indicated at the conclusion
of the message. Every second word will be found in your code."

Like most amateurs dabbling in cryptography, Her Majesty was delighted by her own cleverness.

"I hope I may live up to Your Majesty's faith in me."

"Ysabel's daughter couldn't disappoint me."

Antonia suddenly remembered the young man at the border inspection. Señor Angiolotti. Or was it Angiolillo? A whole chapter of his Spanish history book had been torn out.

"Your Majesty, there may be trouble at customs. Don't the censors remove sections of recent Republican history from our books?"

"But yours will not contain the history of those brief tragic years."

Her Majesty, it seemed, amateur or not, thought of everything. She added now, "You need not concern yourself with your newspaper acquaintance, this Señor Kemp. I am told he arrived at Cádiz in a ship captained by a filibuster named Juan Diego. Advisers of mine are debating whether the man should be taken and hanged while he is in Spain, in spite of his so-called aid to General Weyler."

Antonia felt as if she had been pelted with ice.

"But he saved me, ma'am, and several Red Cross ladies. He brought a shipload of food to the army."

Captain Diego's fate did not particularly interest the regent. She shrugged. "Very well, I'll remind Prime Minister Cánovas. But I can guarantee nothing."

She stood up, and Antonia quickly followed.

"Well now, Antonia, I must let you go. I have a long and I am afraid highly uncomfortable journey ahead. We must both pray for a fair peace. Anything else would be a disaster to all of us."

"Yes, Your Majesty."

"Good. My dear old dragon, the *condesa*, will take you back to your hotel."

Antonia curtsied, touched the queen's fingertips, watched her turn away, her skirts and petticoats rustling over the ground as she walked around the cheerful, bubbling fountain to the interior of the house.

Startled and upset by the new danger to Juan Diego, Antonia wondered how she could ever contact him, warn him to leave Spain at once before the queen's councillors made up their minds to hang him. Her thoughts were interrupted by the *condesa*, who came on like a prison warden with her gruff orders.

"Come, it is growing late, we must go..."

The two women went back through the narrow streets, followed at a discreet distance by two casual strollers that Antonia rightfully assumed were their guards. The *condesa* commented on the historical landmarks of Córdoba but ignored the most interesting thing Antonia saw, a troop of gypsies folding up their carnival games and fortune-telling tables and tents in an open space beyond the hotel too bare to be called a park. Everyone worked, including the children, and at this hour there were no dazzling clothes, no shining satin skirts turned inside out with the fresh side showing. There was no laughter, no flash of fine solid teeth. Everything was dark around them as they melted into the Spanish night like phantoms.

When the *condesa* and Antonia parted at the door of Antonia's room the *condesa* said, "I have some books for you to read on your voyage home. They will teach you much about Spain."

Antonia's fingers shook slightly as she reached for the door latch . . . A fine spy I'll make, she thought . . . I can't even handle a code book . . . She said aloud, "Thank you, I want to learn as much as possible about my ancestors and how they lived. What they stood for. Part of them, at any rate."

One lamp had been lighted by the maid and was smoking a little. It also cast weird, flickering shadows on the whitewashed walls of this room that she called her parlor. The bedroom was dark with a few bars of moonlight sending low black-and-silver patterns of the grillwork across the floor.

Antonia bolted the door behind her, then stood leaning back against it, with the distinct feeling that she was not alone. She had heard a movement, a subtle rubbing of cloth against a wall . . . No, not in this little boxlike room with its small barred window, but in the bedroom, perhaps swallowed up by the shadows of the dark, overpowering Spanish furniture. The bed, the enormous armoire, even the two chairs with their tall lean backs could hide an intruder. Someone waiting to finish off the last of the Guzman-Maguires . . . ?

She edged along the wall, trying to see into the bedroom by the light of the single lamp in the sitting room. Could this have something to do with her becoming the queen's spy? Maybe someone in the queen's confidence had talked, or was a traitor . . .

A man's tall, trim figure was silhouetted against one of the grilled bedroom windows. He was looking out at the dismantled gypsy camp. Antonia opened her mouth to scream—

And then she recognized him, even in the dark.

Juan. He turned, saw her and came toward her out of the moonlight. He was smiling as he held his arms out.

Against all her firm conviction that he belonged to the enemy, she found that her body betrayed her, overwhelmed her. She loved him, there was no fighting *that*. She went into his arms and returned his kiss with a fervor that made them both dizzy. But the instant their mouths parted and he tilted her head to get a better look at her, she remembered what he had to know immediately.

Before she could get her warning out he told her, "Your eyes are enormous, do you know that? And you are—"

"Never mind all that... I heard them talking about hanging you. *Here. In Spain.*"

He smiled, but his fingers tightened on the soft flesh at the sides of her throat. "Who told you?"

She lied quickly. "An old *condesa* who has been acting as our duenna. She knew Mama."

His fingers relaxed. "It was inevitable, I suppose. But Stewart Woodford knows me. He is in Spain now with messages, warnings from the United States. Woodford knows Quincy Kemp and I are here with a positive message. To help..."

She found herself looking anxiously at the window, which had no glass, in the ancient fashion. Though they were on the Continental first floor, one story above the street, there was always a chance someone could overhear them. She allowed herself to enjoy the delight of his lips on her ear, her cheek and throat, and then she could no longer resist asking him in a whisper, "You came here to see someone in the government, the Cortes? Or the prime minister?"

"Among others." He backed away a few inches to look down at her. "You are being very political, sweetheart. Are you interested in Cánovas del Castillo? What do you know about him?"

"I've never even met the prime minister, but you said the message was positive. That sounds good. Is it?"

He kept one arm around her. "We think so. We want the Spanish government to know the majority of the American juntas are willing to settle for autonomy under moderate Spanish rule. Prime Minister Cánovas del Castillo is a conservative. They would prefer Sagasta, who is liberal. But they are willing to talk. They want something similar to the British in Canada and the Antipodes."

And the murderers of my family . . . will they be given amnesty? "What about those who committed crimes against innocent people?"

Obviously, he heard the deeper, implacable note in her voice. He hesitated, chose his words carefully. "Criminals will be punished, of course. By local Cuban courts. Only a few of the wildest anarchists are still preaching their bloody filth. None of the junta members I am acquainted with would support assassins like Angiolillo and his sort."

"Who?"

He was amused by her excitement. "Tana, my sweet, men like that aren't likely to find you, hidden away here in Córdoba."

"No. The name. Who is he?"

"Don't you remember the *fonda* where we stopped to eat that day we ran through the jungle? The *patrón* spoke of an anarchist that some comrades wanted to hire for an assassination in Spain. The *patrón* said he and his friends voted against hiring the anarchist. His name was Angiolillo."

"What is he like?"

Plainly, her interest struck him as excessive.

"I don't know the man *personally*. Slight and young, I think. Dark. I saw a sketch of him some weeks ago when he was chased out of the Austro-Hungarian Empire. Probably he is hiding in France or Italy, waiting for his next . . . assignment."

"I think he has found it," she said slowly. If the juntas, or any part of them were back of Angiolillo's entrance into Spain, then the target must be the queen regent, or the little king, or someone high in the government. In any event such a crime would only make the present situation a thousand times worse. And now that she had met María Cristina, her interest was far more personal than it might have been a few weeks ago.

CHAPTER
EIGHTEEN

SHE LOOKED up at him, studying his face and every line of it.

"Darling, how would you feel if you knew this Angiolillo were already in Spain, under another name?"

She couldn't mistake his surprise and more importantly, his anger.

"But that would be disastrous for us, for our purposes."

"For *your* purpose?"

"Of course. When the Yankee president was murdered at the end of the American Civil War it provoked such fury there was no chance for a just peace or a reconstruction of the southern states. The same would happen here."

"Then, Juanito, we must stop him, and they . . . his targets . . . will owe you their lives for the warning."

He shook her. "What the devil do you mean? What do you know about this Angiolillo? It is Miguel Angiolillo you are talking about?"

"Caris and I stood behind him in the customs office at Irun."

"But you couldn't have. He isn't fool enough to use his own name."

She was pulling him into the sitting room by his wrist. "He called himself Angiolotti."

"There may be a hundred Angiolottis, all innocent, in Spain at this minute."

"Perhaps he counts on that to protect him. But he has a book whose nameplate reads Angiolillo. And he fits your description."

"Are you *sure?*"

"I'll get Caris to repeat it. But first I want the Condesa de Montemayor to hear this. She can get a message through to the queen."

He was already unbolting the door for her. She rushed into the silent, dimly lighted hall with its Moorish archway at either end of the whitewashed walls, then ran under the nearest archway and up the stone steps to wake the *condesa*.

The queen's friend, it turned out, was still up, sitting at a walnut desk writing with an old-fashioned quill pen. She carried the pen to the door and kept tickling her cheek with the aging feather while Antonia poured out her story in bits and pieces.

"An assassin is loose here. Captain Diego came to warn me. He thought I might reach the right people sooner. Caris and I saw him at Irun, he traveled under the name of Angiolotti..."

"Captain Diego?" The *condesa* remained calm, but the goose quill stopped moving.

"No, *no*. The assassin. His real name is Angiolillo. A few, a very *few* of the Cuban rebels may have hired him." The condesa kept staring at her as she hurried on. "What other reason would this assassin have for entering Spain under a different name?"

"A thousand reasons." But seeing Antonia's desperation she added in her matter-of-fact way, "I'll talk to this Diego. I have very little faith in your sister-in-law's powers of observation, however. An addlepate if ever I saw one."

Still, the *condesa* evidently shared Antonia's worry. She followed Antonia down the stairs to Antonia's sitting room, where she introduced herself to Juan Diego and Antonia went to rout Caris out of the wooden tub of warm water she was submerged in. For a minute or two it looked as though Caris would refuse to leave her liquid cocoon, but Antonia nodded urgently and Caris dismissed the maids, who went out carrying the clay pots with which they had been pouring water over Caris' lily-white shoulders.

"What is it, Tana? You do look as if you knew something absolutely awful." Her voice raised as an idea occurred to her. "They've arranged an audience for you! When do we leave for San Sebastián? I love resorts like that. They're wonderfully adapted for meeting old acquaintances—"

"Never mind that. Come with me. Where's your robe? I'll get something to cover your hair." It was rather charmingly skewered on top of her head, and Antonia threw one of Caris' lace mantillas over it while Caris got into a quilted satin robe and sashed it tightly to accentuate her slender waist.

"I can't wait," Caris bubbled. "Is it someone from the palace? Male or female?"

She fell from these heights of anticipation when she walked into Antonia's room. "You!" Apparently this was addressed to Juan Diego. Caris abruptly turned around with every intention of sweeping out again. The *condesa's* deep, crackling voice stopped her.

"Señora Maguire, what did you observe about a young man named Angiolillo?"

"I never heard of him. Really, Tana, did you have to take me from my bath just to ask me stupid questions?"

Diego stepped forward then. "Señora, forgive us, but it may be a very serious matter. Did you see a man named Miguel Angiolillo at the customs barrier in Irun? A young man, dark, with a sallow complexion."

Light dawned. "Oh, the gentleman who called himself Angiolotti. Yes. What about him?"

The *condesa* asked casually, "Was the description the captain just gave correct?"

Caris looked at Antonia, reached behind her and dropped into one of the hard, high-backed chairs. She licked her lips and tried to think back. "He was just the way the captain described him."

"Where was he going? Did you hear that?" the captain asked.

She nodded. "While Tana was unfastening our cases for the inspector I heard the other inspector ask him. He said Bilbao."

Antonia put in, hopefully, "But not San Sebastián..." She felt stupid when both the *condesa* and Juan looked at her and the *condesa* said, "San Sebastián is only a skip and a jump from Bilbao. And very close to Irun."

"But the queen, she's nowhere near—"

The *condesa* cleared her throat. "There is the little king. He might well be the target. A child who represents Spain's future."

"What about the prime minister?" Juan Diego put in. "Señor Cánovas is unpopular in the Western Hemisphere. Many Cubans and Yankees too blame him for General Weyler's excesses."

The *condesa* said crisply, "He is at a spa in the western Pyrenees and should be safe."

Diego reminded her, "If my geography is correct, that region of the Pyrenees is also near San Sebastián. The queen, His Majesty and the prime minister should all be warned."

"To be sure, to be sure. Leave that to me. Meanwhile"—the *condesa*'s long, haughty face softened ever so slightly—"Her Majesty and the Spanish government will not forget what it owes you for your warning, *capitán*. You will stay in the hotel while we proceed about your warning?" She held out her hand and Juan, the supposed "filibuster ex-pirate," bowed over it. At the same time he added, "I should warn you, *condesa*, that my sympathies are still with the people of Cuba and a liberal home rule."

The *condesa*'s wrinkled mouth widened in an unexpected grimace that threatened to be a smile. "We understand each other perfectly, *capitán*. You will forgive me if I hurry off. There are messages to send, plans to be made. Above all, there is the little king to be protected."

Caris watched her go, then reverted to character. "I should be angry with you all for taking me from my bath, but since my observations may have saved the royal family, I suppose I must forgive you." She got up and extended her own hand to Diego, who followed through, smiled, raised it and kissed her knuckles. He also escorted Caris back to her room and fortunately, considering Antonia's annoyance and vivid imagination, returned almost at once.

Antonia tried not to show her jealousy, but her tone gave her away as she asked him abruptly, "Where is your dear friend?"

"Friend?"

"If Quincy Kemp knows about the assassin I'd be surprised if he hadn't warned him already."

She saw his mouth tighten, then, watching her carefully, he softened and held out his arms.

"Sit down, sweetheart. We'll both sit down. Here." He had maneuvered her onto the hard divan that was more like a rigid settle. "What's this? Mutiny in the ranks?"

She looked away, at the bare white wall across the room, at the beamed ceiling, anywhere but at him. "Not mutiny. It seems we aren't really even in the same boat."

"Aren't we? Feels to me as though we are closer than we were when I left Havana."

She faced that. "All right, Juan. You did remind the *condesa* that you were still on the side of the rebels. Then are you sorry you may have saved the life of the queen and of the little boy, the king?"

"No, darling. And you should know better. My beliefs don't justify murders, assassinations, hired killers. All I want for my homeland—and yours, incidentally—is self-rule with ties to Spain. Look at me. You can't seriously think I approve the monstrous thing that was done to your family."

"No..."

"Then why do you behave as though we have no future together? We're going to spend our lives together... well, aren't we?"

"It was you who said when the rebellion is over. You have so much responsibility." A glorious idea occurred to her. She brightened then. "Unless you're sincere in working for the Spanish army and the captain-general of Cuba. That would make things very clear and simple."

He shook his head. "Would you ever respect me if I betrayed everything I believe in? Betrayed my mother and sister?"

"But you would defend the people who murdered my family..."

His hand had been caressing her cheek, but his finger flexed at this.

"No. I wanted to kill them myself when I heard. I want them caught and punished as much as you do. You will not be alone when you return to Cuba. I intend to see that you are guarded at all times during their capture and trial."

She remembered then the queen's commission, which he knew nothing about and which she was obliged to keep secret, even from this man that she loved. "As soon as Cousin Rafael Guzman reads Papa's will to Caris and me I'll be living at Revelstoke in Virginia."

Still holding her, he pulled away to stare at her in surprise. "Well, thank God for that. At least until sentence is carried out on the assassins."

She was relieved; he seemed to feel it was natural for her to be in the United States. She'd dreaded the lies she would have to tell him, or the lie she had to live with while she had those histories of Spain in her safekeeping.

"There's little to take me back to Havana just yet, except to make a deposition when they capture the guitarist and the others. Of course they'll have to prove he was involved, I realize that."

"Carlos Melina is involved," he said grimly. "Quincy has information that a lottery peddler and a beggar in the plaza witnessed a meeting between Melina and one of the wanted tobacco hands immediately after you and your family left for the *merienda* that morning. The worker left on a mare, headed for the crossroads. And your caretaker, Pablo, has run away."

"*Madre de Dios,* I hate that Melina," she whispered. "I'd do anything to destroy that man. *I don't care what I have to do to destroy him.*"

He brought her nearer. "Don't think of it now, my love. Think of the future, when all of this bloodshed is over."

She turned in his arms and kissed him, anxious to blot out the horror that the memory of the guitarist had raised. For a moment he was all gentle as he returned her kiss, then the heat of their desire took over their bodies as it had in the past, and he lifted her, his mouth still on hers, and carried her across the room to her austere bedchamber. Her arms were locked around his neck and she clung to him.

"Love me, love me and make me forget."

Forget . . . in this passionate act, in this mimosa-scented darkness, at least blur memories of her beloved dead, push away that in the queen's service she would be working against her lover's cause when she returned to Virginia . . .

He laid her down on the hard ancient bed and began to undress her slowly with patient fingers whose knowing touch aroused her whole body. She reached around his broad shoulders, let her fingers move slowly under his seaman's jacket, under his shirt. The act of disrobing had been so seductive that when they found themselves flesh to flesh he entered her at once. They climaxed together, laughing in delight at the perfection of their union.

"I love you so much..." she whispered as they lay there afterward, tingling with the aftermath of their rapid, hungry lovemaking.

He turned his head. His lips lingered on her nose, then each of her eyelids. When he raised his head she opened her eyes and said with a kind of astonishment, "I never stopped loving you. Not even... not once."

"Did you ever want to stop?"

She said quickly, "Never."

"I fell in love with you the day you staged an assault on Quincy Kemp's office." He smiled. "Do you know, I had never seen anything so lovely in my life, and I have seen a few continents and quite a few women."

She wasn't sure she liked so much the latter part of that and reminded him, "That night in Aunt Sybil's garden, you seemed to like and hate me all at the same time."

He shrugged. "I hated what I thought you were that night...a deceptive tease. Deception. I guess I dislike that more than anything..." He looked at her, running a finger along a strand of her hair. "That is another reason why I despised that guitarist who signaled to your family's murderers. He wasn't even an honest assassin...sweetheart, don't look that way. You are everything I ever wanted in my life. That is the truth. If we must wait, we will wait. Tana, there is only you. There will only be you."

She went into his arms again, holding tight—

They were jarred back to the present by an imperative pounding on the door. Antonia scrambled across him, his hands closed around her naked waist.

"Sweetheart, careful. Be more calm."

"Let me go, it must be Caris, she can't see you here." She wrenched herself out of his clasp, started to run. He laughed and threw her gown at her. "Better wear something." She stopped, got into her gown and tried to button it as she stumbled to the sitting room, where she demanded angrily, "Who's there?"

"Child? Open the door. Surely, you know my voice by this time."

This was almost as bad as Caris. But at least the Condesa de Montemayor wouldn't rush into her rooms without permission. Antonia opened the door a few inches.

"I'm not dressed, ma'am."

"That is neither here nor there. Take this with you."

Antonia stared at her, finding it curious that the *condesa* hadn't sent a maid if this was a mere errand. Then she saw the handful of books, six of them, in the crook of the *condesa*'s arm and understood. She accepted the heavy books with their marbled covers and gilt-edged pages.

"Thank you. I'll take good care of them."

The *condesa* nodded. "We expect you to. Go with God." She added this in her salty way that in other circumstances would have made Antonia laugh.

Antonia called after her, "Have you sent the warning, ma'am? Are they safe?"

"The telegraph is useful, my child. Her Majesty and the king are safe. We are still trying to reach Señor Cánovas at the spa."

She studied the books in her hands: *A History of Spain in Her Days of Glory*, *A Short History of Imperial Spain* (an exceedingly heavy tome), a history of the Alhambra and King Boabdil, and three others of similar nature. She had no idea which of the six was to be used as her half of the code. She didn't even know how the code was to be operated, and she rather hoped that no one would ever explain it to her.

Hugging the books to her breasts, she shot the bolt on the door, leaned against it and closed her eyes, so nervous her fingers began to ache as they clutched the innocent-looking books.

A shadow crossed her face and she opened her eyes. Juan Diego was there in front of her, dressed now and watching her with concern.

"Are you all right, sweetheart? You look odd. You mustn't let that woman frighten you. Was she a friend of your mother's?"

"They knew each other when mother was a girl."

He reached for the heavy books.

"Here. Let me help you. Why in God's name did she saddle you with all this? Surely you have books of your own."

Without thinking she moved to take back the books, and as she did the books slipped out of her hands and hit the floor with heavy thuds, though nothing, she was relieved to see, fell out of them. Whatever the code, it seemed to be part of the books themselves.

A baffled Juan piled the books up and placed them in her arms. He looked at her closely. "What is it, sweetheart? Are you afraid that old woman will find me here? I'll leave as soon as I see you are all right. Is it something to do with the books? Do they mean that much to you?"

She fumbled for the first excuse he might believe. "The *condesa* thinks they belonged to my mother. When I keep them near me, I feel better, as if she were somehow close."

"Oh? I didn't know your mother was a history scholar."

"Well, she *was*." It seemed inadequate but so emphatic he had to accept it.

"I'll go and let you sleep." He kissed her forehead and when she didn't respond, he went around her to the door.

She recovered to say quickly, "I'll see if it's safe."

She set the books down on the divan and unbolted the door. The hall remained deserted, dimly lighted by a lamp on a taboret in the Moorish archway.

Just as he was leaving she touched his cheek briefly with her lips, then before he could react she closed the door and bolted it.

I'm lying to him, she thought . . . I love him more than anyone, but I'm going to be a spy for people against what he believes in . . .

In the morning she met him having breakfast with Caris in the sunlit patio of the hotel.

Caris explained with evident amusement, "I told Capitán Diego you were having breakfast in your room. Naturally, it wouldn't be proper for him to join you there, so here we are. The sugar buns are very good. And the orange slices. The poor *capitán* doesn't take chocolate but it's too late now."

"What a pity." Antonia took the chair on the other side of her sister-in-law and unfolded the soft, much-laundered napkin.

Juan seemed undisturbed by her sulky mood. He gave her a smile and his lively dark eyes reminded her of their lovemaking the night before. "Did you sleep well?"

"Very well, thank you. I read myself to sleep."

The insufferable Caris took up the conversation there, so that Antonia's chilly attitude was scarcely noticed.

"Tana, Señor Guzman will explain Papa Maguire's will this morning. Don't be late."

Antonia pretended she hadn't heard. She accepted the tray of breakfast from a trim, elderly Spaniard and began to drink her chocolate while she watched Caris and Juan Diego over her cup.

It was Caris, of course, who first saw the new man when he arrived a few minutes later. But to Antonia's surprise she said, "That man, what's he doing here?" Since Caris seldom referred in a derogatory way to any man, Antonia set her cup down and looked around.

She didn't know why the sight of Quincy Kemp should surprise her. She had known he was traveling with Juan, but here he was, with his good-natured, animated Irish face, toddling toward the three of them on the patio.

Thinking of her secret agreement with the queen, she knew she would encounter Quincy often at Washington and Virginia receptions, and it might be helpful to María Cristina if she kept on good terms with this too friendly American columnist-spy.

She put on her best smile. "Good morning, Señor Kemp."

The columnist took the hand she offered and shook it, but for once his light easy charm was absentminded. He gave Caris a nod, ignoring her aloofness, and spoke over the women's heads to Juan Diego. "Great God, man ... excuse me, ladies, but Juan, wait till you get this. I've just heard a story that's going to shake every country in the civilized world. And I'm the first Western Hemisphere newsman to hear it. In fact, I'll be there for first person reports in a very few days. So this is farewell for the nonce, as the ladies' novels say."

Everyone stared at him.

Juan seemed to suspect something. To Antonia's close observation he looked alarmingly serious.

"What is this earthshaking story?"

"Assassination."

Antonia felt sick. "No. Not the queen. Or her little son ..."

Juan reached for Quincy Kemp's arm, gave it a hard wrench. "Who?"

"Spain's prime minister. Cánovas del Castillo. Poor devil had just returned from church, was just sitting there, minding his business, reading the paper—a nice point of irony if it was my column—

and this little pipsqueak shoots him three times. The cafe proprietor telegraphed me."

"Is he dead?" Antonia barely got the words out. Her mouth was dry.

"Died in a matter of minutes. As I understand it, right in front of his wife. So I'm on my way to that damned spa. They must have captured the assassin. They seemed to know who he is. Named Angiolillo, or some such."

He left them staring at each other as he rustled off, jingling the Spanish coins in his pocket.

Caris spoke first. "It seems pretty evident to me that this assassin was hired by the Cuban rebels, no matter who he is."

Antonia had been drawing on the tablecloth with her fork. She looked at Juan. "What do you think?"

He shook his head. "It is going to be bad for the Cuban cause. They would be the last to order such a thing."

Antonia had to wonder about that. The Cubans hated Cánovas, the man who had ordered "Butcher" Weyler into Cuba. She suspected it was wishful thinking that made Juan cling to his hope.

Meanwhile, the horrible act had made Antonia more than ever aware of what she owed her family and María Cristina. The sooner she made herself available to translate the queen's code messages to President McKinley, the better.

She turned her attention back to the tablecloth, but she couldn't seem to avoid Juan. She watched his dark, lean, well-shaped fingers close to hers across the cloth.

. . . We may meet, and kiss, and pretend, my darling, but how can I marry you after this. Isn't there, after all, too much bloodshed between us . . . ?

CHAPTER
NINETEEN

$\mathbf{R}$AFAEL GUZMAN cleared his throat while his fingers locked and unlocked in front of him on his desk. He studied his hands as if the answer to everything lay in those stubby fingernails.

"Cousin Antonia tells me she is more or less aware of Señor Patrick Maguire's intentions when he executed his will. This relieves us all and, if I may say so, keeps us all good friends. You agree, Antonia?"

"Oh, certainly." She was airy about it. This sort of brusque indifference made it easier to avoid the memories that hovered so close and so painfully behind her offhand manner.

Guzman flipped the pages of Patrick Maguire's will.

"Then, if I may simplify..."

Caris was obviously wild with curiosity. "Please. The point of it. How is the estate divided?"

"Señor Maguire, if I may phrase it so, followed the age-old family tradition, probably in deference to the wishes of our dear cousin, Doña Ysabel."

"And that was?" Caris prompted.

"The entire Guzman estates, including small properties in Seville and a share of the Guzman Córdoba mausoleum, are transmitted from father to son, in this case, from mother and father to son."

"But—"

Rafael Guzman waved the papers, slightly annoyed by Caris' eagerness.

"And to the son's heirs and issue."

His dark eyes twinkled as he proceeded cautiously. "I am assured that Felipe Patricio Maguire y Guzman had no issue, as of the moment of his demise. But this leaves his heir, who is indisputably Doña Caris."

Much relieved, Caris sat back, out of the hot sun that slashed across the room in this August afternoon. She did not look at her sister-in-law.

Antonia had known, almost from the day of Felipe's birth, that he would be the Guzman heir. She was amused by Caris' relief and genuinely surprised when the solicitor turned his attention to her.

"As for the Maguire end of the estate, there are certain American properties and investments, dollar investments. They total something just under one hundred thousand United States dollars, as of April tenth of this year, you will be happy to know, dear cousin."

Antonia had known she would receive a handsome annuity of some kind, but to be given the dollar investments, at a time when the dollar was moving higher every day, was unexpected and proof that her father had thought well of her, even when he was faced with the ancient privileges of the male heir.

Rafael Guzman went on. "Stock in numerous corporations, Cuban sugar, cigars, shipping... but these are in dollar currency. Also the estate called Revelstoke. The American percentage of the Maguire fortune goes to you, cousin Antonia, with the exception of the ten thousand in United States government bonds which become the property of Señor Maguire's sister, Sybil Maguire Revelstoke. Señor Maguire also asks that his sister be permitted the use of the estate for her lifetime, if you so desire, upon the understanding that you, his daughter, Antonia, will have her own apartment in Revelstoke at any time she chooses."

"We are very fond of each other," Antonia assured her cousin.

"We have no problems about living in the same house. Heaven knows it's big enough."

"Excellent. But naturally, a beautiful young lady like you will be marrying at any time. You will want your own home. It is a pity about Revelstoke, it would have been quite perfect as your home."

"You need not concern yourself, cousin. I have no plans for marriage..."

He looked at her but she had spoken so firmly and quietly he could not argue.

Caris spoke up. "You haven't mentioned the Palacio Guzman in Havana. Or the hacienda in Camagüez Province."

"The hacienda is yours, Doña Caris, as part of the Guzman estate."

"But the *palacio* is also Guzman."

Frowning, Rafael consulted the sheets under his hands.

"The Palacio Guzman... ah, yes, the *palacio* becomes the property of Patrick Maguire's two children and their heirs. Equally." He gave them his expansive, avuncular smile. "It is fortunate that you two young ladies are friends. It makes it so much simpler."

"I still don't see why—" Caris began and broke off to start again. "I mean to say, it *is* a Guzman property, after all."

Guzman blinked but avoided a direct answer. "Let me see, after the bequests to servants, associates and several relations, including the ten thousand dollars to Sybil Maguire Revelstoke, your estate, Doña Caris, will amount to upward of two million."

"*Pesetas?*"

"Dollars."

Caris' eyes opened wide.

Antonia was impressed too. She remembered Sybil's stories of her early days with Patrick Maguire, their poverty in the Old Country, the miserable voyage across the Atlantic as steerage passengers, their near starvation before the war began in Virginia... "Think of what father accomplished in one lifetime. It's incredible. He truly was a great man."

Rafael Guzman reminded her gently, "With some help from the Guzmans and Pontalvos, my dear."

"But he was a millionaire when he met mother."

"True."

Caris clapped her hands. She had decided to make the best of

220 TANA MAGUIRE

her two million. In dollar value. "If you are sailing to the United States, Tana, then I had better return to Cuba and see to my properties."

Antonia felt sure Caris' first task would be to make over the Palacio Guzman into her property. No matter. Antonia knew her own duty lay at Revelstoke with Aunt Sybil's Washington friends. She owed it to her dead and martyred family. She owed it to the queen, who had given her trust as well as this important commission.

When she met Juan an hour later he asked no questions about her father's will but assumed that she would return with him to Cuba in the *Baracoa*.

She knew she could never stay with him during weeks at sea without betraying that she felt she could never marry him. Worse, there was every likelihood that his love, which she had never doubted, and hers would have her marrying him anyway. She felt terrible to see Juan's upset and confusion at her decision, and tried all manner of explanations, well aware of how false they were.

"The truth is, you are letting outside events ruin our life together," he told her in a voice whose edginess she had never heard before. She avoided looking at him. She might have coped with the angry look in his eyes, but there was pain too, and doubt. He must think she no longer loved him . . . All the same, he was right. Outside events were the culprits.

The Condesa de Montemayor had arranged for her brother's wife, Señora Villedo, a shy, round-faced little woman of amiable disposition, to act as Antonia's duenna on the steamer's next trip across the Atlantic, but Juan insisted on escorting both ladies to Cádiz, where Captain Villedo had anchored after circling Spain from the Bay of Biscay.

Antonia's farewell to her sister-in-law had been a relief to both women. Before returning to Cuba to her inheritance, Caris would see her uncle, General Weyler in Madrid, where he was being feted by the conservatives for his "chastisement of the Cuban rebels." Antonia had no doubt Caris' first words to her uncle would be an animated description of the Guzman fortune. No matter. It was worth it, just to be free of her company.

But the hot dusty trip through Andalusia in late summer was

made more uncomfortable by the now painfully cool relations between her and Juan. He left her and Señora Villedo alone whenever
possible and was as scrupulously polite as any Spanish grandee.
The señora remarked on his excellent manners the day they boarded
the *Santa Cruz* and said good-bye to them.

"What a charming man! I'd heard he was once a filibusterer.
Virtually a pirate. But surely that is not possible."

Antonia murmured something unintelligible. She couldn't help
noting how Juan kissed her hand in a polite farewell, with no more
passion than he'd shown when he touched Señora Villedo's stout
hand. He even gave the señora a warm smile, conspicuously absent
when he spoke to Tana. And as she thought such things she knew
she was being unfair. After all, it was she who had cooled matters
between them.

He left them quickly, jumping off the gangplank to the dock,
giving a distant salute to Captain Villedo, who had just come up
on deck.

The *Santa Cruz* sailed with the tide, and Antonia stood on the
afterdeck with both elbows on the rail watching the bare masts of
the *Baracoa* until she could no longer make out even the foremast
of the little sailing vessel. She was deep in her depression when
the stout, gruff first officer of the *Santa Cruz* stopped behind her
and cleared his throat.

She turned, putting on a smile, then was startled as he stuffed
a piece of paper into her gloved hand and blurted out, "Not my
notion, Doña Antonia. Given to me. Very insistent."

She unfolded the creased and wrinkled paper:

> Meet you at the stile beyond the Revelstoke garden. I promise
> you more romance and less talk than last time we met at the
> stile.

She thought... *My darling, I'll meet you, but it's no use...*
She burst into tears, which was all very confusing to the first
officer.

After two seasick, heartsick days in her narrow, coffinlike state-
room, Antonia came out on deck to join the ever-cheerful Señora
Villedo and the quiet, efficient and handsome Captain Villedo. The

captain's looks confounded her. He certainly did not resemble his
sister, the *condesa*, that basilisk with a core of humanity.

The captain was a competent man, not very talkative, but his
wife more than made up for it, and in many ways helped to cheer
Antonia up so that she could take some pleasure in the great, gray
Atlantic with its awesome power and expanse.

She still had Juan Diego's note in her pocket (often in her hand
when she was alone), and she told herself it was a sort of talisman.
Maybe one day, when the bloody rebellion had been put down,
she and Juan might marry, after all... Meanwhile, though nerve-
wracking, there was the idea of possessing half of a royal code that
would aid the royal cause.

She even told herself she was a born spy... Who would imagine
that pretty, protected Tana Maguire had anything to do with secret
messages passed between Her Majesty in Europe and the United
States president in another hemisphere? No one had guessed her
mission so far, even those most intimate with her, like Caris who
left her still complaining that she hadn't met with the queen, as
she had promised, and Juan, who probably would never believe
her capable of such deception. If she continued to be herself, the
Tana Maguire everyone in Washington and Virginia was familiar
with could be quite a success as a spy... Well, why not, I come
by my talent honestly, she told herself. I'll bet anything that Aunt
Sybil is a lobbyist or spy for some political interests. Maybe it
helped make up for being married to that unctuous Uncle Bernard,
an underhanded sneak who would love to have gotten familiar with
his niece. Antonia remembered how at the age of thirteen she had
to threaten him with telling Aunt Sybil about his advances. After
that he only smirked but never tried anything more than a friendly
squeeze around her waist. She knew from their curled lips and
rolled eyes that her school friends had also experienced his advances, but he still remained the squire of Revelstoke, and much
sought after by women over forty...

Meanwhile, Antonia studied the six books given to her by the
condesa and found not one mark on any page that might be considered part of a code. She could only assume that her friend
Enrique Dupuy de Lôme, the Spanish minister to Washington
who looked a little like an operatic Mephistopheles, would explain
her half of the code, since he possessed the other half.

* * *

By the time Aunt Sybil and Uncle Bernard had collected Antonia at the Baltimore dock and taken her away to the New York-Washington train, Antonia was in reasonably good spirits. Her aunt seemed to have recovered reasonably well from the blow of her brother's death, though she did look thinner and older, a bit more nervous. How could it be otherwise? She seemed to have turned to politics, as always, to blur the painful memories, and she could hardly wait to move her niece away from the dead and into the lively realm of politics.

"I know I should be wearing solid black for Patrick and the family, but Paddy was always so understanding; he would know that complete mourning puts off politicians. I think white with black bands and my bonnet and veil will be appropriate. As for you, dear, you really look like a crow in black. What about lavender. To match your eyes?" She added after an instant's hesitation, "I know you don't give a fig for politics, but you can do wonders in shades of lavender and violet. That is, if you want to sway anyone's votes." She gave her pleasant, tinkling laugh, as if to say she was well aware of how little her niece cared about swaying the opinions of politicians.

Antonia surprised her by the quick assurance, "I'd love to sway men's politics. Especially about the Cuban problem. Mainly to remind them that what happens in Cuba is none of their business in the States."

Her aunt and uncle exchanged glances. Uncle Bernard suggested in his jovial way, "Except that more flies are captured by honey than by vinegar. Not that anyone expects our little girl to delve into sordid political deals, but let's say it's advice from an old campaigner."

Antonia wondered just what campaigns he had in mind. Certainly nothing to do with running for office. Bernard Revelstoke was much more successful behind the scenes. Antonia sat in the newly spruced-up Revelstoke carriage facing Bernard, studying his slightly plump, good-humored face with its small, close-set eyes and heavy lips. He might be useful. She had no doubt he was involved in numerous Cuban affairs. If she played out the line very carefully she might learn something useful that she could use against murderous rebels.

She smiled at him, putting on an innocent, eager, wide-eyed
expression.

"Uncle, you're right. You know so much about things like that.
I'll have to get your advice before I dabble in politics. Or the stock
market. I'll bet you know all about stocks and bonds."

This suggested a sour point, and Bernard Revelstoke lowered
his voice, as though Asa Mangum, the elderly black coachman,
could not hear him despite that he was only a few feet away in the
open carriage.

"I understand that we . . . that is, your aunt, was left ten thousand
dollars in your father's will. That's a goodly sum. A very pleasant
little nest egg to build on. Of course, it was not to be compared
with the Guzman estate that he seemed bound and determined to
leave away from the family entirely."

"Bernard," his wife said gently.

He went on, trying to smooth away any misapprehension. "It
should have gone to you, Tana. No, Sybil, I *will* say it. Young
Hastings was shocked when he heard, and I can hardly blame him.
These medieval Spanish notions of male primacy. Most unfair."

It might have seemed unfair if Antonia hadn't always known it
was so . . . Felipe was the last of the Guzman-Pontalvo connections,
and Caris, for good or ill, was his widow. "Personally," she told
her relations, "I feel that Father was extremely generous to me.
All my estate is in dollars. All the stocks, the government bonds,
the bonds on various companies. I still haven't examined it all."

"We can help you there," her uncle told her. "When you feel
the need of sound advice I flatter myself that my own experience
may be of some service, wouldn't you say, my dear?"

Aunt Sybil said, "Mmm. Is that the Abernethy boy in the horse-
less carriage that just passed us? That foolish child will break his
neck yet."

Antonia smiled at the way she had turned off her husband's
question. When they left the Washington-Alexandria highway and
the horses cantered along the estate road she felt a quickening of
her pulse. She had always loved Revelstoke. Although she knew
her aunt and uncle would like to have had it left in their own name,
she was glad it would ultimately belong to her. There was no bad
memory connected with this estate, as there was, of course, with
the Havana *palacio*.

* * *

The first place Antonia visited after being settled in her own bed-sitting room was the old, warped stile at the far end of the garden. And she went there once every day afterward. Sitting on the top step, peeling off the weathered gray slivers of wood, she thought of Juan, and wondered if they would ever ride together across the green pasture beyond the garden and the stile. A small brook wound its way through the pasture and a herd of milk cows had congregated at one bend in the brook about half a mile away. In her younger days she had often wandered along the path that bordered the brook. Would she ever show Juan that walk, either under bright blue skies or caught in an exhilarating downpour?

She remembered the strange, solemn grandeur of Córdoba with its high, dry air and compared it to this moist, humid section of Virginia. Each was beautiful in its own different way and she loved them both, but at this moment she thought of Revelstoke as life, Havana as purgatory and Córdoba as death.

When she turned back toward the house one autumn morning two weeks after her arrival, still without having heard from Juan, or from anybody about the code, she saw Aunt Sybil motioning to her from the terrace. At the same time she glimpsed Uncle Bernard and a blond young man busily studying a map in Bernard's study.

"I'm sure I know that man," Antonia began as she joined her aunt. "He's a friend of Captain Diego's."

"I know. Captain Felix Leidner. A fairly well-known filibuster. But that's just between you and me."

"Everyone in Cuba knows that. There's no point in our protecting him here. He's among friends when he wanders around this country. It's Cuba that would like to get hold of him." She looked back toward the study, adding, "I used to consider myself one of his friends, but that was before my family was murdered by his friends..."

"Tana," Aunt Sybil began, "don't be bitter. He is actually a likable, well-meaning young man. It's simply that he believes in the cause of the Cuban people."

"Oh? I think he believes in what he is paid for. Especially when he's paid in dollars."

Sybil, older and more experienced in such matters, shrugged off quick judgments. "It is not a matter we can prove or disprove, dear. Come along, something very important has come up. I don't pretend to understand it, but they want you."

"Who?"

"Well, Lloyd Hastings, for one."

Antonia made a face. "How exciting. Where is he?"

"In the breakfast parlor. Across from the dining room. Now, take a deep breath and don't let anything surprise you."

"Well, I can't quite see Lloyd as very important to me these days."

They were passing the closed hall door of Uncle Bernard's study, but even in the shadowy recesses of the hall Antonia could see that her aunt was upset.

"But, my dear, it's *important* that you work together. Why do you dislike him so much? You very nearly married him last year."

Antonia stopped abruptly. "I'll make a bet with you, Aunt Sybil, that Lloyd will marry my sister-in-law as soon as her year of mourning ends."

"You are joking."

"Not at all. He was obviously taken with her when they met in Havana, and that was *before* he knew she would inherit the Guzman estates. I always felt that my greatest attraction for him was his belief that I was an heiress. Now he really has a rich woman, and one who finds him attractive."

Her aunt was silent a moment, then: "Do you mind? Emotionally, I mean."

"To be honest, I deserve it. I never loved him. I never loved anyone but . . . anyway, I knew I was being unfair to Lloyd." Antonia remembered too well how that betrothal had begun. "Every girl in my senior class had her eye on him and he seemed to prefer me. It flattered my infernal conceit. And, of course, on the surface he was a credit to any girl—handsome, close to the president, good manners. He had, as they say, everything. *But* he was so stuffy and boring.

"Hush, I hope they can't hear you. Ah, luckily they've got the door closed."

The music room door was open, however, and Antonia could see the long terrace windows across the room. Uncle Bernard sauntered past. The breakfast parlor was two rooms away. She said out loud, but mostly to herself, "I hope Lloyd has closed the windows."

"What on earth do you mean?"

Antonia shook her head. Aunt Sybil knocked on the breakfast room door. Lloyd opened it a few inches, looking a bit owlish, with one eye visible.

"Did you find her?"

Aunt Sybil nodded and urged Antonia forward.

Antonia resented all this secrecy on Lloyd Hastings' order. She held back like a balky mule until the door opened wider and she saw the man seated across the room. She knew that stocky, serious man with the forbidding air of infallibility.

President William McKinley.

On catching her eye, he smiled, the dictatorial facade vanished and she saw a kindly man whose devotion to his epileptic wife was near-legendary. The powerful chief executive might be the man Queen María Cristina had asked her to act as liaison for, but the man she wanted to help was this man with the rather sad, gentle smile.

Lloyd shut the door behind her, closing out Aunt Sybil. Apparently Sybil understood, but Antonia didn't much like it that Lloyd Hastings was included in the secret correspondence between the queen and the president. He might mean well, but she wasn't at all sure he could be trusted to keep a secret.

She looked around the little room as she offered the president her hand. "Sir, I thought Señor Dupuy de Lôme would be here."

Lloyd and the president obviously had an understanding on this matter. The president waved to Lloyd. "Explain our difficulty to the young lady, Hastings."

Lloyd came forward with his irritatingly officious air of knowing everything. "Now, Antonia, listen very carefully. I don't pretend to understand why Her Majesty chose an inexperienced young woman like you to participate in anything that may settle national policy for two nations..."

Pompous and patronizing, as always.

She said evenly, "But you were the one who encouraged me to ask an audience with the queen."

"An audience, yes. But such a complicated matter... forgive me, Antonia... shouldn't be left in the hands of someone so young—"

"Señor Dupuy will help me. He's very responsible and he's loyal to Her Majesty. I also *trust* him."

With a little cough the president put in, "I'm afraid that is our difficulty, Miss Maguire. We have received a message in answer to our man Woodford's audience with Her Majesty. It seems to be important. Obviously, she prefers that it should not come to us through regular channels."

She could only stare at them, waiting for one of them to explain.

"For some reason," Lloyd said, "this Dupuy de Lôme took it into his head to visit Montreal this very week. Or so the Spanish department tells us. And because of the nature of this business we can't tell anyone why we need him. We can't even reach the fellow."

Antonia was sure all the color left her face. She dropped into one of the little captain's chairs around the lace-covered oblong table. "Please don't look to me. I've no idea how to decode anything."

"See here, Tana . . . Antonia, you must help us. This may be a matter of life and death."

She laughed angrily. "What a cliché. And I resent your trying to frighten me."

The president took over. "Miss Maguire, it is quite possible that if we do not reply to Her Majesty within a matter of hours we will have forfeited our chance of setting the Cuban dispute peaceably."

"But the queen told me she didn't want war."

"I'm afraid the queen is not the final authority in the Spanish government. They're a democracy too. And the assassination of their prime minister seems to have set the whole country on fire. They're in a real fury against us. And against Cuba. The people who count are saying there will be no appeasement in Cuba."

Worse and worse. Now, the president of the United States, the queen of Spain, and probably Juan too, would blame *her* if war broke out.

CHAPTER
TWENTY

ANTONIA TRIED to get hold of herself and consider the steps to be taken. She looked about, wondering how to get upstairs and back without showing her aunt and uncle and especially Felix Leidner the books that contained the queen's private code.

The president and Lloyd Hastings watched her.

"I take it Her Majesty didn't give you the key to the code," the president said. "But Hastings here has unraveled such things before. A matter of probable usage, I believe."

Lloyd explained. "Substitutions of letters, numerals and so forth. Her Majesty's message will be in Spanish, but the law of usage still prevails. Unfortunately her previous correspondence to His Excellency has been reported to newspaper people. That's why we must go through such a rigmarole."

"Couldn't you get the Secret Service or the Treasury to help out?" she asked. "After all, codes are in their domain."

The president shook his head. "You must remember that what

we are doing is contrary to the general views of both the Spanish Cortes and our own Congress. Any messages that exchange a hope of peace will likely be compromised."

"It could even mean the fall of the Spanish monarchy," Lloyd put in.

They'd thrown down a challenge to her. Well, she accepted.

"Please wait. And Lloyd, if you can, see that neither Uncle Bernard nor Captain Leidner hears any of this."

She opened the door, walked into the hall. No one was in sight. She took a few steps, glanced at the double doors that opened into the west end of the long dining room. They were ajar. Sunlight streamed in through the south windows, and it became clear to Antonia that something was preventing that light from reaching the hall. Felix Leidner was standing there? Or Aunt Sybil? She passed the butler, Calvin, on the front staircase and he gave her a surprised look. Obviously, the nervous way he reacted when she saw him aroused her curiosity.

She realized that she was behaving like an amateur . . . well, she *was* an amateur. *And* she was terrified that on account of some foolish action of her own she might help plunge two countries into a war that their leaders didn't want.

The upper floor with its bright sunlit hall was illuminated by aureole windows at both front and back staircases. Antonia entered her room and looked around. Everything seemed to be in place. She had put the six books from the *condesa* onto her bookshelves between the two long windows with their gold drapes and gently moving lace curtains. Outside in the warm autumn sunlight a breeze blew across the northern paddock, where a groom was out walking Aunt Sybil's favorite mare. Aunt Sybil herself was nowhere to be seen . . . Or did I see her a moment ago, hiding behind those double doors?

Antonia bolted her door before going to pick up the books, then rummaged in the big, old-fashioned wardrobe, got out one of her travel valises and dropped in the six books. But that made a conspicuous gap in her small bookshelves so she rearranged the others, put a music box and a letter-opener sword from Córdoba beyond the bookends and left the room.

A maid she didn't recognize was busy dusting the master bedroom at the far end of the hall but seemed uninterested in her as she hurried down to the breakfast parlor, noting as she did so that both sets of double doors at the ends of the dining room were now closed.

Her nerves were not exactly soothed by the reaction of both the president and Lloyd. The latter took the valise from her so quickly she almost dropped it.

"You were damned long." He glanced at the president, who frowned and shook his head. Lloyd apologized, slung the carpetbag valise up onto the breakfast table and began to unfasten it. President McKinley, for all his outward calm, moved across the table from him and reached for the first of the books.

Tana began, "I thought you ought to know—"

Lloyd interrupted her, talking to the president. "I think the key will be somehow indicated on the pages, sir."

The president nodded. "Always these complications. I was sure we could handle the situation, solve this whole Cuban problem. Well, Cleveland warned me..."

Antonia tried again. "I think we really should be very careful in this house."

Lloyd riffled through the pages of the Alhambra history while referring to the page in his left hand. "I don't understand it, no indications whatever. Just the innocuous letter in Spanish by this *condesa*, with this list of numbers. She calls them 'words that will comfort all men of goodwill.'"

The president picked up the thought. "Meant to refer to the Good Book, but which? The queen's Catholic Bible or ours. This *condesa* pretty clearly hints at the books belonging to Miss...er ...Maguire. The key has got to be in one of these."

The two ignored her so completely she picked up one of the histories discarded by Lloyd, almost praying she would find what these brilliant male brains had missed. She had, though, already looked through the books and found nothing except the inscriptions. The only surprise about them was their language. They were written in English: "With deep sympathy, Albinia." Another read: "Deep sympathy, Montemayor." Then one inscribed: "Her Majesty's deepest sympathies to Antonia." The fourth book read simply: "Antonia." The fifth said: "Antonia Maguire," and the last: "The daughter of Ysabel Guzman."

She wondered what her own purpose in this might be. As of the moment she seemed to be nothing but a mail carrier. She had brought the books home. Otherwise, she might as well retreat to the dining room and join the other eavesdropper. While the two men made what she considered not exactly brilliant speculations, taking up the first book, turning to page eighteen and counting lines, she left the other books open to the inscriptions, since they bore the only handwriting in each book.

Curious that none of the inscriptions was like any other. The one that said merely "Antonia" puzzled her more than the ones with longer inscriptions. Wouldn't most of the inscriptions have been similar? Since they were meant to be given to her at the same time they'd probably have been written at the same time. Why were they so different? One word. Then an inscription of six, then one of five.

She saw that the next inscription had two words, merely her first and last names. A faint idea buzzed about in her head as the president said, "I don't pretend to understand the whys and where-fores of codes. It may be we will have to keep trying for Dupuy after all. Even if we find the key, it's all in Spanish. I grant that you two know Spanish better than I do, but still... all we have are numbers. Big ones, little ones, no rhyme or reason—"

"No, sir. Excuse me, but there is rhyme. Maybe reason," Lloyd said pointing to the childish set of numbers. "For example, what do we have here as the first group? Twenty-bar, nine-bar, 351-bar, six. Since the key is in these books—"

"And Señor Dupuy's books," Antonia put in.

The president nodded. "Yes. We have only half the key."

"Well, it seems reasonable to assume 351 is a page number. The first twenty may be the number of a line."

"Or or a word."

Lloyd dropped into the nearest chair, still studying the coded letter. "We'll just have to try each book, line twenty, page three fifty-one, word so-and-so, until we can make sense of it."

The president took up one of the books. "I can barely translate this one: *A History of Modern Spain from the Catholic Sovereigns to Alfonso the Twelfth of ... of Blessed Memory.* That's the queen's late husband. The father of the present boy king?"

"Yes, sir. You realize, Mr. President, if it comes out that Her

Majesty's ideas differ with the Cortes or the new Liberal party, both she and Alfonso the Thirteenth may be dethroned."

McKinley showed something of his irritation with the whole matter. "Her government has been far better for the country than the warmongers of both conservatives and liberals. Even my predecessor thought so, and he was a *Democrat*."

Antonia agreed, but was still thinking on her notion that had been momentarily tabled... "The last number in each group, Lloyd. Are there any numbers above six?"

Lloyd waved her off, but the president responded politely, "Nothing above six. Probably these six books. But we will have to try each book to find out how she numbered them."

"Not necessarily, sir." Antonia pointed to the book with her single name. "Look at the inscriptions. This may be number one. That book with two words, number two. Then, here are three words. Is this book number three?"

Lloyd, ignoring her, was repeating to himself, "The three numerals refer to the pages. We have to find out which numbers refer to lines, which to words and which, above all, to the book involved in that word. It certainly would be simpler if the queen could just put a call to you over Mr. Bell's telephone wire."

"And what would prevent certain of her so-called advisers from overhearing?" the president reminded him. "They are not all on her side, as we know." He looked at Antonia. "I think this little lady may have hit on the answer." He pointed to the first series of numerals. "Let's say the last number refers to the book inasmuch as none of the last numbers go above six..."

Just then a shadow passed across the room. Antonia looked quickly at the nearest window. Nothing. A passing cloud in front of the sun?

Lloyd had turned to Antonia's suggestion, since it was now buttressed by the president's pointing finger. "Six it is. And you'd say this book has an inscription of six words. Let's assume 'Catholic Sovereigns to Alfonso et cetera' is number six. Look up page three fifty-one. Line twenty. Ninth word."

With Antonia peering over his shoulder, the president turned pages to 351, his finger moving down to the twentieth line and the ninth word.

"Vote." The full line read, *Upon the wishes of the Spanish People the vote of the parliament or Cortes...*"Well, the rest doesn't concern us. 'Vote' is the word."

There were twenty-six combinations of numbers in the message. Having followed the same method to find each word, Lloyd dipped a pen into the inkwell on the sideboard and wrote down the thirteenth and last word of the first group. He and the president looked at each other. There were still thirteen more combinations of numbers and certainly the thirteen already translated made little sense.

"So much for that idea." The president sighed.

The thirteen sets of numbers that were left added nothing but the same jibberish. Lloyd mused over the paper. "Perhaps Dupuy's half of the message is sandwiched in between the words given to Antonia."

"Señor Dupuy's perhaps start the combination," she suggested diffidently. "And if he has the first word, it would be logical, because Her Majesty hinted that I should cooperate with Señor Dupuy and not vice versa."

Lloyd was displeased. Amateurs meddling in his province were an occupational hazard. Still... "All right, try it this way, 'Blank [for Dupuy's first word]—vote—[blank]—Cortes'..." He stopped, read the message back to himself. "We may have something. The blank after María, for instance, is undoubtedly Cristina. The blank after 'prime' could be 'minister.'" He went on, jotting down words. "How does this sound? 'Something—vote Cortes and new prime minister, María Cristina wishes Your Excellency believe—she?—endorses—something and—sale—Cuba or negotiation'?"

The president read it several times. "It makes sense. The Cortes and the new prime minister... that would be this liberal Señor Sagasta... wish one thing but the queen endorses—probably peace—and the sale of Cuba or negotiation. She wants me to know that no matter what the Spanish Cortes and the new prime minister says, she is holding out for either the sale of Cuba or negotiation. Probably home rule. What they are calling autonomy. But after the assassination of Señor Cánovas she doesn't dare go publicly against the pro-war sentiments."

"In other words, patience. Why couldn't she have said so?"

"She is in a very ticklish spot," McKinley reminded Lloyd.

Antonia thought, And so are we. She pointed silently toward the window that opened on a little brick walk and beyond the kitchen herb garden, the north paddock. "I'm almost sure someone was out there."

Lloyd crumpled up the scrawled page of decoded notes. The president held up one hand.

"Don't worry. Unless I miss my guess you'll find my Secret Service friends out there. In any case, they'd better be." He raised his voice. "Wilkinson. Medrano. Show yourselves."

After only a moment's delay one of the open windows was abruptly filled by a compact, thirtyish man with a large friendly mouth and intense eyes.

"Medrano, sir. You wanted me? Wilkinson's around front. Somebody new arriving. Had to check him out. New arrival was around here a minute ago."

"He can't have overheard much if anything," the president said. "Who was our prowler?"

Medrano turned away from the window and called out, "Wilk, that fellow we caught by the drawing room doors that open on the walk here. Who is he?"

"One of Mrs. Revelstoke's guests," the unseen Wilkinson answered back. "Sea captain. Name's Juan Diego."

Antonia's first reaction was, of course, pure pleasure . . . he'd come to see her, just as he'd promised. She heard the president and his Secret Service man discuss the matter, dismissing Juan as "probably all right. Sybil Revelstoke vouches for him," but they couldn't know what Antonia knew, that Juan was as strongly pro-rebel as ever . . . What had he been up to when he was found within a few yards of President McKinley's secret conference? Had he heard anything? Was it a deliberate act on his part? If he now knew María Cristina's message to the president . . .

Lloyd turned to Antonia. "Can he be trusted, do you think? Miss Caris—that is, young Mrs. Maguire—happened to write about your Spanish voyage. She said this Captain Diego and his friend the columnist, came to Córdoba. Do you still feel his conversion is genuine? Couldn't he still be playacting, working for those cut-throats—"

"Don't be ridiculous," she snapped. "Do you think I would tolerate anyone who helped my family's murderers?" She started to pick up the six books, grabbing them out of Lloyd's hands. "The queen gave these into my care. Or at least, the *condesa* did. It's the same thing."

The president, ever the peacemaker, put in gently, "Miss Maguire, for the moment the books are certainly safe in your hands. As for the other matter, if you vouch for Captain Diego, I think we may assume he is on the side of peace." He motioned to Medrano at the window. "I'm afraid I am due back in the Capitol. Another function to put us all to sleep. I wish I could delegate these things to the vice-president. Or better yet, the assistant secretary of the navy. That rambunctious Teddy Roosevelt would feel right at home. He has a real fondness for noise and confusion, and how busy he is, promoting a war. The greatest confusion of all."

Medrano turned away from the window and went around to join the president at the front door. The president thanked Antonia, shook hands with her and went out with Lloyd, who told her in the doorway, "You were splendid, my dear. We owe you our thanks." Then he offset the compliment when he put his finger to his lips, to remind her to keep silent. As if she needed that...

She said with some bite, "I'll give your regards to Caris next time I write to her."

He refused to let her ruffle his complacency. "Thank you. Remarkable young woman, the way she has handled her tragedy."

Her tragedy, Antonia thought. She continued to have a low opinion of her sister-in-law's suffering. The president, accompanied by Lloyd Hastings and the two Secret Service operatives, left by the front door, where Aunt Sybil and Uncle Bernard wished them well on their ride back to Washington. Antonia stayed in the breakfast parlor long enough to gather up her books and replace them in the valise. She had just fastened it when a lively male voice said, "Remember me, Miss Maguire? Quite an exciting voyage in that old tub, wasn't it?"

Felix Leidner stood in the doorway, looking exactly as she had first remembered him in Juan's substitute *Baracoa*. He was grinning, his windblown light hair making him look younger than ever. But there was also a devil-may-care quality that reminded her of his true profession.

"Exciting was the least of it," she told him coolly as she passed him in the doorway.

He reached for her valise. "May I help you, ma'am?"

She started to pull the valise away, then realized that would only harden any suspicions he might already have.

"Thank you. The president wanted to see the...souvenirs I brought back from Spain." Her nervousness increased. It would be disastrous for a gunrunning mercenary like Felix Leidner to get a hint of the six volumes that formed half of the queen regent's code. He could command an enormous price from the powerful New York Cuban junta for the information.

They walked down the hall, away from the front of the house, where presumably the Secret Service had questioned Juan. She desperately wanted to turn around but kept going. She was not fooled by Felix Leidner's attentions at this moment, but what disturbed her was the possibility that Juan might conceivably try to use her for the same purposes. Was that possible? She tried to convince herself it wasn't.

They started up the stairs. To get his mind off the subject of the valise and move him onto the defensive she said, "I suppose you're making another profitable arrangement to deliver the guns to some Cubans so they can kill other Cubans. I even wonder if some captain like you perhaps took my family's killers off the island. Someone did, including that guitarist who betrayed my family." She stopped a minute at the head of the stairs. "Would you carry a creature like that?"

"For Yankee dollars? You Spanish have an expression, *quién sabe?*" He laughed, a chilly sound. "I'm carrying a friend of yours on my next voyage. He may prove useful when he lands in Santiago de Cuba."

"Useful against...whom?"

"Let's say, against Cuba's Spanish rulers..."

No matter, this mercenary wouldn't hesitate to help anybody for a fee. She needed to stop him some way. She forced herself to play-act, to pretend she didn't care... "Since my family died, I've really little interest in my homeland. Actually, I feel more at home right here in the United States." She went on airily, "So you may tell me who your passenger is, or you may not. It doesn't matter to me."

"Oh, well, I wouldn't want you to be angry with me." He smiled when he said it.

Felix lingered upstairs at her door, probably, she thought, hoping to see the contents of her valise. She forced herself to show him a big smile.

"I expect I'll see you at dinner, Captain Leidner."

"You surely will." His blue eyes appraised her, insolently, she thought, though he wasn't without his damned charm. "I must say, I admire Juan Diego's taste." He added quickly, "I mean that in the most respectful way, señorita. I am too good a friend of Juanito's to flirt with the girl who is the center of his whole life."

"I believe Señor Diego has a cause that is more the center of his life. Like you..."

"Me?"

"Yes. Your Cuban Freedom Cause, I believe you call it."

"Not I, ma'am. I haven't a single pennyworth of passion for the Cuban cause or any other. My passion is all for the fortune I'm making out of this so-called rebellion."

"I suppose Juan Diego knows how you feel?"

She had started to close the door, but he reached out and held it open long enough for him to tell her in a voice suddenly full of ice, "My friend Juanito knows how I feel. I don't lie to the man who saved my life many times. And the other way around, too. *Hasta la vista.* Isn't that what you Cuban aristocrats say?"

Before she could answer he had closed the door and left her alone. It was just as well... he'd put her in her place, at least for the time being.

She replaced the books, jamming them between several Godey's magazines, a romance and the portraits of her mother, Felipe, her father and her Revelstoke relatives. When she shifted the silver-framed portrait of her young brother with his laughing mouth and romantic brown eyes, her fingers curled around the frame. She saw that her knuckles were white with the pressure as she gently set the frame back. Felipe would be living today if not for the likes of Captain Leidner's "friends," and one of them, it seemed, would be sailing with him on his next voyage, and more dead Felipes would follow.

"*No,* not if I can help it."

She stood off, studying the bookshelves, decided they looked all right, natural. She wondered if Lloyd Hastings had gotten too far away for her to stop him. Hurrying down the front stairs, she ran out on the veranda just in time to see the carriage of President McKinley and two horsemen disappear in the distance, swallowed up by the colorful autumn woods.

She went back to the house looking for a pen and paper. Lloyd had left a pen and inkwell in the breakfast parlor, and when she opened the door she found them pushed to one end of the sideboard. She remembered distinctly that Lloyd had left them in the middle of the sideboard on top of the flat green blotter also borrowed from the study.

The green blotter was gone.

She looked around the room. Nothing else seemed to have been touched. She knew at once why the blotter was gone. Such a spotless blotter, *before* Lloyd used it. No other blotted messages to confuse the issue . . . who had the blotter now?

She went at once to Uncle Bernard's study and found him sucking the sharp end of his own pen while he sighed over a well-worn ledger. He looked up at her, surprised. "Sorry, I thought you were that pirate fellow, Leidner. Wants me to stand good on the insurance bond for his next voyage. I wonder just how risky that is." He shrugged to relieve the tension between his heavy shoulders, then bestowed on her his patient smile. "But I'm sure pretty young heiresses aren't interested in the tiresome problems of businessmen. May I help you, my dear?"

"Just looking for an envelope, do you mind?" She reached over the end of his desk and began to rummage among piles of bills, correspondence, a checkbook and a stack of Bernard Revelstoke's creamy personal stationery. "While I'm at it, could you give me a sheet of paper and one of those pens?"

"Of course. Help yourself."

She found nothing incriminating. His papers were messy but they hid nothing suspicious. His own blotter was also green but full of old blotting impressions.

She gave him a breezy "thanks" and began to scribble her message to Lloyd:

Lloyd,

Two matters, One: Someone here has removed the blotter you used.

Two: Captain Felix Leidner takes a Cuban rebel on his next

voyage. Their port is Santiago de Cuba. I think the rebel's job
is a threat to the legal government of Cuba. They also carry
guns. Please notify the U.S. patrols.

Don't let it get beyond U.S. jurisdiction. A jail term is better
than a long-drawn-out Cuban court trial, as you must know.

She scrawled a big "Tana" before she remembered that Lloyd
always called her by her formal name. No matter.

"Uncle Bernard, may I borrow one of your servants? I forgot to
tell Lloyd Hastings something. He'll need a horse, or a horse and
buggy. Whatever can overtake the president's party."

Bernard considered a minute, but his mind still seemed to be
on the "unbalanced" figures in his ledger. "I'll send Harry Burns.
He often runs errands for your Aunt Sybil and me between here
and Washington. He's a regular Paul Revere on horseback."

"Wonderful. Thank you, Uncle." She would see Harry Burns off
on his Paul Revere ride. No last-minute instructions by dear, tricky
Uncle Bernard . . .

It was less difficult than she had expected. Having put aside his
own work to locate the messenger, Uncle Bernard now left him to
Antonia and went back to his profits and losses in Cuban tobacco
and seagoing insurance investments.

Harry Burns was an athletic young man whose round face seemed
all innocence. Who would ever guess he carried important messages of state? He asked, "You want me to stop the president
himself, ma'am?"

"Not necessarily. But be sure this gets to Mr. Lloyd Hastings.
He will be riding in the carriage with the president."

He took the sealed envelope, didn't look at it but folded it between two fingers and stuck it into an inside pocket of his worn
cotton jacket.

Someone, probably Uncle Bernard, had ordered Harry Burns'
mount saddled, and he quickly rode off on the sorrel mare, seeming
to dissolve among the russet colors of the woods.

Antonia stood there a moment, upset by her fears, torn by her
feelings for Juan Diego, her love . . . and intrusive suspicion. Suddenly she was startled by two muscular arms that caught her in a
vise, drawing her back. Lips brushed her ear.

"Sweetheart, I went out to the stile. You weren't there—"

She turned her head, pressed herself against him, but all the same, at the same time, the thought kept spinning in her mind...

...*Was your visit to the stile, darling, before or after you spied on the president?*...

CHAPTER
TWENTY-ONE

SHE VOICED none of such thoughts. She was a woman yielding to the desires of her body, not the warning of her mind. She turned until her lips touched his. The contact banished doubts.

She teased him. "You aren't angry with me any more?"

His head shifted far enough away from her so he could scowl down at her. "When was I angry at you?"

She smiled at the convenient shortness of his memory. "I seem to remember a day in the Cádiz harbor when we said good-bye, your very proper good-bye. You were warmer to Señora Villedo."

He kept a straight face. "Well, the señora was very gracious. A delightful lady. It was she who suggested I leave that message with you." He pretended to shake her as he said anxiously, "You did get my message, didn't you?"

She had a notion to make him suffer the way she had the day the *Santa Cruz* sailed, but life was too short and certainly their happiness was too short to waste time on games.

"If you could see how unhappy I was the day we sailed, and how quickly I changed after I read that scrap the sailor pressed into my tear-stained palm you wouldn't ask such damn foolish questions."

"Then come along to the stile. I believe that was our point of reference."

They started off the veranda arm in arm. On the pebbled walk he turned to the north and the walk that separated the house from the herb garden and the north paddock.

Antonia stopped abruptly. "Wrong direction. It's the south path. Around the south terrace."

He considered the path. "So that's why those two yeggs wrestled with me. Was I on sacred soil?"

He must have heard by now, even if he hadn't seen President McKinley himself . . . "You were intruding on the president of the United States. He was in one of those north rooms." She hesitated an instant. "He and Lloyd were talking. They asked me in and questioned me about public opinion in Spain. As if I know what Spaniards think."

He seemed uninterested in her explanations as he swung her around and headed in the opposite direction. "We are wasting time. The stile calls us."

With arms locked around each other they walked along the foot of the terrace, then across the lawn toward the distant stile. Halfway to their destination they discovered that one of the calves had wandered out of the herd that moved across the pasture. The calf contentedly nuzzled the rickety old stile and raised his sad eyes to stare when Diego lifted Antonia to the top of it.

Antonia's suspicions had now begun to seep away with Juan's telling her his mistake about the north walk. The calf, and her relief, made her smile tenderly at him.

"I like that look," he said just before he kissed her.

"Do you, my darling? Why?" It sounded like a teasing, conceited question, but she had lived with such deception since her audience with the queen that she tended to question everything—including her own motives and reactions, never mind his.

"Why? Because this is the passionate, honest girl I met in Quincy Kemp's office, not the glamorous beauty, the seductive charmer I sometimes catch on this face."

"You make me self-conscious. Do I always have to be plain Tana Maguire to get your approval?"

"You could never be plain anything. I didn't say plain. I said honest and passionate . . . Do you love me?"

It startled her for a moment. "You know I do."

"So you see? Honest. Now, test number two. Kiss me." She leaned forward, put her hands on his shoulders and pressed her mouth hard on his.

The calf nudged Antonia, pushing her sideways so that she almost fell off the stile. She and Juan laughed as he caught her and pulled her back onto her low perch.

"*And* passionate. I told you so, my honest, passionate love."

She'd never thought of herself as dishonest, until recently. But he couldn't know about that . . . Her conscience wasn't much appeased by the sight of Felix Leidner striding across the grass toward them. She wished now that she hadn't reported his voyage to Lloyd. He didn't belong in jails. Like Juan he should be out on the free, windblown quarterdeck of a ship. She tried to tell herself that he was taking a spy to Cuba to further the crimes of people who'd murdered her family, but all this had nothing to do with honesty . . . *She* had become dishonest with herself, but even worse, with Juan . . .

At dinner she tried hard to be friendly to Leidner, and during the evening even listened without argument to his talk with Juan about the blind stupidity of the Spanish ruler in Cuba.

Aunt Sybil caught Antonia and Juan exchanging long good-night embraces just before midnight and apologized.

"If you two take my advice, you will be married at once in a quiet ceremony. Then I can give you one delightful room instead of witnessing all these romantic transports every time you are to be separated for a few hours."

Juan studied Antonia for a long moment, his eyes warm. "I am beginning to think it is a mistake to wait. Should we? I mean, soon?"

Felix Leidner had just come up the servants' stairs in time to hear his friend's proposal, and he called to them cheerfully as he opened his door, "Say yes, Miss Maguire, life, so they say, is uncertain. And far too short, to my way of thinking."

The first sharp wind of late autumn had burst through the aureole window behind the young captain, and Antonia shivered.

"Here, sweetheart," Juan Diego said, smiling at her seriousness, "it won't be so bad. You may even grow to enjoy marriage, after a few years."

"What an idiot you are!" She hugged him, not wanting ever to let go, to let him go back to his "work"...

Aunt Sybil, highly amused by the sight of what she called "romantic transports," turned her attention to Leidner. "Must you leave so early, Captain? Bernard said you were devil-bent on leaving just after sunup."

"I have a cargo waiting. Mustn't be late. My whole future depends on this one."

Juan held Antonia tighter. "Tana, are you cold? You're shivering."

"No... but if we're to be married soon, I do think your best friend should be present. Señor Capitán, stay and be Juanito's best man. *Do stay.*"

Leidner shook his head. "A schedule's a schedule. But don't look so sad. I'm not going to the ends of the earth. Only across the straits, as you two well know."

"Bring my husband back some Cuban cigars," Aunt Sybil reminded him.

"And bring yourself back," Diego called.

He nodded, waved and went into his room.

Antonia caught at Juan's sleeve. "Don't let him go. He's your friend... I can't help feeling it's a sort of bad omen, letting him go when so many know about the sailing..."

"My sweet, every voyage has its dangers. There are omens all the time. I didn't know you were superstitious. Besides, these Americans who know about the sailing are our friends, the friends of Cuban freedom. Why would they betray what they themselves give him to deliver?"

She couldn't agree, but she also felt she couldn't object any further. And if caught, a short jail term might actually save Felix Leidner's life. It would certainly keep him off the treacherous Florida Straits for a little while, and his capture might warn Juan away from his dangerous game. That last she honestly doubted, no matter how much she tried to convince herself.

She kissed him good-night and closed her door, but that night her sleep was badly troubled. She dreamed of a blissful wedding to Juan and then, in the middle of the ceremony, Captain Leidner appeared looking very pale, his clothing, his hands and feet dripping saltwater on the carpet in front of the altar. He said nothing but one long arm pointed at her, and still the salt drops fell, some of them touching her own hand.

The drops were hot. They scalded her flesh.

She woke up with a start.

The oil lamp on her bedstand had tipped over, and a drop of oil had fallen on the heel of her hand. She jumped up, righted the lamp, relieved that the opaque globe had not broken.

Getting back to sleep proved more difficult. . . .

Before the household was up the next morning Captain Leidner had already gone, and after a day of soul-searching Antonia sent a message to Lloyd Hastings:

> Forget my first letter. Captain Leidner is apparently guilty of nothing more than carrying cargo with the encouragement of half the members of Congress.

Indeed, more than half of them favored independence for Cuba, even at the cost of war with Spain. And almost all the newspapers that shaped American opinion likewise favored the rebels.

She heard nothing from either message. Harry Burns returned, nodded when she asked if he had put the first letter into Mr. Hastings' hands. Then he was sent off to Chicago with messages from both Aunt Sybil and Uncle Bernard on the subject of Cuban sugar investments, sugar imports from the island having fallen to one-fourth of their prerevolutionary quota. So Antonia's second letter was sent by the postal system.

Juan, with Aunt Sybil as a romantic chorus, had decided that their lives were being wasted apart. He should marry Antonia now instead of at the end of the Cuban rebellion.

"I know," Antonia taunted him lightly. "You realize your beloved rebels are going down in defeat and you've given up."

She felt that he was about to say "quite the reverse," but he stopped in time to prevent an argument and kissed her instead.

They were interrupted in their breakfast on the terrace by Quincy Kemp, whom Aunt Sybil presented with great cheer.

"Isn't it divine? Look who's here. Quincy, these two silly children are debating marriage."

Quincy's chunky body sank into a Duncan Phyfe chair beside Antonia, the chair giving a protesting squeak.

"Hot for this late in the season. But a good time for weddings. Those gorgeous, overpowering hats you ladies wear today were made to dominate the crumbling, sugar-man bridegroom."

"You are impossible, Quincy," Sybil said. "If I'd known you were such a misogynist I'd never have let you in today."

The repartee went on, but for Antonia the day had lost its glory. Somehow she sensed that the columnist was here to make trouble, and that the trouble was directed at her.

Kemp waited until Diego went off with Uncle Bernard to discuss the rumor about the kaiser's ships in the Caribbean. It seemed that whenever the Imperial German Navy dropped anchor lately they had stirred up trouble with the locals while ostensibly on goodwill visits.

Kemp seemed determined to ignore this interesting discussion, and Antonia quizzed him about why. "Doesn't the kaiser interest you at all? I thought your column thrived on international gossip like that. Maybe the kaiser will end by having his own war with Spain and save your country from such a calamity."

"I doubt it..." He settled back in his chair, balancing it on two legs against the brick balustrade of the terrace. "Miss Maguire, has it occurred to you that if you marry Captain Diego you're going to be in an excellent position to know all his movements."

"What makes you think I want to know all his movements?"

"Don't you?" She sat up in a hurry but he went on without waiting for her protest. "Isn't that all part of your deal with the Spanish queen regent?"

"*No*. He had nothing to do—"

"But there was a deal, of some sort."

She sat down abruptly. "That's absurd. I'm not exactly spy material. And I certainly wouldn't spy on Juan, not for any queen or anyone else."

She found his blue eyes much too observant, and avoided them, which he noticed as he took out his cigar case and considered the contents."

"Well, Miss Maguire, you say you wouldn't spy on old Juan, and I believe it, but do you think he will?"

She felt the stillness of the afternoon close in around her. "Do you mean to tell him such a lie?"

His response was, "Cigars, bah... they'll never replace the Cubans. I wish to heaven we owned the damned place. At least maybe we'd get some decent cigars."

"Answer me."

He closed the cigar case without selecting a cigar.

"All right, Tana my girl. I don't intend to tell Diego anything about you. I figure if you hate his rebel friends, nobody's got a better reason." He stared at her while she looked back, speechless. "And for what it's worth, I don't believe you would use him."

Her mouth was dry. "Thank you. I wouldn't. But I do want to help Her Majesty keep the peace, and there won't be any peace if the rebels persist in their crimes—"

"What about the crimes committed by the Spanish rulers of Cuba? Butcher Weyler and his reconcentration camps, for example."

"General Weyler had been recalled."

"Does that change the 100,000 women, children and old people who have died in his camps?"

"Of course not, but they've nothing to do with me." She got up again and this time left the table.

To her surprise he called after her, "I told you I believed you. Why don't you marry him? It will do you both good."

She said over her shoulder, "I suppose you think he'll reform me?"

"I'm sure of it. You mean well, Tana... beg pardon, Miss Maguire. And as the good captain's wife you'd soon get over that Hamlet act of yours."

"Hamlet?"

"That desire for revenge. It's no good. It eats you up if you're a decent, outgoing person, and I think you are." He reached for her hand, stopping her. "Hasn't it been that way with you since you began this campaign to avenge your family?"

She swallowed hard and managed a firmness that sounded false even to her own ears. "I know your methods, Mr. Kemp. You make accusations until you anger your victims. Then they admit anything to be rid of you."

His big jovial face creased unhappily. "I'm sorry. I don't want to be someone you get rid of. What do you say we just become friends, based on a mutual respect for Captain Diego and what he's doing."

"I wish I could believe you." She looked at him very carefully and added, "You accused me of being a spy. *If* that were true, all I would really want is peace and honor for my countries, all three of them. That isn't quite the same as spying for one branch of a foreign government that's trying to make trouble so it can pick up the prize—Cuba."

"By foreign I suppose you mean the American government."

"I mean the United States. Cuba is in America. So is Brazil. So is Mexico."

"Yes, we Americans do make that mistake. I beg your pardon. But do you think I'm somehow connected with the State Department. The president?"

"No. Naval intelligence."

She expected him either to deny this or to ignore it as he once had. Instead he studied her with a provocative grin.

"Now, I wonder where you got that idea. You've said it before, it isn't any truer now. The point is, we in the United States know war is inevitable so we try to be prepared. But that's beside the point. I think I know your kind of woman. Once you're married to Captain Diego you'll do everything in your power to keep him safe. You won't betray him, *or* his people."

"I'm not betraying them now. His people are Cubans. The only betrayers are those who stir up discontent and rebellion."

He let her go after a brief pause. His palm slapped the table so hard the sound made her jump. "All right, I give up. But one day you'll go too far, do something there's no turning back from. And then, my girl, how you'll wish you had this minute back."

She said, "Don't be silly. I'm not in a position to do anything earthshaking. And I would never hurt Captain Diego. Even you understand that."

But later in the days that followed she thought a good deal about their conversation, especially when the Spanish minister, Enrique Dupuy de Lôme, sent her a message to meet him and Lloyd Hastings in Washington at the L'Enfant House, a hotel whose conservatory-tearoom was the rendezvous for many meetings, both romantic and business. Fortunately the Spanish minister had not been so obvious. She would meet Lloyd in the businesslike atmosphere of the lobby.

She found it relatively easy to dissemble to Juan and the Revelstokes. Juan had finished his own business in Washington and Baltimore and was about to leave for New York, and Antonia would visit Washington for fittings of her winter wardrobe. Though still in mourning, she agreed that Aunt Sybil was right. The wardrobe would be in shades of violet, lavender and white with black bands. She cared little about the subject of clothes. Her conscience still troubled her over the deceptions she had practiced on the man she loved, and was half a mind to lay everything in the hands of Señor Dupuy.

Juan, who was on his way to New York to confer with the active Cuban junta, escorted Antonia to the dressmakers's establishment in Washington and then caught the train to New York.

The owner of the shop, Madame Lucréce, seemed to understand all too well when Antonia explained her luncheon "with the wife of the Spanish minister."

"We are going to discuss Captain Diego's advancement," she explained, and madame nodded wisely.

"*Bien entendu,* mademoiselle. It shall be as you say, a small secret between us. You wish to further the captain's advancement without his knowledge. So. You will return to my shop before the captain arrives back from New York this evening?"

Antonia knew that no matter what she told Madame Lucréce, this woman would still suspect that there could be only one reason for a secret meeting: a romantic interlude.

Carrying her valise with the queen's books, Antonia was met in the lobby of L'Enfant House by Lloyd Hastings and Miss Jackman, a severe-looking young woman with thin red hair and a superior manner that instantly rubbed Antonia the wrong way. She proved to be Lloyd's "associate," someone exceedingly knowledgeable about government affairs. She wore a puce-colored suit, which was not the happiest shade with her hair, but it fitted her so tightly with its draped skirt and close jacket that she left no doubt that she was proud of her matchstick figure. Her being there made it impossible for Antonia to ask Lloyd what he had done about her two messages concerning Felix Leidner.

"Miss Maguire," the woman began at once as Lloyd took up the valise and the three stepped into the elevator, "you will be relieved to know that this can be taken out of your hands now." She pointed to the valise, ignoring the male elevator operator who looked straight ahead at the elevator doors. "You must have been very nervous, handling something so unfamiliar in your life."

"Quite the contrary, Miss—ah—Miss." Antonia's smile was big and glittering. "I seem to have found a vocation for the work. And Lloyd, I mean Mr. Hastings, will vouch for the fact that I solved the little impasse he reached the other day at Revelstoke."

Lloyd put in somewhat offhandedly, "Miss Maguire has been of some assistance. The president said to me only yesterday..."

He went on in the same vein, with a few references to her but a great deal about the confidences *he* shared with William McKinley. As he did, Antonia let her mind wander. She wished she hadn't come. She wished she'd never gotten into a conspiracy. At night she often awoke with a curious, haunting notion that her mother would not have approved of this sort of vengeance she'd set herself to accomplish...

The Spanish minister, Enrique Dupuy de Lôme, met them in the foyer of his suite, looking as darkly distinguished as ever, his Mephistophelean appearance enhanced rather than diminished by his polite greeting to Antonia.

"Ah, Señorita Maguire, I have heard how helpful you were recently."

They had barely entered the elaborate, heavily furnished suite before Miss Jackman was dismissed to transcribe to the typewriter a sheaf of notes from the Spanish minister's Montreal visit. No one else was in the suite.

"You brought the books. Excellent. We have another message. But do sit down. Here, on the divan. My translation is here with blanks for the words to be found in your books. I think we may have the burden of the message already. Nevertheless, let us have the entire story."

Lloyd was already deep in the job of searching her books for the first word, while Dupuy de Lôme confessed, "Between ourselves, I find Her Majesty's efforts very much like most amateurs. Many complications but so easily unraveled once one has the clue."

Antonia looked at him curiously. "You do approve of what Her Majesty and the president are trying to do? To find a peaceful solution rather than war?"

"Certainly. Who am I to disagree with my sovereign? Well then, Señor Hastings, am I right? Have I read the sense of it even before we decode the señorita's half?"

"So it would seem." Something had disturbed Lloyd and he added stiffly, "There are those who unwisely underestimate the intelligence of President McKinley."

Dupuy smiled. "I would say, it is impossible to underestimate the intelligence of—but there, I make a little joke and I have upset you. A joke, señor. No more."

Antonia, as well as Lloyd, found that Dupuy's little "joke" and attitude were not to her liking. But what had happened to her? Why should she care what the Spaniard thought of the slow, careful American president? The surprise was that she did care.

Lloyd and Dupuy read the results of their work together:

"The Cortes and the Liberal Prime Minister agree that nothing should be sacrificed. They refuse autonomy, local rule. Believe me, Excellency, my profound desire is for peace, if we remember always the honor of Spain."

"Much the same as her previous message," Lloyd said.

The Spanish minister was not enthusiastic. "Pointless, I am afraid ... this president of yours has little power over the overwhelming sentiment of your jingoist Congress and your fire-eating public. They are all so eager for war—"

"The Spanish Cortes seems just as eager," Antonia pointed out, surprising herself again.

Dupuy contradicted her. "Our government is eager to preserve

Spanish honor. That is a very different thing. Death before dishonor
is no idle boast to anyone with a drop of Spanish blood. And if we
surrender Cuba without a fight, it would be the basest form of
dishonor."

She now realized that Dupuy was not in sympathy with the
queen's efforts to preserve the peace. Dupuy went on. "My opinion, however, has nothing to do with the matter. I take my orders
from Her Majesty, so we proceed with the absurdity of these secret,
coded messages. Meanwhile, let us hope we may have more good
fortune, like the Leidner affair."

Antonia looked up at him, with sudden fear. Before she could
speak Lloyd turned to her. "That reminds me, Antonia. I never
did understand what that letter of yours was all about. You mentioned a Leidner. But we knew nothing about it."

Dupuy smiled. "Well, fortunately, someone did. Captain Felix
Leidner, unlike our turncoat friend Diego, remained in the filibustering business. He was captured by our Spanish patrol boats
outside the harbor of Santiago de Cuba. He not only carried contraband weapons and ammunition for the rebels, but a young spy,
so we were informed. The young fellow was to be dropped off in
Cuba dressed as a female, with orders to report the movements of
government troops in Santiago province."

"How"—Antonia had to begin again, her voice was so husky she
scarcely recognized it—"how did you find all this out?"

"An informant gave us our first clue. The Spanish patrols did the
rest. Leidner was strong, refused to talk, but the young spy broke
quickly under questioning." He saw a little of the distaste in Lloyd's
eyes and added a half-apology. "I am afraid our army in Cuba is
not overly gentle in its interrogation. They remember what has
happened to their fellow soldiers when they were captured by
rebels."

Antonia felt sick. She wanted nothing so much as to escape from
this room and from herself.

Lloyd was shocked too, though with less reason.

"What will be done with Captain Leidner and his crew?"

Dupuy shrugged. "It no longer concerns us."

Antonia managed to ask why.

"My dear young lady, the matter was settled some eight hours
after the capture of the *Frederika*. Having been found guilty of

treason and piracy against the Royal Spanish Colony of Cuba,
Captain Leidner, the young spy Timothy Burford and three of the
ship's crew were hanged at Santiago prison on Monday last."

While Antonia huddled on one corner of the divan with her eyes
closed and her fists clenched, Lloyd received this news with suitable revulsion and disgust.

"This is certainly not the way of our courts. I daresay there were
no defense attorneys and no hope of a fair trial."

Dupuy dismissed the matter. "But they were guilty. The result
of a trial would have been the same, and think of their suffering
while they waited out the verdict."

"In fact," Lloyd said with heavy irony, "I suppose you might say
that hanging them was the Christian thing to do."

Dupuy was growing a trifle impatient. "Have we any other matters to discuss? Your president plays the cards close to the waist-
coat, as my poker friends say."

"Our business in concluded, I believe. Are you ready, Antonia?"

She nodded, reached out for Lloyd's hand when she got up. She
suddenly felt very old. If she'd had a penitent's flagellating whip
she would have lashed herself, but she also knew even that wouldn't
erase her guilt.

Nor would her guilt be lessened when she discovered who had
put her note to Lloyd into the hands of the Spanish government
in Cuba. She was fairly certain now that Uncle Bernard was responsible... When she had proof she would try to see him punished in a way to make him suffer as that poor Tim Burford must
have under torture. Thank God she had one weapon against him.
She owned Revelstoke, and few things would hurt him more than
to lose his precious home...

Every time she closed her eyes she saw those men she had known
and liked, even the boy Tim Burford, dangling from a long gibbet,
and her impulsive behavior and tardy attempt to undo it.

Lord, how would Juan Diego feel when he knew her part in it?
He would hate and despise her, but no more than she hated and
despised herself.

While they waited for the elevator, Lloyd looked at her closely.
"Are you all right? You look white as a sheet. You mustn't think
about Dupuy's gruesome stories. These tragedies do happen. God
knows what the newspapers here will do with it. They've already

made heroes out of Leidner and the others. Your friend Diego used to be one of them, but he seems to be safely in the Spanish camp for the moment."

She said nothing. There was nothing to say. She was numb with horror.

In the lobby he suggested that they stop in the Conservatory Tearoom. "You look as though a cup of tea might just give you a little color."

"No, thanks." The hoarseness remained in her voice. She coughed, shook her head and turned to leave him.

"Let me walk with you to . . . what is it? A dressmaker?"

"Don't bother. I want to window shop."

She walked rapidly down the street toward Madame Lucréce's shop. And Lloyd had been right. The local newspapers plus the New York *Journal* and the *Telegraph* blasted the news in thick, funereal black:

HERO HANGED BY SPAIN

SPAIN BOASTS TORTURE DEATHS

LEIDNER EXECUTED—NO TRIAL

She wondered if Juan had seen the headlines yet. She longed to comfort him, and at the same time was terrified of his reaction when he discovered her part in Felix Leidner's awful death.

CHAPTER
TWENTY-TWO

THE MEETING she at once hungered for and dreaded was
easier than she had any right to expect. She decided to meet Juan
at the station instead of at Madame Lucréce's shop. Juan had read
the news in New York, and when he walked into the big, echoing
marble station looking sticken and suddenly older, she held her
arms out to him and for one of the few times in their lives up to
this moment, it was he who found refuge in her arms and not the
other way around.

The moment helped them both. She too felt older, maybe even
a little wiser, and now she had the exquisite knowledge that she
was necessary to him. His well-being and happiness depended at
least in some ways on her. In the instant of that realization she
determined never to let him down.

They walked out of the station arm in arm, found the old heavy
Revelstoke carriage and horses waiting, the dignified Revelstoke
coachman dozing on his high perch in the growing chill of the

autumn night. He had carefully timed his arrival, but the train was twenty minutes late. He snapped to attention at their arrival, ignoring Juan's apology for keeping him waiting. He saluted the two of them with the stock of his whip, started to get down to help Antonia into the closed carriage but was forestalled by Diego.

Riding home through the quiet Virginia landscape, Juan brought back the subject that had so deeply depressed them both.

"Felix would never take advice. Remember, we both pressed him to stay, but he had the head of a bull."

". . . Did he have a family?"

"It's the only thing we can be glad of. He talked about marrying a German girl. She lives in some Rhineland town. Koblenz, he said. But it wasn't definite. His mother is still living. I'll write to her, of course . . . You liked him, didn't you?"

"I learned to. That last evening, I think."

He was quiet for a while, perhaps remembering, she thought, the good times, and the dangerous times, with his friend who had been betrayed and brutally executed. He surprised her suddenly by the abruptness of his next question.

"Will you marry me? Within the week?"

She looked at him, aching to say yes, but afraid too. If he married her and then found out her part in his friend's death, he would hate her even more for deceiving him . . . "I want to, more than anything—"

"Then why not?"

"It's hard to explain, I . . ."

"All right, sweetheart, we won't talk any more about it now. But we won't forget it—I won't allow it."

She could only smile through her tears and kiss him in a fashion that couldn't leave any doubt in his mind about her overwhelming feelings.

The moment they reached Revelstoke that evening they were met by Aunt Sybil and Uncle Bernard on the east terrace. They were all sympathy, they had heard about Felix Leidner and as far as Antonia could judge her aunt seemed genuinely sorry. "He was a delightful guest, as you know, a dear young man . . ."

While she went on in this manner, Antonia watched Uncle Bernard. It seemed he was an excellent actor. He nodded at everything his wife said. His small eyes looked suitably mournful, but his fingers flexed, closing into fists and opening as if he were agitated by some emotions considerably beyond this concern for a casual acquaintance who had recently visited his house.

How close had he been to Felix Leidner? They had spent an hour or two together discussing... holy Mother of God... they had discussed Leidner's insurance on his ship's cargo.

She challenged him. "In an odd sort of way, Uncle Bernard, you should profit by the capture of the *Frederika*. Didn't you put up the money to insure it?"

"I? My dear child, certainly not. A cargo of guns? I am not that reckless."

"I thought you told me—"

"You misunderstood, my dear."

Sybil and Diego had stopped talking as they began to take note of this peculiar conversation, full of unspoken venom, between Antonia and her uncle, who went on smoothly, his voice dripping sorrow...

"And, my dear, not that my money losses can possible compare with the taking of a vital young life like Felix Leidner's, but I did lend him money to insure a cargo of oranges and tobacco he intended to bring back from Cuba. Now, well, it's a loss but I can surely live with it..." He shrugged magnanimously.

"And Harry Burns?"

His eyebrows went up. "Oh, yes. Our boy Harry. The one you sent to Washington with that urgent message of yours."

Bastard. But she had always suspected he was dangerous. This latest treachery shouldn't surprise her. She forced herself to a calm she was far from feeling, aided by Juan and her aunt, who were in no mood for what they must think was her petulance.

She reached for Juan's arm.

"We have plans to make, darling. Remember?" Because he must still be thinking of Leidner's death, she added, "He wanted us to be married, he would be glad."

Juan seemed to hesitate. Had he changed his mind?

"The señora must have guessed that we are agreed on an early marriage. But I haven't told my Tanita why it is so important." His hand closed over her fingers on his arm. "I learned something else in New York. From the junta. They did *not* approve the murders of the Guzman-Maguire family."

Aunt Sybil looked pale, and angry. "I should hope not. I have never believed it was a part of the rebellion."

"What has this to do with me, and our marriage?" Antonia wanted to know.

"I was told by members of the junta I trust that Melina, the guitarist who betrayed the family, has been captured and is being held for identification by Señora Caris Maguire, and by you, Antonia. I don't want my Tanita to venture into Havana without me by her side at all times. If we are married, it would facilitate matters."

Aunt Sybil was delighted. "A quiet affair, because Tana is still in mourning. Then the two of you can steal into Havana long enough to identify that monster and then get back again to safety."

"But any rebel in the city might kill Juan as a traitor," Antonia protested, then stopped because Juan was purposefully pressing her fingers.

"Not at all. They know nothing will be gained, since I have given up the business that got poor Felix killed."

Uncle Bernard was listening to all this with interest, Antonia noted as Sybil linked her arm in her husband's and hustled him into the house babbling in her charming fashion . . . "We must make plans, this takes away something of the pall left by Captain Leidner's murder . . ."

When they were alone Juan tried to calm Antonia's apprehensions. "Believe me, my love, our people who give the orders in Havana know why I will be there. The word has gone out. Neither my wife nor I are to be touched."

"I hope . . ." and then her fears were, temporarily, quieted by his lingering kiss.

Between them, Aunt Sybil and Antonia made preparations for the quiet, very private wedding. Diego left all these matters in the women's hands. She had no doubt that in back of his confidence was a secret knowledge shared with the powerful Cuban juntas in New York and Washington. She asked no questions because she was afraid to know the answers. Somehow Lloyd, the president and even Dupuy de Lôme might learn something that would harm or even destroy Juan.

She strongly suspected . . . in effect, he'd told her so . . . that Juan was still closely allied to the cause he had sworn to uphold, no matter how much the queen and the Spanish government in Havana believed in his "reformation." She also realized that his marriage to a known partisan of the royal cause would help his masquerade. She wasn't so cynical as to believe this was his motive for marrying her, but she was not unhappy that the marriage would be of help to him.

For all her intentions to make the wedding private, word leaked out, and by the day of the ceremony there were forty-two guests. Even this was referred to by Washington society columnists as "an intimate, private affair," due to the recent deaths in the Maguire-Guzman y Pontalvo family of the bride.

While Antonia was being fitted with her wreath of muguet in place of the customary yards of Pontalvo veiling, Aunt Sybil, elegant in lavender taffeta, rustled into the crowded bed-sitting room of the bride to announce that President McKinley had arrived with Lloyd Hastings and his Secret Service army, as well as, of course, Bernard.

Antonia was less than thrilled. Every time she thought of President McKinley and her promise to the queen regent, her conscience moved on to the intercepted letter to Lloyd Hastings. She still had a strong suspicion that dear Uncle Bernard had the letter and would use it against her if she caused him any difficulty. It also checkmated any ideas she might have of avenging herself by throwing Bernard Revelstoke off the estate. Perhaps it was just as well. She knew she could never throw Aunt Sybil out. Aunt Sybil was the last Maguire relation left to her... Still, she loathed the idea of Uncle Bernard walking alongside her to the improvised altar. The very touch of him made her flesh crawl, but he was her only male relative. A dismal prospect.

She tried to receive the news about the president with a big smile and a rather feeble "that's nice, I hope he has a good seat."

"You may be sure of that, dear. Bernard has him collared, as it were, and every chair in the house has been commandeered." Sybil stood back and looked her over.

"Tanita, you are *ravishing*. And the rest of you girls too."

The four girls from Antonia's Female Academy were a soft bouquet of lilac, and the bride provided a stunning sight in violet satin that nearly matched her eyes. In the society pages much would be made of this astonishing match, but its only importance to Antonia had occurred when Juan glimpsed a bit of the material in Sybil's hands and announced that he saw no resemblance. His Tana's eyes were far more beautiful. This might not be true, but Antonia loved him for saying it.

The processional music was played on the Revelstoke grand piano by the musical wife of the local Methodist-Episcopal minister. To meet the requirements of the bride and groom, a priest had been borrowed from Washington, where the Roman Catholic religion was slightly more prevalent. He was Father Ernesto de Plana and had been the Spanish minister's confessor for years. Antonia admitted her own prejudice, but ever since Dupuy de Lôme's dismissal of Captain Leidner's death she had disliked any connection with the distinguished and popular diplomat and felt that even his confessor was suspect.

Juan, on the other hand, found nothing wrong with the priest, who was a man of surprisingly liberal views and, as Juan explained to Antonia, "The padre is a rare man. He supports the royalist governors of Cuba but he spends much time giving aid to Cuban exiles and even junta members."

There was nothing for it but to accept Father de Plana.

Uncle Bernard waited in the upper hall with elbow extended. As always he looked jovial, handsome in his well-endowed way. "Dear child," he whispered, "there never was so lovely a bride."

She barely touched his arm with her icy fingertips. She would not feel safe until she and Juan were beyond his reach. They descended the front stairs as the end of the procession headed by her four academy friends whose lilac taffeta charm in swanlike silhouettes was received by the staring, straining guests below with suitable ohs and ahs. The matron of honor came next, Aunt Sybil looking handsomer than ever, her lavender gown bringing out all the beauty of her freshly burnished red hair. She and Antonia each wore an unobtrusive black grosgrain ribbon around their necks, the single tribute to the memory of their murdered family, but the somber note did not detract from the overall picture.

At any other time, the gasps and whispers in praise of the bride would have been gratifying to Antonia, but today she wanted only to get the ceremony over and to leave this house with Juan, get away from the memory of her part in Captain Leidner's death, away from the smug, proud smile of Uncle Bernard.

She looked at Juan, at the far end of the double living room near the altar that had been set up in front of the fireplace. Since Quincy Kemp was unavailable, having been stationed in Havana at the news source, Juan's best man was his mate from the *Baracoa*, William Pullitt, a Yankee, taciturn and unruffled by any emergency, even a wedding. His lean, leathery face revealed little if any emotion as the procession moved between the seated rows of guests, but just for a moment, when Uncle Bernard released her to Juan, Antonia took her eyes off the bridegroom to see a ghost of an approving grin flicker over those seamy features. She remembered William Pullitt's calm handling of the old ship the day the Spanish patrol came aboard. He had been a man to count on during that emergency. And now this event.

Juan was all in black-and-white, one of his slim-fitting black suits with an immaculate white shirt and tie. The trim power of his body was only slightly concealed by his "respectable business suit," but the sight of him without those familiar, form-fitting seaman's sweaters and jackets startled her at first. He held out a hand to her, and she felt his fingers close around hers and imagined his strength coursing through her.

Father de Plana smiled on them and began the service in his deep, sonorous voice with its magical accent. The shortness of the service surprised, and relieved, Antonia. Her own responses came hoarsely and with a surprising accent that she had lost during her later academy days. Juan, on the other hand, spoke as clearly as if he were on a quarterdeck. The ring had been his mother's, and he set great store by it, which meant it had special meaning for Antonia. She kissed the heavy gold band when he placed it on her finger, a gesture that made Juan stumble in his vows for the first time.

"Now, *capitán*," Father de Plana said, "if you please, you will salute the bride."

Juan raised his bride's chin and to everyone's surprise, "saluted" Antonia on each eyelid, his lips warm and careful. She savored this, then raised her arms, locked her hands behind his head and tilted it until her mouth was on his.

By this time the guests and the wedding party felt that the bride and groom had enjoyed enough privacy. Several dozen of them eagerly clustered around them. William Pullitt brushed her cheek, then stood far back from the crush, arousing considerable interest in the bridesmaids, who giggled and whispered to one another, attracted by his leathery look and, to them, forbidding aura.

Antonia kissed Father de Plana, he blessed her, wished her all things good in God's eyes and went on to discuss charity for homeless Cuban women and children with some of the wealthier guests. He was replaced by Enrique Dupuy de Lôme, who kissed her hand with his stylized elegance. His touch, his very presence reminded her of the people who had warned the Spanish governor about Captain Leidner's voyage, and it was all she could do to remain civil, though she had no real evidence he was personally guilty.

It was easier to feel kindly toward President McKinley, who looked tired, worn and worried. He took her hand and wished her well, but he obviously wanted to be elsewhere. He did manage to separate her from the others long enough to suggest quietly, "If your little library is packaged, Hastings will take it from you."

"I told him before the ceremony, sir. He probably has the books by this time."

He seemed relieved. "In that way no one else need be involved beyond Dupuy. Do you think Her Majesty would be satisfied?"

"Mr. Hastings represents you. Señor Dupuy and I represent the queen regent. That should keep the matter from becoming public. I know Your Excellency and Mr. Hastings are far more efficient than an amateur like me."

"Well, you have done your country a good service, Mrs. Diego. In the long run, let's hope, you might have helped prevent a war."

He soon left with his entourage of protective guards. Hastings was the last to congratulate her, but he assured her this was not due to any dog-in-the-manger attitude.

"So long as you're happy, Antonia. And I must say, you look like you are. I imagine you must have missed your sister-in-law, but you'll see her in Havana, for the identification proceedings. She would have been a great comfort to you, I'm sure."

"I'm sure."

There were more kisses, many from people whose faces were a blur but whose good wishes were welcome, the more the better. She and Juan could use every bit of goodwill in the dangerous months to come.

At last, to her intense relief, Juan was there beside her, taking her arm. For Antonia the ceremony had been a jumbled picture of crowds, words, late autumn sunlight and a deep, haunting fear that was not banished until after she had thrown her sprig of muguet from the top of the front staircase to the most eager of her bridesmaids, Mary-Ellen Hancock, who made an impressive leap to win it.

With Aunt Sybil's help she changed rapidly to a taffeta-and-velvet suit with a velvet tam-o'-shanter that fitted over half of her thick black hair. She then came out in the hall into her *husband's* arms.

They were driven to Washington in style by the Revelstoke carriage and team, and spent their wedding night on the train, making love, getting newly acquainted after their long period of abstinence. The jolting of the train and the narrow size of the berth only made them laugh as it somehow raised the sensual delight of their lovemaking.

There was a hunger between them that they thought would never be satisfied. His firm but gentle fingers began their exploration at the nape of her neck, reaching beneath the mass of her tousled hair, then moved downward along her spine and around to her breasts and nipples, which stiffened at the touch of his lips. She felt the shudders of excitement throughout her body and slipped her own hands around his back to his firm muscled hips and tried to draw her own body closer to him. She touched at his groin as he entered her, and they reached their climax together.

"I dreamed of this, every night," she told him when her breathing had quieted some. And then, "Darling, love me again, please, again..."

There was little left of the night by the time they lay back, though still within each other's touch, and slept in loving exhaustion.

The following afternoon they reached Key West and sailed on the dawn tide for Havana.

"A honeymoon not to forget," Antonia told Juan as they stood, arms linked, watching the crossing of the Florida Straits in the blue dawn.

William Pullitt passed behind them on the *Baracoa's* afterdeck. "Not much of a honeymoon, if you'll excuse me, Miss... Mrs. Out

there looks pretty empty now, but I heard tell on the docks today
that us Yanks are thinkin' of sending a battleship out into these
waters."

"What's this?" Juan turned to challenge him. "Are they going to
war with Spain without even an announcement?"

"She's a fine new battleship, they say. Name of the *Maine*. But
she'll be sent to patrol in peace. So it's said."

Antonia reached out and drew Juan Diego back to her. "Don't
think about it. It needn't concern us. We won't *let* it."

Juan, looking serious, tried to go along.

"You are right, sweetheart. We won't let it concern us. Pullitt,
take your *Maine* and send it to kingdom come."

CHAPTER
TWENTY-THREE

HAVANA, "THE Paris of the New World."

Though the city was jammed with refugees, and more poured into the city daily, these starving remnants of a once thriving peasantry and of the burned-out sugar mills still did not diminish the excitement of the ancient city.

As soon as the *Baracoa* had passed within the narrow neck of Havana harbor Antonia was sure she smelled orange blossoms and wild jungle blooms undisturbed by the autumn climate elsewhere.

As always there was someone, this time the mate William Pullitt, who remarked, "Dead fish, garbage and decay, that's what I smell."

Antonia would not listen. Even from the *Baracoa*'s anchorage near the Castello de la Fuerza, the oldest edifice in the New World, she could hear the noise, the metallic clang of church bells, the deafening toot of the boats ferrying people and merchandise across the harbor, and through it all the clip-clop of horses on paving stones. Sufficient time had elapsed, including the visits to Spain and the crushing guilt she associated with Revelstoke, so that she could be sentimental about her birthplace.

The new trolley cars seemed noiser then she remembered, and the *Malecón* was crowded with strolling government soldiers in pale summer uniforms, loose kerchiefs, open jackets, trousers too big and swords clanking as they walked. Their wide-brimmed hats of palmetto straw did not quite conceal their new mustaches, worn stiffly to make them look older. Even the hats did not protect them from the broiling tropic sun. The young Aragonese, Castilian and Andalusian faces looked nervous and hunted.

"They're just boys," Antonia said to Juan. "Hardly old enough to lift one of those rifles. And you can see they don't hate anyone. But if they're sent out into the countryside they'll be butchered. And so far from home. Do you suppose they even know what they are fighting for?"

"Who knows? A lot of them, probably not." He looked unhappy but she knew he hadn't swayed in his feelings about his rebels.

They reached the Palacio Guzman to find Caris de Correña Maguire entertaining Captain-General Blanco's aide, Hernán de Noriega. He might be a handsome young man, and obviously Caris thought so, but he would always remind Antonia of the ghastly days after the death of her parents and Felipe.

Caris presented her cheek to Antonia but greeted Juan with more enthusiasm than usual. This was his final test, as he told Antonia later. If Señora Caris and the queen of Spain accepted him as a loyalist, anyone would. It was made easier by the shipload of refrigerated meat that the *Baracoa* had unloaded for General Blanco's troops. Antonia suspected that William Pullitt had stayed aboard to unload more than government meat.

Caris introduced Juan to Señor de Noriega, all suave and friendly. "As though I didn't recognize the distinguished Capitán Diego... we are fortunate to have your help against these misguided rebels. The stories I could tell you of their crimes against our young soldiers..."

Antonia quickly got them off this subject. "I was afraid things would be changed but mother's vines over there smell sweet as ever. And the whole garden, just as it was."

Caris grimaced. "If you like that insufferable sweetness. By the way, you're certain we can identify this Carlos Melina?"

Antonia, following Juan and the new gatekeeper to their bedroom with the luggage, mostly hers, said over her shoulder to Caris, "absolutely."

There were a few bad minutes when Antonia and Juan came in to dinner in the high-ceilinged, seventeenth-century dining room with its old, scarred, but treasured furniture, all of it reminding Antonia of the happy meals she and her family had shared in the company of those heavy Spanish heirlooms. Caris automatically took the host's chair. She had evidently already trained the servants. Well, Antonia decided, she'd not open hostilities until the main business of their visit was done.

It was not to be the first depressing experience of their return. María-Rosa Guttierez had left a note chiding Antonia for marrying only six months after "our dear Felipe's murder," and Adelaide Heffernan arrived at the Palacio Guzman long enough to mourn the death of young Tim Burford, something that would always haunt Antonia.

At dinner Caris behaved as usual. Perhaps to arouse the jealousy of the good-looking Noriega, she persisted in describing her great love for Felipe and how she missed him, especially in this room where he had first "asked me to be his," as she put it.

It occurred to Antonia that Caris talked more about Felipe tonight than she had during the entire Spanish sojourn, and her glib tongue seemed to be borrowing all the phrases of a romantic novelist to help her paint a portrait of this Romeo and Juliet love. At all events, Lloyd Hastings had definitely lost out in the race for Caris' fickle heart. There was no denying, however, that Caris looked well in black lace against her blonde hair, and that she was an expert in the language of the fan.

The best moments were spent in the huge mahogany four-poster bed, an oasis and escape from all the horrors of memory and the suffering island.

But as the rainy season ended and the dry winter days set in they found it impossible to walk through the narrow, crowded streets without coming on scores of refugees huddled under the laurel and palm trees, begging for food or waiting in their ragged lines for bowls of soup made up of lentils, a little square of pork and sometimes a bit of potato.

It was Adelaide Heffernan, visiting the Palacio Guzman on one of her rare free times from her work with Miss Barton, who suggested that the tiny square beyond the gates of the Palacio Guzman be used by these victims of fights they had never understood.

Juan thought it was an excellent idea, and Antonia was soon busy with the practical aspects of the charity. "We can have Zerlina make up nourishing soup for them," she told Juan. "A regular stew with healthy vegetables. With bananas and pomegranates and oranges they can at least survive . . . I wish I could be sure the money we give to house them is going to the right people, I keep wondering if . . ."

Adelaide said she wished she could help, "but we are swamped, night and day. Miss Barton insists on giving help to the rebels as well, you know. And we are in trouble with the Havana authorities."

It was Juan whose praise meant most to her. Respect and admiration had been added to passion since their separation in Spain, and each day in Havana it seemed to increase.

One day when she was ladling out bowls of Zerlina's lamb and pork stew, with its vegetables of all colors, red peppers, green beans, faded lentils, bright carrots, Noriega came to announce that the prisoners were ready for identification . . . They had been sufficiently "quizzed" . . . "The guitarist and one of the assassins," he said quietly.

Antonia immediately went to change for the trip to the offices of the *jefatura*. While she dressed, Juan asked her, "Tana . . ." He rarely called her by her name, even the familiar nickname. It was usually "sweetheart," and she looked her surprise. "Do you still feel the way you did in the hospital that day?"

"You mean my passionate craving for revenge?" She shook her head. "No . . . but I realize they must be punished."

He kissed her hair. "I know. Gentle Caris is hot to hang them personally—not that they don't deserve it," he added.

All during the ride in the big old open carriage to the ancient building across the square from the captain-general's headquarters, Caris chattered away in ghoulish detail about her feelings on the day of the massacre. Hernán de Noriega's black-fringed eyes seemed to sparkle with excitement as she talked.

"You have been incredibly brave, Señora Maguire. And you must be braver still. It will be necessary to swear to the identification of the men. There are two of them, of course."

"Has the guitarist said anything yet?" Juan asked.

"Certainly, Captain. He was induced to confess his part. The motive was the death of the two who threw the infernal machine into the wedding crowd last spring. They were cousins or blood brothers or something of the sort. Bound in their sacred cause, so he said. The original plan was for him to open the courtyard gate to the assassins at night, but the *merienda* seemed a safer way, with less likelihood of interference."

Antonia shuddered.

The palace currently in use for trials and questioning relieved the captain-general of the trip to Morro Castle, whose thick walls and horrifying reputation embarrassed General Blanco. He preferred not to be seen entering what Diego had called a hellhole. But to Antonia the *jefatura* looked every bit as forbidding as the old fortress that greeted Antonia every time she sailed into the harbor from the Florida Straits.

She moved nearer to Juan. He held her close, but she felt the tension in his body.

"Sweetheart, only the truth. Not guesses, but what you are certain of. And don't be afraid of what will happen if you identify them. Compassion is fine, but as I told you, I also believe in justice. If they are guilty and went unpunished I would want to execute them myself. For what they've made you suffer."

She was thinking of others whose deaths she had caused. Would Juan call *that* justice?

A remarkably thin, tall, languid-looking man who spoke with a Castilian lisp took the party in hand when they had entered the guardroom, a huge stony hall used in the days of the conquistadores as a gathering place for the officers of Spain's armies. The languid man was addressed by Hernán de Noriega as Don Francisco Caballo, who represented the captain-general at the questioning. His position surprised Antonia. He looked so harmless, much too relaxed to supervise the use of torture.

Don Francisco Caballo explained that the two prisoners would stand in the sunken well of a room in a great deal of light, electric and lantern and even lamplight. The two women and their escorts would remain in semidarkness, watching the prisoners move, noting them from every direction. When they were ready they would signal to Caballo's six soldiers, who would bring out the prisoners and then record the reactions of the witnesses.

It satisfied Antonia some to note that when they reached the darkened room in which the prisoners would appear, Caris held back, her Lady Macbeth bravura having collapsed. Reassured by both Noriega and Don Francisco, she allowed herself to be led into the room, but she pressed back against the cold stucco wall and covered her eyes when the prisoners were marched into a circle of blazing light. The two youthful men blinked and swayed, one of them, the guitarist, shuffling beside a guard while the room echoed eerily with the rattle of his chains.

Antonia stood straight, squeezing Juan's hand tightly. It was the same guitarist who had waved his guitar as a signal the day of the *merienda* and recently confessed the real intention had been to murder the Maguires in their beds. She hadn't seen him commit a crime, but she had normal feelings. He looked bruised and something was wrong with his legs.

The other was different. Either a cane or tobacco worker, he still looked unusually tall, and to Antonia there was a kind of madness in his eyes. She could never forget him... like some fiery creature out of hell... seeing him when she looked up and saw him towering above her and her mother with a machete...

More of her old, burning hatred returned. How could it not? She was ready with her identification.

The prisoners squinted, trying to see the vague, shadowy spectators beyond the blinding light. Their physical condition shocked Antonia, and she had to admit she was glad when they were taken away. Caris was even more relieved. She took her hands from her eyes and waved vaguely, asking to be removed from this place.

"And what is the verdict of the ladies?" Don Francisco wanted to know when the witnesses had moved to Caballo's own office with its glassless barred window, typical of Havana, where they received a blast of fresh, flower-scented air.

"My dear señora," Noriega told Caris, "we are proud of you." He indicated Antonia belatedly... "And of the Señora Diego, naturally. It was difficult."

Caballo nudged him and he went on quickly. "What is your verdict? Are they the men?"

Caris glanced at Antonia. "What do you think, Tana?"

Antonia had no hesitation. "They are the men. The taller one killed my mother." She looked at Juan. "It is true."

He nodded. "You're right to say so."

"If the ladies will be so kind as to sign these statements, all is in readiness."

Antonia signed at once with a pen that spattered ink, and eventually Caris did likewise, then murmured that "I feel quite... weak..."

Both Caballo and Noriega rushed to hold her up.

Juan offered his arm to Antonia, who took it instantly and they went out of the building, out into the ancient plaza where they passed several peasants. One of them literally hissed Juan and Antonia, but to Antonia's surprise, the fellow was silenced by his companions. A thin, middle-aged man in a big palmetto hat leaned toward Juan.

"Well done, Capitán. We don't make war on families. We're not royalists."

Antonia felt the gibe, but after what she had seen of the *reconcentrados* and the recent hundreds of homeless, starving people, she understood the truth of the man's statement.

Caris and Noriega took the Maguire carriage back to the *palacio* while, at Juan's suggestion, he and Antonia walked over to the Inglaterra Hotel, home of the endless procession of international correspondents.

"Quincy Kemp," he told her, "is bound to be out on the *terrasse* drinking."

She agreed to meet Quincy, although he made her uneasy. She'd always suspected the jolly-faced correspondent could read her mind. But she had an added incentive that she confessed now with some shame.

"The minute I get back to the *palacio* I know I must roll up my sleeves again... it's depressing to know those poor people will be just as hungry tomorrow."

"Sweetheart, you have certainly earned a different view for at least a few hours. I've never been more proud of anyone."

She pushed back those awful memories of the note to Lloyd Hastings.

They saw then Quincy Kemp sprawled in a wicker chair at the

front table of a French-looking sidewalk cafe. He hailed them, started to get up. Antonia waved him back to his seat while she and Juan joined him.

Juan studied his bland, innocent face. "What's happened?"

Quincy had set his sherry down and reached for Antonia's hand. She smiled at him, finding it impossible not to like him even if, in some ways, she was leery of him. He signaled the waiter and gave his guests' order for coffee, then sipped at his sweet sherry, peering over the lip of the glass at them.

"First, would you like to know who betrayed our gallant friend Captain Leidner?"

Antonia thought her heart would stop.

Juan, looking grim as she'd ever seen him, said in Spanish, "Very much, *mi amigo*."

"Do you happen to remember a mate on the *Frederika*, a brute with an eye for the girls called—"

"*Bagley*." Juan slapped his palm on the table. "I had trouble with the fellow myself. That may have been why he betrayed Felix, because Felix had helped us . . . me, in particular."

Quincy overlooked the hint about Antonia. "Well, don't you be worrying about Master Bagley. Several members of the *Frederika's* crew escaped and they'll hunt him down." Their steaming coffee had come by this time, so he raised his glass. "Here's to justice. She's never all blind. Always sees out of at least one eye."

They drank, Antonia intensely relieved, yet ashamed as well. Her own note might have done equal damage.

"But that's not all the news." Quincy settled back, reached into his vest pocket and pulled out his heavy pocket watch. "Just about now, turn your head a little to the right, my old friend, and look down into the channel. It's just about passing Morro Castle at this minute."

Juan craned his neck. "I see the crowded harbor. All the masts of the deepwater ships. A busy place these days. Some steamers too. I think the *City of Washington* got in this morning."

"Keep looking. What I'm talking about is probably blocked by these buildings along the street. Wait until it passes."

Juan caught his breath. "*Madre de Dios*."

Antonia half-rose in her chair to get a better view of the harbor. A long, sleek battleship moved majestically through the sparkling blue waters of Havana harbor. Many of the ship's crew stood at attention on her decks.

Antonia asked, "Is it one of the kaiser's ships? They say his ships were in Haiti recently."

"Oh, no," Quincy told her, "she's Yankee, all right. Our spandy new battleship. The U.S.S. *Maine* . . . on a peaceful visit, so they say. But the gossip is that the Spanish queen has given up the fight for peace. The latest word delivered to our Ambassador Woodford is that Spain requests McKinley to denounce the rebels here in Cuba. Even the queen says so. And you know my country is never going to hold for that. Not with the press and the public and Congress in favor of Cuban independence."

Antonia and Juan looked at each other. Antonia's eyes flashed. There was still hope, and maybe she and Juan could be a part of that attempt at peace. "Juanito, can't we try to make friends of the *Maine*'s crew. We're fairly well known. We'll make the people of Havana see they aren't savages and vice versa. . ."

Quincy seemed amused, but Juan was with her. He told the columnist now, "You news people thrive on disaster, but we may fool you. That ship is going to represent the United States to these Spaniards. In the end this visit of the *Maine* may be remembered not as the threat of a foreign power but as a goodwill gesture."

CHAPTER
TWENTY-FOUR

REGARDLESS OF the mitigating effect of Quincy Kemp's news of Bagley's duplicity on Antonia's guilty conscience, she was still convinced she wanted no more to do with Uncle Bernard. She would never really know whether he had or hadn't sold her information about Captain Leidner, but since Lloyd hadn't received it, and she couldn't get hold of Harry Burns, the reasonable conclusion was he may well have.

"I'm going to sell Revelstoke to Aunt Sybil. I don't like visiting there these days. I don't trust Uncle Bernard, for one thing," she told Juan one morning just before they went to act as friendly ambassadors between General Blanco, his staff and the officers and crew of the *Maine*.

Juan thought the sale was an excellent idea. "We'll have our own home when this business is over."

She hugged him, delighted by the thought, and sorry only that she would be separated from Juan for several days while she discussed the sale with Aunt Sybil. She suggested that she should go at once to get it over and done, but he asked her to make it later. "I need you to come back to. This place would be a hell without you."

So she put off her trip back to Virginia, hoping that he could get free of his own still mysterious duties to accompany her.

Meanwhile, there was the entertainment of the *Maine*'s crew to keep them busy. Making friends of the great battleship's officers and crew was easier than Antonia expected. The men did not act the part of insolent conquerors. Nor did they make enemies by their arrogance, like Kaiser Wilhelm's men of the Imperial German Navy's training ships, news of whose actions in Haiti and elsewhere had soon drifted across the narrow channel separating Cuba from Hispaniola. Following the rumors came the ships themselves, to further congest Havana harbor.

The Yankee officers were gentlemanly, and like their Captain Sigsbee a bit reserved in the beginning. As Juan speculated, they were feeling their way, trying hard to carry out their orders for "friendly and dignified contact with the natives of this Spanish colony."

The crew proceeded to the *Malecón*, arriving back with their shore boats loaded down with Spanish dolls and vases, ivory fans, minature Toledo sword letter openers and felt pillows with the words "Souvenir de Habana" hastily sewn on in georgette or chiffon, which tore off or unraveled the next day. Business began to boom. The city was more crowded than ever with refugees.

Caris told Antonia, "We're like an island within the city. Havana is surrounded by rebel sympathizers. An island. Any day they may rush into the city and run over us."

"Rubbish."

All the same Antonia felt the excitement that pervaded the ancient city. Juan had the benefit of his seagoing experience and soon made friends with various members of the crew. A few held out, objecting to comradeship with a man who they said had sold out his old friends, the Cuban rebels. Juan wasn't about to persuade them otherwise. Not now, not yet...

Caris confided to Antonia that Señor Noriega had asked her to marry him when her year of mourning was over. Before Antonia could react she went rushing on, "He's the heir to a tidy fortune in sherry, I believe. From Jerez. So don't think he's marrying me for my own fortune—"

"Are you quite sure of your facts?" Juan put in.

"He's related to the Albas, through his mother."

Juan looked at Antonia, who shook her head at him and merely said, "Then I guess that should settle matters..."

In bed that night, Juan said, "Shouldn't we look more closely into the matter of our Señor Noriega and his fortune?"

Antonia shrugged. "General Blanco has boasted several times that he had connections with the Albas, so at least he can't be a candidate for our soup lines." Something more important was troubling her and she turned her head on the pillow to ask him, "What happened to the two we identified?"

"...They were hanged an hour after we left the *jefatura*."

She shivered, but couldn't honestly say she was sorry they were dead. "Tell me, darling, what do you do all day on the waterfront when I am virtuously feeding the poor?"

"You don't want to know," he said, and pulled her to him.

He was right, she thought, at least in some ways. She certainly didn't want to know that he was contacting seamen-rebels, probably exchanging information with them. She didn't want to know that he could be taken and hanged for what he was doing.

He tried to be less provocative later: "I am also making myself useful. Today I finally persuaded Captain Sigsbee of the *Maine* to attend the bullfights on Sunday. That will very probably put him in excellent favor with our esteemed captain-general. Not to mention you and me."

"Very clever of you, darling." She snuggled up to him, not letting on that she meant her comment in more than one way.

The next evening she was less than pleased when she found him in a low-voiced conversation with a young man, a conversation that ended abruptly as she stepped out into the garden to see what had delayed him.

"It's nothing. Young Raul Lacosta here has gotten himself into service as a secretary to José de Canalejas. I was just congratulating him."

"Who is Canalejas?" she asked as soon as the wiry fellow slipped away into the warm February night.

He took her arm, leading her into the house. "Don José is visiting

Havana. He is the editor of *El Heraldo* in Madrid. A very powerful and influential paper." He paused for an instant and she felt sure he was thinking twice about telling her the rest. "You happen to share an old friend with him."

"Me?"

"Señor Enrique Dupuy de Lôme."

"I don't see how his friendship with Señor Dupuy matters to you."

"How right you are."

"Well, then?"

"Señor Dupuy writes letters to his friends."

"He hasn't written any to you."

"Quite true. Still, he has a way of bearing his soul to his friends. His other friends. Now, isn't it bedtime?"

The next day she considered writing to the Spanish minister, warning him to be discreet, but memory of the disastrous warning to Lloyd Hastings, a message that never reached its intended destination, made her dismiss the idea.

The following Sunday Caris managed to rouse herself to make one of the Sigsbee parties, as the bullfighting expedition came to be known. Hernán de Noriega went along on the ferryboat across to the arena, obviously to keep an eye on Caris, who behaved charmingly to each of the youngish *Maine* officers in the party and was, in turn, treated with great favor by the Americans.

Antonia was soon calling them by their nicknames, at their request. The fact that she spoke English, slightly glossed over with the soft accent of Virginia, made them feel at home with her. It was a bit disconcerting to find that her husband didn't seem at all jealous of her popularity. He even smiled when the sailors made a fuss over her.

Juan was a very smart man.

There were problems with the very first *corrida*. Several of the younger men who had come out into the countryside expecting something like an American rodeo were revolted by the cruelty toward the unfortunate horses of the picadors and of course the unfortunate bull, an attitude that Antonia had come to understand. It had been the subject of the first attack on her by the girls at the academy when she was ten. All her arguments about the sacredness of the ceremonies, the glorification of truth and life and death eluded them. Now, so many years later, she found her arguments weakening. She could understand the reaction of an Ensign Gallegher, who had to leave the arena before the second bull had been dispatched.

The first *torero* had been admirable in Antonia's eyes. No tricks, no playing to his claque of admirers. A straight kill. The second *torero* was a show-off and a daredevil who delighted the Spaniards in the crowd. He gave the aficionados their money's worth. But the third was a butcher, a man past his prime who had lost his immunity from fear.

Unlike Caris and Noriega, Antonia left the arena with a resolution not to attend another *corrida*. The Americans looked "pale around the gills," as Captain Sigsbee said with a smile to excuse his slang. A quiet man, a little older than his officers, he politely praised the view and the weather. Havana harbor, in fact, had never looked more beautiful as the group headed across the waters and then to town through the train station. Soon they could make out the sleek and beautiful *Maine* as it rode at anchor between the flagship of the Spanish fleet, a German training ship, and the popular Ward Line tourist dock.

"Quite a sight, isn't she?" Captain Sigsbee said proudly. "I'll wager in ten years there will hardly be a single mast of a sailing vessel out there. All steam. Its time is here."

Juan spoke up. "I for one will be sorry to see that time. My *Baracoa* is enough speed for me."

"Where is she now?" Noriega asked.

Antonia tensed, wondering, but Juan said easily, "Carrying coffee and meat to the troops marching on Oriente Province, I imagine."

Suddenly, as the party was herded into deep-seated, old-fashioned *volantes* for the ride back to their ship, a fiery-eyed young man thrust a wadded paper into Captain Sigsbee's hand and ran back into the crowd heading toward the suburban train station.

"Something political, I suppose," Captain Sigsbee said as he unfolded the paper. Antonia read it over his shoulder:

DEATH TO THE AMERICANS!
DEATH TO AUTONOMY!
LONG LIVE SPAIN!

And at the bottom of the page: LOOK TO YOUR SHIP!

While the men were rereading the warning, Antonia put in doubtfully, "We all saw the fellow who gave it to you. He looked to me more like one of the rebels, in that field hat and nothing else but those torn trousers." She tried to sound more convincing than she felt.

The men looked at one another. It was hard to say...

Caris insisted it couldn't be real. Spaniards would never be so impolite to honored guests, and so forth.

"Of course not," Captain Sigsbee said, still remembering his manners. But he would double the guard that night. Live ammunition at every gangway.

Back at the Palacio Guzman, Antonia said, "Suppose the fellow was one of the rebels, trying to make trouble between the *Maine's* crew and the people of Havana?"

"Sweetheart, all terrorists are contemptible. I've come to that idea more and more as this business builds. There are things I wish now that I hadn't—" He broke off, then said, "I felt this way after your family was murdered, I feel it even more today."

They slept well that night, sharing their feelings. But the next morning old fears multiplied. Before noon Juan was met by a wiry man whom Antonia recognized as the new "secretary" to the Spanish newsman Don José de Canalejas. When they had finished their business Juan returned to Antonia, shaking his head.

"It's too late, the thing is done."

"What thing? What's happening? *Tell me.*"

"There's nothing we can do now but hope the United States dismisses it as malicious gossip."

He would say nothing more.

The bad news was brought to the Palacio Guzman by the least likely source—Adelaide Heffernan. She was breathless when she got to the garden gate the next afternoon with her news and an armful of newspapers.

"Tana, it's terrible... that awful man Señor Dupuy. I believe he must have lost his mind. Ah... Captain Diego, such an outrage..."

Antonia dismissed the gatekeeper and ushered Adelaide into the garden with an arm around her shoulder. Juan slipped the newspapers out from under the nurse's arm and snapped open the top paper, the New York *Journal*.

"Dios!"

She turned back. "Juanito, what is it?"

For a moment he looked as if he would tear up the sheet, then thought better of it. She read the huge headline:

WORST INSULT TO UNITED STATES IN ITS HISTORY

She took the paper from him and walked into her mother's old sitting room, followed by Juan and Adelaide.

"A letter," Adelaide said, still trying to catch her breath. "The Spanish minister wrote that letter to a friend here in Havana and someone from the New York junta stole it. He must have sent the letter to the Hearst papers, and the other papers too. They all have the story."

"What story...?" Antonia said.

But it was clear enough. Snatches of Enrique Dupuy de Lôme's stolen letter to his friend and confidant leaped at her:

> McKinley...weak, and popularity-seeking...a hack politi-
> cian...Journalistic rabble who infest this hotel concern our-
> selves with commercial relations and send here a man of
> importance to make propaganda among senators and others
> who oppose the junta and to go on gathering support of exiles
> (from Cuba)...

It sounded so like the Enrique Dupuy she knew. He had always held these opinions. But the letter was private, the opinions personal. The letter had been stolen, used to arouse the volatile Yankee press.

She looked at Juan, and she knew without asking. Meanwhile, she had to wait until they were alone.

The rest of the afternoon passed slowly. The house was full of pronouncements, pompous opinions by people who knew little or nothing about it.

Only two people really knew. Antonia, who knew Enrique Dupuy de Lôme, and Juan, who had caused the Spanish minister's private letter to be stolen and then delivered to Spain's enemies.

Juan and Antonia were scrupulously careful with each other but nothing could save them from the tension and foreboding they felt during the hours when politeness prevented them from talking about their real problem.

Every time Antonia thought of Juan's "crime," she remembered her own. Now was the time to tell him. Sooner or later he had to know. She had been, in a different way, as guilty as he was.

Shortly after sunset Adelaide Heffernan returned to the local hospital, where she and another of Miss Barton's trainees were teaching operating room procedures to the young local nurses. Juan sent one of Zerlina's nephews along to protect the nurse, and Noriega took Caris off to a concert at the governor's palace.

"Where we will all thumb noses at the gringos," Caris said. "These papers with their vile lies... the Spanish minister would never be so foolish to put in writing what we all know is true. No ... it is the Yankees trying to drag us into war so they can steal Cuba."

She was still giving loud voice to such sentiments when they drove off in Noriega's horse and buggy, leaving Juan and Antonia to face each other in the shadows of the portico.

CHAPTER
TWENTY-FIVE

Antonia SURPRISED herself by her quiet tone, the tired inevitability of this moment which must have been shaping itself for months.

"It *was* you, wasn't it?"

He looked pale, unlike himself. "It was. I agreed to send the letter. It went up from Key West. Quincy Kemp saw to it."

"I'm only surprised he didn't use the story himself, in his precious column."

"He couldn't. It was too big. Besides, he has another job and it suited his . . . associates to handle it this way."

"U.S. naval intelligence?"

That surprised him. "You knew?"

"So does Aunt Sybil."

"Ah . . . well, your aunt is equally busy in such matters. She sells information to the Secret Service. They're rivals of naval intelligence." He motioned her toward the sitting room again. "Sweet-

heart, there is no way I can undo what has been done. I thought
at the time that it was for the best. For Cuba. I thought it might
make the Spanish government offer autonomy and end this business
with home rule. I never wanted screaming headlines, I never
thought it would bring talk of war. Can you understand any of this
... how much I regretted it afterward...?"

She walked back into the room with him. The time for some
truth from her had come too.

"I know. I can understand, Juanito, because I committed the
same... wrong. Or crime. Whatever you want to call it."

They sat down together, and he took her fingers, which she had
nervously balled in a fist.

"Now, that is crazy talk. What have you done that is so shocking?"

She glanced at her hand in his, then said quietly, "Captain Leidner
said that he was carrying a spy to Santiago de Cuba. I thought that
spy might act against Her Majesty's troops. I sent a message to
Lloyd Hastings asking that the Americans stop him. Lloyd never
received it."

He sat there, staring at her. Finally: "I may have gotten us into
war, and you helped to hang Felix—"

"Dear Uncle Bernard deserves some credit too. I at least never
wanted the Spanish gunboat to get Felix."

"Does it matter now? Besides, your letter may have given the
Spaniards the information, but they already had that information
from Bagley. And my meddling gave the United States an excuse
for... We're a fine pair."

"Uncle Bernard should be caught," she insisted. "Someone should
catch him in the act and turn him over to the American authorities.
I'm positive he buys and sells information—"

"I don't doubt it. Quincy believes your aunt permits him to
discover secrets the government wants leaked out. But in your case
he found a gold mine. Not, I'm afraid, that Felix wouldn't have
talked in front of him sooner or later. Felix was always a daredevil.
Your uncle backed Felix on some cargoes. But General Blanco and
the Spanish government must have offered Revelstoke a bigger
bribe."

"Can Uncle Bernard be finished? Can't we make him pay?"

He looked at her. "Leave your uncle to his own devices. He'll
stumble. Somewhere, somehow, he will pay. But don't let yourself

be taken up by hate. I did that, and it almost destroyed me."

The room was very silent for a few minutes. She got up.

"Where are you going?" he said.

"Somewhere away from here. I see it in your eyes. You can't forgive me for Felix, can you?"

He said perhaps too quickly, "I love you, *querida*. I can't stop loving you in a minute..."

She looked around the room and through the barred window at the garden greenery. She had put off the sale of Revelstoke too long. Perhaps a separation from her would convince Juan that he really did still love her in spite of what had happened. She might even blackmail Uncle Bernard into a confession.

"I'm going back to sell Revelstoke to Aunt Sybil. I can never live near Bernard again. After that, if you still want me..."

It was like a blow to the heart, his brief hesitation.

"Yes... you won't feel secure until that's settled." He added, "You'll also be safer in the States, if war comes..."

He was really trying to get rid of her, she was convinced. She nodded tiredly. "I'll pack a few things. The Ward liner *City of Washington* sails tomorrow morning. If I go down to the docks tonight they may let me go aboard."

"Quincy is returning to the States as well. He can look after you ... It won't be long, sweetheart. Only weeks, maybe days."

"Thank you."

How careful and polite they were, she thought. But she still felt he wanted to be rid of her... all that talk about war... what he really wanted was to be free of the woman who may have killed his best friend...

When she had thrown things into a suitcase, without seeing them through her tears, she came out of the bedroom with a fake smile and presented the case and smaller valise to Juan. "All ready," she said brightly, "you can't say I'm a typical female, taking an age to pack."

"Very true. You... certainly were anxious to leave." He took the cases. "Take care, sweetheart. Promise me."

"I promise. I mean to sell Revelstoke at any price. I want to be rid of Uncle Bernard."

The carriage was not waiting. They had to get the coachman out of bed, harness the team and then ride through the cloudy but radiantly lighted February night to the docks. The city itself was noisy as ever. Its twenty-four-hour liveliness only pointed up the silence between Antonia and Juan. They said very little to each other. Words could find no place in their emotionally charged thoughts.

In mid-evening the harbor appeared to be rings with lights in contrast to the windblown clouds. The busy *Malecón* and the streets rising gradually to the century-old plazas swarmed with strollers. The steamer *City of Washington,* looking staid and proper and rather squat with only a masthead light and a few faint running lights, did not look very receptive. Other ships in the harbor, sailing vessels, warships and steamers, were pale silhouettes around the big, white-hulled American battleship *Maine.*

As Juan and Antonia descended from the carriage and started down to the Ward Line docks, they were hailed by Quincy Kemp, seated at his usual table close to the wharfside activity. He had a snap-top valise beside his feet and was wearing his green derby.

"Don't tell me I'm to have company on my long lonely voyage over the bounding main. Come, sit. You might as well. There was a crowd down there a while ago. I'm waiting here where the beer is cool and the sherry's warm until ten o'clock. Then I'll amble up the gangplank and into my bunk."

Juan hesitated. "Tana is the one who is sailing. Family business. But if we can have a few more minutes together . . . shall we, sweetheart?"

They joined the columnist who then spoiled things by saying, "I've been having trouble getting things past the censor here. Most of us have. I've got a ratty-looking fellow over in that cantina watching me now. You, on the other hand, are free to come and go on the *Maine.*" Juan sighed; Quincy waved aside his impatience. "Only a minute. It's vital. I want a message sent through Captain Sigsbee's channels, avoiding the Spanish censor. He'll send out a boat tonight—"

"Another try at starting a war?" Juan asked sardonically.

"Just the reverse. I've got to get this thing off tonight. I'm pointing to the strong opinion here that Spain may sell Cuba. Save us from a war. It's damned important. Read it yourself on the way but it has to get out tonight. Tomorrow there will be more trouble stirred up by the Hearsts and the Pulitzers."

"And the Kemps?"

Quincy shrugged his heavy shoulders. "Not this time."

Juan and Antonia looked at each other.

Quincy fished in his vest pocket, pulled out a stained square of paper along with his watch. "Here, it should take you half an hour at the longest. Fifteen or twenty minutes, more like."

Antonia put in, "If you aren't back in twenty minutes I'll personally be down there on the docks to get you."

"She will," Juan told Quincy, half smiling.

Quincy consulted his watch, "Nine-fifteen. About nine-thirty we'll both come along, then the three of us can board the *Washington*.

They watched Juan go off along the dock toward the big battleship.

"A sherry?" Quincy asked. Antonia shook her head. Her concentration on Juan, who had already disappeared, was interrupted by a pounding, rattling noise that had begun to rise beyond the waterfront.

"Sounds like cavalry." Quincy got up in his seat, impressed by the horses who appeared suddenly at the far end of the street under the expert control of their Spanish riders, who, returning from maneuvers, paraded among the strollers of a dozen nations. The harbor itself had never been quieter; hardly a ripple as the night-blue waters swept up to the wharves and back.

From the *Maine*, across the calm water, she heard the melancholy note of taps.

"Bugler Newton," Quincy murmured, stifling a yawn. "Musically that boy has a great future. We had best be on our way to meet your beloved."

She was already starting off when he caught up with her, panting a little. "Have some compassion for my weight and years, Mavourneen."

She turned abruptly, staring at the cantina across the street. The electric lights that ringed the harbor were certainly bright enough, but the fellow with the long, dragging mustache had seated himself just out of the range of light—looking what Quincy claimed him to be . . . a spy.

Like all the pedestrians, tourists and other strollers on the wide street, however, he had been attracted by the skilled horsemen and their mounts now showing off their paces before this enthusiastic audience.

"Navy yard looks pretty dark," Quincy said. "Only a few lights. You see any shore boat from the *Maine*?"

"Not yet," She squinted into the darkness of the harbor, wondering what time it was and how long Juan would have with her before he left her cabin tonight. Or would he stay until the *City of Washington* sailed in the morning?

They had just passed a cantina on the edge of the dock area, vaguely aware of the noise made by the cavalry troop on the street above, when the night world of Havana seemed to turn upside down. Antonia was still peering out across the harbor waters as she heard a booming sound like a giant cannon shot, and then before her disbelieving gaze the huge superstructure of the *Maine* leaped into the air like a giant leviathan of the deep, then sank back in a great spout of fire and smoke and foaming water.

The noise roared onward, deafeningly, as the city shook. At the same time the electricity went off and the city was dark. Only the gasoline and oil lamps made tiny oases of light throughout the harbor area.

Sudden darkness made the cavalry horses panic, plunging into the screaming crowds, making the terrible night more hellish.

Quincy and Antonia picked themselves up from the street. Quincy was cradling his arm. "Busted, by gum."

Antonia winced at the long red bruise on her own arm, and in the darkness raised her skirts. A bad scrape along her thigh.

"What *happened*?"

Quincy was staring out across the waters where the great battleship seemed to dissolve into a massive rain of steel and wood and humanity that spread over the harbor waters where the Spanish flagship and the *City of Washington* were already running out their boats for a rescue. His usually calm voice was shaky.

"It would appear that the *Maine* has blown up."

"Juanito! He was on board."

Holding his arm against his stomach, Quincy scowled at the confusion around them. "What the hell else is going on? Can you see?"

"The horses, they're stampeding... *Juanito*..." She began to run along the dock calling out his name.

A hand grasped and tightened around her bruised arm and dragged her to the edge of the wharf. The man told her in Spanish, "We've taken some from the water, you will help us, señorita?"

Juanito, where are you?

But there was no way to refuse. She knelt at the end of the wharf and took one end of a blanket while the Spaniard held another corner. The sailor in the waist of the shore boat held the other two ends of the blanket. They were boosting up a sailor from the *Maine*. He was soaking wet, apparently had been blown into the harbor waters.

While Antonia knelt over the youth—he was hardly more than eighteen—another sailor in wet singlet was brought up. And then, another was laid beside them. All of them must have been asleep when the explosion rocked the harbor. And all were dead. She realized that when she bundled up her handkerchief to stanch the blood of the boy.

The Spanish sailors shoved off again to pick up more bodies. From the glimmer of lights in the little boats and the great inferno of the *Maine*, Antonia could see that the water was littered with bodies. There must have been hundreds. Two-thirds of the ship's company. The monumental size of the disaster blurred its horror.

Antonia hurried back from the wharf, up past the first cantina, the front of which had collapsed onto the screaming patrons. She ignored that as she ignored the panic among the cavalry horses and pedestrians farther along the street. She rushed into the first untouched cafe where the patrons were beginning to shuffle back to their tables and the bar. Most of the glasses had broken, but the diehards were already slapping the counter, demanding refills.

She raised her voice. She sounded hoarse and panic-stricken. She *was* panic-stricken. "Help us, some of you. Please. There are so many casualties..."

Two of the patrons were Americans and didn't understand her. The man, middle-aged and amiable, asked her to explain. She did so and was rewarded by his quick agreement.

"I'm a baby doctor. Wilfred Blinn. But I *am* a doctor. Get me some cloth and anything we can use to wash the wounds. Alcohol, anything."

The doctor's wife rushed to gather articles. Dr. Blinn hurried back down to the wharves with Antonia, followed by his wife. She was gathering more articles as she went and doing a good job of shaming other passersby to join the volunteers.

Antonia led the procession but her thoughts were all on her husband.

The horror of the disaster grew. Bodies retrieved from the water now lined the docks. Every ship in the harbor seemed to have lowered boats, and the dripping oars picked their way carefully among the debris and the bodies. Only the after-quarter of the *Maine* remained afloat. The entire forward area, including all the crew's quarters, was gone. The human losses must be incredibly high.

And Juan Diego?

Antonia obeyed Dr. Blinn's instructions, relieved at the few successes, the lives perhaps saved as he bandaged and treated the sailors with white powders in folded papers that he said would relieve anything from headaches and fevers to stomach upsets. Nobody was in a position to argue.

The night air was now pierced by the brassy sound of bugles that summoned to arms most of the troops in the city. Antonia momentarily stopped bandaging a sailor's head wound to clap her hands over her ears, but was recalled to her task by the sailor, who told her in a surprisingly chipper voice for someone whose cranium had received a possibly lethal blow, "At least, ma'am, this time I ain't throwin' up."

Lord... it was the boy who had been sickened by the carnage of the bullfight. Her throat closed and she had to try twice before she could get out an answer. "You certainly aren't, Ensign Gallegher. I'm sorry about the *corrida*. I think you'd have preferred one of those Yankee baseball games."

"Right..."

She patted his hand, then signaled to the arriving nurses and their male aides among Miss Barton's trainees. At the last minute she asked Gallegher, "Did you see my husband Captain Diego on the ship tonight...?"

Gallegher made a feeble motion with one hand. "Sure. Vis-visited our skipper... little while ago..."

Which gave her some hope... Captain Sigsbee's cabin was in the after-part of the ship, the only section not yet under water. Meanwhile there were more victims, more oil-covered bodies coming in. Every shore boat or dinghy or landing craft of any kind had been devoted to the search and rescue.

In spite of the prompt arrival of Spanish officials, from the captain-general through all levels of government, with what was obviously a frantic concern, various hangers-on had already started the insidious gossip, and American tourists were in the forefront of it.

"Spain is back of this."... "You can thank the queen regent for this monstrous crime."... "Mark me, who else profits? It's Spanish arrogance, no question..."

"Who else profits?" Antonia asked the question out loud. It stopped Dr. Blinn, who was hurrying by to set the broken elbow of a spectator on the docks.

"Can't see that it profits this government, miss. Maybe the rebels might want more trouble between Spain and us Americans. But I wonder if they could have worked out such a great crime."

"But what else is possible?"

Quincy Kemp was squatting on the ground, nursing his arm. "Stick to the theories about Spain and the rebels. Just remember, it didn't come from any internal explosion. *You two got that?*"

Dr. Blinn grunted. "A danged sight of ammunition must have been stored kind of careless-like all over that ship, what with the danger and all."

"Just don't speculate."

Dr. Blinn had no time for any more speculations one way or the other. Two stretcher-bearers rushed by, bearing a blanket-covered form up to the nearest temporary hospital. One of the running men accidentally kicked out as he passed. Quincy screamed, then tried to get back on the ragged edge of humor.

"Did you find old Juan?"

"Not yet. Have you—" She looked up from the chilled boy she was wrapping in a military cape. "Quincy, tell me, have *you* seen Juanito...?"

Dr. Blinn knelt to help Quincy, who groaned but also managed to get out, "Lots of activity along the docks and down near the Ward Line. You know our Juan, he's probably playing here somewhere..."

She didn't doubt that... *if* he had reached shore.

CHAPTER
TWENTY-SIX

I T STILL lacked a few minutes of midnight, but the docks were covered with motionless bodies as far as she could see in the flickering lamp and lantern lights. No new bodies had been brought in during the last ten minutes, and Antonia got to her feet with an effort. Blood and saltwater and oil stained her from her tangled hair to her shoes.

Dr. Blinn shook her gently. "Here, here, don't faint on me. We'll be needing you later. You're doing some job."

"Just sitting too long. I seem to be locked into one position. Ah ... that's better."

The doctor raised the lantern that glowed beside Quincy. "Go up to the nearest cantina. I prescribed strong coffee and milk for you."

She shook her head. "If I get out of here I may never come back."

"Yes you will. You're lots stronger than you think. You've already proved that."

Not really, she thought as she trudged along the dock and up the sloping streets that were still teeming with running men, oxen drawing coffins, confused onlookers who seemed to suffer more from emotional than physical injury.

... How long before I know? she asked herself... must I look at every one of those bodies just to be sure? How can I bring myself to do it? Even if Juan were dead, she had to know...

She followed the doctor's prescription, ordered coffee with milk and sat down to keep from shaking so much. She was so deep in her own thoughts she didn't notice the two curiosity-seekers who wandered into the cantina, the woman asking a waiter in her elegant Spanish with a Castilian lisp for "your best sherry, please."

Caris de Correña Maguire, being carefully seated by Hernán de Noriega, had forgotten to wear her gloves. Her carefully fitted new linen suit was wrinkled and strained. She took a long, deep breath. "I am exhausted. Where can she be? She should have been on the steamer, according to that gypsy cook of hers."

Noriega was reassuring. "I don't think we need concern ourselves. General Blanco said the *Washington* was untouched."

"The poor general..." Caris murmured, brightening a little as the glass of pale sherry was set before her. "He must be in dreadful trouble. The Yankees are sure to think the worst. What can have happened? How could anyone commit such an atrocity?"

"Perhaps no one," Noriega said. "Maybe it was an accident. But the Yankees have been on the alert ever since the *corrida* and those threats they received. What more logical than that *they* blew themselves up and put the blame on us."

"How awful! We will be at war in no time. I wonder how Tana will feel about her beloved Yankees then."

Hearing her name, Antonia raised her head and looked over at them and called out, "Where were you when it happened?"

Startled, they got up, calling her name, and came over to her. Caris would have hugged her but apparently was put off by Antonia's disheveled condition.

"What's *happened* to you, Tana? Don't tell me you were in the explosion. You look dreadful. Come, beloved"—this to her fiancé—

"we must get her home where she belongs. We've been looking everywhere for you. Hernán, we must get the carriage and horses back."

"Impossible, *querida*. They've commandeered everything to carry away the bodies. But perhaps after Señora Diego finishes the coffee she can walk."

Caris was less than entranced by that notion. "You know I couldn't walk so far. I'm in French heels."

Antonia shook her head in disbelief. Caris was nothing if not consistent. "Don't worry, I appreciate your concern but I can't leave the waterfront until I know what happened to Juanito—"

"Oh, Tana, I'm sure he is fine. He's probably down there doing some noble job of rescue..."

Noriega hesitated, glancing uneasily at the street beyond the last table. "We need to be on our way. General Blanco will be wondering why I've not returned to lend some...diplomatic assistance. There are regrets to be expressed, discussions about the investigation. The empire is in serious danger..."

All of which was of little interest to Antonia, her thoughts being filled with Juan, his black-clad figure dissolving in the darkness near the shore boats of the U.S.S. *Maine*...

"I'm sorry," she said. "I'll have to go back. Dr. Blinn is expecting me.

Caris protested briefly but in the end went off with Noriega, shaking her head over her sister-in-law's stubbornness.

Antonia was a little surprised that Caris had made any effort at all to find her. It was quite a human gesture for that lady...When she started to walk she felt stiffer than ever, but she knew she could never rest at home. There was nothing for it but to go back into that inferno.

It had to be nearly one in the morning by now, but the city remained in the grip of panic. People bumped into her as they rushed past, but she was scarcely conscious of it as she looked out along the docks at the covered bodies.

Was Juan among them?

She passed the Ward Line docks where the *City of Washington*'s crew was still working hard over the remaining wounded, along with the Spaniards of the flagship *Alfonso XII*. She thought of what

Noriega had said, but it just seemed incredible that the catastrophe
to the *Maine* could be anything but accidental. She prayed that it
was.

She was heading toward Dr. Blinn when a woman called out her
name. She turned around to see Adelaide Heffernan, puffing hard
but carrying one corner of a blanket on which a young Spanish
sailor writhed with a leg broken in the rescue attempt.

"Adelaide, have you seen Juan?"

In the red lamplight Adelaide Heffernan looked stricken. "He
. . . I thought . . ."

She had her answer. All her senses seemed to die. "You saw
him . . ."

"Sprawled on the wharf over there. Blood on . . . on his hair and
hands. Oh, Tana, I couldn't stop, I had this patient—"

Antonia said abruptly to Dr. Blinn, "Excuse me," and started to
run along the dock to the wharf used by the German training ship
Charlotte. Dr. Blinn was shouting that he needed her but she
pretended not to hear.

She made out the . . . body. An arm dangled over a warped piling
above the dark oily water. The other was curved under his head.
The black hair was soaking wet. She knelt down beside him.

"Juanito, look at me, please . . ."

He was *alive*. He raised his head, eyes open. The distant lantern
glow caught their light.

"*Querida mia* . . . I've looked everywhere . . . where were you?"

Her laugh was close to hysteria. "Just up the wharf. Near the
buoy where the Yankee sailors bring in their boats. Darling, are
you badly hurt?"

She tried to frame his face between her palms. He winced.
Trickles of blood had dried on the left side of his face.

"From the glass and steel, I guess . . . I was in the shore boat
when the *Maine* blew up. I've been pulling some of the poor devils
from the water. Most of this gore isn't even mine." He drew himself
up to his knees, then with a small assist from her, he stood up and
stretched. "I spent about an hour looking for you. No one seemed
to have seen you so I went back to what I was doing." He looked
around at the harbor, then took her arm. "Nothing more I can do
here. I think we've got the last of them. Come on."

"You know . . . I thought you *wanted* me to leave you, you seemed so anxious to have me go back to the States."

"You seemed anxious to go. I felt terrible."

"Because of Felix?"

"Because you wanted to leave me."

"Never. You should know that by now."

"Well, I wanted to get you out of what I guessed would be a dangerous situation . . ." He looked around. "And God knows, it is."

"I'm not leaving you. Believe that."

He forced a smile.

"I do. I know when to surrender."

"Then we go home to the *palacio?*"

He had his arm around her and was moving her along the wharf, limping badly. "No, sweetheart, we're going to the *City of Washington*. This explosion and Dupuy's letter are all the United States will need to declare war. We may be in it before the month is out."

"All the more reason why I'm staying. You need me, darling."

He admitted he did. "All the same, I want you out of any war zone, which will be here, not in Virginia."

"Juan, do you think the Spanish government did it?" It was a terrible thought but she had to ask.

"I doubt it."

"The rebels, or their American sympathizers? They'll profit if there's a war with the United States . . ."

He shrugged. "Or an accident, or some group we don't even know about . . ."

"Then it could have been *anyone.*"

"True. We may never know . . ."

They had just passed a ring of lights where the last of the bodies were being removed when she stopped him abruptly.

"*Look* at me, Juanito. Do you see anything different about me?"

He looked at her face and hair, at her now filthy beaded taffeta gown and jacket. "*Por Dios*, you look as if you had bathed in—"

"Blood? Dirt? Water and oil? I have, darling. I've been in it. Like you."

He put a hand under her elbow and piloted her along. She

glanced at him, saw that his jaw looked set, but then he smiled at her. "I've got an idea you're trying to tell me something."

"I am . . . we made our vows *together*. We need each other."

They headed for the collapsed cantina at the end of the docks. Workers, freed at last from their rescue work, were squatting among the debris, drinking liquor rescued from the collapse. Juan waved her to a broken tabletop that had settled on the floor.

"Sit, *amigo*. You have just been inducted into the Battle for Cuba."

"As you say, Captain."

She sat down as ordered, playing to his game, but also aware of the tiredness etched in his face and that must be in his whole body. She knew because she shared it, and he understood that. They sat there on that broken tabletop, holding each other and wondering at the marvel that had allowed them to stay alive for each other and . . . who knew, perhaps some other purpose that the horrors of this night could neither deny nor reveal.